A Woman of Genius

A Woman of Genius

Mary Austin

Afterword by Nancy Porter

The Feminist Press
Old Westbury, New York

© 1985 by The Feminist Press
All Rights Reserved. Published in 1985.
Printed in the United States of America.
89 88 87 86 85   6 5 4 3 2 1

First Feminist Press edition

Library of Congress Cataloging in Publication Data

Austin, Mary Hunter, 1868-1934.
    A woman of genius.

    Reprint. Originally published: Garden City, N.Y. :
Doubleday, Page, c1912.
    I. Title.
PS3501.U8W6 1985   813′.52   85-7069
ISBN 0-935312-44-7 (pbk.)

Cover Design: Gilda Hannah
Cover Art: *Self-Portrait* by Kate Freeman Clark, Kate
    Freeman Clark Art Gallery, Holly Springs, Mississippi.
    Reproduced by permission of the Marshall County
    Historical Society.
Text Design: Barbara Heineman
Typesetting: ComCom
Manufacturing: Haddon Craftsmen, Inc.

Contents

BOOK I

Chapter 1

It is strange that I can never think of writing any account of my life without thinking of Pauline Mills and wondering what she will say of it. Pauline is rather given to reading the autobiographies of distinguished people—unless she has left off since I disappointed her—and finding in them new persuasions of the fundamental rightness of her scheme of things. I recall very well, how, when I was having the bad time of my life there in Chicago, she would abound in consoling instances from one then appearing in the monthly magazines; skidding over the obvious derivation of the biographist's son from the Lord Knows Who, except that it wasn't from the man to whom she was legally married, to fix on the foolish detail of the child's tempers and woolly lambs as the advertisement of that true womanliness which Pauline loves to pluck from every feminine bush.

There was also a great deal in that story about a certain other celebrity, for her relations to whom the writer was blackballed in a club of which I afterward became a member, and I think it was the things Pauline said about one of the rewards of genius being the privilege of association with such transcendent personalities on a footing which permitted one to call them by their first names in one's reminiscences, that gave me the notion of writing this book. It has struck me as humorous to a degree, that, in this sort of writing, the really important things are usually left out.

I thought then of writing the life of an accomplished woman, not so much of the accomplishment as of the woman; and I have never been able to make a start at it without thinking of Pauline Mills and that curious social warp which obligates us most to impeach the validity of a woman's opinion at the points where it is most supported by experience. From the earliest I have been rendered highly suspicious of the social estimate of women, by the general social conspiracy against her telling the truth about herself. But, in fact, I do not think Mrs. Mills will read my book. Henry will read it first at his office and tell her that he'd rather she shouldn't, for Henry has been so successfully Paulined that it is quite sufficient for any statement of life to lie outside his wife's accepted bias, to stamp it with insidious impropriety. There is at times something almost heroic in the resolution with which women like Pauline Mills defend themselves from whatever might shift the centres of their complacency.

But even without Pauline, it interests me greatly to undertake this book, of which I have said in the title as much as a phrase may of the scope of the undertaking, for if I know anything of genius it is wholly extraneous, derived, impersonal, flowing through and by. I cannot tell you what it is, but I hope to show you a little of how I was seized of it, shaped; what resistances opposed to it; what surrenders. I mean to put as plainly as possible how I felt it fumbling at my earlier life like the sea at the foot of a tidal wall, and by what rifts in the structure of living, its inundation rose upon me; by what practices and passions I was enlarged to it, and by what well meaning of my friends I was cramped and hardened. But of its ultimate operation once it had worked up through my stiff clay, of triumphs, profits, all the intricacies of technique, gossip of rehearsals, you shall hear next to nothing. This is the story of the struggle between a Genius for Tragic Acting and the daughter of a County Clerk, with the social ideal of Taylorville, Ohianna, for the villain. It is a drama in which none of the characters played the parts they were cast for, and invariably spoke from the wrong cues, which nevertheless proceeded to a successful dénouement. But if you are looking for anything ordinarily called plot, you will be disappointed. Plot is distinctly the province of fiction, though I've a notion there is a sort of order in my story, if one could look at it from the vantage of the gods, but I have never rightly made it out. What I mean to go about is the exploitation of the personal phases of genius, of which when it refers to myself you must not understand me to speak as of a peculiar merit, like the faculty for presiding at a woman's club or baking sixteen pies of a morning, which distinguished one Taylorvillian from another; rather as a seizure, a possession which overtook me unaware, like one of those insidious Oriental disorders which you may never die of, but can never be cured. You shall hear how I did

4

successfully stave it off in my youth for the sake of a Working Taylor and Men's Outfitter, and was nearly intimidated out of it by the wife of a Chicago attorney who had something to do with stocks; how I was often very tired of it, and many times, especially in the earlier periods when I was trying to effect a compromise between it and the afore-mentioned Taylorvillian predilections, I should have been happiest to have been quit of it altogether.

I shall try to have you understand that I have not undertaken to restate those phases of autobiography which are commonly suppressed, because of an exception to what the public has finally and at large concurred in, that it does not particularly matter what happens to the vessel of personality, so long as the essential fluid gets through; but from having gone so much farther to discover that it matters not a little to Genius to be so scamped and retarded. I have arrived at seeing the uncritical acceptance of poverty and heartbreak as essential accompaniments of Gift, very much of a piece with the proneness of Christians to regard the early martyrdoms as concomitants of faith, when every thinking person knows they arose in the cruelty and stupidity of the bystanders. Hardly any one seems to have recalled in this connection, that the initial Christian experience is a baptism of Joy, and it was only in the business of communicating it that it became bloody and tormenting. If you will go a little farther with me, you shall be made to see the miseries of genius, perhaps also the bulk of wretchedness everywhere, not so much the rod of inexplicable chastisement, as the reaction of a purblind social complacency.

I shall take you at the sincerest in admitting the function of Art to be its re-kneading of the bread of life until it nourishes us toward greater achievement, as a basis for proving that much that you may be thinking about its processes is wrong, and most that you may have done for its support is beside the mark. If I have had any compunction about writing this book, it has been the fear that in the relation of incidents difficult and sordid, you might still miss the point of your being largely to blame for them. And even if you escape the banality of believing that my having lived for a week in Chicago on 85 cents was in any way important to my artistic development, and go so far as to apprehend it as it actually was, a foolish and unnecessary interference with my business of serving you anew with entertainment, you must go a little farther honestly to accept it, even when it came—this revitalizing

5

fluid of which I was for the moment the vase, the cup—in circumstances which in the rule you live by, appear, when not actually reprehensible, at least ridiculous.

Looking back over a series of struggles that have left me in a frame when no man under forty interests me very much, still within the possibility of personal romance, and at an age when most women have the affectional value of a keepsake only, the arbiter and leader of my world, I seem to see my life not much else but a breach in the social fabric, sedulously bricked up from within and battered from without, through which at last pours light and the fluid soul of Life. Something of all this I shall try to make plain to you, and incidentally how in the process I have perceived dimly this huge coil of social adjustment as a struggle *against* the invasive forces of blessedness, the smother of sheep in the lanes stupidly to escape the fair pastures toward which a large Friendliness herds them. If you go as far as this with me, you shall avoid, who knows, what indirection, and that not altogether without entertainment.

Chapter 2

Of Taylorville, where I grew up and was married, the most distinguishing thing was that there was nothing to distinguish it from a hundred towns in Ohianna. To begin with, it was laid out about a square, and had two streets at right angles known as Main and Broad. Broad Street, I remember, ran east and west between the high school and the railway station, and Main Street had the Catholic cemetery on the south, and the tool and hoe works on the north to mark—there was no other visible distinction—the points at which it became country road. There were numerous cross streets, east and west, called after the Governors, or perhaps it was the Presidents, and north and south, set forth on official maps as avenues, taking their names from the trees with which they were falsely declared to be planted, though I do not recall that they were ever spoken of by these names except by the leading county paper which had its office in one corner of the square over the Coöperative store, was Republican in politics, and stood for Progress.

The square was planted with maples; a hitching rack ran quite around it and was, in the number and character of the vehicles attached to it, a sort of public calendar for the days of the week and the seasons. On court days and elections, I remember, they quite filled the rack and overflowed to the tieposts in front of the courthouse, which stood on its own ground a little off from the square, balanced on the opposite side by the Methodist Church. It was a perfect index to the country neighbourhoods that spread east and north to the flat, black corn lands, west to the marl and clay of the river district, and south to the tall-weeded, oozy Bottoms. Teams from the Bottoms, I believe, always had cockleburs in their tails; and spanking dapple grays drove in with shining top-buggies from the stock farms whose flacking windmills on the straight horizons of the north, struck on my childish fancy as some sort of mechanical scarecrow to frighten away the homey charms of the wooded hills. I recall this sort of detail as the only thing in my native town that affected my imagination. When I saw the flakes of black loam dropping from the tires, or the yellow clay of the river district caked solidly about the racked hubs, I was stirred by the allurement of travel and adventure, the movement of human enterprise on the fourwent ways of the world.

From my always seeming to see them so bemired with their recent passages, I gather that my observations must have been made chiefly in winter on my way to school. From other memories of Taylorville arched in by the full-leaved elms and maples, smelling of dust and syringas, and never quite separable from a suspicion of boredom, I judge my summer acquaintance with its streets to have been chiefly by way of going to church, for, until the winter I was eleven years old, Taylorville, the world in fact, meant Hadley's pasture.

It lay back of that part of the town where our house was, contiguous to a common of abandoned orchard and cow lot, and if it lacked anything of adventurous occasion and delight, we, Forrie and Effie and I, the McGee children, and the little Allinghams, did not know it. There was a sort of convention of childhood that we should never go straight to it by the proper path, but it must always be taken by assault or stealth: over the woodhouse and then along the top of the orchard fence as far as you could manage without falling off, and then tagging the orchard trees; I remember there were times when we felt obliged to climb

7

up every tree in our way and down on the other side, and so to the stump lot where the earliest violets were to be found—how blue it would be with them in April about the fairy ring of some decaying trunk!—and beyond the stump lot, the alder brook and the Stone-pit pond where we caught a pike once, come up from the river to spawn. Up from the brook ranged a wood over the shallow hills, farther and darker than we dared, and along its banks was every variety of pleasantness. There was always something to be done there, springs to be scooped out, rills to be dammed; always something to eat, sassafras root, minnows taken by hand and half cooked on surreptitious fires, red haws and hazelnuts; always some place to be visited with freshness and discovery, dark umbrageous corners to provide that dreaded and delighted panic of the wild.

But perhaps the best service the pasture did us was as a theatre for the dramatization of the bourgeoning social instinct. We played at church and school in it, at scalping and Robinson Crusoe and the Three Bears. We went farther and played at High Priests and Oracles and Sacrifice—and what were we at Taylorville to know of such things?

If this were to be as full an account of my Art as it is of myself, I should have to stop here and try to have you understand how at this time I was all awash in the fluid stuff of it, buoyed and possessed by unknowledgeable splendours, heroisms, tenderness, a shifty glittering flood. I am always checked in my attempt to render this submerged childhood of mine by the recollection of my mother in the midst of the annoyance which any reference to it always caused her, trying judicially to account for it on the basis of my having read too much, with the lurking conviction at the bottom of all comment that a few more spankings might have effectually counteracted it. But though I read more than the other children, there was never very much to read in Taylorville at any time, and no amount of reading could have put into my mind what I found there—the sustaining fairy wonder of the world.

I was not, I think, different in kind from the other children, except as being more consistently immersed in it and never quite dispossessed. I have lost and rediscovered the way to it some several times; have indeed, had to defend its approaches with violence and skill: this whole business of the biography has no other point, in fact, than to show you how far my human behaviour has been timed to keep what I believe most people part with

8

no more distressfully than with their milk teeth. Effie, I know, has no recollection of this period other than that there was a time when the earth was hung with vestiges of splendour, and if my brother has kept anything of his original inheritance, he would sooner admit to a left over appetite for jujubes and liquorice; for Forester is fully of the common opinion that the fevers, flights and drops of temperament are the mere infirmity of Gift. There was a time, before I left off talking to Forester at all about my work, when he visibly permitted his pity to assuage his disgust at the persistence of so patent a silliness in me, and still earlier, before I owned three motor cars, an estate in Florida and a house on the Hudson, there were not wanting intimations of its voluntary assumption as a pose; pose in Forester's vocabulary standing for any frame of behaviour to which he is not naturally addicted. But there it was, the flux of experience rising to the surface of our plays, the reservoir from which later, without having personally contemplated such an act, I drew the authority for how Lady Macbeth must have felt, about to do a murder, from which if I had had a taste for it, I might have drawn with like assurance the necessity of the square of the hypothenuse to equal the squares of the other two sides.

It is curious that, though I cannot remember how my father looked nor who taught me long division, I recall perfectly how the reddening blackberry leaves lay under the hoar frost in Hadley's pasture, and the dew between the pale gold wires of the grass on summer mornings, and the very words and rites by which we paid observance to Snockerty. I am not sure whether Ellen McGee or I invented him, but first and last he got us into as much trouble as though we had not always distinctly recognized him for an invention. The McGees lived quite around the corner of the pasture from us, and, as far as my memory serves, the whole seven of them had nothing to do but lie in wait for any appearance of ours in the stump lot; though in respect to their father being a section boss, and the family Catholic, we were not supposed, when we put on our good clothes and went out of the front gate, to meet them socially. I think there must have been also some parental restriction on our intercourse of play, for they never came to our house nor we to theirs; the little Allinghams, in fact, never would play with them. They came to play with us and only included the McGees on the implication of their being our guests. If at any time we three Lattimores were called away,

9

Pauline, who was the eldest, would forthwith marshal her young tribe in exactly the same manner in which she afterward held Henry Mills in the paths of rectitude, and march them straight out of the big gate to their home. I remember how I used perfectly to hate the expression of the little Allinghams on these occasions and sympathize with the not always successfully repressed jeers of the McGees. Mrs. Allingham was the sort of woman who makes a point of having the full confidence of her children—detestable practice—and I have always suspected, in spite of the friendliness of the families, that the little Allinghams used to make a sort of moral instance of us whenever they fell into discredit with their parents. At any rate the report of our doings in Hadley's pasture as they worked around through her to our mother, would lead to episodes of marked coolness, in which we held ourselves each loftily aloof from the other, until incontinently the spirit of play swirled us together again in a joyous democracy.

At the time when the Snockerty obsession overtook us, Ellen McGee was the only real rival I had for the leadership of the pasture; if she had not had, along with all her Irish quickness, a touch of Irish sycophancy, I should have lost all my ascendency after the advent of Snockerty. I feel sure now that Ellen must have invented him; she was most enviably furnished in all the signs of lucky and unlucky and what it meant if you put your stocking on wrong side out in the morning, with charms to say for warts, and scraps of Old World song that had all the force of incantations. Her fairy tales too had a more convincing sound, for she got them from her father, who had always known somebody who knew the human participators. It was commonly insisted by Mrs. Allingham that the McGee children would never come to anything, and I believe, in fact, they never did, but they supplied an element of healthful vulgarity in our lives that, remembering Alfred Allingham's adolescent priggishness, I am inclined to think was very good for us.

If I have said nothing of my parents until now, it is because the part they played in our lives for the first ten years was, from our point of view, negligible. Parents were a sort of natural appendage of children, against whose solidarity our performance had room and opportunity. They kept the house together; they staved off fear—no one, for instance, would think of sleeping in a place where there were no parents—they bulked large between us and the unknown. There was a general notion of our elders toward rubbing it into us that we ought to be excessively grateful to them for not having turned us adrift, *sans* food and housing, but I do not think we took it seriously.

Parents existed for the purpose of rendering the world livable for children, and on the whole their disposition was friendly, except in cases like Mrs. Allingham, who contrived always to give you a guilty sense of having forgot to wipe your feet or tramped on the flower borders. I do not think we had a more active belief in our parents' profession of absorption in our interests than in my father's pretence to be desperately wounded by Forester's popgun, or scared out of his wits when Effie jumped at him from behind the syringa bush. It was admittedly nice of them and it kept the game going, but there were also times when they did not manage it so successfully as we could have wished. I think that we never questioned their right to punish us for disobedience, perhaps because there is, after all, something intrinsically sound about the right of might, though we sometimes questioned the occasion, as when we had been told we might play in the pasture for an hour, of the passage of which we knew as much as wild pigeons. There was always, to me at least, an inexplicableness about such reprisals that mitigated against their moral issue. There was one point, however, upon which we all three opposed an unalterable front; we would *not* kiss and make up after our private squabbles. We fought, or combined against neighbouring tribes, or divided our benefits with an even handedness that obtains nowhere as among children, but we would not be tricked into a status which it might be inconvenient to maintain. I am sure, though, that Mrs. Allingham used rather to put it over my mother for her inability to make little prigs of us.

"Mothers," she would say on the rare occasions when she came to call in the beaded dolman and black kid gloves which other Taylorvillians wore only on Sunday, "MOTHERS," with the effect of making it all capitals, "have an inestimable privilege in shaping their children's characters." This was when we had had our faces surreptitiously washed and been brought in for ceremonial inspection; and a little later she would add, with the air of having tactfully conveyed advice under the guise of information, "I always insist"—here Forester would kick me furtively—"*insist* on having the full confidence of mine," at which point my mother would make excuses to get me out of the room before I, who never could learn that people are not always of the mind they think they are, made embarrassing disclosures.

Up to this time my mother figures chiefly as a woman who tied up our hurts and overruled my father when he tried to beg us off from going to church. I suppose it was the baby always in arms or expected that kept us from romping all over her as we did with my father; and much of her profession of interest in us, which came usually at the end of admonitory occasions, had the cold futility of the family prayers that my mother tried to make appear part of the habitual order when Cousin Judd came to stay with us.

I do not know whether he suspected the hollowness of our morning worship, but I am sure I was never in the least imposed upon by the high moral attitude from which my mother attempted to deal with my misbehaviours. She used to conduct these interviews on the prescription of certain books by the reading of which I was afterward corrupted, on a basis of shocked solemnity that, as she was not without a sense of humour, often broke down under my raw disbelief. Forester, always amenable to suggestion, was sometimes reduced to writhing contrition by these inquisitorial attempts, but I came away from them oftenest not a little embarrassed by her inability to bring anything to pass by them.

I do not think our detachment was greater than is common with young children in families where they are pushed out of their privilege of cuddling as fast as they were in ours. There were thirteen months between Forester and me, another brother, early dead, before Effie, and two that came after. The children who died were always sickly; I think it probable in the country phrase, so appalling in its easy acceptance, my mother had "never seen a well day"; and what was meant to be the joy of loving was utterly swamped for her in its accompanying dread. I seem to have been born into the knowledge that the breast, the lap, and the brooding tenderness were the sole prerogative of babies; it was imperative to your larger estate not to exhibit the weakness of wanting them. There comes back to me in this connection an evening with us three, Forester, Effie and I, squeezed on to the lowest step of the stairs for company, my mother in the dusk, rocking and singing one of those wildly sweet and tragic melodies that the men brought back out of the South as seeds are carried in a sheep's coat. To this day I cannot hear it without a certain swelling to let in the smell of the summer dusk and the flitter of the bats outside and the quaver of my mother's voice. I could see the baby's white gown hanging over her arm—it was the next one after Effie, and already she must have been expecting the next—and the soft screech of the rocker on the deal floor, and all at once I knew, with what certainty it hurts me still to remember, how it felt to be held so close . . . *close* . . . and safe . . . and the swell of the breast under the song, and the swing of the rocker . . . knew it as if I had been but that moment dispossessed . . . and the need . . . as I know now I have always needed to be so enfolded.

I do not remember just what happened; I seem to have come to from a fit of passionate crying, climbed up out of it by a hand that gripped me by the shoulder and shook me occasionally by way of hastening my composure. I was struggling desperately to get away from it . . . away from the mother, who held me so to the mother I had just remembered . . . and there was Jule, the maid, holding up the lamp, ordering me to bed in the dark for having spoiled our quiet evening. Then after what seemed a long time, Effie snuggled up to me under the covers, terrified by my sudden accession of sobs but too loyal to call down the household upon us.

It came back . . . the need of mothering. There was a time when I had lain abed some days with the measles or whatever. I was small enough, I remember, to lie in the crib bed that was kept downstairs for the prevalent baby . . . and my mouth was dry with fever. I recall my mother standing over me and my being taken dreadfully with the need of that sustaining bosom, and her stooping to my stretched arms divinely . . . and then . . . I asked her to put me down again. I have had drops and sinkings, but nothing to compare with this, for there was nothing there you understand . . . the release, the comforting . . . it wasn't there . . . *it was never there at all!*

Chapter 3

But I began to tell you how Ellen McGee and I invented Snockerty and arrived at our first contact with organized society, at least Forrie and Effie and I did, for it led to our being interdicted the society of the McGee children for so long that we forgot to inquire what inconvenience, if any, they suffered on account of it.

You will see for yourself that Ellen must have invented him—where, indeed, should a saint-abhorring, Sunday-schooled Taylorville child get the stuff for it? God we knew, and were greatly bored by His inordinate partiality for the Jews as against all ancient peoples, and by the inquisitorial eye and ear forever at the keyhole of our lives, as Cousin Judd never spared to remind us; and personally I was convinced of a large friendliness brooding over Hadley's pasture, to the sense of which I woke every morning afresh, was called by it, and to it; walking apart from the others, I vaguely prayed. But Snockerty was of the stripe of trolls, leprechauns, pucks, and hobgoblins.

We began, I remember, by thinking of him as resident in an old hollow apple tree, down which, if small trifles were dropped, they fell out of reach and sound. There was the inviting hole, arm high in the apple trunk, into which you popped bright pebbles, bits of glass—and I suppose He might have sprung very naturally from the need of justifying your having parted with something you valued and couldn't get back again, at the prompting of an impulse you did not understand. Very presently the practice grew into the acknowledgment of a personality amenable to our desires.

We took to dropping small belongings in the tree for an omen of the day: whether the spring was full or not, or if we should find any pawpaws in the wood, and drew the augury from anything that happened immediately afterward: say, if the wind ruffled the leaves or if a rabbit ran out of the grass.

It was Ellen who showed the most wit in interpreting the signs and afterward reconciling their inconsistencies, but it was I conceived the notion of propitiating Snockerty, who by this time had come to exercise a marked influence on all our plays, by a species of dramatic entertainment made up of scraps of school exercises, Sunday hymns, recitations, and particularly of improvisations in which Ellen and I vied. There were times when, even in the midst of these ritualistic observances, we would go off at a tangent of normal play, quite oblivious of Snockerty; other times we were so worked upon by our own performance as to make sacrifices of really valuable possessions and variously to afflict ourselves.

It was I, I remember, who scared one of the little Allinghams almost into fits by my rendering in the name of Snockerty of an anathema which I had picked up somewhere, but it was Ellen who contrived to extend His influence over the whole of our territory by finding in every decaying stump and hollow trunk, a means of communication, and deriving therefrom authority for any wild prank that happened to come into her head. It is curious that in all the escapades which were imposed on us in the name of our deity, for which we were duly punished, not one word of the real cause of our outbreaks ever leaked through to our parents. It was the only thing, I believe, the little Allinghams never told their mother, not even when the second youngest in a perfect frenzy of propitiation, made a sacrifice of a handful of his careful curls which I personally hacked off for him with Forester's pocket knife. He lied like a little gentleman and said he had cut them off himself because he was tired of looking like a girl baby.

I think it must have been about the end of Snockerty's second summer that Ellen's wild humour got us all into serious trouble which resulted in my first real contact with authority.

Along the west side of Hadley's pasture, between it and the county road, lay the tilled fields of the Ross property, corn and pumpkins and turnips, against which a solemn trespass board advised us. It was that board, no doubt, which led to our always referring to the owner of it as old man Ross, for except as he was a tall, stooping, white-bearded, childless man, I do not know how he had deserved our disrespect. I have suspected since that the trespass sign did not originate wholly in the alleged cantankerousness of farmer Ross, and that the McGees knew more of the taste of his young turnips and roasting ears than they admitted at the time when Snockerty announced to Ellen through the hollow of a dark, gnarly oak at the foot of Hadley's hill, that he would be acceptably served by a feast of green corn and turnips out of Ross's field. This was the first time the idea of such a depredation had occurred to us, I believe, for we were really good children in the main, but I do not think we had any notion of disobeying. Personally I rather delighted in the idea of being compelled to desperate enterprises. I recall the wild freebooting dash, the scramble over the fence, the rustle of the corn full of delicious intimations of ambush and surprise, the real fear of coming suddenly on old man Ross among the rows, where I suspect we did a great deal of damage in the search for ears suitable to roast, and the derisive epithets which we did not spare to fling over our shoulders as we escaped into the brush with our booty. There was a perfect little carnival of wickedness in the safe hollow where we stripped the ears for roasting—fires too were forbidden us—where we dared old man Ross to come on, gave dramatic rehearsals of what we should do to him in that event, and revelled in forbidden manners and interdicted words. I remember the delightful shock of hearing Alfred Allingham declare that he meant to get his belly full of green corn anyway, for belly was a word that no well brought up Taylorville child was expected to use on any occasion; and finally how we all took hands in a wild dance around the fire and over it, crying,

"Snockerty, Snockerty, Snockerty!"

in a sort of savage singsong.

Following on the heels of that, a sort of film came over the performance, an intimation of our disgust in each other at the connivance of wrongdoing. I remember, as we came up through the orchard rather late, this feeling grew upon us: the sense of taint, of cheapness, which swelled into a most abominable conviction of guilt as we discovered old man Ross on the front porch talking to our father. And then with what a heaviness of raw turnips and culpability we huddled in about our mother, going with brisk movements to and fro getting supper, and how she cuffed us out of her way, not knowing in the least what old man Ross had come about. Finally the overwhelming consciousness of publicity swooped down upon us at my father's coming in through the door, very white and angry, wanting to know if this were true that he had heard—and it was the utmost limit of opprobriousness that our father should get to know of our misdeeds at all. Times before, when we downrightly transgressed by

16

eating wild crabs, or taking off our stockings to wade in the brook too early in the season, we bore our mother's strictures according to our several dispositions. Forester, I remember, was troubled with sensibility and used fairly to give us over to wrath by the advertisement of guilty behaviour. He had a vocation for confession, wept copiously under whippings which did him a world of good, and went about for days with a chastened manner which irritated me excessively. I believe now that he was quite sincere in it, but there was a feeling among the rest of us that he carried the admission of culpability too far. Myself, since I never entered on disobedience without having settled with myself that the fun of it would be worth the pains, scorned repentance, and endured correction with a philosophy which got me the reputation of being a hardened and froward child. That we did not, on this basis, get into more serious scrapes was due to Effie, who could never bear any sort of unpleasantness. Parents, if you crossed them, had a way of making things so very unpleasant.

It was Effie who, if we went to the neighbours for a stated visit, kept her eye upon the clock, and if she found us yielding to temptation, was fertile in the invention of counter exploits just as exciting and quite within the parental pale, and when we did fall, had a genius for extrication as great as Forester's for propitiatory behaviour. So it fell out that our piratical descent on Ross's field was our first encounter with an order of things that transcended my mother's personal jurisdiction.

Up to this time contact with our parents' world had got no farther than vainglorious imaginings of our proper entry into it, and now suddenly we found that we *were* in it, haled there by our own acts in the unhappy quality of offenders. I think this was the first time in my life that I had been glad it was Forester who was the boy and not I who was made to go with my father and Mr. Allingham to Ross's field to point out the damage, for which they paid.

It was this which sealed the enormity of our offence, money was paid for it, and came near to losing its moral point with Forrie, who felt himself immeasurably raised in the estimate of the other boys as a public character. It served, along with my father's anger, which was so new to us, to raise the occasion to a solemn note against which mere switchings were inconsiderable. No doubt my brother has forgotten it by now, along with Effie, who got off with nothing worse than the complicity of having been one of us, but to me the incident takes rank as the beginning of a new kind of Snockertism which was to array itself indefinitely against the forces inappreciably sucking at the bottom of my life.

It was as if, on the very first occasion of my swimming to the surface of my lustrous seas, I was taken with a line at the end of which I was to be played into shoals and shallows, to foul with my flounderings some clear pools and scatter the peace of many smaller fry—I mean the obligation of repute, the necessity of being loyal to what I found in the world because it had been founded in sincerity with pains. For what my father made clear to us as the very crux of our transgression, was that we had discredited our bringing up. Old man Ross could be paid for his vegetables, but there was nothing, I was given to understand, could satisfy our arrears to our parents' honour, which, it transpired, had been appallingly blackened in the event.

Nothing in my whole life has so surprised me as the capacity of this single adventure for involving us in successive coils of turpitude and disaster; though it was not until we followed my father into the best room the next morning after he had seen Mr. Allingham, still rather sick, for the turnips had not agreed with us, that we realized the worst, rounding on us through a stream of dreadful, biting things that, as my father uttered them, seemed to float us clear beyond the pale of sympathy and hope. I remember my father walking up and down with his hands under his coat behind, a short man in my recollection, with a kind of swing in his walk which curiously nobody but myself seems to have noticed, and a sort of electrical flash in his manner which might have come, as in this instance, from our never being brought up before him except when we had done something thoroughly exasperating: I am not sure that I did not tell Ellen McGee, in an attempt to render the magnitude of our going over, that he rated us in full uniform, waving his sword, which at that moment hung with his regimentals over the mantelpiece.

"Good heavens," he said, "you might have been arrested for it—my children—*mine*—and I thought I could have trusted you. Good heavens!"

Suddenly he reached out as it were over my brother's shoulder, to whom in his capacity as the eldest son most of this tirade was addressed, with a word for me that was to go tearing its way sorely to the seat of memory and consciousness, and, lodging there, become the one point of attachment to support the memory of him beyond his death.

18

"As for you, Olivia," I started at this, for I had been staying my misery for the moment on a red and black table cover which my mother valued, and I was amazed to find myself still able to hate —"as for you, Olivia May"—he would never allow my name to be shortened in the least—"I *am* surprised at you."

He had expected better of me then; he had reached beyond my surfaces and divined what I was inarticulately sure of, that I was different—no, not better—but somehow intrinsically different. He was surprised at me; he did not say so much of Forester, and he *did* say that it was exactly what he had expected of the McGees, but he had had a better opinion of me. I recall a throb of exasperation at his never having told me. I might have lived up to it. But with all the soreness of having dropped short of a possible estimate, that phrase, which might have gone no deeper than his momentary disappointment, is all I have on which to hang the faith that perhaps . . . perhaps some vision had shaped on his horizon of what I might become. I was never anything to my mother, I know, but a cuckoo's egg dropped in her creditable nest. "But," said my father, "I *am* surprised at *you.*"

He was, I believe, one of those men who make a speciality of integrity and of great dependability in public service, which is often brought to answer for the want of private success; an early republican type fast being relegated to small towns and country neighbourhoods. He had a brilliant war record which was partly responsible for his office, and a string of debts pendent from some earlier mercantile enterprise, which, in the occasion they afforded of paying up under circumstances of great stringency, appeared somehow an additional burnish to his name. He was a man everybody liked; that he was extremely gentle and gay in his manner with us on most occasions, I remember very well, and I think he must have had a vein of romance, though I do not know upon what grounds except that among the few books that he left, many were of that character, and from the names of his children, Forester, Olivia May, and Ephemia, called Effie for short, which were certainly not Taylorvillian. Forester grew out of a heroic incident of his soldiering, of which I have forgotten all the particulars except that the other man's name was Forester, and my father's idea of giving it to his son who was born about that time, was that when he should grow up, and be distinguished, the double name of Forester Lattimore should serve at once as a reminder and a certificate of appreciation. I recall that we children, or perhaps it was only I, used to abound in dramatic ima-

19

ginings of what would happen when this belated recognition took place, though in fact nothing ever came of it, which might have been largely owing to my brother's turning out the least distinguished of men.

Whether if my father had lived he would have remained always as much in the dark as to the private sources of my behaviour, I try not to guess, but this incident picked him out for me among the ruck of fathers as a man distinguished for propriety, produced, in the very moment of pronouncing me unworthy of it, the ideal of a personal standard. If he hadn't up to this time affected greatly my gratitude or affections, he began to shine for me now with some of the precious quality which inheres in dreams. And before the shine had gone off I lost him.

Chapter 4

My Father's death, which occurred the March following, came suddenly, wholly fortuitous to the outward eye, and I have heard my mother say, in its inconsequence, its failure to line up with any conceivable moral occasion, did much to shake her faith in a controlling Providence; but affects me still as then, as the most incontrovertible of evidences of Powers moving at large among men, occupied with other affairs than ours. A little while ago, as I sat writing here on my veranda, looking riverward, an ant ran across my paper, which I blew out with my breath into space, and I did not look to see what disaster. It reminded me suddenly of the way I felt about my father's taking off. He was, he must have been, in the way of some god that March morning; that is one of the evidences by which you know that there are gods at all. You play happily about their knees, sometimes they play with you, then you stumble against a foot thrust out, or the clamour of your iniquity disturbs their proper meditations, and suddenly you are silenced. My mother was doubtless right; it would have been better if he had stayed with her and the children, certainly happier, but he got in the way of the Powers.

It is curious that until I began just now to reconstruct the circumstances in which the news of his death came to me, I never realized that I might have been looking on, but high above it, at the very instant and occasion, for, from the window of my room in the second story of the Taylorville grammar school I could see the unfinished walls of the Zimmern block aglimmer with the light which the wind heaped up and shattered against their raw pink surfaces, and a loose board of the scaffolding allowed to remain up all winter, flacking like a torn leaf in the mighty current in which the school building, all the buildings, shook with the steady tremor of reeds in a freshet. Between them the tops of the maples, level like a shorn hedge, kept up an immensity of tormented motion that invaded even the schoolroom with a sense of its insupportable fatigues. I remember there were few at their desks that day, and all the discipline relaxed by the confusion of the wind. At the morning recess there had been some debate about dismissing the session, and one of the young teachers on the third floor had grown hysterical and been reprimanded by the principal.

It must have been about eleven of the clock, while I was watching the little puffs of dust that rose between the planks of the flooring whenever the building shuddered and ground its teeth, divided between an affectation of timorousness which seemed to grow in favour as a suitable frame of behaviour, and the rapid rise of every tingling sense to the spacious movement of the weather and my private dramatization of the demolition of the building, from which only such occupants as I favoured should be rescued by my signal behaviour. Already several children had been abstracted by anxious parents, so that I failed to be even startled by another knocking until my attention was attracted by the teacher opening the door, and opening it wide upon my Uncle Alva.

I saw him step back with a motion of his head sidewise, to draw her after him, but it took all the suggestive nods and winks that, as she drew it shut behind her, were focussed on my desk, to pull me up to the realization that his visit must have something to do with me. It was not, in fact, until I was halfway down the aisle after Miss Jessel called me, that I recovered my surprise sufficiently to assume the mysteriously important air that was proper to the fifth grade on being privileged to answer the door.

There was not, I am sure, in the brief information that I was wanted at home, one betraying syllable; nothing sufficiently unusual in the way Miss Jessel tied me into my hood, nor in finding Effie tied into hers on the first floor, nor in the way her teacher kissed her—everybody kissed Effie who was allowed— nothing in Forester's having already cleared out without waiting for us. We got into the town in the wake of Uncle Alva and between the business blocks where the tall buildings abated the wind. There was no traffic in the streets that day. Here and there a foot passenger with his hat held down by both hands and his coat tails between his legs, staggered into doorways which were snapped to behind him, and from the glass of which faces looked out featureless in the blur of the wind. As we passed the side door of a men's clothing establishment one of these pale human orbs approached to the pane, exhibited a peering movement, rapped on the glass and beckoned. I know now this must have been the working of an instinct to which Taylorville was so habituated that it seemed natural to Uncle Alva—he was only my mother's half brother, not my father's—to send us on with a word about over- taking us, while he crossed the street at the instance of that beckoning finger to be chaffered with in the matter of my father's grave clothes. All this time there was not a word spoken that could convey to us children the import of our unexpected re- lease. We drifted down the street, Effie and I, sidling against the blasts that drove furiously in the crossways, and finally as we caught our breath under a long red sandstone building, I recall being taken violently, as it were, by knowledge, and crying out that my father was dead, that he was dead and I should never see him again. I do not know how I knew, but I knew, and Effie accepted it; she came cuddling up to me in the smother of the wind, trying to comfort me as if, as I think did not occur to her, he had been my father only and not hers at all. I do not recall very well how we got across the town between the shut houses, high shouldered with the cold, except that Uncle Alva did not come up with us, and the vast lapping of the wind that swirled us together at intervals in a community of breathlessness, seemed somehow to have grown out of the occasion and be naturally commensurate with its desolating quality. I do not think it oc- curred to us as strange that we should have been left so to come to the knowledge that grew until, as we came in sight of our home, we were fairly taken aback to find it so little altered from what it had been when we left it three hours before. It had never been an attractive house: yellow painted, with chocolate trim- mings and unshuttered windows against which the wind contrived. It cowered in a wide yard full of unpruned maples that now held up their limbs protestingly, that shook off from their stretched boughs, disclaimers of responsibility; the very smoke wrenched itself from the chimney and escaped, hurryingly upon the wind; the shrubbery wrung itself; whole flights of fallen leaves that had settled soddenly beside the borders all the winter, having at last got a plain sight of it, whirled up aghast and fled along the road. The blinds were down at the front windows, and no one came in or out.

I remember our hanging there on the opposite side of the street for an appreciable interval before trusting ourselves to a usualness which every moment began to appear more frightening, and being snatched back from the brink of panic by the rattle of wheels in the road behind us as a light buggy, all aglitter from point to point of its natty furnishings, drew up at our gate and discharged from the seat beside the driver a youngish man, all of a piece with the turnout, in the trim and shining blackness of his exterior, who, with a kind of subdued tripping, ran up the walk and entered at the door without a knock. I am not sure that Effie identified him as the man who had taken away the babies, indeed, the two who came after Effie were so close together and went so soon, that I have heard her say that she has no recollection of anything except a house enlivened by continuous baby; but she had the knowledge common to every Taylorville child of the undertaker as the only man who was let softly in at unknocked doors, with his frock coat buttoned tight and the rim of his black hat held against his freshly shaven chin. We snatched the knowledge from one another as we caught hands together and fairly dove into the side entrance that opened on the living room.

The first thing I was aware of was the sound of Forester blubbering, and then of the place being full of neighbours and my mother sitting by the fire in a chair out of the best room, crying heartily. We flung ourselves upon her, crying too, and were gathered up in a violence of grief and rocking, through which I could hear a great many voices in a kind of frightened and extenuating remonstrance, "Come now, Mrs. Lattimore. Now Sally—there, there—" at every word of which my mother's sobbing broke out afresh. I remember getting done with my crying first and being very hot and uncomfortable and thinking of nothing but how I should wriggle out of her embrace and get away, anywhere to escape from the burden of having to seem to care; and then, but whether it was immediately after I am not sure, going rather heavily upstairs and being overtaken in the middle of it by the dramatic suggestion of myself as an orphan child toiling through the world—I dare say I had read something like that recently—and carrying out the suggestion with an immense effect on Uncle Alva, who happened to be coming down at that moment. And then the insidious spread through all my soul of cold disaster, out of which I found myself unable to rise even to the appearance of how much I cared.

Of all that time my father lay dead in the best room, for by the usual Taylorville procedure the funeral could not take place until the afternoon of the second day, I have only snatches of remembrance: of my being taken in to look at him as he lay in the coffin in a very nice coat which I had never seen him wear, and the sudden conviction I had of its somehow being connected with that mysterious summons which had taken Uncle Alva away from us that morning in the street; of the "sitting up;" which was done both nights by groups of neighbours, mostly young; and the festive air it had with the table spread with the best cloth and notable delicacies; and mine and Forester's reprisals against one another as to the impropriety of squabbling over the remains of a layer cake. And particularly of Cousin Judd.

He came about dusk from the farm—he had been sent for—looking shocked, and yet with a kind of enjoyable solemnity, I thought; and the first thing he wished to do was to pray with my poor mother.

"We must submit ourselves to the will of God, Sally," he urged.

"O God! *God!*" said my mother, walking up and down. "I'm not so sure God had anything to do with it."

"It's a wrong spirit, Sally, a wrong spirit—a spirit of rebellion." My mother began to cry.

"Why couldn't God have left him alone? What had he done that he should be taken away? What have *I* done—"

"You mustn't take it like this, Sally. Think of your duty to your children. 'The Lord giveth'—"

"Go tell Him to give me back my husband, then—"

Effie and I cowered in our corner between the base burner and the sewing machine; it was terrible to hear them so, quarrelling about God. My mother had her hands to her head as she walked; her figure touched by the firelight, not quite spoiled by childbearing, looked young to me.

"Oh! Oh! Oh!" she cried with every step.

"You mustn't, Sally; you'll be punished for it—"

Cousin Judd shook with excitement; he was bullying her about her Christian submission. I went up to him suddenly and struck him on the arm with my fist.

"You let her alone!" I cried. "Let her alone!"

Somebody spoke out sharply, I think; a hand plucked me from behind—to my amazement my mother's.

"Olivia, Olivia May! I *am* surprised . . . and your father not out of the house yet. Go up to your room and see if you can't learn to control yourself!"

After all there was some excuse for Cousin Judd. There was, in the general estimate, something more than fortuitous circumstance that went to my father's taking off. Early in the winter, when work had been stopped on the Zimmern building, there had been a good deal of talk about some local regulations as to the removal of scaffolding and the security of foot passengers. That the contractors had not been brought to book about it was thought to be due to official connivance; my father had written to the paper about it. But the scaffolding had remained until that morning of the high wind, when it came down all together and a bit of the wall with it. That my father should have been passing on his way to the courthouse at the moment, was a leaping together of circumstances that seemed somehow to have raised it to the plane of a moral instance. It provided just that element of the dramatic in human affairs, which somehow wakens the conviction of having always expected it; though it hardly appeared why my father, rather than the contractor or the conniving city official, should have been the victim. If it wasn't an act of Providence, it was so like one that it contributed to bring out to the funeral more people than might otherwise have ventured themselves in such weather.

It was also thought that if anything of that nature could have made up to her, my mother should have found much to console her in the funeral. The Masons took part in it, as also the G. A. R. and the Republican Club, though they might have made a more imposing show of numbers if all the societies had not been so largely composed of the same members. In addition to all this, my mother's crape came quite to the hem of her dress and Effie and I had new hats. I remember those hats very well; they had very tall crowns and narrow brims and velvet trimmings, and we

25

tried them on for Pauline Allingham after we had gone up to bed the night before the funeral. Mrs. Allingham had called and Pauline had been allowed to come up to us. I remember her asking how we felt, and Effie's being as much impressed by the way in which I carried off the situation as if she had not been in the least concerned in it. And then we sat up in bed in our nightgowns and tried on the hats while Pauline walked about to get the effect from both sides, and refrained, in respect to the occasion, from offering any criticism.

It was the evening after the funeral and everybody had gone away but one good neighbour. The room had been set in order while we were away at the cemetery; the lamp was lit and there was a red glow on everything from the deep heart of the base burner. The woman went about softly to set a meal for us, and under the lamp there was a great bowl of quince marmalade which she had brought over neighbourly from her own stores; the colour of it played through the clear glass like a stain upon the white cloth. It happened to have been a favourite dish of my father's.

For the last year it had been a family use, he being delicate in his appetite, to make a point of saving for him anything which he might possibly eat, and taking the greatest satisfaction in his enjoyment. Therefore it came quite natural for me to get a small dish from the cupboard and begin to serve out a portion of Mrs. Mason's preserves for my father. All at once it came over me . . . the meaning of bereavement; that there was nobody to be done for tenderly; the loss of it . . . the need of the heart for all its offices of loving . . . and the unavailing pain.

Chapter 5

It followed soon on my father's death that we gave up the yellow house with the chocolate trimmings and took another near the high school, and that very summer my mother lengthened my skirts halfway to my shoe tops and began to find fault with my behaviour "for a girl of your age." We saw no more of the McGees after that except as Ellen managed to keep on in the same class at school with me; and Pauline and I found ourselves with a bosom friendship on our hands.

I went on missing my father terribly, but in a child's inarticulate fashion, and it is only lately that I have realized how much of my life went at loose ends for the loss out of it of a man's point of view and the appreciable standards which grow out of his relation to the community. Ever since the Snockerty episode there had been glimmers on my horizon of the sort of rightness owing from a daughter of Henry Lattimore, but now that I had no longer the use of the personal instance, I lost all notion of what those things might be; for though I have often heard my mother spoken of as one of the best women in the world, she was the last to have provided me with a definite pattern of behaviour.

Pauline had struck out a sort of social balance for herself grounded on the fear of what was "common." Her mother had a day at home, from which seemed to flow an orderly perspective of social observances, for which my mother, never having arrived at the pitch of visiting cards, afforded me no criterion whatever.

She had been a farmer's daughter in another part of the state, and had done something for herself in the way of school teaching before she married my father. My grandparents I never saw, but I seem to recall at such public occasions as county fairs and soldiers' reunions, certain tall, farmer-looking men and their badly dressed wives, who called her cousin and were answered by their Christian names, whom I understand to be my mother's relatives without accepting them as mine. They were all soldiers though, the men of our family; you saw it at once in the odd stiffness sitting on their farmer carriage like the firm strokes of a master on a pupil's smudged drawing. I think I got my first notion of the quality of experience in the way they exalted themselves in the memories of marches and battles. There had been a station of the underground railway not ten miles from Taylorville, and there had gone out from the town at the first call, a volunteer company with so many Judds and Wilsons and Lattimores on the roster that it read like the record of a family Bible. They had gone out from, they had come back to, a life as little relieved by adventure as the flat horizon of their corn lands, but in the interim they had stretched themselves, endured, conquered. I have heard political economists of the cross roads account variously for the prosperity of Ohianna in the decade following the civil outbreak, but I have never heard it laid to the

27

revitalizing of our common stock by the shock of its moral strenuosities.

To this day I question whether Cousin Judd got more out of his religion than out of this most unchristian experience, from which he had come back silver tipped as it were, from that empyrean into which men pass when they are by great emotions a little removed from themselves, to kindle in my young mind a realization of the preciousness of passion over all human assets. It came to me, however, in the years between twelve and fifteen that my mother's relations did things with their knives and neglected others with their forks that were not done in circles that by virtue of just such observances, got themselves called Good Society. I was aware of a sort of gracelessness in their vital processes, in much the same way that I knew that the striped and flowered carpet in my mother's best room did not harmonize with the wall paper, and that the curtains went badly with them both. I have to go back to this, and to the fact that my clothes were chosen for wearing qualities rather than becomingness, to account for a behaviour that, as I began to emerge from the illumined mists of play, my mother complained of under the head of my "not taking an interest."

How else was I to protect myself from the thousand inharmonies that chafed against the budding instinct of beauty: the plum-coloured ribbons I was expected to wear with my brown dress, the mottled Japanese pattern upon the gilt ground of the wall paper, against which I had pushed out a kind of shell, hung within with the glittering stuff of dreams.

For just about the time I should have been absorbed in Cousin Lydia's beaded dolman and the turning of my mother's one silk, I was regularly victimized by the fits and starts of temperament, instinctive efforts toward the rehearsal of greater passions than had appeared above my horizon, flashes of red and blue and gold thrown up on the plain Taylorville surface of my behaviour, with the result of putting me at odds with the Taylorvillians.

It was as if, being required to produce a character, I found myself with samples of a great many sorts on my hands which I kept offering, hopeful that they might be found to match with the acceptable article, which, I may say here, they never did. They were good samples too, considering how young I was, of the Magdas, Ophelias, Antigones I was yet to become, of the great lady, good comrade and lover, but the most I got by it was the

28

suspicion of insincerity and affectation. I sensitively suffered the more from it as I was conscious of the veering of this inward direction, without being able to prove what I was sure of, its relevance to the Shining Destiny toward which I moved. If you ask how this assurance differed from the general human hope of a superior happiness, I can only say that the event has proved it, and as early as I was aware of it, moved me childishly to acts of propitiation. I wanted gratefully to be good, with a goodness acceptable to the Powers from which such assurance flowed, but it was a long time before I could separate my notion of this from my earliest ideal of what would have been suitable behaviour to my father, so that all the upward reach of adolescence was tinged by my sense of loss in him.

It was when I was about thirteen and had not yet forgotten how my father looked, that I made an important discovery; on the opposite side of the church, and close to the Amen corner, sat a man with something in the cut of his beard, in the swing of his shoulders, at which some dying nerve started suddenly athrob. I must have seen him there a great many times without noticing, and perhaps the likeness was not so much as I had thought, and I had had to wait until my recollection faded to its note of faint suggestion, but from that day I took to going out of my way to school to pass by Mr. Gower's place of business for the sake of the start of memory that for the moment brought my father near again. I even went so far as to mention to my mother that I liked sitting in church where I could look at Mr. Gower because he reminded me of somebody. We were on our way home on Sunday night—we were always taken to church twice on Sunday—Forester was on ahead with Effie, and just as we came along under the shadow of the spool factory, I had reached up to tuck my hand under my mother's arm and make my timid suggestion.

"Well, somebody who?" said my mother.

"Of my father—"

"Oh," said my mother, "that's just your fancy." But she did not shake off my hand from her arm as was her habit toward proffers of affection, and the moment passed for one of confidence between us. I was convinced that she must have taken notice of the likeness for herself. That was in the spring, and all that summer vacation I spent a great deal of time playing with Nettie Gower for the sake of seeing her father come at the gate about five in the afternoon the way mine had done.

29

Nettie was not an attractive child, and of an age better suited to Effie, who couldn't bear her; the relation, it seemed, wanted an explanation, but it never occurred to me that so long as I withheld my own, another would be found for it. Nettie's brother found it about the time that my friendship with his sister was at its most flourishing. He was no nicer than you would expect a brother of Nettie's to be, though he was good-looking in a red-cheeked way, with a flattened curl in the middle of his forehead, and of late he had taken to hanging about Nettie and me, looking at me with a curious sort of smirk that I was not quite arrived at knowing for the beginning gallantry. He knew perfectly well that I did not come to see Nettie because I was fond of her, but it was yet for me to discover that he thought it was because I was fond of him. I remember I was making a bower in the asparagus bed; I was too old to play in the asparagus bed, but I was making a point of being good enough to do it on Nettie's account, and I had asked Charlie for his knife to cut the stems.

"Come and get it." He was holding it out to me hollowed in his palm; and he would not let go my hand.

"You don't want no knife," he leered sickeningly. "I know what you want." Suddenly I caught sight of Nettie's face with its straight thick plaits of hair and near-sighted eyes narrowed at me behind her glasses, and it struck me all at once that she had never taken my interest in her seriously either.

"Well, what?" I began defensively.

"This!" He thrust out his face toward mine, but I was too quick for him. That was my first sex encounter, and it didn't somehow make it any the less exasperating to realize that what lay behind my sudden interest in Nettie couldn't now be brought forward in extenuation, but I am always glad that I slapped Charlie Gower before the paralyzing sense of being trapped by my own behaviour overtook me. I hadn't found the words yet for the unimagined disgust of the boy's impertinence when, as I was helping to wipe the dishes that evening after supper, I tried to put it to my mother on a new basis which the incident seemed to have created, of our being somehow ranged together against such offences. It was the time for us to have emerged a little from the family relation to the freemasonry of sex, but my mother missed knowing it.

"I am not going to Nettie Gower's any more," I began.

"No?" said my mother; and of course I could not conceive that she had forgotten the confidence in which the connection with Nettie began.

"That Charlie . . . I just hate him. You know, he thought I was coming to see Nettie because of him."

"Well," said my mother, turning out the dishwater, "perhaps you were."

And that, I think it safe to say, is as near as my family ever came to understanding the processes at work behind the incidents of my growing up. Yet I think my mother very often did know that the key to my behaviour did not lie in the obvious explanation of it; and a sort of aversion toward what was strange, which I have come to think of as growing out of her unsophistication, kept her from admitting it. It was less disconcerting to have my springs of action accounted for on the basis of what Mrs. Allingham would have called "common," than to have it arraigned by her own standard as "queer." There was always in Taylorville a certain caddishness toward innovations of conduct, which we youngsters railed at as countrified, which I now perceive to have been no worse than the instinctive movement to lessen by despising it, the terror, the deep, far-rooted terror of the unknown. The incident served, however, to supersede with resentment the sense of personal definite loss in which it had begun.

Before the year was out I had so far forgotten my father that I saw no resemblance to him in Mr. Gower and would not have recognized it had I met it anywhere, though the want of fathering had its share no doubt in landing me, as I cast about for an appreciable rule to live by, in what I have already described as a superior sort of Snockertism. The immediate step to it was my getting converted. That very winter all Taylorville and the six townships were caught up in one of those acute emotional crises called a Revival. It had begun in the Methodist, and gradually involved the whole number of Protestant churches, and had overflowed into the Congregational building as affording the greatest seating room; by the middle of February it was possible to feel through the whole community the ground swell of its disturbances. Night after night the people poured in to it to be flayed in spirit, striped, agonized, exalted at the hands of a practised evangelist, which they *liked*; as it had the cachet of being supernaturally good for them, they liked it with a deeper, more soul-

31

stretching enjoyment than the operas, theatres, social adventure of cities, supposing they had been at hand.

It hardly seems possible with all she had to do, and yet I think my mother could not have missed one of those meetings, going regularly with Cousin Judd, who drove in from the farm more times than you would have thought the farm could have spared him, or with Forester, who had been converted the winter before, though I think he must have regretted the smaller occasion. Left at home with Effie who was thought too young to be benefited by the preaching and too old to be laid by in an overcoat on the Sunday-school benches with dozens of others, heavy with sleep and the vitiated air, late, when I had finished my arithmetic and was afraid to go to bed in the empty house, I would open the window a crack toward the blur on the night from the tall, shutterless windows of the church, and catch the faint swell of the hymns and at times the hysteric shout of some sinner "coming through," and I was as drawn to it as any savage to the roll of the medicine drums.

The backwash of this excitement penetrated even to the schoolroom, as from time to time some awed whisper ran of this and that one of our classmates being converted, and walking apart from us with the other saved in a chastened mystery. And finally Pauline Allingham and I talked it over and decided to get converted too. Pauline, I remember, had not been allowed to attend the meetings and considered her spiritual welfare jeopardized in the prohibition. We knew by this time perfectly well what we had to do, and had arranged to get excused from our respective rooms—Pauline was a grade behind me on account of diphtheria the previous winter—and to meet in the abandoned coal-hole between the boys' and girls' basement. Pauline, who had always an aptitude for proselyting, brought another girl from the sixth grade, who was also under conviction—we had the terms very pat—a thin, hatchet-faced girl who joined the Baptist Church and afterward married a minister, so that she might very easily have reckoned the incident at something like its supposititious value in her life. I remember that we knelt down in the dusty coal-hole where the little children used to play I-spy, and prayed by turns for light, aloud at first, and then, as we felt the approach of the compelling mood, silently, as we waited for the moment after which we might rather put it

32

over our classmates on the strength of our salvation.

It came, oh, it came! the sweep up and out, the dizzying lightness—not very different, in fact, from the breathless rush with which on a first night of *Magda* or *Cleopatra* I have felt my part meet me as I cross between the wings—the lift, the tremor of passion. "Oh," I said, "I'm saved! I'm saved! I know it."

"So am I," said Flora Haines. "I was a long time ago, but I didn't like to say anything." And if I hadn't just been converted I should have thought it rather mean of her. In the dusk of the coal-hole we heard Pauline sniffling.

"I suppose it's because I'm so much worse a sinner," she admitted, "but I just can't feel it."

"You must give yourself into the Lord's hands, Pauline dear." Flora Haines had heard the evangelist. I began to offer myself passionately in prayer as a vicarious atonement for Pauline's shortcomings.

"Don't you feel anything?" Flora urged, "not the least thing?"

"Well . . . sort of . . . something," Pauline confessed.

"Well, of course, that's it."

"Yes, that's it," I insisted.

"Well, I suppose it is," Pauline gave in, mopping her eyes with her handkerchief, "but it isn't the least like what I expected."

We heard the school clock strike the quarter hour, and got up, brushing our knees rather guiltily. Flora Haines and I were kept in all that afternoon recess for exceeding our excuse, but Pauline saved herself by bursting into tears as soon as she reached her room, and being sent home with a headache.

That was on Thursday, and Saturday afternoon we were all to meet at our house and go together to a great children's meeting, where we were expected to announce that we were saved. Pauline was a little late. I was explaining to Flora Haines that I was to join our church on probation on Sunday, but Flora, being a Baptist, had been put off by her minister until the Revival should be over and he could attend to all the baptisms at once. We naturally expected something similar from Pauline.

"I hardly think," she said, stroking her muff and looking very ladylike, "that I shall take such an important step in life until I am older."

"But," I objected, "how can anything be more important?"

"It's your *soul,* Pauline!" Flora Hines was slightly scandalized.

"That's just the reason; it's so important my mother thinks I ought not to take any steps until I can give it my most mature judgment."

Flora Haines and I looked at one another silently; we might have known Pauline's mother wouldn't let her do anything so common as get converted.

Chapter 6

I was duly taken into the church on the following Sabbath, to the great relief of my family, having for once exhibited the normal reaction of a young person in my circumstances, and though I have laid much to the door of that institution of the retarding of my development and the dimming of the delicate surface of happiness, I think now it was not wholly bad for me. If I hadn't up to this time found any way of being good by myself, I was now provided with a criterion of conduct toward which even those who hadn't been able to manage it for themselves, moved a public approbation. I have heard my mother say that even Mr. Farley, the banker, who read books on evolution and was a Freethinker (opprobrious term), had been known to pronounce the church an excellent thing for women.

The church left you in no doubt about things. You attended morning and evening service; as soon as you were old enough for it, which was before you were fit, you taught in Sunday school; you waited on table at oyster suppers designed for the raising of the minister's salary, and if you had any talent for it you sang in the choir or recited things at the church sociables. And when you were married and consequently middle-aged, you joined the W. F. M. S. and the Sewing Society.

It was after the incident of the coal-hole that I began to experience this easy irreproachability, and to build out of its ready-to-hand materials a sort of extra self, from which afterward to burst was the bitter wound of life. For my particular church went farther and provided a chart for all the by-lanes of behaviour. "You were never," said the evangelist, whose relish of the situation on the day that a score or so of us had renounced the devil and all

34

his works, gave me a vague sensation of having made a meal and licked his lips over us, "you should never go anywhere that you could not take your Saviour with you," and when I saw Cousin Judd wag at my mother and she smile and pat her hymn book, I was apprised that we had come to the root of the whole matter.

I have wondered since to how many young converts in Ohianna that phrase has been handed out and with what blighting consequences.

For a Saviour as I knew Him at thirteen and a half, was a solemn presence that ran in your mind with the bleakness of plain, whitewashed walls and hard benches and a general hush, a vague sensation of your chest being too tight for you, and a little of the feeling you had when you had gone to call at the Allinghams and had forgotten to wipe your feet; and it was manifest if you took that incubus everywhere you went you wouldn't have any fun.

It was fortunate at that time that it was not the desire for entertainment that moved me so much as the need of my youth to serve; the unparented hunger for authority. But with the pressure of that environment, if there had been anybody with the wit to see where my Gift lay, what anybody could have done about it is difficult to say. When all that Taylorville afforded of the proper food of Gift, brightness, music, and the dance, was of so forlorn a quality, it has been a question if I do not owe the church some thanks for cutting out the possible cheapening of taste and the satisfaction of ill-regulated applause—that is, if Gift can be hurt at all by what happens to the possessor. It can be cramped and enfeebled in expression, rendered tormenting in its passage and futile to the recipient, but to whom it comes its supernal quality rises forever beyond all attainder.

What happened to the actress during all the time I was undertaken by the church to be made into the sort of woman serviceable to Taylorville, was inconsiderable; what grew out of it for Olivia was no small matter, and much of it I lay without bitterness to Cousin Judd, who, from having got himself named adviser in my father's will, was in a position to affect my life to the worse.

And yet, in so far as I am not an unprecedented sport on the family tree, I had more in common with this shrewd-dealing, loud-praying, twice-removed soldier cousin than with any of my kind, though I should hardly say as much to him, for he has never been in a theatre, and if he still considers me a hopeful subject for prayer it is because his Christian duty rises superior to his conviction.

He is pricked out in my earlier recollections by the difficulty he seems to have had in effecting a compromise between the traditional distrustfulness of the Ohianna farmer toward the Powers in general, and particularly of the weather, and his obligation of Christian Joy, and for a curious effect of not belonging to his wife, a large, uninteresting woman with a sense of her own merit which she never succeeded in imposing on anybody but Cousin Judd. She had a keen appreciation of worldly values which led her always to select the best material for her clothes, and another feeling of their expensiveness which resulted in her being always a little belated in the styles. She approved of religion, though not active in it, and in twenty years she and Cousin Judd had arrived at a series of compromises and excuses which enabled her to appear at church one Sunday in five and still keep up the interest of the clergyman and congregation as to why she didn't come the other four.

Whenever the days were short or the roads too heavy, Cousin Judd would put up over night at our house, and I remember how my mother would always be able to say, looking about the empty democrat wagon as though she expected her in ambush somewhere:

"And you didn't bring Lydia?" and Cousin Judd being able to reply to it as if it were something he had expected up till the last moment, and been keenly disappointed:

"Well, no, Liddy ain't feeling quite up to it," which my mother received without skepticism. After this they were free to talk of other things.

What there was between Cousin Judd and me, with due allowance for the years, was the spark, the touch-and-go of vitality that rose in me to a hundred beckonings of running flood and waving boughs—music and movement; and only the moral enthusiasms of war and religion raised through his heavy farmer stuff. We should have loved one another had we known how; as it was, all our intercourse was marked on his part by the gracelessness of rusticity, and by the impertinence of adolescence on mine. I used regularly to receive his pious admonitions with what, for a Taylorville child, was flippancy; nevertheless there were occasions when we had set off of summer Sunday mornings together to early class, when the church was cool and dim and the smell of

36

the honey locusts came in through the window, that I caught the thrill that ran from the pounding of his fist where he prayed at the other end of the long bench; and there was a kind of blessedness shed from him as with closed eyes and lifted chin he swung from peak to peak of the splendid measure of "How Firm a Foundation," that I garnered up and hugged to myself in place of Art and the Joy of Living. All of which was very good for me and might have answered if it had not come into Cousin Judd's head that he ought to overlook my reading.

By this time I had worked through all my father's books and was ready to satisfy the itch of imagination even with the vicious inaccuracies of what was called Christian literature. The trouble all came of course of my not understanding the nature of a lie. Not that I couldn't tell a downright fib if I had to, or haven't on occasion, but a lie is to me just as silly a performance when it is about marriage or work as about the law of gravitation, and when it is presented to me in the form of human behaviour it makes me sick, like the smell of tuberoses in a close room; and I failed utterly to realize then that there are a great many people capable of living sincerely and at the same time blandly misrepresenting the facts of life in the interests of what is called morality. I do not think it probable that Cousin Judd accepted for himself the rule of behaviour prescribed by the books he recommended—I shall not tell you what they were, but if there are any Sunday-school libraries in Ohianna you will find them on the shelves—but I know that he and my mother esteemed them excellent for the young.

So far as they thought of it at all, they believed that in surrounding me with intimations of a life in which there was nothing more important than settling with Deity the minor details of living, and especially how much you would pay to His establishment, they had done their utmost to provide me with a life in which nothing more important could happen. If you were careful about reading the Bible and doing good to people—that is, persuading them to go to church and to leave off swearing—all the more serious details such as making a living, marrying and having children would take care of themselves; and the trouble was, as I have said, that I believed it. And that was how I found myself farthest from Art and Life at the time when I found myself a young lady.

I had to make this discovery for myself, for there were no social occasions in Taylorville to give a term to your advent into the grown-up world, though there was a definite privilege which marked your achievement of it. There was a period prior to this in which you bumped against things you were too old for, and carromed to the things for which you were quite too young, and about the end of your high-school term you had done with hair ribbons and begun to have company on your own account, and the sort of things began to happen which marked the point beyond which if you fell upon disaster it was your own fault. They happened to me.

By dint of my doing her compositions and of her doing my arithmetic, Pauline Allingham and I had managed to keep together all through the high school, and it was in our last year, when we used to put in the long end of the afternoons at Pauline's, playing croquet, that I first took notice of Tommy Bettersworth. The Bettersworth yard abutted on the Allingham's for the space of one woodshed and a horse-chestnut tree, and it was along in October that I began to be aware that it was not altogether the view of the garden that kept Tommy on the woodshed or in the chestnut tree the greater part of the afternoon. It may be that the adventure with Charlie Gower had sharpened my perception, at any rate it had aroused my discretion; I was carefully oblivious to the proximity of Tommy Bettersworth. But there came a day when Pauline was not, when she wanted to tell me something about Flora Haines which she was afraid he might overhear.

"Come around to the summer-house," she said, "Tommy's always hanging about; I can't think what makes him."

"Always?" I suggested.

"Why, you know yourself he was there last Saturday, and Thursday when we . . ."

"Is he there when you and Flora are there, or only . . ."

"Oh," Pauline gave a gasp, "No—Oh, I never thought . . . Olive . . . I do believe . . . that's it!"

"Well, what?"

"It's *you*, Olive," solemnly. "It must be that . . . he really is . . ." Pauline's reading included more romance than mine.

"Well, he can't say I gave him any encouragement."

"Oh, *of course* not, darling," Pauline was sympathetic. "You couldn't . . . it is *so* interesting. What would the girls say?"

"Pauline, if you ever . . ."

"Truly, I never will. . . . But just *think!*"

But we reckoned without Alfred Allingham. Alfred was not a nice boy at that age; he had come the way of curled darlings to be a sly, tale-bearing, offensive little cad, and the next Saturday, when Pauline turned him off the croquet ground for ribaldry, he went as far as the rose border and jeered back at us.

"I know why you don't want me," he mocked; "so's I can't see Olive and Tommy Bettersworth makin' eyes." He executed a jig to the tune of

> "Olive's mad and I am glad,
> And I know what'll please her—"

At this juncture the wrist and hand of Tommy Bettersworth appeared over the partition fence armed with horse-chestnuts which thudded with precision on the offensive person of Alfred Allingham. Pauline and I escaped to the summer-house. I thought I was going to cry until I found I was giggling, at which I was so mortified that I did cry.

"He'll tell everybody in school," I protested.

"What do you care?" soothed Pauline, "besides, you have to be teased about somebody, you know, and have somebody to choose you when they play clap in and clap out. You just *have* to. Look at me." Pauline had been carrying on the discreetest of flirtations with Henry Glave for some months. "Tommy Bettersworth is a nice boy, and besides, dear, we'll have so much more in common."

Pauline was right. Unless you had somebody to be teased about you were really not in things. I was furiously embarrassed by it, but I was resigned. Tommy sent me two notes that winter and a silk handkerchief for Christmas which I pretended was from Pauline. I am not going to be blamed for this. It was at least a month earlier that I had observed Tommy Bettersworth's inability to get away from Niles's corner on his way home from school until I had passed there on mine. It struck me as a very interesting trait of masculine character; I would have liked to talk it over with my mother on the plane of human interest; it seemed possible she might have noted similar eccentricities. I remember I worked around to it Saturday morning when I was helping her to darn the tablecloths. My mother was not unprepared; she did her duty by me as it was conceived in Taylorville, and did it promptly.

39

"You are too young to be thinking about the boys," she said. "I don't want to hear you talking about such things until the time comes."

This was so much in line with what was expected of parents, that I blinked the obvious retort that the time for talking about such things was when they began to happen, and went on with the tablecloths. But I couldn't tell her about the handkerchief after that. It would have been positively unmaidenly. And after he had sent me a magnificent paper lace valentine, I distinctly encouraged Tommy Bettersworth.

This being the case, I do not know just how it began to be conveyed to me, as in the lengthening evenings of spring, Tommy took to church-going, that his hands were coarse and his ears too prominent, and as I confided solemnly to Pauline, though I had the greatest respect for his character, I simply couldn't bear to have him about. This was the more singular since the church-going was the visible sign of the good influence that, according to the books, I was exercising; and though Tommy was as nearly inarticulate as was natural, I was in no doubt on whose account this new start proceeded. If I had not disliked Tommy very much at this period, why should I have taken to tucking myself between Forester and Effie on the way home, embarrassedly aware of Tommy, whose way did not lie in our direction, scuffling along with the Lawrences on the other side of the street? I seem to remember some rather heroic attempts on Tommy's part to account for his presence there on the ground of wanting to speak privately to Forester, certain shouts and sallies toward which my brother displayed a derisive consciousness of their not being pertinent to the occasion.

I have often wondered how much of these tentative ventures toward an altered relation were observed by our elders; not much, I should think. At any rate no mollifying word drifted down from their heights of experience to our shallows of self-consciousness.

My mother adhered to her notion of my not being at an age for "such things," borne out, I believe, by the consensus of paternal opinion that she might too easily "put notions" in my head; not inquiring what notions might by the natural process of living be already there. Perhaps they were not altogether wrong in this, so delicate is the process of sex development that nature herself obscures the processes. To this day I do not know how much my taking suddenly to going home with Belle Endsleigh by a short cut was embarrassment, and how much a discreet feminine awareness that in my absence Tommy would better manage to make the family take his walking with them as a matter of course, but I remember that I cried when my mother, who did not approve of Belle Endsleigh, scolded me. And then quite suddenly came the click and the loosened tension of the readjustment.

Along about Easter Alfred Allingham told Pauline that Tommy had thrashed Charlie Gower, and though it was supposed to be the strictest secret, it was because Charlie had teased him about me. Pauline was rather scandalized by my insistence that Charlie wouldn't have done it if Tommy hadn't rather conspicuously brought it on himself.

"I call it truly noble of him . . . like a knight." Pauline could always throw the glamour of her reading around the immediate circumstance. "At any rate, after this you can't do anything less than treat him politely," she urged.

Whether it would have made any difference in my attitude or not, it did in Tommy's. I saw that when he came out of the church with us next Sunday. There was a certain aggressive maleness in the way he strode beside me, that there was no mistaking. I looked about rather feebly for Belle.

"I don't see her anywhere," Tommy assured me, "besides, we don't want her." As I could see Tommy in the light that streamed from the church windows, it occurred to me that if he was not good-looking he certainly looked good, and he had a moustache coming.

Forester, who was going through a phase himself, had gone home with Amy Lawrence; Effie lagged behind with mother, talking to Mrs. Endsleigh about the prospects of the Sewing Society raising the money for repainting the parsonage. Looking back to see what had become of them I tripped on the boardwalk.

"If you would take my arm" . . . suggested Tommy. I was aware of the sleeve of his coat under my fingers.

The next turn took us out of sound of the voices; the street lamps flared far apart in the long, quiet avenue. The shed pods of the maples slipped and popped under us with the sweet smell of the sap.

41

"How did you like the sermon?" Tommy wished to know. What I had to say of it was probably not very much to the point. No one overtook us as we walked. There was a sense of tremendous occasions in the air, of things accomplished. I had established the privilege. I was walking home from church with a young man. I was a young lady.

Chapter 7

As often as I think of Olivia Lattimore growing up, I have wondered if there was really no evidence of dramatic talent about, or simply no one able to observe it. There was no theatre at Taylorville, and when from time to time third-rate stock companies performed indifferent plays at the Town Hall, Forrie and Effie and I heard nothing of them except that they were presumably wicked.

Occasionally there were amateur performances in which, when I had won a grudging consent to take part, I failed to distinguish myself. Effie had a very amusing trick of mimicry, and if you had heard her recite "Curfew Shall Not Ring To-night," you would have thought that the Gift on its way from whatever high and unknowable source, in passing her had lighted haphazard on the most unlikely instrument. I was not even clever at my books except by starts and flashes.

I graduated at the high school with Pauline, and afterward we had two years together at Montecito. This was the next town to Taylorville, and its bitter rival. Montecito had a Young Ladies' Seminary, a Business College, and the State Institution for the Blind, for which Taylorville so little forgave it that the new railroad was persuaded to leave Montecito four miles to the right and make its junction with the L. and C. at Taylorville. This carried the farmer shipping away from Montecito, but the victory was not altogether scathless; young ladies were still obliged to go to the seminary, and it enabled Montecito to put on the air of having retired from the vulgar competition of trade and become the Athens of the West.

Pauline and I went over to school on Mondays and home on

Fridays. The course of study was for three years, but because there was Effie to think of and my mother's means were limited, I had only two, and was never able to catch up with Pauline by the length of that extra year. She was always holding it out against me in extenuation and excuse; when she tried to account for my marriage having turned out so badly on the ground of my not having had Advantages, I knew she was thinking of Montecito. She thinks of it still, I imagine, to condone as she does, I am sure, with an adorable womanliness, what in my conduct she no longer feels able to countenance. And yet I hardly know what I might have drawn from that third year more than I took away from the other two, which was, besides the regular course of study, an acquaintance with a style of furnishings not all gilt wall paper and plush brocade, and a renewed taste for good reading. They made such a point of good reading at the seminary that I have always thought it a pity they could not go a little farther and make a practice of it.

The difficulty with most of our reading was that it had no relativity to the process of life in Ohianna; we had things as far removed from it as Dante and Euripides, things no nearer than "The Scarlet Letter" and "David Copperfield," from which to draw for the exigencies of Taylorville was to cause my mother to wonder, with tears in her eyes, why in the world I couldn't be like other people. I read; I gorged, in fact, on the best books, but I found it more convenient to go on living by the shallow priggishness of Cousin Judd's selection. All that splendid stream poured in upon me and sank and lost itself in the shifty undercurrent that made still, by times, distracting eddies on the surface of adolescence.

But whatever was missed or misunderstood of its evidences, the Gift worked at the bottom, throve like a sea anemone under the shallows of girlishness, and, nourished by unsuspected means, was the source no doubt of the live resistance I opposed to all that grew out of Forester's making a vocation of being a good son. I do not know yet how to deal with sufficient tenderness and without exasperation with the disposition of widowed women, bred to dependence, to build out of their sons the shape of a man proper to be leaned upon. It is so justified in sentiment, so pretty to see in its immediate phases, that though my mother was young and attractive enough to have married again, it was difficult not to concur in her making a virtue, a glorification of

43

living entirely in her boy. I seem to remember a time before Forrie was intrigued by the general appreciation, when it required some coercion to present him always in the character of the most dutiful son. He hadn't, for instance, invariably fancied himself setting out for prayer meeting with my mother's hymn book and umbrella, but the second summer after my father died, when he had worked on Cousin Judd's farm and brought home his wages, found him completely implicated. We were really not so poor there was any occasion for this, but mother was so delighted with the idea of a provider, and Forester was so pleased with the picture of himself in that capacity, that it was all, no doubt, very good for him.

He always did bring home his wages after that, which led to his being consulted about meals, and the new curtains for the dining-room, and to being met in the evening as though all the house had been primed for his return, and merely gone on in that expectation while he was away. Effie, I know, had no difficulty in accepting him as the excuse for any amount of household ritual, making a fuss about his birthdays and trying on her new clothes for his approval, but Effie was five years younger than Forester and I was only twenty-two months. It was more, I think, than our community in the gaucheries and hesitancies of youth that disinclined me to take seriously my brother's opinions on window curtains and to sniff at my mother's affectionate pretence of his being the head of the family. At times when I felt this going on in our house, there rose up like a wisp of fog between me and the glittering promise of the future, a kind of horror of the destiny of women; to defer and adjust, to maintain the attitude of acquiescence toward opinions and capabilities that had nothing more to recommend them than merely that they were a man's! I could be abased, I should be delighted to be imposed upon, but if I paid out self-immolation I wanted something for my money, and I didn't consider I was getting it with my brother for whom I smuggled notes and copied compositions.

It never occurred to my mother, until it came to the concrete question of spending-money, that there was anything more than a kind of natural perverseness in my attitude, which only served to throw into relief the satisfactoriness of her relations to her son. Forester, it appeared, was to have an allowance, and I wanted one too.

"But what," said my mother, tolerantly, for she had not yet

44

thought of granting it, "would you do with an allowance?"

"Whatever Forester does."

"But Forester," my mother explained, waving the stocking she had stretched upon her hand, "is a boy." I expostulated.

"What has that got to do with it?"

"Olivia!" The ridiculousness of having such a question addressed to her brought a smile to my mother's lips, which hung fixed there as I saw her mind back away suddenly in fear that I was really going to insist on knowing what that had to do with it.

"I give you twenty-five cents a week for church money," she parried weakly.

"That's what you think I ought to give. I want an allowance, and then I can deny myself and give what I like."

"Forester earns his," said my mother; she hadn't of course meant the discussion to get on to a basis of reasonableness.

"Well," I threatened, "I'll earn mine."

That was really what did the business in the end. All the boys in Taylorville worked as soon as they were old enough, but it was the last resort of poverty that girls should be put to wages. Before that possibility my mother retreated into amused indulgence. She paid me my allowance, appreciably less than my brother's, on the first of the month, with the air of concurring in a joke, which I think now must have covered some vague hurt at my want of sympathy with the beautiful fiction of Forester's growing up to take my father's place with her. They had achieved by the time Forester was twenty, what passed for perfect confidence between them, though it was at the cost of Forester's living shallowly or not at all in the courts of boyhood which my mother was unable to reënter, and her voluntary withdrawal from varieties of experience from which his youth prevented him. My mother always thought it was made up to her in affection; what came out of it for Forester is still on the knees of the gods.

I began to say how it was that the Gift took care of itself while Forester was engrossing the family attention. He had had a year at the business college in Montecito, which was considered quite sufficient, and rather more, in fact, than his accepted vocation as the support of his mother seemed to call for. Any question that might naturally come up of a profession for him, seemed to have been quashed beforehand by the general notion of an immediate salary as the means to that end. I do not recall a voice lifted on behalf of a life of his own. He had worked up from driving the

45

delivery wagon in vacations to being dry goods clerk at the Coöperative, where his affability and easy familiarity with the requirements of women, made him immensely popular. Everybody liked to trade with Forester because he took such pains in matching things, and he was such a good boy to his mother. He paid the largest portion of his salary for his board, and took Effie, who adored him, about with him. I don't mean to say that he was not also good friends with Olivia, or that there was anything which prevented my doing my best with the three chocolate layer cakes and the angel's food I made for his party on his twenty-first birthday.

The real unpleasantness on that occasion came of my mother's notion of distinguishing it among all other birthdays by paying over to Forester a third of the not very considerable sum left by my father, derived chiefly from his back pay as an officer, which she had always held as particularly set aside for us children. It was owing perhaps to a form of secretiveness that in unprotected woman does duty for caution, that Effie and I had scarcely heard of this sum until it was flourished before us on the day before the birthday, much as if it had been my father's sword, supposing the occasion to have required it being girded on his son.

Forester was to have a third of that money in the form of a check under his plate on the morning of his birthday. Effie and I did full justice to the magnificence of the proposal. I was beating the whites of thirteen eggs by Pauline's recipe for angel food—mine called for only eleven—and Effie was rubbing up Mrs. Endsleigh's spoons, which had been borrowed for the party.

I was always happier in the kitchen than in any room of the house, with its plain tinted walls, the plain painted woodwork (the parlour was hideously "grained"), and the red of Effie's geraniums at the window ledge. The stir of domesticity, all this talk of my father, intrigued me for the moment into the sense of being a valued and intrinsic part of the family.

"His father would have wanted Forester to have that money," said my mother, "Now that he's of age."

"And when," I questioned, raised by the mention of thirds to the joyous inclusion, "are Effie and I to have ours?"

"Oh," my mother's interest waned, "when you are married, perhaps."

It had grown in my mind as I spoke, that I had been of age now more than a year and nothing had come of it. The suggestion that

46

my father could have taken a less active interest in the event on my behalf, pressed upon a dying sensibility; I resented his being so committed to this posthumous slight and meant to defend him from it.

"He'd have wanted me to have mine on my birthday, the same as Forester," I insisted.

"Oh, Olivia!" My mother's tone intimated annoyance at my claim to being supported by my father in my absurdities, but her good humour was proof against it. "Girls have theirs when they are married," she soothed.

I held up the platter and whisked the stiff froth with the air of doing these things very dexterously; I wasn't going to admit by taking it seriously, that my brother's coming of age was any more important than mine, but I spare you the flippancies by which I covered the hurt of realizing that to everybody except myself, it was.

"It is so like you, Olivia," said my mother, with tears in her eyes, "to want to spoil everything." What I had really spoiled was the free exercise of partiality by which she was enabled to distinguish Forester over her other children, according to her sense of his deserts; and, besides, what in the world would the child do with all that money?

"The same thing that Forester does," I maintained, and then quickly to forestall another objection which I saw rising in her face. "If you were old enough to be married at nineteen, I guess I am old enough to be trusted with a few hundred dollars."

But there I had struck again on the structure of tradition that kept Taylorville from direct contact with the issues of life; anybody was old enough to be married at eighteen, but money was a serious matter. Whenever I said things like that I could see my mother waver between a shocked wonder at having produced such unnaturalness, and the fear that somebody might overhear us. And I didn't know myself what I wanted with that money, except that I craved the sense of being important that went with the possession of it. And of course now that I had been refused it on the ground of sex, it was part of the general resistance that I opposed to things as they were, to have it on principle. Just when I had mother almost convinced that she ought to give it to me, she made it nearly impossible for me to accept, by asking Forester what she ought to do about it. When I had demanded it as the evidence of my taking rank with my brother as a personage, it was insufferable that it should come to me as a concession of his amiability.

What I really wanted of course was to have it put under my plate with an affectionate speech about its being the legacy of a soldier and the witness of his integrity, coupled with the hope that I would spend it in a manner to give pleasure to my dear father, who was no doubt looking on at this happy incident.

There was nothing in me then—there is nothing now—which advised me of being inappropriately the object of such an address, or my replying to it as gallantly as the junior clerk of the Coöperative. To do Forester justice, he came out squarely on the question of my being entitled to the money if he was, but he contrived backhandedly to convey his sense of my obtuseness in not deferring sentimentally to a male ascendancy that I did not intrinsically feel; and I can go back now to these disquieting episodes as the beginning of that maladjustment of my earlier years, in not having a man about toward whom I could actually experience the deference I was expected to exhibit.

Well, I had my check for the same amount and on the same occasion as my brother's, but the feeling in the air of its being merely a concession to my frowardness, prevented me from making any return for it that interfered with Forester's carrying off the situation of coming into his father's legacy on coming of age, quite to my mother's satisfaction. What it might have made for graciousness for once in my life to have been the centre of that dramatic affectionateness, I can only guess. Firm in the determination that since no sentiment went to its bestowal none should go to its acknowledgment, I carried my check upstairs and shook all of the rugs out of the window to account for my eyes being red at ten o'clock in the morning. And that was the way the Powers took to provide against the complete submergence of the actress in the young lady, for though it turned out that I did spend the greater part of the money on my wedding clothes, a portion of it went for the only technical training I ever had.

The real business of a young lady in Taylorville was getting married, but to avoid an obviousness in the interim, she played the piano or painted on satin or became interested in missions. If my money had fallen in eight months earlier I should undoubtedly have spent it on the third year at Montecito; as it was I decided to study elocution. It appeared a wholly fortuitous choice. I was not supposed to have any talent for it, but I burned to spend some of my money sensibly, and it was admittedly sensible for a young lady to take lessons in something. Effie was having music, Flora Haines painted plaques; when Olivia joined Professor Winter's elocution classes at Temperance Hall mother said it looked like throwing money away, but of course I could teach in case anything happened, which meant in case of my not being married or being left a widow with young children.

Professor Winter was the kind of man who would have collected patch boxes and painted miniatures on ladies' fans; not that he could have done anything of the sort on his income, but it would have suited the kind of man he was. He had small neat ways and nice little tricks of discrimination, and microscopic enthusiasms that hovered and fluttered, enough of them when it came to the rendering of a favourite passage, to produce a kind of haze of appreciation like a swarm of midges. Not being able to afford patch boxes or Louis XV enamels, he collected accents instead. The man's memory for phonic variations was extraordinary; all our accustomed speech was a wild garden over which he took little flights and drops and humming poises, extracting, as it were by sips, your private history, things you would have probably told for the asking, but objected to having wrested from your betraying tongue. He would come teetering forward on his neat little boots, upon the toes of which he appeared to elevate himself by pressing the tips of his fingers very firmly together, and when you committed yourself no farther than to remark on the state of the weather or the election outlook, he would want to know if you hadn't spent some time of your youth in the South, or if it was your maternal or paternal grandfather who was Norwegian. Either of which would be true and annoying, particularly as you weren't aware of speaking other than the rest of the world, for if there was anything quite and completely abhorrent to the Taylorville mind it was the implication of being different from other Taylorvillians.

Somewhere the Professor had picked up an adequate theory and practice of voice production, though I never knew anything of his training except that he had been an instructor in a normal school and was aggrieved at his dismissal. After he had advertised himself as open for private instruction and tri-weekly classes at Temperance Hall, there was something almost like a concerted effort at keeping him in the town, because of the credit he afforded us against Montecito. With the exception of a much-

49

whiskered personage who came over from the business college in the winter to conduct evening classes in penmanship, he was the only man addressed habitually as Professor, and the only one who wore evening dress at public functions.

His dress coat imparted a particular touch of elegance to occasions when he gave readings from "Evangeline" and "The Lady of the Lake" (Taylorville's choice), and thoroughly discredited a disgruntled Montecitan who, on the basis of having been to Chicago on his wedding trip, insisted that such were only worn by waiters in hotels.

It would be interesting to record that Professor Winter lent himself with alacrity to the unfolding of my Gift, but, in fact, his imagination hardly strayed so far. He taught phonics and voice production and taught them very well; probably he had no more practical acquaintance with the stage than I had. Certainly he never suggested it for me, and for my part I could hardly have explained why with so little encouragement I was so devoted to the rather tedious drill. Pauline was still at the seminary, and the regular hours of practice made a bulwark against an insidious proprietary air which Tommy Bettersworth began to wear. Besides the voice training, I had a system of physical culture, artificial and unsound as I have since learned, but serving to restrain my too exuberant gesture, and much memorizing of poems and plays for practice work. I hardly know if the Professor had any dramatic talent or not; probably not, as he made nothing, I remember, of stopping me in the middle of a great passion for the sake of a dropped consonant, and deprecated original readings on my part.

It was his relish for musical cadence as much as its intellectual appreciation that led him to select the Elizabethan drama, in the great scenes of which I was letter perfect by the time I had come to the end of the Professor's instruction, and at the end too, it seemed, of my devices for dodging the destiny of women.

Chapter 8

I have tried to sketch to you how in Taylorville we were allowed to stumble on the grown-up consciousness of sex, but I can give you no idea of the extent to which we were prevented from the grown-up judgment.

Somewhere between the ages of sixteen and eighteen, one was loosed on a free and lively social intercourse from which one was expected to emerge later, triumphantly mated. This was obligatory; otherwise your family sighed and said that somehow Olivia didn't seem to know how to catch a husband, and then painstakingly refrained from the subject in your presence; or your mother, if she was particularly loyal, said she had always thought there was no call for a girl to marry if she didn't feel to want to. But anything resembling maternal interference in your behalf was looked upon as worldly minded, or at the least unnecessary. The custom of chaperonage was unheard of; girls were supposed to be trusted.

I do not recall now that I ever had any particular instruction as to how to conduct myself toward young men except that they were never on any account to take liberties. Whatever else went to the difficult business of mating you were supposed to pick up. That I did not pass through this period in entire obliviousness was due to Pauline, who had the keenest appreciation of her effect on the opposite sex. She was the sort of girl who is described as having always had a great deal of attention; she had a nice Procrustean notion of the sort of young man to be engaged to—our maiden imagination hardly went farther than that—and her young ladyhood appeared to be a process of trying it on the greatest possible number of eligible Taylorvillians. When she came home from Montecito she had already met Henry Mills at the house of a roommate where she had spent the Easter vacation, and he had sent her flowers at commencement and verses of his own composition.

It was Pauline who explained to me that unless I had some young man like Tommy Bettersworth who could be counted on,

I could hardly hope to be "in" things—when they made up a party to go sleighing, for instance, or a picnic to Willesden Lake. I liked being in things and did not altogether dislike Tommy Bettersworth. He was a thoroughly creditable beau and required very little handling, for even as early as that I had an inkling of what I have long since concluded, that a man who requires over-much to be played and baited, held off and on, is rather poor game after you have got him. It worried Pauline not a little that I forgave Tommy so lightly for small offences; she was afraid it might appear that I liked him too much, when in truth it was only that I liked him too little. And for complacence, if I had had any disposition toward it, I was saved by the shocking example of Forester, all of whose relations were tinged by his vocation of model son. He had acquired by this time a manner, by the intimacy, greater than is common in boys, with which he lived into the feminine life of the household, and by his daily performance of measuring off petticoats and matching hose, which admitted him to families where we visited, on a footing that enabled him to flirt with the daughters under the very apron-strings of their mothers. You couldn't somehow maintain a strict virginal severity with a young man who had just taken an informed and personal interest in your mother's flannelette wrappers, the credit of whose dutifulness was a warrant for his not meaning anything in particular. In short, Forrie spooned.

I think now there was some excuse for him; he had been wrenched very early by his affections from the normal outbreaks of adolescence; he had never to my knowledge been "out with the boys." Unless he got it in the business of junior clerk at the Coöperative, he could hardly be said to have a male life at all; he was being shaped to a man's performance at the expense of his mannishness. But against his philandering rose up, not only the fastidiousness of girlhood, but some latent sense of rightness, as keen in me as the violinist's for the variation of tone; something that questioned the justice of pronouncing thoroughly moral a young man who, if he never went over the brink, was willing to spend a considerable portion of his time on the edge of it. I should have admired Forester more at this juncture if he had been a little wild—and I knew perfectly that my mother would have interdicted any social life for me whatever if I had permitted a tithe of the familiarities allowed to my brother.

Among the other things which a girl was expected to "pick up," along with the art of attracting a husband, was the vital information with which she was expected to meet the occasion of marrying one. It was all a part of the general assumption of the truth as something not suitable for the young to know, that nobody told us any of these things if they could help it. I do not mean to say that there was not a certain amount of half information whispered about among the girls, who by the avidity for such whisperings established themselves as not quite nice. But Pauline Allingham and I were nice girls. What this meant was that nothing that pertained to the mystery of marriage reached us through all the suppression and evasions of the social conspiracy, except the obviousness of maternity. I remember how intimations of it as part of our legitimate experience, began to grow upon us with a profound and tender curiosity toward very young children, and, particularly on Pauline's part, a great shyness of being seen in their company. But we were not expected to possess ourselves of accurate information until we were already involved in it.

We had reached the age when matrons no longer avoided references to its most conspicuous phases in our presence, before we found words for mentioning it to one another. There was a young aunt of Pauline's lent something to that.

She was a sister of Mr. Allingham, come to stay with them while her husband was absent somewhere in the West. Pauline told me about it one of the week-ends she spent at home from Montecito; this was Saturday afternoon, and she had found the aunt in the house on her return the evening before.

"Do you know," she said, "it is very queer the way I feel about Aunt Alice—the way she is, you know. Mamma hadn't told me, and when I came into the sitting room and saw her, I thought I was going to cry; and it wasn't that I was sorry either . . . I'm awfully fond of her. I just felt it."

"Yes, I know," I admitted.

"Aunt Alice is so sensible," Pauline explained a few weeks later, "she talks to me a great deal; she's only a few years older than I am. She has shown me all her things for the baby. Mamma didn't think she ought . . . you know how mothers are. They're in the bureau drawer in the best room. I'll show them to you some time; Alice won't mind."

Alice didn't mind, it appeared, so it must have been shyness that led us to select the afternoon when the married women were away, and though I cannot forgive the conditions which led us so surreptitiously to touch the fringe of the great experience, I own still to some tenderness for the two girls with their heads together that bright hot afternoon, over the bureau drawer in Mrs. Allingham's best room. Pauline showed me a little sacque which she had crocheted.

"Mother thought I was too young, but Alice said I might."

"You must have liked to, awfully," I envied.

"That's one of the nice things about having children, I should think"—Pauline fingered a hemstitched slip—"you can make things for them."

"Which would you rather have, girls or boys?" I hazarded.

"Oh, girls; you can always dress them so prettily."

"But boys . . . they can do so many things when they grow up." I felt rather strongly on that point.

"Alice says"—Pauline folded the little frock—"that she's so glad to have it she doesn't care which it is." Something, perhaps an echo of my mother's experience, pricked in me.

"They aren't always as glad as that."

"I suppose not. Alice is having this one because she wants it."

We looked at one another. We would have liked to have spoken further, to have defined ourselves, despoiled ourselves of tenderness, nobilities, but around the whole subject lay the blank expanse of our ignorance. We locked the drawer again and went out and played croquet. And that was how we stood toward our normal destiny that summer when Pauline was wondering if Henry Mills meant to propose to her, and I was wondering how much longer I could keep Tommy Bettersworth from proposing to me.

I managed to stave it off until the end of September. On the twenty-second of that month there was a picnic at Willesden Lake. There were ten couples of us, and Flora Haines, who was wanted to count even with a young man who was to join us at the lake, a stranger to most of us, nephew to one of the wealthiest farmers in the township. We had always wished there might have been young people at the Garrett farm, and there was some talk of this nephew, who was to come on a visit, being adopted.

Some of our brothers had made his acquaintance, and Pauline, who had met him at Montecito, had warranted him as "interesting." I believe Flora Haines was invited to pair with him because every girl felt that Flora would be eminently safe to trust her own young man to in the event of Helmeth Garrett proving more worth while.

Henry Mills, who was reading law at the county seat of the adjoining county, had come over for the picnic and was expected to bring matters to a crisis with Pauline, and Forester had a day off to take Belle Endsleigh, who was at the point of pitying him because, though he had such an affectionate disposition, so long as his mother depended on him he couldn't think of marrying. We had no chaperone of course; several of the couples were engaged, and there were brothers; we wouldn't have to put up with the implication that we were not able to manage by ourselves.

It was the sort of day . . . soft Indian summer, painted woodlands, gossamer glinting high in the windless air . . . on which Forester found it necessary to hope brotherly that I should be able to get through it without being silly. By that he meant that the submerged Olivia, however interestingly she might read in a book, was highly incomprehensible and nearly always ridiculous to her contemporaries.

Willesden Lake was properly a drainage pond of four or five acres in extent, drawn like a bow about the contour of two hills; water-lilies grew at the head where a stream came in, and muskrats built at the lower end. The picnic ground was in the hollow between the two hills, by a spring, where the grass grew smooth like a lawn to the roots of oaks burning blood red from leaf to leaf. As it turned out, though we put off lunch for him for an hour, young Mr. Garrett did not come, and as the party sat about on the mossy hummocks in the quiet of repletion, I thought nothing could be so much worth while as to leave Tommy in care of Flora Haines and get away into the woods by myself. The soul of the weather had got into my soul and I felt I should discredit myself with Forester if I stayed. There was a little footpath that led down by a rill to the lake, and as I took it, there was scarcely a sound louder than the soft down-rustle of the painted leaves. There were two or three old boats, half water-logged, tied at the head of the lake, and one of these I found and paddled across to the opposite bank. I had not known there was a path there opening from the dewberry bushes that dipped along the border, but the spirit in my feet answered to its invitation. I followed it up the hill through the leaf drift that heaped whispering in the smoky wood. I spread out my arms as I went and began to move to the rhythm of chanted verse. Where the red and gold and russet banners brushed me I was touched delicately as with flame. I had on a very pretty dress that day, I remember, a thin organdy with a leaf pattern, made up over yellow sateen, and the consciousness of suitability worked happily on my mind. At the top of the hill I struck into an old wood road where it passed through a grove of young hickory, blazing yellow like a host. Here I went slowly and dropped the chanting to the measure of classic English verse; it was the only means of expression Taylorville had provided me. Scene after scene I went through happy and oblivious. I had been at it half an hour perhaps, moving forward with the natural impetus of the play, in the faint old wagon tracks, and had got as far as

—Flowers that affrighted she let fall
From Dis's wagon!—

When I was startled by the clapping of hands, and looked up to see a young man sitting on the top of a rail fence that ran straight across the way, as though he might have stopped there to rest in the act of climbing over.

"I knew you would see me the next minute," he said, "and I wanted to be discovered in the act of appreciation." He sprang down from the fence and came toward me, taking off his hat. "I suppose you are from the picnic; I expected to find you somewhere about. I am Helmeth Garrett."

"They're at the spring—we waited lunch for you. I am Miss Lattimore; Olivia May," I supplemented. I was a little doubtful about that point, for at Taylorville we called one another by our first names. I was pleased with the swiftness with which he struck upon a permissible compromise.

"I owe you all sorts of apologies, Miss Olivia, but the mare I was to ride went lame and uncle couldn't spare me another, so I had an early lunch at the house and walked over." As he stood looking down at me I saw that he had a crop of unruly dark hair and what there was in his face that Pauline had found interesting. He wore a soft red tie, knotted loosely at the collar of a white flannel shirt, and for the rest of him was dressed very much as other young men. All at once a spark of irrepressible friendliness flashed up in smiles between us.

56

It seemed the merest chance then that I had come across the wood to meet him. In the light of what has happened since, I see that the guardian of my submerged self was doing what it could for me; but against the embattled social forces of Taylorville what could even the gods do!

"If you will take me to the others," he suggested, "I can make my excuses, and then we can talk." It was remarkable, I thought, that he should have discovered so early that we would wish to talk. We began to move in the direction of the lake.

"Were you doing a play?" he asked. I nodded.

"How long were you watching me?"

"Since you passed the plum brush yonder; it was bully! Are you going on the stage?" I explained about Professor Winter and the elocution lessons.

"They don't approve of the stage in Taylorville," I finished, touched by the vanishing trace of a realization that up to this moment the objection would have been stated personally.

"And with all your talent! Oh, I know what I'm saying. I lived in Chicago four years and saw a lot of the theatre."

He began to talk to me of the stage, probably much of it neither informed nor profitable, but I had never heard it talked of before in unembarrassed relevancy to living, and he had that trick of speech that goes with the achieving propensity, of accelerating his own energy as he talked, so that its backwater fairly floated us into the ease of intimacy. There was no doubt we were tremendously pleased with one another. I was throbbing still with the measure of verse and moved half trippingly to the rhythm of my blood.

"Do you dance too?" What went with that implied something personal and complimentary.

"Oh, no—a few steps I've picked up at school. That's another of the things we don't approve at Taylorville."

"I say, what a lot of old mossbacks there must be about here anyway. Take my uncle, now. . . ." He went on to tell me how he had tried to induce his uncle, who could afford it, to advance the money for technical training in engineering. Uncle Garrett was of the opinion that Helmeth would do better to get a job with some good man and "pick up things. . . . always managed to get along by rule of thumb himself," said the nephew, "and thinks all the rest of us ought to. I said, 'How would it be with a doctor, now, just to scramble up his medicine?' but you can't get through

57

to my uncle. He thinks a man who can run a thrashing machine is an engineer."

I remember that we found it necessary to sit down on the slope of the hill toward the pond while he sketched for me his notion of what an engineer's career might be. "But you've got to have technical training . . . got to! Talk about rule of thumb . . . it's like going at it with no thumbs at all." In the midst of this we remembered that we ought to be looking for the rest of the picnickers. Once in the boat, however, there was a muskrat's nest which, as something new to him, had to be poked into, and we stopped to gather lilies, which I could not have done by myself without wetting my dress. When we came at last to the spring, we found the lunch baskets huddled under the oak and nobody about.

I think we must have been very far gone by this time in the young rapture of intimacy. The wood was smokily still, and we scuffed great heaps of the leaves together as we walked about pretending to look for the others. I remember it seemed a singular flame-touched circumstance that the leaves flew up from under our feet and fell lightly on our faces and our hair.

"I suppose we can't help finding them; the wonder is they haven't been spoiling our good talk before now."

"Oh," I protested, "if you hadn't been coming to look for them you wouldn't have met me."

"And now that we have met, we are going to keep on. I'm coming to see you. May I?"

"If you care so much. . . ." A little spiral of wind rising fountain-wise out of the breathlessness whirled up a smother of brightening leaves; it caught my skirts and whipped them against his knees. It seemed to have blown our hands together too, though I am at a loss to know how that was.

"Care!" he said. "If I care? Oh, you beauty, you wonder!" All at once he had kissed me.

The electrical moment hung in the air, poised, took flight upward in dizzying splendour. Suddenly from within the wood came a little snigger of laughter.

Chapter 9

I do not know how long it took for the certainty that I had been kissed by an utter stranger in the presence of the entire picnic, to work through the singing flames in which that kiss had wrapped me. We must have walked on almost immediately in the direction of the snigger; I remember a kind of clutch of my spirit toward the mere mechanical act of walking, to hold me fast to the time and place from which there was an inward rush to escape. We walked on. They were all sitting together under a bank of hazel and the girls' laps were filled with the brown clusters. Out of my whirling dimness I heard Helmeth Garrett explaining, as I introduced him, how he had come across me in the wood, looking for them.

"And of course," suggested Charlie Gower, "in such good company you weren't in a hurry about looking for the rest of us." I remembered the asparagus bed and was glad I had slapped him.

"No," my companion looked him over very coolly, "now that I've seen some of the rest of you I'm glad I didn't hurry." Plainly it wasn't going to do to try to take it out of Helmeth Garrett.

As we began by common consent to move back to the spring, Forester drew me by the arm behind the hazel. He was divided between a brotherly disgust at my lapse, and delight to have caught the prim Olivia tripping.

"Well," he exclaimed, "you *have* done it!" Considering what I knew of Forester's affairs this was unbearable.

"Oh! it isn't for *you* to talk—"

"What I want to know is, whether I am to thrash him or not?"

"Thrash him?" I wondered.

"For getting you talked about . . . off there in the woods all afternoon!"

"We weren't—" I began, but suddenly I saw the white bolls of the sycamores redden with the westering sun; we must have been three hours covering what was at most a half hour's walk. "Don't be vulgar, Forester," I went on, with my chin in the air.

"Oh, well," was my brother's parting shot, "I don't know as I

59

ought to make any objection, seeing you didn't."

That, I felt, was the weakness of my position; I not only hadn't made any objection, I hadn't felt any shame; the annoyance, the hurt of outraged maidenliness, whatever was the traditional attitude, hadn't come. Inwardly I burned with the woods afire, the red west, the white star like a torch that came out above it. On the way home Helmeth Garrett rode with us as far as the main road and was particularly attentive to Pauline and Flora Haines. I remember it came to me dimly that there was something designedly protective in this; there was more or less veiled innuendo flying about which failed to get through to me. Pauline put it quite plainly for me when she came to talk things over the day after the picnic. She was sympathetic.

"Oh, my dear, it must be dreadful for you," she cooed; "a perfect stranger, and getting you talked about that way!"

"So I am talked about?"

"My *dear,* what could you expect? And in plain sight of us. If you had only pushed him away, or something."

"I couldn't," I said, "I was so . . . astonished." In the night I had found myself explaining to Pauline how this affair of Helmeth Garrett had differed importantly from all similar instances; now I saw its shining surfaces dimmed with comment like unwiped glass.

"That's just what I *said!*" Pauline was pleased with herself. "I told Belle Endsleigh you weren't used to that sort of thing . . . you were *completely* overcome. But of course he wasn't really a gentleman or he wouldn't have done it." I do not know why at this moment it occurred to me that probably Henry Mills hadn't proposed to Pauline after all, but before I could frame a discreet question she was off in another direction.

"What will Tommy Bettersworth say?"

"Why, what has he got to do with it?"

"O-*liv*-ia! After the way you've encouraged him . . ."

"You mean because I went to the picnic with him? Well, what can he do about it?" Pauline gave me up with a gesture.

"Tommy is the soul of chivalry," she said, "and anybody can see he is crazy about you, simply crazy." What I really wanted was that she should go on talking about Helmeth Garrett. I wanted ground for putting to her that since all we had been sedulously taught about kissing and all "that sort of thing"—that it was horrid, cheapening, insufferable—had failed to establish itself, had in fact come as a sword, divining mystery, it couldn't be dealt with on the accepted Taylorville basis. I felt the quality of achievement in Helmeth Garrett's right to kiss me, a right which I was sure he lacked only the occasion to establish. But when the occasion came it went all awry.

It was the next Sunday morning, and all down Polk Street the frost-bitten flower borders were a little made up for by the passage between the shoals of maple leaves that lined the walks, of whole flocks of bright winged, new fall hats on their way to church. Mother and Effie were in front and two of my Sunday-school scholars had scurried up like rabbits out of the fallen leafage and tucked themselves on either side of my carefully held skirts. Suddenly there was a rattle of buggy wheels on the winter roughed road; it turned in by Niles's corner and drove directly toward us; the top was down and I made out by the quick pricking of my blood, the Garrett bays and Helmeth with his hat off, his hair tousled, and a bright soft tie swinging free of his vest. You saw heads turning all along the block in discreet censure of his unsabbatical behavior. He recognized me almost immediately and turned the team with intention to our side of the street. He was going to speak to me . . . he was speaking. My mother's back stiffened, she didn't know of course. Forrie wouldn't have had the face to tell her, but how many eyes on us up and down the street did know? A Sunday-school teacher in the midst of her scholars. . . . and he had kissed me on Thursday!

"Olivia," said my mother, "do you know that young man? Such manners . . . Sunday morning, too. Well, I am glad that you had the sense to ignore him;" and I did not know until that moment that I had.

It was because of my habit of living inwardly, I suppose, that it never occurred to me that the incident could have any other bearing on our relations than the secret one of confirming me in my impression of our intimacy being on a superior, excluding footing. He had come, as I was perfectly aware, to renew it at the point of breaking off, and this security quite blinded me to the effect my cold reception might have upon him. That he would fail to understnad how I was hemmed and pinned in by Taylorville, hadn't occurred to me, not even when he passed us again on the way home from church, driving recklessly. His hat was on this time, determinedly to one side, and he was smoking, smoking a cigar. I thought at first he had not seen me, but he turned suddenly when he was quite past and swept me a flourish with it held between two fingers of the hand that touched his hat.

At that time in Taylorville no really nice young man smoked, at least not when he would get found out. This offensiveness in the face of the returning church-goers was too flagrant to admit even the appearance of noticing it, but that it would be noticed, taken stock of in the general summing up of our relation, I was sickeningly aware.

Tommy Bettersworth put one version of it for me comfortingly when he came in the evening to take me to church.

"I saw you turn down that Garrett fellow this morning. Served him right . . . that and the way you behaved Thursday . . . just as if you did not find him worth rowing about. A lot of girls make a fuss, and it's only to draw a fellow on; and now you're going to church with me the same as usual; that'll show 'em what *I* think of it." Now, I had clean forgotten that Tommy might come that evening. I was whelmed with the certainty that Helmeth Garrett had gone back to the farm after all without seeing me; and the moment Tommy came through the gate I had one of those rifts of lucidity in which I saw him whole and limited, pasted flat against the background of Taylorville without any perspective of imagination, and was taken mightily with the wish to explain to him where he stood, once for all, outside and disconnected with anything that was vital and important to me. But quite unexpectedly, before I could frame a beginning, he had presented himself to me in a new light. He was cover, something to get behind in order to exercise myself more freely in the things he couldn't understand.

Something more was bound to come out of my relation to Helmeth Garrett; the incident couldn't go on hanging in the air that way; and in the meantime here was an opportunity to put it out of public attention by going out with Tommy. It did hang in the air, however, for three days, during which I pulsed and sickened with expectancy; by Thursday it had reached a point where I knew that if Helmeth Garrett didn't come and kiss me again I shouldn't be able to bear it. It was soon after sundown that I felt him coming.

I took a great many turns in the garden, which, carrying me occasionally out of reach of the click of the gate latch, afforded me the relief of thinking that he might have arrived in the interval when I was out of hearing. His approaching tread was within me.

When it was just seven my mother came out and called:

"Olivia, I promised Mrs. Endsleigh a starter of yeast; I have just remembered. Could you take it to her?"

The Endsleigh backyard was separated from ours by a vacant lot, the houses fronting on parallel streets; there was no sound at the gate and mother had the bowl in a white napkin held out to me, with a long message about where the sewing circle was to meet next Thursday.

"If any body comes,"—for the life of me I couldn't have kept that back,—"you can tell them I'll be back in a minute," I cautioned her.

"Are you expecting anybody?"

"Only Tommy," I prevaricated, instantly and unaccountably. I saw my mother look at me rather oddly over the tops of the glasses she had lately assumed. On the Endsleigh's back porch I found Belle in evening dress gathering ivy berries for her hair.

"Oh," she said, to my plain appearance, "aren't you going?"

"Going where?"

"Oh, if you don't know . . . to Flora's." Belle was embarrassed.

"I hadn't heard of it."

"It's just a few friends," Belle wavered between sympathy and superiority. "Flora is so particular. . . ."

"I couldn't have gone anyway," I interpolated, "I have an engagement." I had to find Mrs. Endsleigh after that and deliver my errand.

When I reached home mother was sitting placidly just outside the circle of the lamp, knitting. She only looked up as I entered and I had to drag it out of her at last.

"Has anybody been here?"

"Nobody that you would care to see."

"But who?"

"That fast-looking young man who tried to speak to you on Sunday. I'm glad you have a proper feeling about such things. Mr. Garrett's nephew, didn't you say? I told him you were engaged."

"Oh, mother!" I was out in panting haste. At the gate I ran square into Tommy Bettersworth.

"Did you see anybody?"

"Nobody. I came through by Davis's. I was coming in," he suggested, as I stood peering into the dark.

"I thought you'd be going to Flora's." A wild hope flashed in

63

me that maybe he was going and I should be rid of him.

"Oh, I don't care much for that crowd. I told her I had an engagement with you." So he had known I was not to be invited. I resented the liberty of his defence. "Let's go down to Niles's and have some ice cream," Tommy propitiated.

"It's too cold for ice cream." I led the way back to the house. I was satisfied there was no one in the street. When we stepped into the fan of light from the lit window, Tommy saw my face.

"Oh, I say, Ollie, you mustn't take it like that. Beastly cats girls are! Flora's just jealous because she thought she was invited to the picnic for that Garrett chap, and you got him; she wants to have a chance at him herself to-night." There was a green-painted garden seat on the porch between the front windows. I sat down on it.

"It's not Flora I'm crying about . . . it is being so misunderstood." I was thinking that Helmeth Garrett would suppose I had stayed away from Flora's on his account; she would never dare to say she had not invited me. Tommy's arm came comfortingly along the back of the bench.

"It's just because they do understand that they are made; they know a fellow would give his eyes to kiss you. Infernal cad! to snatch it like that; and I've never even asked you for one." His voice was very close to my ear. "I tell you, Olivia, I've thought of something. If you were to be engaged to me . . . you know I've always wanted . . . then nobody would have a right to say anything. They'd see that you just left it to me."

"Oh," I blurted, "it's not so bad as that!"

"You think about it," he urged. "I don't want to bother you, but if you need it, why here I am." It was because I was thinking of him so little that I hadn't noticed where Tommy's arm had got by this time. That unfulfilled kiss had seemed somehow to leave me unimaginably exposed, assailed. I was needing desperately then to be kissed again, to find myself revalued.

"It's awfully good of you, Tommy. . . ."

I do not know how it was that neither of us heard Forester come up from the gate; all at once there was his foot on the step; as he came into the porch a soft sound drew him, he stared blankly on us for a moment and then laughed shortly.

"Oh! it's you this time, Bettersworth. I thought it might be that Garrett chap."

That was unkind of Forester, but there were extenuations. I

found afterward that Belle had teased Flora to ask him and he had refused, thinking it unbrotherly when I was not to be invited, and he and Belle had quarrelled.

"I don't know as it matters to you"—Tommy was valiant—"whom she kisses, if I don't mind it."

"You? What have you got to do with it?"

"Well, a lot. I'm engaged to her."

BOOK II

Chapter 1

The first notion of an obligation I had in writing this part of my story, was that if it is to be serviceable, no lingering sentiment should render it less than literal, and none of that egotism turned inside out which makes a kind of sanctity of the personal experience, prevent me from offering it whole. And the next was that the only way in which it could be made to appear in its complete pitiableness, would be to write it from the point of view of Tommy Bettersworth. For after all, I have emerged—retarded, crippled in my affectional capacities, bodily the worse, but still with wings to spread and some disposition toward flying. And when I think of the dreams Tommy had, how he must have figured in them to himself, large between me and all misadventure, adored, dependable; and then how he blundered and lost himself in the mazes of unsuitability, I find bitterness augmenting in me not on my account but his. The amazing pity of it was that it might all have turned out very well if I had been what I seemed to him and to my family at the time when I let him engage himself to me to save me from imminent embarrassment.

My mother, though she took on for the occasion an appropriate solemnity, was frankly relieved to have me so well disposed. Tommy had been brought up in the church, had no bad habits, and was earning a reasonable salary with Burton Brothers, Tailors and Outfitters.

There was nobody whose business it was to tell me that I did not love Tommy enough to marry him. I have often wondered, supposing a medium of communication had been established between my mother and me, if I had told her how much more that other kiss had meant to me than Tommy's mild osculation, she would have understood or made a fight for me? I am afraid she would only have seen in it evidence of an infatuation for an undesirable young man, one who smoked and drove rakishly about town in red neckties on Sunday morning. But in fact I liked Tommy immensely. The mating instinct was awake; all our world clapped us forward to the adventure.

If you ask what the inward monitor was about on this occasion, I will say that it is always and singularly inept at human estimates. If, often in search of companionship, its eye is removed from the Mark, to fix upon the personal environment, it is still unfurnished to divine behind which plain exterior lives another like itself! I took Tommy's community of interest for granted on the evidence of his loving me, though, indeed, after all these years I am not quite clear why he, why Forester and Pauline couldn't have walked in the way with me toward the Shining Destiny. I was not conscious of any private advantage; certainly so far as our beginnings were concerned, none showed, and I should have been glad of their company . . . and here at the end I am walking in it alone.

About a month after my engagement, Henry Mills proposed to Pauline, and she began preparations to be married the following June. Tommy's salary not being thought to justify it so soon, the idea of my own marriage had not come very close to me until I began to help Pauline work initials on table linen.

The chief difference between Pauline and me had been that she had lived all her life, so to speak, at home; nothing exigent to her social order had ever found her "out"; but Olivia seemed always to be at the top of the house or somewhere in the back garden, to whom the normal occasions presented themselves as a succession of cards under the door. I do not mean to say that I actually missed any of these appointed visitors, but all my early life comes back to me as a series of importunate callers whose names I was not sure of, and who distracted me frightfully from something vastly more pleasant and important that I wanted very much to do, without knowing very well what it was. But it was in the long afternoons when Pauline and I sat upstairs together sewing on our white things that I began to take notice of the relation of what happened to me to the things that went on inside, and to be intrigued away from the Vision by the possibility of turning it into facts of line and colour and suitability. It was the beginning of my realizing what came afterward to be such a bitter and engrossing need with me, the need of money.

Much that had struck inharmoniously on me in the furnishings of Taylorville, had identified itself so with the point of view there, that I had come to think of the one as being the natural and inevitable expression of the other; now, with the growing appreciation of a home of my own as a medium of self-realization, I accepted its possibility of limitation by the figure of my husband's income without being entirely daunted thereby. For I was still of the young opinion that getting rich involved no more serious matter than setting about it. As I saw it then, Men's Tailoring and Outfitting did not appear an unlikely beginning; if Tommy had achieved the magnificence I planned for him, it wouldn't have been on the whole more remarkable than what has happened. What I had to reckon with later was the astonishing fact that Tommy liked plush furniture, and liked it red for choice.

I do not know why it should have taken me by surprise to find him in harmony with his bringing up; there was no reason for the case being otherwise except as I seemed to find one in his being fond of me. His mother's house was not unlike other Taylorvillian homes, more austerely kept; the blinds were always pulled down in the best room, and they never opened the piano except when there was company, or for the little girls to practise their music lessons. Mrs. Bettersworth was a large, fair woman with pale, prominent eyes, and pale hair pulled back from a corrugated forehead, and his sisters, who were all younger than Tommy, were exactly like her, their eyes if possible more protruded, which you felt to be owing to their hair being braided very tightly in two braids as far apart as possible at the corners of their heads.

They treated me always with the greatest respect. If there had been anybody who could have thrown any light on the situation it would have been Mr. Bettersworth. He was a dry man, with what passed in Taylorville for an eccentric turn of mind. He had for instance, been known to justify himself for putting Tommy to the Men's Outfitters rather than to his own business of building and contracting, on the ground that Tommy wanted the imagination for it. Just as if an imagination could be of use to anybody!

"So you are going to undertake to make Tommy happy?" he said to me on the occasion of my taking supper with the family as a formal acknowledgment of my engagement.

"Don't you think I can do it?" He was looking at me rather quizzically, and I really wished to know.

"Oh! I was wondering," he said, "what you would do with what you had left over." But it was years before I understood what he meant by that.

About the time I was bridesmaid for Pauline, Tommy had an advantageous offer that put our marriage almost immediately within reach. Burton Brothers was a branch house, one of a score with the Head at Chicago, to whom Tommy had so commended himself under the stimulus of being engaged, that on the establishment of a new store in Higgleston they offered him the sales department. There was also to be a working tailor and a superintendent visiting it regularly from Chicago, which its nearness to the metropolis allowed.

All that we knew of Higgleston was that it was a long settled farming community, which, having discovered itself at the junction of two railway lines that approached Chicago from the southeast, conceived itself to have arrived there by some native superiority, and awoke to the expectation of importance.

It lay, as respects Taylorville, no great distance beyond the flat horizon of the north, where the prairie broke into wooded land again, far enough north not to have been fanned by the hot blast of the war and the spiritual struggle that preceded it, and so to have missed the revitalizing processes that crowded the few succeeding years. Whatever difference there was between it and Taylorville besides population, was just the difference between a community that has fought whole-heartedly and one that stood looking on at the fight.

It was not far enough from Taylorville to have struck out anything new for itself in manners or furniture, but the necessity of going south two or three hours to change cars, and north again several hours more, set up an illusion of change which led to a disappointment in its want of variety. Tommy went out in July, and in a month wrote me that he would be able to come for me as soon as I was ready, and hoping it would not be long. If I had looked, as in the last hesitancies of girlhood I believe I did, for my mother to have raised an objection to my going so far from home, I found myself, instead, almost with the feeling of being pushed out of the nest. It seemed as if in hastening me out of the family she would be the sooner free to give herself without reproach to a new and extraordinary scheme of Forester's. What I guess now to have been in part the motive, was that she already had been touched by the warning of that disorder which finally carried her off, which, with the curious futility of timid women, she hoped, by not mentioning, to postpone.

For a long time now Forester had found himself in the situation of having grown beyond his virtues. That assumption of mannishness which sat so prettily on his nonage was rendered inconspicuous by his majority. People who had forgotten that he had never had any boyhood, found nothing especially commendable in the mild soberness of twenty-three. I have a notion, too, that the happy circumstance of my marriage lit up for him some personal phases which he could hardly have regarded with complacence, for by this time he had passed, in his character of philanderer, from being hopefully regarded as reclaimable to constancy, to a sort of public understudy in the practice of the affections. However it had come about, the young ladies who still took on Forester at intervals, no longer looked on him so much as privileged but as eminently safe; and the number of girls in a given community who can be counted on for such a performance, is limited. That summer before I was married, after Belle Endsleigh had run away from home with a commercial traveler who disappointed the moral instance by making her a very good husband afterward, my brother found himself, as regards the young people's world, in a situation of uneasy detachment. And there was no doubt that the Coöperative, where he had been seven years, bored him excessively. It was then he conceived the idea of reinstating himself in the atmosphere of importance by setting himself up in business.

Adjacent to Niles's Ice Cream Parlours, there was a small stationery and news agency which might be bought and enlarged to creditable proportions. There was, I believe, actually nothing to be urged against this as a matter of business; the difficulty was that to accomplish it my mother would be obliged to hypothecate the whole of her small capital. What my mother really thought about her property was that she held it in trust for the family interest, and that, with the secret intimation of her end which I surmise must have reached her by this time, she believed to be served by Forester's plan. It was so much the general view that by marrying I took myself out of the family altogether, that I felt convinced that she meant, so soon as that was accomplished, to undertake what, in the face of my protesting attitude, she had not the courage to begin. I remember how shocked she was at my telling her that this tying up of the two ends of life in a monetary obligation, would put her and Forester very much in the situation of a young man married to a middle-aged woman. I mention this here because the implication that grew out of it, of my marriage being looked forward to as a relief, had much to do with the failure out of my life at this juncture, of informing intimacy.

A great deal of necessary information had come my way through Pauline's marriage, through the comment set free by Belle Endsleigh's affair, through the natural awakening of my mind toward the intimations of books. Marriage I began to perceive as an engulfing personal experience. Until now I hadn't been able to think of it except as a means of providing pleasant companionship on the way toward that large and shining world for which I felt myself forever and unassailably fit. It began to exhibit now, through vistas that allured, the aspect of a vast inhuman grin. Somewhere out of this prospect of sympathy and understanding, arose upon you the tremendous inundation of Life. Dimly beyond the point of Tommy's joyous possession of me, I was aware of an incalculable Force by which the whole province of my being was assailed, very different from the girlish prevision of motherhood which had floated with the fragrance of orris root from Aunt Alice's bureau drawer in the Allingham's spare room.

I don't say this is the way all girls feel about the approach of maternity, but I saw it then like the wolf in the fairy tale, which as soon as its head was admitted, thrust in a shoulder and so came bodily into the room and devoured the protestant. Long afterward, when I was in a position to know something of the private experience of trapeze performers, I learned that they came to a point sometimes in midspring when the body apprised them of inadequacy, a warning sure to be followed in no long time by disaster. I have thought sometimes that what reached me then was the advice of a body instinctively aware of being unequal to the demands about to be imposed upon it.

I hardly know now by what road I arrived at the certainty that some women, Pauline for instance, were able to face this looming terror of childbearing by making terms with it. Life, it appeared, waited at their doors with respect, modified the edge of its inevitableness to their convenience. If Pauline had been accessible— but she was living in Chicago with Henry Mills, going out a great deal, and writing me infrequent letters of bright complacency. It was only in the last frightened gasp I fixed upon my mother. You

74

must imagine for yourself from what you know of nice girls thirty years ago, how inarticulate the whole business was; the most I can do is to have you understand my desperate need to know, to interpose between marriage and maternity never so slight an interval in which to collect myself and leave off shrinking.

About a week before my wedding we were sitting together at the close of the afternoon; my mother had taken up her knitting, as her habit was when the light failed. Something in the work we had been doing, putting the last touches to my wedding dress, led her to speak of her own, and of my father as a young man. The mention pricked me to notice what I recall now as characteristic of Taylorville women, that, with all she had been through, the war, her eight children, so many graves, there was still in her attitude, toward all these, a kind of untutored virginity. It made, my noticing it then and being touched by it, a sort of bridge by which it seemed for the moment she might be drawn over to my side. On the impulse I spoke.

"Mother," I said, "I want to know. . . . ?"

It seemed a natural sort of knowledge to which any woman had a right. Almost before the question was out I saw the expression of offended shock come over my mother's reminiscent softness, the nearly animal rage of terror with which the unknown, the unaccustomed, assailed her.

"Olivia! Olivia!" She stood up, her knitting rigid in her hands, the ball of it speeding away in the dusk of the floor on some private terror of its own. "Olivia, I'll not hear of such things! You are not to speak of them, do you understand! I'll have nothing to do with them!"

"I wanted to know," I said. "I thought you could tell me. . . ."

I went over and stood by the window; a little dry snow was blowing—it was the first week in November—beginning to collect on the edges of the walks and along the fences; the landscape showed sketched in white on a background of neutral gray. I heard a movement in the room behind me; my mother came presently and stood looking out with me. She was very pale, scared but commiserating. Somehow my question had glanced in striking the dying nerve of long since encountered dreads and pains. We faced them together there in the cold twilight.

"I'm sorry, daughter"—she hesitated—"I can't help you. I don't know . . . I never knew myself."

Chapter 2

It is no doubt owing to the habit of life in Higgleston being so little differentiated from Taylorville that I was never able to get any other impression of it than as a place one put up at on the way to some other; always it bore to my mind the air of a traveller's room in one of those stops where it is necessary to open the trunks but not worth while to unpack them. Nor do I think it was altogether owing to what I left there that my recollection of it centres paganly about the cemetery. In Taylorville, love and birth, though but scantily removed from the savour of impropriety, were still the salient facts of existence, but in Higgleston a funeral was your real human occasion. It was as if the rural fear of innovation had thrown them back for a pivotal centre upon the point of continuity with their past.

It was a generous rolling space set aside for the dead, abutting on two sides on the boardwalks of the town, stretching back by dips and hollows to the wooded pastures. Near the gates which opened from the walk, it was divided off in single plots and family allotments, scattering more and more to the farthest neglected mounds that crept obscurely under the hazel thickets and the sapling oaks, happiest when named the least, assimilated quickliest to their native earth. It was this that rendered the pagan touch, for though nearly all Higgleston was church-going and looked forward to a hymn-book heaven, they seemed to me never quite dissevered from the untutored pastures to which their whole living and dying was a process of being reabsorbed.

Higgleston, until this junction of railroads occurred, had been a close settled farming community, and a vague notion of civic improvement had ripped through the centre of its wide old yards and comfortable, country looking dwellings, a shadeless, unpaved street lined with what were known as business blocks, with a tendency to run mostly to front and a general placarded state of being to let, or about to be opened on these premises.

Beyond the railway station there was a dingy region devoted to car shops and cheap lodgings, known locally as Track Town, whose inhabitants were forever at odds with the older rural population, withdrawing itself into a kind of aristocracy of priority and propriety; and between these an intermediary group, self styled, "the leading business men of the town," forever and trivially busy to reconcile the two factions in the interests of trade. That Tommy was by reason of his position as managing salesman of Burton Brothers, generically of this class, might have had something to do with my never having formed any vital or lasting relations with either community; and it might have been for quite other reasons. For in the very beginning of my stay there, life had seized me; that bubbling, frothing Force, working forever to breach the film of existence. I was used by it, I was abused by it. For what does Life care what it does to the tender bodies of women?

My baby was born within ten months of my marriage and most of that time I was wretchedly, depressingly ill. All my memories of my early married life are of Olivia, in the mornings still with frost, cowering away from the kitchen sights and smells, or gasping up out of ingulfing nausea to sit out the duty calls of the leading ladies of Higgleston in the cold, disordered house; of Tommy gulping unsuitable meals of underdone and overdone things, and washing the day's accumulation of dishes after business hours, patient and portentously cheerful, with Olivia in a wrapper, half hysterical with weakness—all the young wife's dreams gone awry! And Tommy too, he must have had visions of himself coming home to a well-kept house, of delicious little dinners and long hours in which he should appear in his proper character as the adored, achieving male. Not long ago I read a book of a man's life written by a man, in which he justified himself of unfaithfulness because his wife appeared before him habitually in curl papers—and there were days when I couldn't even do my hair!

In the beginning we had taken, in respect to Tommy's position among those same live business men, a house rather too large for us, and we hadn't counted on the wages of a servant. Now with the necessity upon us of laying by money for the Great Expense, we felt less justified in it than ever. This pinch of necessity was of the quality of corrosion on what must have been meant for the consummate experience. I have to dwell on it here because in this practical confusion of my illness, was laid the foundation of our later failure to come together on any working basis. We hadn't, in fact, time to find it; no time to understand, none whatever in which to explore the use of passion and react into that superunion of which the bodily relation is the overt sign—young things we were, who had not fairly known each other as man and woman before we were compelled to trace in one another the lineaments of parents, all attention drawn away from the imperative business of framing a common ideal, to centre on the child.

What this precipitance accomplished was, that, instead of being drawn insensibly to find in the exigencies of marriage the natural unfolding of that inward vitality, always much stronger on me than any exterior phase, I was by the shock of too early maternity driven apart from the usual, and I still believe the happier, destiny of women.

With all this we were spared the bitterness of the unwelcoming thought. Little homely memories swim up beyond the pains and depressions to mark, like twigs and leafage on a freshet, the swelling of the new affection: Effie at Montecito, overruling all my mother's shocked suggestions as to her supposed obliviousness of my condition, sitting up nights to sew for me . . . the dress I tried to make myself . . . the bureau drawer from which I used to take the little things every night to look at them . . . the smell of orris.

"See, Tommy; I've done *so* much to-day. Isn't it pretty?"

"My dear, you've shown that to me at least forty times and I've always said so."

"Yes, but isn't it? . . . the little sleeves . . . did you think anything *could* be so small? Tommy, don't you wish it would *come?*"

We had to make what we could of these moments of thrilled expectancy, of tender brooding curiosity.

I scarcely recall now all the reasons why it was thought best for me to go back to my mother in August, and to the family physician, but I find it all pertinent to my subject. Whatever was done there was mostly wrong, though I was years finding it out. I mean that whatever chance I had of growing up into the competent mother of a family was probably lost to me through the inexactitudes of country practice. We hadn't then arrived at the realization that the well or ill going of maternity is a matter of septics rather than sentiment. Taylorville was a town of ten thousand inhabitants, but at that time no one had heard of such a thing as a trained nurse; the business of midwifery was given over in general to a widow so little attractive that she was thought not to have a chance of marrying again, and by the circumstance of having had two or three children of her own, believed to be eminently fit. To Olivia's first encounter with the rending powers of Life, there went any amount of affectionate consideration and much old wives' lore of an extraordinary character. It seems hardly credible now, but in the beginning of things going wrong, there were symptoms concealed from the doctor on the ground of delicacy.

My baby, too, poor little man, was feeble from birth, a bottle baby; the best that could have been done would hardly have been a chance for him. Lying there in the hot, close room, all the air shut out with the light, in the midst of pains, I made a fight for him, tried to interpose such scraps of better knowledge as had come to me through reading, but they made no headway against my mother's confidential, "Well, I ought to know, I've buried five," and against Forester, who by the added importance of having invested all her fortune, had gained such way with my mother that she listened respectfully to his explication of what should be done for the baby. It was Forester who overbore with ridicule my suggestion that he should be fed at regular hours, for which I never forgave him. But I had enough to do to fortify my racked body against the time when I should be obliged to get up and go on again, as it seemed privately I never should be able.

And they were all so fond and proud of my little Thomas Henry —he was named so for his father and mine—Effie simply adored him; the wonder of his smallness, the way in which he moved his limbs and opened and shut his eyes; quite as if there had never been one born before. The way they hung over him, and the wrong things they did! Even Cousin Lydia drove into church the first Sunday after, for the purpose of holding him for a quarter of an hour in her large, silk poplin arms, at the end of which time she had softened almost to the point of confidence.

"I thought I was going to have one once," she admitted, "but somehow I couldn't seem to manage it." She looked over to where Cousin Judd sat with my mother. "He was always fond of young ones. . . ." It occurred to me then that Cousin Lydia was probably a much misunderstood woman.

Of the next six months at Higgleston after I returned to it with a three months' old baby I have scarcely any recollection that is not mixed up with bodily torment for myself and anxiety for the child. I think it probable that most of that time my husband found the house badly kept, the meals irregular and his wife hysterical. I hadn't anything to spare with which to consider what figure I might have cut in the eyes of the onlooker. Tommy shines out for me in that period by reason of the unwearying patience and cheerfulness with which he successfully ignored the general unsatisfactoriness of his home, and at times for a certain exasperation I had with him, as if by being somehow less quiescent he might have opposed a better front to the encroachments of distress. We did try to help in the kitchen after our finances had a little recovered from the strain of my confinement, a Higgleston girl of no very great competence and a sort of back-door visiting acquaintance with two thirds of the community. Her chief accomplishments while she stayed with us, were concocted out of the scraps and fag ends of our private conversations. I could always tell that Ida had overheard something by the alacrity with which she banged the pots about in the kitchen in order that she might get through with her work and go out and tell somebody. In the end Tommy said that when it came to a choice between getting his own meals and losing his best customers he preferred the former.

All this time I did not know how ill I was because of the consuming anxiety for the baby. I remember times in the night—the dreadful momentary revolt of my body rousing to this new demand upon it, before the mind waked to the selfless consideration; and the failure of composure which was as much weakness as fear; the long watching, the walking to and for, and the debates as to whether we ought or ought not to venture on the expense of the doctor. And for long years afterward what is the bitterest of bitterness, finding out that we had done the wrong thing. To this day I cannot come across any notices of the more competent methods for the care of delicate children, without a remembering pang.

All the time this was going on I was aware by a secondary detached sort of self, that there was a point somewhere beyond this perplexity of pain, at which the joyful possession of my son should begin. I was anxious to get at him, to have speech with him, to realize his identity—any woman will understand—and along about the time the blue flags and the live-for-evers and the white bridal wreaths were at their best in the cemetery, it came upon me terrifyingly that I might, after all, have to let him go without it. We were walking there that day, the first we had thought it safe to take the baby out, for it was customary to walk in the cemetery on Sunday and almost obligatory to your social standing. The oaks were budding, and the wind in the irises and the shadow of them on the tombstones, and the people all in their Sunday best, walking in the warm light, gave an effect of more aliveness than the sombre yards of the town could afford.

Tommy had taken the baby from me, for, though I could somehow never get enough of the feel of him, his head in the hollow of my shoulder, his weight against my arm, I was so little strong myself that I was glad to pretend that it was because he was really getting heavy, and just then we passed a little mound, so low, where a new headboard had been set up with the superscription, "Only son of———and———aged eight months," and it was the age, and the little mound was just the length of my boy. I think there was a rush of tears to cover that, the realization by a kind of prevision that it was just to that he was to come, tears checked in mid-course by the swift up-rush of the certainty, of the reality, of the absoluteness of human experience. For by whatever mystery or magic he had come to identity through me, he was my son as I knew, and not even death could so unmake him.

I dwell upon this and one other incident which I shall relate in its proper place, as all that was offered to me of the traditional compensation for what women are supposed to be. If a sedulous social ideal has kept them from the world touch through knowledge and achievement, it has been because, sincerely enough, they have not been supposed to be prevented from world processes so much as directed to find them in a happier way. This would be reasonable if they found them. What society fails to understand, or dishonestly fails to admit, is that marriage as an act is not invariably the stroke that ushers in the experience of being married.

Whatever proportions the change in my life had assumed to the outward eye, it was only by the imagined pain of loss that I began to perceive that I could never be quite in the same relation to things again, and to identify my experience with the world adventure. I had become, by the way of giving life and losing it, a link in the chain that leads from dark to dark; I had touched for the moment a reality from which the process of self-realization could be measured. It was the most and the best I was to know of the incident called maternity, that whether it were most bitter or most sweet it was irrevocable.

I suppose, though he was always so inarticulate, that Tommy must have caught something of my mood from me. He didn't seem to see anything ridiculous in my holding on to a fold of the baby's skirt all the way home; and when we had come into the house and the boy was laid in his crib again, so wan and so little, I sat on my young husband's knee and cried with my face against his, and he did not ask me what it was about.

I think, though, that we had not yet appreciated how near we were to losing him until my mother came to visit us along in the middle of the summer. She was quite excited, as she walked up from the station with Tommy, and for her, almost gay with the novelty of spending a month with a married daughter, and then as soon as she had sight of the child, I saw her checked and startled inquiry travel from me to Tommy and back to the child's meagre little features, and a new and amazing tenderness in all her manner to me. That night after I was in bed she came in her night-dress and kissed me without saying anything, and I was too surprised to make any motion of response. That was the first time I remember my mother having kissed me on anything less than an official occasion . . . . but she had buried five herself.

Notwithstanding, my mother's coming and the care she took of the baby, seemed to make me, if anything, less prepared for the end. There were new remedies of my mother's to be tried, which appeared hopeful. I recovered composure, thought of him as improving, when in fact it was only I who was stronger for a few nights' uninterrupted sleep. Then there was a day on which he was very quiet and she scarcely put him down from her lap at all. I do not know what I thought of that, nor of the doctor coming twice that day, unsummoned. I suppose my sensibilities must have been blunted by the strain, for I recall thinking when Tommy came home in the middle of the afternoon, how good it was we could all have this quiet time together. It was the end of June. I remember the blinds half drawn against the sun and the smell of lawns newly cut and the damask rose by the window; I was going about putting fresh flowers in the vases, a thing I had of late little time to do . . . suddenly I noticed Tommy crying. He sat close to my mother trying to make the boy's poor little claws curl round his finger, and at the failure tears ran down unwiped. I had never seen Tommy cry. I put down my roses uncertain if I ought to go to him . . . . and all at once my mother called me.

Chapter 3

Very closely on the loss of my baby, of which I have spared you as much as possible, came crowding the opening movement of my artistic career. Within a month I was in a hospital in Chicago, recovering from the disastrous termination of another expectancy that had come, scarcely regarded in the obsession of anxiety and overwork during the last weeks of my boy's life, and had failed to sustain itself under the shock of his death. And after the hospital there was a month of convalescence at Pauline's. It was the first time I had seen her since her marriage.

I found her living in one of those curious, compressed city houses, one room wide and three deep, which, after the rambling, scattered homes of Higgleston, induced a feeling of cramp, until I discovered a kind of spaciousness in the life within. It was really very little else than relief from the accustomed inharmonies of rurality, a sort of scenic air and light that answered perfectly so long as you believed it real. Pauline's wall papers were soft, unpatterned, with wide borders; her windows were hung with plain scrim and the furniture coverings were in tone with the carpets. When ladies called in the afternoon, Pauline gave them tea which she made in a brass kettle over a spirit lamp. You can scarcely understand what that kettle stood for in my new estimate of the graciousness of living: a kind of sacred flamen, round which gathered unimagined possibilities for the dramatization of that eager inward life which, now that the strictures of bodily pain were loosed, began to press toward expression. It rose insistently against the depressing figure my draggled and defeated condition must have cut in the face of Pauline's bright competency and the quality of assurance in her choice of things among which she moved. Whatever her standards of behaviour or furniture, they were always present to the eye, not sunk below the plane of consciousness like mine, and she could always name you the people who practised them or the places where they could be bought and at what price. My expressed interest in the teakettle, led at once to the particular department store where I saw rows

83

of them shining in the ticketed inaccessibility of seven dollars and ninety-eight cents. From point to point of such eminent practicability I was pricked to think of preëmpting some of these new phases of suitability for myself, finding myself debarred by the flatness of my purse. The effect of it was to throw me back into the benumbing sense of personal neglect with which the city had burst upon me. From the first, as I began to go about still in my half-invalided condition, I had been tremendously struck with the plentitude of beauty. Here was every article of human use made fair and fit so that nobody need have lacked a portion of it, save for an inexplicable error in the means of distribution. I, for instance, who had within me the witness of heirship, had none of it.

That I should have felt it so, was no doubt a part of that Taylorvillian fallacy in which I had been reared, that all that was precious and desirable was shed as the natural flower and fruit of goodness. Here confronted with the concrete preciousness of the shop windows, I realized that if there had been anything originally sound in that proposition, I had at least missed the particular kind of goodness to which it was chargeable. I wanted, I absurdly wanted just then to collect my arrears of privilege and consideration in terms of hardwood furniture and afternoon tea-kettles, in graceful, feminine leisure, all the traditional sanctity and enthronement of women, for which I had paid with my body, with maternal anxieties and wifely submission. What glimmered on my horizon was the realization that it was not in such appreciable coin the debt was paid, the beginning of knowledge that seldom, except by accident, is it paid at all. What I learned from Pauline was that most of it came by way of the bargain counter. Not even the Shining Destiny was due to arrive merely by reason of your own private conviction of being fit, but demanded something to be laid down for it; though if you had named the whole price to me at that juncture, I should have refused to pay.

Besides all this, the most memorable thing that came of my visit to Pauline was that I went to the theatre. It was Henry's suggestion; the thought I wanted cheering. Pauline was not going out much that season and her reluctance to claim my attention, in the face of my bereavement, to her own approaching Event, threw at times a shadow of constraint on our quiet evenings. Henry had fallen into a way of taking me out for timid and Higglestonian glimpses of the night sights of the city, but I am not sure it was the obligation of hospitality which led him to propose the theatre. I recall that he displayed a particular knowingness about what he styled "the attractions." What surprised me most was that I discovered no qualms in myself over a proceeding so at variance with my bringing up; and the piece, a broad comedy of Henry's selection, made no particular impression on me other than the singular one of having known a great deal about it before. My criticism of the acting brought Pauline around with a swing from the City Cousin attitude in which she had initiated the experience for me, to one aesthetically sympathetic.

"The things men choose, my dear—and to anybody who has been saturated in Shakespeare as you have! You really must see Modjeska; it will be an inspiration to you. Henry, you must take her to see Modjeska."

I had not yet made up my mind as to whether I liked Henry Mills, but I was willing to go and see Modjeska with him; we had orchestra seats and Pauline insisted on my wearing her black silk wrap. On the way, Henry told me a great deal about Madam Modjeska with that same air of knowingness which fitted so oddly with his assumption of the model husband. I had accustomed myself to think of Henry as an attorney, which in Taylorville meant a man who could be trusted with the administration of widows' property and Fourth of July orations. Henry, it transpired, was a sort of junior partner in one of those city firms whose concern is not with people who have broken the law, but with those who are desirous to sail as close to the wind as possible without breaking it. They had a great deal to do with stock companies, in connection with which Henry had found some personal advantage. He always referred to it as "our office" so that I am in doubt still as to the exact nature of his connection with it; its only relation to his private life was to lead to his habitually appearing in what is known as a business suit, and an air of shrewd reliability. If in the beginning he had any notions of his own as to what a husband ought to be, he had discarded them in favour of Pauline's, and if as early as that he had devised any system of paying himself off for his complicity in her ideals, I didn't discover it.

I saw Modjeska with Henry, in "Romeo and Juliet," and afterward stole away to a matinée by myself and saw her as Rosalind. I do not know now if she was the great artist she seemed, it is so long since I have seen her, but she sufficed. I had no words in which to express my extraordinary sense of possession in her, the profound, excluding intimacy of her art. Long after Henry Mills had gone to his connubial pillow I remained walking up and down in my room in a state of intense, inarticulate excitement. I did not think concretely of the stage nor of acting; what I had news of, was a country of large impulses and satisfying movement. I felt myself strong, had I but known the way, to set out for it. When I found sleep at last, it was to dream, not of the theatre, but of Helmeth Garrett. I was made aware of him first by a sense of fulness about my heart, and then I came upon him looking as he had looked last in the Willesden woods, writing at a table, a pale blur about him of the causeless light of dreams. I recognized the carpet underfoot as a favourite Taylorvillian selection, but overhead, red boughs of sycamore and oak depended through the dream-fogged atmosphere. I stood and read over his shoulder what he wrote, and though the words escaped me, the meaning of them put all straight between us. He turned as he wrote and looked at me with a look that set us back in the wrapt intimacy of the flaming forest . . . . somehow we had got there and found it softly dark! In the interval between my dream and morning, that kiss which had been the source of so much secret blame and secret exultation was somehow accounted for: it was a waif out of the country of Rosalind and Juliet. The sense of a vital readjustment remained with me all that day; there had been after all, in the common phrase, "something between us." But I explained the recrudescence of memory on the basis that it was from Helmeth Garrett that I had first heard of Chicago and Modjeska.

I came back to Higgleston reasonably well, with some fine points of achievement twinkling ahead of me, to have my newfound sense of direction put all at fault by the trivial circumstance of Tommy's having papered the living room. The walls when we took the house, had been finished hard and white, much in need of renewing, from the expense of which our immediate plunge into the cares of a family had prevented us. Casting about for any way of ridding it against my return, of the sadness of association, Tommy had hit upon the idea of papering the room himself in the evenings after closing hours, and by way of keeping it a pleasant surprise, had chosen the paper to his own taste. Any one who kept house in the early 80's will recall a type of paper then in vogue, of large unintelligent arabesques of a liverish bronzy hue, parting at regular intervals upon Neapolitan landscapes of pronounced pinks and blues. Tommy's landscapes achieved the added atrocity of having Japanese ladies walking about in them, and though the room wanted lighting, the paper was very dark. It must have cost him something too! From the amount of his salary which he had remitted for my hospital expenses he could hardly have left himself money to pay for his meals at Higgleston's one doubtful restaurant. The appearance of the kitchen, indeed, suggested that he had made most of them on crackers and tinned ham.

I was glad to have discovered this before I said to him how much better it would have been for him to send me the money and let me select the paper in Chicago. What leaped upon me as he waved the lamp about to show me how cleverly he had matched the borders, was the surprising, the confounding certainty that after all our shared sorrow and anxiety we hadn't in the least come together. I had lived in the house with him for two years, had borne him a child and lost it, and he had chosen this moment of heartrending return, to give me to understand that he couldn't even know what I might like in the way of wall papers.

I suppose all this time when the surface of my attention was taken up with the baby, I had been making unconscious estimates of my husband, but that night just as we had come from the station, the moment of calculating that on a basis of necessary economy, I should have to live at least three years with the evidence of his ineptitude, was the first of my regarding him critically as the instrument of my destiny. And I hadn't primarily selected him for that purpose. I do not know now exactly why I married Tommy, except that marriage seemed a natural sort of experience and I had taken to it as readily as though it had been something to eat, something to nourish and sustain. I hadn't at any rate thought of it as entangling. I did not then; but certainly it occurred to me that for the enlarged standard of living I had brought home with me, a man of Tommy's taste was likely to prove an unsuitable tool.

Slight as the incident of the wall paper was, it served to check my dawning interest in domesticity, and set my hungering mind looking elsewhere for sustenance. We were still a little in arrears on account of the funeral expenses and my illness, and no more improvements were to be thought of; Tommy and I were of one mind in that we had the common Taylorvillian horror of debt. There were other things which seemed to put off my conquest of

87

the harmonious environment, things every woman who has lost a child will understand . . . starting awake at night to the remembered cry . . . the blessed weight upon the arm that failed and receded before returning consciousness. I recall going into the bedroom once where a shawl had been dropped on the pillow, like . . . so like . . . and the memories of infinitesimal neglects that began to show now preposterously blamable.

In my first year at Higgleston I had been rather driven apart from the community by the absorption of my condition and the intimation that instead of being the crown of life it merely saved itself by not being mentioned. Now, in my desperate need of the social function, I began to imagine, for want of any other likeness between us, a community of lack. I thought of Higgleston as aching for life as I ached, and began to wonder if we mightn't help one another.

As the colder weather shut me more into the haunted rooms, Tommy thought it might be a good thing if I took an interest in the entertainment which the I. O. O. F., of which he was a Fellow, was undertaking for the benefit of their new hall. As the sort of service counted on from the wives of prominent members, it might also be beneficial to trade. On this understanding I did take an interest, with the result that the entertainment was an immense success. It led naturally to my being put in charge of the annual Public School Library theatricals and a little later to my being connected with what was the acute dramatic crisis of the Middle West.

There should be a great many people still who remember a large, loose melodrama called "The Union Spy," or "The Confederate Spy," accordingly as it was performed north or south of Mason and Dixon's line, participated in by the country at large; a sort of localized Passion play lifted by its tremendous personal interest free of all theatrical taint. There was a Captain McWhirter who went about with the scenery and accessories, casting the parts and conducting rehearsals, sharing the profits with the local G. A. R. The battle scenes were invariably executed by the veterans of the order, with horrid realism. Effie wrote me that there had been three performances in Taylorville and Cousin Judd had been to every one of them.

With the reputation I had acquired in Higgleston, it came naturally when the town, by its slighter hold on the event, achieved a single performance, for me to be cast for the principal part, unhindered by any convention on behalf of my recent mourning. Rather, so close did the subject lie to the community feeling, there was an instinctive sense of dramatic propriety in my sorrow in connection with the anguish of war-bereaved women. One can imagine such a sentiment operating in the choice of players at Oberammergau. In addition to my acting, I began very soon to take a large share of the responsibility of rehearsals.

I do not know where I got the things I put into that business. Where, in fact, does Gift come from, and what is the nature of it? I found myself falling back on my studies with Professor Winter, on slight amateurish incidents of Taylorville, on my brief Chicago contact even, to account to Higgleston for insights, certainties, that they would not have accepted without some such obvious backing. Nevertheless the thing was there, the aptitude to seize and carry to its touching, its fruitful expression, the awkward eagerness of the community to relive its most moving actualities. Never in America have we been so near the democratic drama.

In the final performance I surprised Tommy and myself with my success, most of all I surprised Captain McWhirter. He was arranging a production of "The Spy" at the twin towns of Newton and Canfield, about two hours south of us, and asked me to go down there for him and attend to alternate rehearsals. Tommy was immensely flattered, pleased to have me forget my melancholy, and the money was a consideration. I saw the captain through with two performances in each town, and three at Waterbury. All this time I had not thought of the stage professionally. I returned to Tommy and the wall paper after the final performance with a vague sense of flatness, to try to pull together out of Higgleston's unwilling materials the stuff of a satisfying existence.

Suddenly in April came a telegram and a letter from Captain McWhirter at Kincade, to say that on the eve of production, his leading lady had run away to be married, and could I, would I, come down and see him through. The letter contained an enclosure for travelling expenses, and a substantial offer for my time. No reasonable objection presenting itself, I went down to him by Monday's train.

89

Chapter 4

On the morning between the second and third performance of "The Spy," for McWhirter never let the people off with less than three if he could help it, as I was sitting in the dining room of the Hotel Metropole at Kincade, enjoying the sense of leisure a late breakfast afforded, I saw the captain making his way toward me through an archipelago of whitish island upon which the remains of innumerable breakfasts appeared to be cast away without hope of rescue from the languid waiters, steering as straight a course as was compatible with a conversation kept up over his shoulder with a man, who for a certain close-cropped, clean-shaven, ever-ready look, might have been bred for the priesthood and given it up for the newspaper business. It was a type and manner I was to know very well as the actor-manager, but as the first I had seen of that species, I failed to identify it. What I did remark was the odd mixture of condescension and importance which the captain managed to put into the fact of being caught in his company. He introduced him to me as Mr. O'Farrell, Mr. Shamus O'Farrell, as though there could be but one of him and that one fully accredited and explained. He defined him further—after some remarks on the performance of the evening before in a key which seemed to sustain the evidence of Mr. O'Farrell's name in favour of his nationality—as manager of the Shamrock Players Company, billed for the first of the week in Kincade.

It turned out in the course of these remarks, which the captain delivered with a kind of proprietary air in us, that Mr. O'Farrell —he called himself The O'Farrell in his posters—had a proposition to make to me. He put it with an admirable mixture of compliment and depreciation, as though either was a sort of stopcock to meet a too reluctant modesty on my part or a too exorbitant demand for payment. I was afterward to know many variations of this singular blend, and to acquaint myself definitely how far it is safe to trust it in either direction before the stop was turned, but for the moment I was under the impression, as no doubt O'Farrell meant I should be, that a thing so perfectly asked for should not be refused.

What he asked was that I should come over to the opera house where the rest of the company awaited us, to assist at a rehearsal in the part left open by the illness of the star. I do not now recall if the manager actually made me an offer in this first encounter, but it was in the air that if I suited the part and the part suited me, I was to regard myself as temporarily engaged in Miss Dean's place.

So naturally had the occasion come about, that I cannot remember that I found any particular difficulty in reconciling myself to a possible connection with the professional stage. There had been no church of my denomination at Higgleston, and I had affiliated with one made up of the remnants of two or three other houseless sects, under the caption of the United Congregations, and there was nothing in its somewhat loosened discipline that positively forbade the theatre. In my work with McWhirter, the play had come to mean so much the intimate expression of life, so wove itself with all that had been profound and heroic in the experience of the people, that it seemed to come quite as a matter of course for me to be walking out between the captain and the manager toward the opera house. O'Farrell, too, must have beguiled me with that extraordinary Celtic faculty for the sympathetic note, for I am sure I received the impression as we went, that his play, "The Shamrock," meant quite as much to the Irish temperament, as "The Spy" could mean to Ohianna. The manager and McWhirter had crossed one another's trails on more than one occasion, which seemed to give the whole affair the colour of neighbourliness.

It transpired in the course of our walk that Laurine Dean, America's greatest emotional actress—it was O'Farrell called her that—had been taken down at Waterbury with bronchitis, and the cast having been already disarranged by an earlier defection, he had been obliged to cancel several one-night stands and put in at Kincade to wait until a substitute could be procured from St. Louis or Chicago, which difficulty was happily obviated by the discovery of Mrs. Olivia Bettersworth.

All this, as I was to learn later, was not so near the truth as it might be, but it served. I could never make out, so insistent was each to claim the credit of it, whether it was O'Farrell or

McWhirter first thought of offering the part to me, but there it was for me to take it or leave it as I was so inclined. Our own performance was in Armory Hall and this was my first entrance of the back premises of a proper stage. I recall as we came in through the stage door having no feeling about it all but an odd one of being entirely habituated to such entrances.

They were all there waiting for us, the Shamrocks, grouped around the prompter's table in a dimly lit, dusty space, with a half conscious staginess even in their informal groupings, men and women regarding me with a queer mixture of coldness and in-gratiation. I had time to take that in, and an impression of shoppy smartness, before Manager O'Farrell with a movement like the shuffling of cards drew us all together in a kind of general intro-duction and commanded the rehearsal to begin. Well, I went on with it as I suppose it was foregone I should as soon as I had smelled the dust of action, which was the stale and musty cloud that rolled up on our skirts from the floor and shook down upon our shoulders from the wings, too unsophisticated even to guess at the situation which the manager's air of genial hurry was so admirably planned to cover. I read from the prompter's book— O'Farrell had sketched the plot to me on the way over—and did my utmost to keep up with his hasty interpolations of the busi-ness. I was feeling horribly amatèurish and awkward in the pres-ence of these second-rate folk, whom I took always far too seri-ously, and suddenly swamped in confusion at hearing the manager call out to me from the orchestra what was meant for instruction, in an utterly unintelligible professional jargon. McWhirter through some notion, I suppose, of keeping his work innocuously amateurish, had used no sort of staginess, and the phrase froze me into mortification. With the strain of attention I was already under I could not even make an intelligent guess at his meaning, as O'Farrell, mistaking my hesitation, repeated it with growing peremptoriness. I could see the rest of the cast who were on the stage with me, aware of my embarrassment, and letting the situation fall with a kind of sulky detachment, which struck me then, and still, as vulgar rather than cruel. Suddenly from behind me a voice smooth and full, translated the clipped jargon into ordinary speech. I had no time, as I moved to obey it, for so much as a grateful glance over my shoulder, but I knew very well that the voice had come from a young woman of about my own age, who, as I entered at the beginning of the rehearsal, had been sitting in the wings, taking in my introduction with the gaze of a tethered cow, quiet, incurious, oblivious of the tether. As soon as I was free from the first act, I got around to her.

"Thank you so much," I began. "You see I am not used—"

"Why do you care?" she wondered. "It is only a kind of slang. They all had to learn it once."

I could see that she sprang from my own class. Taylorville, the high school, the village dressmaker, might have turned her out that moment; and by degrees I was aware that she was beautiful; pale, tanned complexion, thick untaught masses of brown hair, and pale brown eyes of a profound and unfathomed rurality. As she moved across the stage at the prompter's call, with her skirts bunched up on her hip with a safety pin, out of the dust, as if she had just come from scrubbing the dairy, I fairly started with the shock of her bodily perfection and her extraordinary manner of going about with it as though it were something picked up in passing for the convenience of covering. It provoked me to the same sort of involuntary exclamation as though one should see a child playing with a rare porcelain. By contrast she seemed to bring out in the others, streaks and flashes of cheapness, of the stain and wear of unprofitable use.

She came to me again at the end of her scene. "Where do you live?" she wished to know. "I can come around with you and coach you with your part."

"I'm not sure," I hesitated: "I don't know if I shall go on with it." She took me again with her slow, incurious gaze.

"Why, what else are you here for?"

That in fact appeared to be Mr. O'Farrell's view of it, and though I went through the form of taking the day to think it over and telegraph to Tommy, I did finally engage myself to the Shamrock Company for the term of Miss Dean's illness. My husband made no objection except that he preferred I should not use my own name, as indeed, O'Farrell had no notion of my doing, as the posters and programmes stood in Miss Dean's name already.

We had from Thursday to Monday to get up my part. With all my quickness I could not have managed it, except for the alacrity with which, after the first day, all the company played up to my business, prompted me in my lines, and assisted in my make-up. There was, if I had but known it, a reason for this extra helpfulness, which, remembering the way the ladies of the United Congregations had pulled and hauled about the Easter entertain-

93

ment, went far with me toward raising the estimate of professional acting among the blessed privileges. Several members of the cast had felt themselves entitled to Miss Dean's place, for the manager had refused to pay an understudy, and found it easier to concede it to me, a brilliant society woman as I had been figured to them—I suspected McWhirter there—a talented amateur who would return to privacy and trouble the profession no more, rather than to one who might be expected to develop tendencies to keep what she had got. Moreover, they had played to small houses of late, most of the salaries were in arrears, and from the first of my taking hold of it, it began to be certain that the piece would go. For I not only played the part of the gay, melodramatic Irish Eileen, but I played with it. There was all my youth in it, the youth I hadn't had, there was wild Ellen McGee and the wet pastures and the woods aflame. With Tommy and a home to fall back upon, with no professional standing to keep, with no bitterness and rancours, I adventured with the part, tossed it up and made sport of it, played it as a stupendous lark. The rest of the company took it from me that it was a lark, and were as solicitous to see it through for me as though I had been an only child among a lot of maiden aunts. And I did not know of course that this charm of good fellowship was based more directly on the box-office returns than on the community of art.

Incidentally a great deal that went on in my behalf threw light on the character and disposition of the star.

"I 'most wore my fingers off, hookin' 'er up," confided the dresser who took in her gowns for me, "but she won't let out an inch, not she. Well, this spell'll pull'er down a bit, that's one comfort."

Cecelia Brune made me up. She was the youngest member of the company and that she was distractingly and unnecessarily pretty didn't obviate the certainty that in Milwaukee where she was born she had been known as Cissy Brown.

"You don't really need anything but a little colour and black around the eyes," she insisted. "Dean is a sight when she's made up; got so much to cover. I'll bet she is no sicker than me, she's just taken the slack time to get her wrinkles massaged. Gee, if I had a face like hers I'd take it off and have it ironed!"

Cecelia, I may remark, lived for her prettiness; she lived by it. She had a speaking part of half a dozen lines and a dance in the Village Green act, and her mere appearance on the street of any town where we were billed, was good for two solid rows clear across the house. In Cecelia's opinion this was the quintessence of art, to attract males and keep them dangling, and to eke out her personal adornment by gifts which she managed to extract from her admirers without having yet paid the inestimable price for them. Married woman as I was, I was too countrified to understand that inevitably she must finally pay it. She had all the dewy, large-eyed softness of look that one reluctantly disassociates from innocence, and a degree of cold, grubby calculation in which she mistook, flaunted about in fact, for chastity. It was she who told me as much as I got to know for a great many years of Sarah Croyden, who had already taken me with the fascination of her Gift, the inordinate curiosity to know, to touch and to prove, which makes me still the victim of its least elusive promise and the dupe of any poor pretender to it. I wanted something to account for, except when she was under the obsession of a part, her marked inadequacy to her perfect exterior, for the rich full voice that, caught in the wind of her genius, gripped and threatened, but ran through her ordinary conversation as flaccid as a velvet ribbon.

She was, by Cecelia's account, the daughter of a Baptist elder in a small New York town, strictly brought up— I could measure the weals of the strictness upon my own heart—and had run away with an actor named Lawrence, after one wild, brief encounter when O'Farrell had been playing in the town. That was before Cecelia's time and she had no report of the said Lawrence except that he was as handsome as they make them and a regular rotter.

"She'd ought to have known," opined Cecelia—though where in her nineteen years she could have acquired the groundwork of such knowledge was more than I could guess—"She'd ought to have known what she was up against by his bein' so willing to marry her. He wouldn't have put his head in a noose like that without he had hold of the loose end of it himself."

That he had so held it, transpired in less than a year, in the reappearance of a former wife who turned up at his lodging one night to wait his return from the theatre, where, no one knew by what diabolical agency, Lawrence had word of her, and made what Cecelia called a "get away." What passed between the two women on that occasion must have been noteworthy, but it was sunk forever under Sarah's unfathomable rurality. O'Farrell, who of his class was a very decent sort, had been so little able to bear the sight of beauty in distress that he offered the poor girl an unimportant part as an alternative to starvation, and Sarah had very quickly settled what was to become of her by developing extraordinary talent.

I think no one of us at that time quite realized how good she was; Cecelia Brune, I know, did not even think her beautiful.

"No style," she said, settling her corset at the hips and fluffing up her pompadour with my comb, "and no figgur." But myself, I seemed to see her the mere embodiment of a gift which had snatched at this chance encounter with an actor, to swing into opportunity, regardless of its host. Whenever I watched her acting, some living impulse deep within me reared its head.

I have set all this down here because with the exception of Manager O'Farrell and Jimmy Vantine, the comedian, who was thirty-five, objectionable, and in love with Cecelia, these two women were all I ever saw again of the Shamrock players. Miss Dean I did not meet on this occasion, for though at the end of three weeks, before I had time to tire of travel and new towns and nightly triumphs, she wrote she would return to her work, it fell out that she did not actually return until I was well on my way home.

"I thought she would have a quick recovery when she found out what a sweep you'd been makin'," remarked Cecelia. That was all the comment that passed on the occasion. If Mr. O'Farrell made no motion toward making me a permanent member of his company, there were reasons for it that I understood better later. I had to own to a little disappointment that nobody came to the station to see me off except Cecelia and Sarah Croyden. It is true Jimmy Vantine was there, but he left us in no doubt that he only came because Cecelia had promised to spend the interval between their train and my own in his company. He fussed about with my luggage in order to get me off as quickly as possible.

The very bread-and-buttery relation of the Shamrocks to what was for me the community of Art, had never struck so sourly upon me as at the casual quality of their good-byes. I remembered noticing that morning how very little hair there was on the top of Jimmy Vantine's head, and that he did not seem to me quite clean. I found myself so let down after the three weeks' excitement that I thought it necessary at Springfield, where I changed, to interpose two days' shopping between me and Higgleston. Among other things I bought there was a spirit lamp and a brass teakettle.

Chapter 5

Understand that up to this time I had not yet thought of the stage as a career for myself. I hadn't yet needed it. I had not then realized that the insight and passion which have singled me out among women of my profession couldn't be turned to render the mere business of living beautiful and fit. I hardly understand it now. Why should people pay night after night to see me loving, achieving, suffering, in a way they wouldn't think of undertaking for themselves? Life as I saw it was sufficiently dramatic: charged, wonderful. I at least felt at home in the great moments of kings, the tender hours of poets, and I hadn't thought of my participation in these things rendering me in any way superior to Higgleston or even different. If I had, I shouldn't have settled there in the first place. If I had glimpsed even at Tommy's exclusion from all that mattered passionately to me, I shouldn't have married him. It was because I had not yet begun to be markedly dissatisfied with either of them that I presently got myself the reputation of having trampled both Tommy and Higgleston underfoot. I must ask your patience for a little until I show you how wholly I offered myself to them both and how completely they wouldn't have me.

The point of departure was of course that I didn't accept the Higglestonian reading of married obligations to mean that my whole time was to be taken up with just living with Tommy. It was as natural, and in view of the scope it afforded for individual development, a more convenient arrangement than living with my mother, but not a whit more absorbing. I couldn't, anyway, think of just living as an end, and accordingly I looked about for a more spacious occupation; I thought I had found it in the directing of that submerged spiritual passion which I had felt in the sustaining drama of the war. I had a notion there might be a vent for it in the shape of a permanent dramatic society by means of which all Higgleston, and I with them, could escape temporarily from its commonness into the heroic movement. It was all very clear in my own mind but it failed utterly in communication.

97

I began wrongly in the first place by asking the Higgleston ladies to tea. Afternoon tea was unheard of in Higgleston, and I had forgotten, or perhaps I had never learned, that in Higgleston you couldn't do anything different without implying dissatisfaction with things as they were. You were likely on such occasions to be visited by the inquiry as to whether the place wasn't good enough for you. As a matter of fact afternoon tea was almost as unfamiliar to me as to the rest of them, but I had read English novels and I knew how it ought to be done. I knew for instance, that people came and went with a delightful informality and had tea made fresh for them, and were witty or portentous as the occasion demanded. My invitations read from four to five, and the Higgleston ladies came solidly within the minute and departed in phalanxes upon the stroke of five. They all wore their best things, which, from the number of black silks included, and black kid gloves not quite pulled on at the finger tips, gave the affair almost a funereal atmosphere. They had most of them had their tea with their midday meal, and Mrs. Dinkelspiel said openly that she didn't approve of eating between meals. They sat about the room against the wall and fairly hypnotized me into getting up and passing things, which I knew was not the way tea should be served. In Higgleston, the only occasion when things were handed about, were Church sociables and the like, when the number of guests precluded the possibility of having them all at your table; and by the time I got once around, the tea was cold and I realized how thin my thin bread and butter and chocolate wafers looked in respect to the huge, soft slabs of layer cake, stiffened by frosting and filling, which, in Higgleston went by the name of light refreshments. The only saving incident was the natural way in which Mrs. Ross, our attorney's wife who visited East every summer and knew how things were done, asked for "two lumps, please," and came back a second time for bread and butter. I think they were all tremendously pleased to be asked, though they didn't intend to commit themselves to the innovation by appearing to have a good time. And that was the occasion I chose for broaching my great subject, without, I am afraid, in the least grasping their incapacity to share in my joyous discovery of the world of Art which I so generously held out to them.

It hadn't been possible to keep my professional adventure from the townspeople, nor had I attempted it. What I really felt was that we were to be congratulated as a community in having one among us privileged to experience it, and I honestly think I should have felt so of any one to whom the adventure had befallen. But I suspect I must have given the impression of rather flaunting it in their faces.

I put my new project on the ground that though we were dissevered by our situation, there was no occasion for our being out of touch with the world of emotion, not, at least, so long as we had admission to it through the drama: and it wasn't in me to imagine that the world I prefigured to them under those terms was one by their standards never to be kept sufficiently at a distance.

Mrs. Miller put the case for most of them with the suggestion thrown out guardedly that she didn't "know as she held with plays for church members"; she was a large, tasteless woman, whose husband kept the lumber yard and derived from it an extensive air of being in touch with the world's occupations. "And I don't know," she went on relentlessly, "that I ever see any good come of play acting to them that practise it."

Mrs. Ross, determined to live up to her two lumps, came forward gallantly with:

"Oh, but, Mrs. Miller, when our dear Mrs. Bettersworth——"

"That's what I was thinking of," Mrs. Miller put it over her.

"Well for my part," declared Mrs. Dinkelspiel, with the air of not caring who knew it, "I don't want my girls to sell tickets or anything; it makes 'em too forward." Mrs. Harvey, whose husband was in hardware, began to tell discursively about a perfectly lovely entertainment they had had in Newton Centre for the missionary society, which Mrs. Miller took exception to on the ground of its frivolity.

"I don't know," she maintained, "if the Lord's work ain't hindered by them sort of comicalities as much as it's helped."

I am not sure where this discussion mightn't have landed us if the general attention had not been distracted just then by my husband, an hour before his time, coming through the front gate and up the walk. He had evidently forgotten my tea party, for he came straight to me, and backed away precipitately through the portières as soon as he saw the assembled ladies sitting about the wall. It was not that which disturbed us; any Higgleston male would have done the same, but it was plain in the brief glimpse we had of him that he looked white and stricken. A little later we heard him in the back of the house making ambiguous noises

99

such as not one of my guests could fail to understand as the precusor of a domestic crisis. I could see the little flutter of uneasiness which passed over them, between their sense of its demanding my immediate attention and the fear of leaving before the expressed time. Fortunately the stroke of five released them. The door was hardly shut on the last silk skirt when I ran out and found him staring out of the kitchen window.

"Well?" I questioned.

"I thought they would never go," he protested. "Come in here." He led the way to the living room as if somehow he found it more appropriate to the gravity of what he had to impart, and yet failed to make a beginning with his news. He shut the door and leaned against it with his hands behind him for support.

"Has anything happened?"

"Happened? Oh, I don't know. I've lost my job."

"Lost? Burton Brothers?" I was all at sea.

He nodded. "They're closing out; the manager's in town today. He told us. . . ." By degrees I got it out of him. Burton Brothers thought they saw hard times ahead, they were closing out a number of their smaller establishments, centring everything on their Chicago house. Suddenly my thought leaped up.

"But couldn't they give you something there . . . in Chicago?" I was dizzy for a moment with the wild hope of it. Never to live in Higgleston any more—but Tommy cut me short.

"They've men who have been with them longer than I have to provide for. . . . I asked."

"Oh, well, no matter. The world is full of jobs." Looking for one appealed to me in the light of an adventure, but because I saw how pale he was I went to him and began to kiss him softly. By the way he yielded himself to me I grasped a little of his lost and rudderless condition, once he found himself outside the limits of a salaried employment. I began to question him again as the best way of getting the extent of our disaster before us.

"What does Mr. Rathbone say?" Rathbone was our working tailor, a thin, elderly, peering man of a sort you could scarcely think of as having any existence apart from his shop. He used to come sidling down the street to it and settle himself among his implements with the air of a brooding hen taking to her nest; the sound of his machine was a contented clucking.

"He was struck all of a heap. They're better fixed than we are." Tommy added this as an afterthought as likely to affect the tailor's attitude when he came to himself. "They" were old Rathbone and his daughter, one of those conspicuously blond and full-breasted women who seem to take to the dressmaking and millinery trades by instinct. As she got herself up on Sunday in her smart tailoring, with a hat "from the city," and her hair amazingly pompadoured, she was to some of the men who came to our church, very much what the brass teakettle was to me, a touch of the unattainable but not unappreciated elegancies of life. Tommy admired her immensely and was disappointed that I did not have her at the house oftener.

"They've got her business to fall back on," Tommy suggested now with an approach to envy. He had never seen Miss Rathbone as I had, professionally, going about with her protuberant bosom stuck full of pins, a tape line draped about her collarless neck, and her skirt and belt never quite together in the back, so he thought of her establishment as a kind of stay in affliction.

"And I have the stage," I flourished. It was the first time I had thought of it as an expedient, but I glanced away from the thought in passing, for to say the truth I didn't in the least know how to go about getting a living by it. I creamed some chipped beef for Tommy's supper, a dish he was particularly fond of, and opened a jar of quince marmalade, and all the time I wasn't stirring something or setting the table, I had my arms around him, trying to prop him against what I did not feel so much terrifying as exciting. We talked a little about his getting his old place back in Taylorville, and just as we were clearing away the supper things we saw Miss Rathbone, with her father tucked under her arm, pass the square of light raying out into the spring dusk from our window, and a moment later they knocked at our door. It was one of the things that I felt bound to like Miss Rathbone for, that she took such care of her father; she did everything for him, it was said, even to making up his mind for him, and this evening by the flare of the lamp Tommy held up to welcome them, it was clear she had made it up to some purpose. It must have been what he saw in her face that made my husband put the lamp back on the table from which the white cloth had not yet been removed, as if the clearing up was too small a matter to consort with the occasion.

I was relieved to have my husband take charge of the visit, especially as he made no motion to invite them into the front room where the remains of the bread and butter and the chairs

101

against the wall would have apprised Miss Rathbone of my having entertained company on an occasion to which she had not been invited. It was part of Tommy's sense of social obligation that we ought never to neglect Mr. Rathbone, whom, though his connection with the business was as slight as my husband's, he insisted on regarding as in some sort a partner. So we sat down rather stiffly about the table still shrouded in its white cloth, as though upon it were about to be laid out the dead enterprise of Burton Brothers, and looked, all of us, I think, a little pleased to find ourselves in so grave a situation.

Miss Rathbone, who had always a great many accessories to her toilet, bags and handkerchiefs and scarves and things, laid them on the table as though they were a kind of insignia of office, and made a poor pretence to keep up with me the proper feminine detachment from the business which had brought them there. We neither of us, Miss Rathbone and I, had the least idea what the other might be thinking about or presumably interested in, though I think she made the more gallant effort to pretend that she did. On this evening I could see that she was full of the project for which she had primed her father, and was nervously anxious lest he shouldn't go off at the right moment or with the proper pyrotechnic.

I remember the talk that went on at first, because it was so much in the way of doing business in Higgleston, and impressed me even then with its factitious shrewdness, based very simply on the supposition that Capitalists—it was under that caption that Burton Brothers figured—never meant what they said. Capitalists were always talking of hard times; it was part of their deep laid perspicacity. Burton Brothers wished to sell out the business; was it reasonable to suppose they would think it good enough to sell and not good enough to go on with?

"Father thinks," said Miss Rathbone, and I am sure he had done so dutifully at her instigation, "that they couldn't ask no great price after talking about hard times the way they have."

It was not in keeping with what was thought to be woman's place, that she should go on to the completed suggestion. In fact, so far as I remember it never was completed, but was talked around and about, as if by indirection we could lessen the temerity of the proposal that old Rathbone and Tommy should buy out the shop on such favorable terms as Burton Brothers, in view of their own statement of its depreciation, couldn't fail to make.

"You could live over the store," Miss Rathbone let fall into the widening rings of silence that followed her first suggestion; "your rent would be cheaper, and it would come into the business."

I felt that she made it too plain that the chief objection that my husband could have was the lack of money for the initial adventure; but because I realized that much of my instinctive resistance to a plan that tied him to Higgleston as to a stake, was due to her having originated it, I kept it to myself. I had a hundred inarticulate objections, chief of which was that I couldn't see how any plan that was acceptable to the Rathbones, could get me on toward the Shining Destiny, but when you remember that I hadn't yet been able to put that concretely to myself, you will see how impossible it was that I should have put it to my husband. In the end Tommy was talked over. I believe the consideration of going on in the same place and under the same circumstances without the terrifying dislocation of looking for a job, had more to do with it than Miss Rathbone's calculation of the profits. We wrote home for the money; Effie wrote back that everything of mother's was involved in the stationery business, which was still on the doubtful side of prosperity, but Tommy's father let us have three hundred dollars.

The necessity of readjusting our way of life to Tommy's new status of proprietor, and moving in over the store, kept my plans for the dramatic exploitation of Higgleston in abeyance. It seemed however by as much as I was now bound up with the interest of the community, to put me on a better footing for beginning it, and on Decoration Day, walking in the cemetery under the bright boughs, between the flowery mounds, the Gift stirred in me, played upon by this touching dramatization of common human pain and loss. I recalled that it was just such solemn festivals of the people that I had had in mind to lay hold on and make the medium of a profounder appreciation. And the next one about to present itself as an occasion was the Fourth of July.

I detached myself from Tommy long enough to make my way around to two or three of the ladies who usually served on the committee.

"We ought to have a meeting soon now," I suggested; "it will take all of a month to get the children ready."

"That's what we thought," agreed Mrs. Miller heavily. "They was to our house Thursday—" She went on to tell me who was to read the Declaration and who deliver the oration.

"But," I protested, "that's exactly what they've had every Fourth these twenty years!"

"Well, I guess," said Mrs. Harvey, "if Higgleston people want that kind of a celebration, they've a right to have it."

"I guess they have," Mrs. Miller agreed with her.

They had always rather held it out against me at Higgleston that I had never taken the village squabbles seriously, that I was reconciled too quickly for a proper sense of their proportions, and they must have reckoned without this quality in me now, for I was so far from realizing the deliberateness of the slight, that I thought I would go around on the way home and see our minister; perhaps he could do something. It appeared simply ridiculous that Higgleston shouldn't have the newest of this sort of thing when it was there for the asking.

I found him raking the garden in his third best suit and the impossible sort of hat affected by professional men in their more human occasions. The moment I flashed out at him with my question about the committee, he fell at once into a manner of ministerial equivocation—the air of being man enough to know he was doing a mean thing without being man enough to avoid doing it. Er . . . yes, he believed there had been a meeting . . . he hadn't realized that I was expecting to be notified. I wasn't a regular member, was I?

"No," I admitted, "but last year—" The intention of the slight began to dawn on me.

"You see, the programme is usually made up from the children of the united Sunday schools . . ."

"I know, of course, but what has that? . . . ." He did know how mean it was; I could see by the dexterity with which he delivered the blow.

"A good many of the mothers thought they'd rather not have them exposed to . . . er . . . professional methods." As an afterthought he tried to give it the cast of a priestly remonstrance which he must have seen didn't in the least impose on me.

I suppose it was the fear of how I might put it to one of his best paying parishioners that led him to go around to the store the next morning and make matters worse by explaining to Tommy that though the children weren't to be contaminated by my professionalism, it could probably be arranged for me to "recite something." To do Tommy justice, he was as mad as a hatter.

Being so much nearer to village-mindedness himself, I suppose my husband could better understand the mean envy of my larger opportunity, but his obduracy in maintaining that I had been offended led to the only real initiative he ever showed in all the time I was married to him.

"I'd just like to *show* them!" he kept sputtering. All at once he cheered up with a snort. "*I'll* show them!" He was very busy all the evening with letters which he went out on purpose to post, with the result that when a few days later he made his contribution to the fireworks fund, he made it a little larger, as became a live business man, on the ground that he wouldn't be able to participate as his wife had "accepted an invitation to take charge of the programme at Newton Centre." Newton Centre was ten miles away, and though I couldn't do much on account of the difficulty of rehearsals, I managed to make the announcement of it in the county paper convey to them that what they had missed wasn't quite to be sicklied over with Mrs. Miller's asseveration of a notable want of moral particularity at Newton Centre. The very first time I went out to a Sunday-school social thereafter it was made plain to me that if I wanted to take up the annual Library entertainment, it was open to me.

"And I always will say," Mrs. Miller conceded, "that there's nobody can make your children seem such a credit to you as Mrs. Bettersworth."

"It's a regular talent you have," Mrs. Harvey backed her up, "like a person in the Bible." This scriptural reference came in so aptly that I could see several ladies nodding complacently. Mrs. Ross sailed quite over them and landed on the topmost peak of approbation.

"I've always believed," she asserted, "that a Christian woman on the stage would have an uplifting influence."

But by this time my ambition had slacked under the summer heat and the steady cluck of old Rathbone's machine and the mixed smell of damp woollen under the iron, and creosote shingle stains. There had been no loss of social standing in our living over the store; such readjustments in Higgleston went by the name of bettering yourself, and were commendable. But somehow I could never ask ladies to tea when the only entrance was by way of a men's furnishing store. The four rooms, opening into one another so that there was no way of getting from the kitchen to the parlour except through the bedroom. I found quite hopeless as a means of expressing my relation to all that appealed to me as inspiring, dazzling. Because I could not go out without making a street toilet, I went out too little, and suffered from want of tone. And suddenly along in September came a letter from O'Farrell offering me a place in his company, and a note from Sarah begging me to accept it. If up to that time I had not thought of the stage as a career, now at the suggestion the desire of it ravened in me like a flame.

Chapter 6

"And you never seem to think I might not *want* my wife to go on the stage?"

I do not know what unhappy imp prompted Tommy to take that tone with me; but whenever I try to fix upon the point of reprehensibleness which led on from my writing to O'Farrell that I would join him in ten days in Chicago, to the tragic termination of my marriage, I found myself whirled about this attitude of his in the deep-seated passionate Why of my life. Why should love be tied to particular ways of doing things? What was this horror of human obligation that made it necessary, since Tommy and I were so innocently fond of one another, that one of us should be made unhappy by it? Why should it be so accepted on all sides that it should be I? For my husband's feeling was but a single item in the total of social prejudice by which, once my purpose had gone abroad by way of the Rathbones, I found myself driven apart from the community interest as by a hostile tide, across which Higgleston gazed at me with strange, begrudging eyes. I recall how the men looked at me the first time I went out afterward, a little aslant, as though some ineradicable taint of impropriety attached in their minds to any association with the stage.

Whatever attitude Tommy finally achieved in the necessity of sustaining the situation he had created for himself by his backing of my first professional venture, was no doubt influenced by the need of covering his hurt at realizing, through my own wild rush to embrace the present opportunity, how far I was from accepting life gracefully at his hands, the docile creature of his dreams.

106

Little things come back to me . . . words, looks . . . sticks and straws of his traditions made wreckage by the wind of my desire, which my resentment at his implication in the general attitude, prevented me from fully estimating. My mother too, to whom I wrote my decision as soon as I had arrived at it, in a long letter designed to convince me that a wife's chief duty and becomingness lay in seeing that nothing of her lapped over the bounds prescribed by her husband's capacity, contributed to the exasperated sense I had of having every step toward the fulfilment of my natural gift dragged at by loving hands. Poor mother, I am afraid I never quite realized what a duckling I turned out to her, nor with what magnanimity she faced it.

"But I suppose you think you are doing right," she wrote at the end, and then in a postscript, "I read in the papers there is a church in New York that gives communion to actors, but I don't expect you will get as far as that."

It was finally Miss Rathbone who relieved the situation by pulling Tommy over to a consenting frame of mind in consideration of the neat little plumlet she extracted from it for herself by making me a travelling dress in three days. She brought it down to the house for me to try on, and it was pathetic to see the way my husband hung upon the effect she made for him of turning me out in a way that was a credit to them both.

"You'll see," she seemed to be saying to him by nothing more explicit than an exclamation full of pins and a clever way of squinting at the hang of my skirt, "that when we two take a hand at the affairs of the great world we can come up to the best of them." And all the time I could hear the Higgleston ladies drumming up trade for her out of Newton Centre with their "Stylish? Oh, very. She makes all her clothes for Mrs. Bettersworth—Olivia Lattimore, the actress, you know."

Just at the end though, when we were lying in bed the last morning, afraid to go to sleep again lest we shouldn't get up early enough to catch the train, I believe if Tommy had risen superior to his traditional objection to a married woman having interests outside her home, and claimed me by some strong personal need of his own. I should have answered it gladly. The trouble with my husband's need of me was that it left too much over.

"But of course," he reminded me at the station, "you can give it up any minute if you want to." I think quite to the last he hoped I would rise to some such generous pretence and come back to him, but we neither of us had much notion of the nature of a player's contract.

I had arranged to stay with Pauline until I could look about me, and from the little that I had been able to tell her of my affairs I could see she was in a flutter what to think of me. During the five days I was in her house I watched her swing through a whole arc of possible attitudes, to settle with truly remarkable instinct on the one which her own future permitted her most consistently to maintain.

"You dear, ridiculous child," she hovered over the point with indulgent patronage, "what will you think of next?"

Pauline herself was going through a phase at the time. They had moved out to a detached house at Evanston on account of its being better for the baby, and there was a visible diminution of her earlier effect of housewifely efficiency, in view of Henry's growing prosperity. You could see all Pauline's surfaces like a tulip bed in February, budding toward a new estimate of her preciousness in terms of her husband's income. When she took me by the shoulders, holding me off from her to give play to the pose of amused, affectionate bewilderment, I could see just where the consciousness of a more acceptable femininity as evinced by her being provided with a cook and a housemaid, prompted her to this gracious glozing of my not being in quite so fortunate a case. I was to be the Wonder, the sport on the feminine bush, dear and extenuated, made adorably not to feel my excluding variation; an attitude not uncommon in wives of well-to-do husbands toward women who work. It was an attitude successfully kept up by Pauline Mills for as long as I provided her the occasion. Just at first I suspect I rather contributed to it by my own feeling of its being such a tremendous adventure for me, Olivia Lattimore, with Taylorville, Hadley's pasture and the McGee children behind me, to be going on the stage. How I exulted in it all, the hall bedroom where I finally settled across from Sarah Croyden, the worry of rehearsals, the baked smell of the streets bored through by the raw lake winds, the beckoning night lights—the vestibule of doors opening on the solemn splendour of the world.

At the rehearsals I met Cecelia Brune, if anything prettier than before, and quite perceptibly harder, and Jimmy Vantine, still in love with her, still with his bald crown not quite clean and the same objectionable habit of sidling about, fingering one's dress, laying hands on one as he talked. I met Manager O'Farrell, not a whit altered, and Miss Laurine Dean. I liked and I didn't like her. She drew by a certain warm charm of personality that repelled in closer quarters by its odours of sickliness. There was a quality in her beauty as of a flower kept too long in its glass, not so much withered as ready to fall apart. She had small appealing hands, such as moved one to take them up and handle them, and served somehow to mitigate a subtle impression of impropriety conveyed by her slight sidewise smile. She was probably good-natured by temperament and peevish through excessive use of cigarettes. She made a point of always speaking well of everybody, but it was a long time before I learned that no sort of blame was so deadly as her commendation. "Such a beautiful woman Miss Croyden is," she would say, "isn't it a pity about her nose," and though I had never thought of Sarah's nose as mitigating against her perfection, I found myself after that thinking of it. You could see that magnanimity, which was her chosen attitude, was often a strain to her. I do not think she had any gift at all, but she had a perception of it that had enabled her to produce a very tolerable imitation of acting and kept her, in a covert way, inordinately jealous of the gift in others. She was jealous of mine.

It was not all at once I discovered it. In the beginning, because I never detected her in any of the obvious snatchings of lines and positions that went on at rehearsals, but even making a stand for me against incursions into my part which I was too unaccustomed to forestall, I thought of her as being of rather better strain than most of the company. I was probably the only member of it unaware of her deliberate measures not to permit me such a footing as might lead to my supplanting her with Manager O'Farrell, toward whom I began to find myself in what, for me, was an interesting and charming relation. It was a relation I should have been glad to maintain with any member of the company, but it was only O'Farrell who found himself equal to it. I was full and effervescing with the joy of creation; night by night as I felt the working of the living organism we should have been, transmitting supernal energies of emotion to the audience, who by the very communicating act became a part of us, I felt myself also warming toward my fellow players. I was so charged I should have struck a spark from any one of them when we met, but for the fact that by degrees I discovered that they presented to me the negative pole.

I was aware of such communicating fluid between particular pairs of them. I saw it spark from eye to eye, heard it break in voices; it flashed like sheet lightning about our horizons on occasions of great triumph; but I was distinctly alive to the fact that the medium by which it was accomplished was turned from me. At times I was brushed by the wing of a suspicion that among the men, there was something almost predetermined in their denial of what was for me, the sympathetic, creative impulse. I was a little ashamed for them of the gaucherie of withholding what seemed so important to our common success, and yet I seemed always to be surprising all of them at it, except Jimmy Vantine and the manager. I couldn't of course, on account of his propensity for laying hands on one, take it from Jimmy, but between Mr. O'Farrell and me it ran with a pleasant, profitable warmth. I was conscious always of acting better the scenes I had with him. The thrill of them was never quite broken in off-the-stage hours. I felt myself sustained by it. For one thing the man had genuine talent, and I think besides Sarah Croyden and Jimmy Vantine, no one else in the company had very much. Jimmy had a gift, besmeared and discredited by his own cheapness, but O'Farrell had a real flowing genius and a degree of personal vitality that sketched him out as by fire from the flat Taylorville types I had known. We used to talk together about my own possibilities and I had many helpful hints from him, but in spite of this friendliness I never made any way with him against Miss Dean. Not that I tried, but by degrees I found that suggestions made and favours asked, were granted or accepted on the basis of their non-interference with our leading lady. I was not without intimations, which I usually disregarded because I found their conclusions impossible to maintain, that she even triumphed over me in little matters too inconsiderable to have been taken into account except on the understanding that we were pitted in a deliberate rivalry. I was hurt and amazed at times to discover that we presented this aspect to the rest of the company. I felt that I was being judged by my conduct of a business in which I was not engaged.

The situation, however, had not developed to such a pitch by the time we played in Kincade, that it could affect my pleasure in the visit Tommy paid me there; I was overjoyed to have the arms of my own man about me again; I was proud of his pride in my success as *Polly Eccles,* and pleased to have him and Sarah pleased with one another. I thought then that if I could only have Tommy and my work I should ask no more of destiny; I do not now see why I couldn't, but I like best to think of him as he seemed to me then, wholesome and good, raised by his joy of our reunion almost to my excited plane, generous in his sharing of my triumphs. It seemed for the moment to put my feet quite on solid ground. I knew at last where I was.

It was about a month after this that I began to find myself pitted against Miss Dean in a struggle for some dimly grasped advantage, with the dice cogged against me. I saw myself in the general estimate, convinced of handling my game badly, and could form no guess even at the expected moves. I smarted under a sense that Manager O'Farrell was not backing up the friendliness of our relations, and I remember saying to Sarah Croyden once that I suspected Miss Dean was using her sex attraction against me, but I missed the point of Sarah's slow, commiserating smile. At the time we were all more or less swamped by the discomforts of our wintry flights from town to town, execrable hotels, irregular and unsatisfying meals. One and another of us went down with colds, and finally toward the end of February, I was taken with a severe neuralgia. It reached its acutest stage the first night we played at Louisville.

I had hurried home from the theatre the moment I was released from my part, to find relief from it in rest, but an hour or two later, still suffering and discovering that I had taken all my powders, I decided to go down to Sarah's room on the lower floor to ask for some that I knew she had. I slipped on my shoes and a thick gray dressing gown, and taking the precaution of wrapping my head in a shawl against the draughty halls, I went down to her. I was returning with the box of powders in my hand when I was startled by the sound of a door lifting carefully on the latch. The hotel was built in the shape of a capital T, with the stair halfway of the stem. I was almost at the foot of it facing the cross hall that gave me a view of the door of Miss Dean's room, and I saw now that it was slightly ajar. I shrank instinctively into the shadow of the recess where the stair began, for I was unwilling that anybody should see the witch I looked in my dressing gown and shawl. In the interval before the door widened I heard the tick of a tin-faced clock just across from me. Part of the enamel was fallen away from the face of it so that it looked as if eaten upon by discreditable sores; a chandelier holding two smoky kerosene lamps hung slightly awry at the crossing of the T, and cast a tipsy shadow. The door swung back slightly, it opened into the room, and a man came out of it and crossed directly in front of me, probably to his room in the other arm of the T.

Once out of the door it snapped softly to behind him, and the man fell instantly into a manner that disconnected him with it to a degree that could only have been possible to an accomplished actor. If I had not seen him come out of it, I should have supposed him abroad upon such a casual errand as my own.

But there was no mistaking that it was Manager O'Farrell. By the tin-faced clock it was a quarter past one. And he would have been home from the theatre more than an hour!

I got up to my room somehow; I think my neuralgia must have left me with the shock; I can't remember feeling it any more after that. You have to remember that this was my first actual contact with sin of any sort. Generations of the stock of Methodism revolted in me. I had liked the man, I had thought of our relation as something precious, to be kept intact because it nourished the quality of our art, and I had all the conventional woman's horror of being brought in touch with looseness. It was part of the admitted business of the men of my class to keep their women from such contacts, and Manager O'Farrell had allowed me to enter into a sort of rivalry with a shameless woman—with his mistress.

I have always been what the country people in Ohianna call a knowledgeable woman. I have not much faculty of getting news of a situation through the facts as they present themselves, but I have instincts which under the stimulus of emotion work with extraordinary celerity and thoroughness. Now suddenly the half-apprehended suggestion of the last few months took fire from the excitement of my mind, and exploded into certainties. I sensed all at once intolerable things, the withholden eyes, the covert attention fixed on my relations with the manager and Miss Dean. I lay on the bed and shuddered with dry sobs; other times I lay still, awake and blazing. About daylight Sarah came up to inquire how my neuralgia did. She found me with the unopened box clutched tightly in my hand. She turned up the smoky gas and noted the dark circles under my eyes.

"What has happened? Something, I know," she insisted gently. I blurted it out.

"Mr. O'Farrell . . . I saw him come out of Miss Dean's room

112

". . . at a quarter of one. He was . . . oh, Sarah . . . he was! . . ."
I relapsed again into the horror of it.

"Oh!" she said. She turned out the light and came and forced
me gently under the covers and got into bed beside me.

"Didn't you know?" she questioned.

"Did you?"

"No one really knows these things. I didn't want to be the first
to suggest it to you."

"Do the others know?"

"As much as we do. It has been going on a long time."

"And you put up with it—you go about with them?" I was
astonished at the welling up of disgust in me. Sarah felt for my
hand and held it.

"My dear, in our business you have to learn to take no notice.
It is not that these things are so much worse with actors, but it
is more difficult to keep them covered up. You must know that
a great many people do such things."

"I know—*wicked* people. I never thought of its being done by
anybody you liked."

"Oh, yes;" she was perfectly simple. "You can like them, you
can like them greatly." I remembered that I oughtn't to have said
that to Sarah Croyden.

"You mustn't think Mr. O'Farrell such a bad man. He is probably fond of her. In some respects he is a very good man. When
I was—left, without a penny, he might have made terms with me.
Some managers would. But he gave me a living salary and left me
to myself. He has been very kind to me."

"But she—" I choked back my sick resentment to get at what
had been tearing its way through my consciousness for the last
three hours. "She must have thought that *that* was what I wanted
of him. . . ."

"Well, it is natural she should be anxious, with other women
about. She is in love with him."

"Did you think so? About me, I mean?"

"No," said Sarah. "No, I didn't think so."

It was light enough now to show the outline of the drifts along
the sills and the fine gritty powder which the wind dashed inter-
mittently against the panes; the filter of day under the scant
blinds brought out in the affair streaks of vulgarity as evident as
the pattern of the paper on the wall. It seemed to borrow cheap-

113

ness from the broken castor of the bureau, as from my recollection of the eaten face of the clock and the leaning chandelier. I sat up in the bed and laid hold of Sarah in my eagerness to get clear of what by my mere knowledge of it, seemed an unbearable complicity.

"I had a feeling for him," I admitted. "I could act better with him; but it was different from that—you know it was different."

"Yes," said Sarah, "I know. I know because I am that way myself; it is *like* that, but it isn't that." I was still, holding my breath while she considered; we were very close upon the twined roots of sex and art.

"There's a feeling that goes with acting, with other sorts of things, painting and music, maybe, a feeling of your wanting to get *through* to something and lay hold of it, and your not being able to leaves you . . . aching somehow, and you think if there's a particular person . . . I think O'Farrell would understand . . . it is being able to act makes you know the difference I suppose. He really can act you know, and you can, but Dean wouldn't understand, nor the others. My—Mr. Lawrence didn't understand!" It was the first time she had ever mentioned him to me. "Sometimes I think they might have felt the difference just at first, but nobody told them and they got used to thinking it is . . . the other thing." She drew me down into the bed again and covered me. "You mustn't take it too hard . . . we all go through it once . . . and you are safe so long as you know."

"But I can't go on with it." I was positive on that point. "Sarah, Sarah, don't say I have to go on with it."

"I know you can't. But you just have to."

"I should never be able to face either of them again without showing that I know."

"And then the others will know and they will think . . ."

I threw out my arms, seeing how I was trapped. I wanted to cry out on them; to despise the woman openly. "And they will think that I am jealous . . . that I wanted it myself. . . ."

I rolled in the bed and bit my hands with shame and anger. Sarah caught me in her arms and held me until the paroxysm passed. I was quieted at last from exhaustion.

"You can stay in your room to-day," she suggested. "I can bring your meals up to you; this neuralgia will give you an excuse, and you needn't see any one until you go to the theatre. That will give you one day. Maybe by to-morrow . . ."

But I had no confidence that to-morrow would bring me any sensible relief. The moral shock was tremendous. All my pride was engaged on the side of never letting anybody know; to have been misunderstood in the quality of my disgust would have been the intolerable last thing. Sarah brought up my breakfast before she had her own; she reported nobody about yet except Jimmy Vantine who had inquired for me. About half an hour later she came softly in again with a yellow envelope open in her hand. I saw by her face that it was for me and that the news it contained put the present situation out of question.

"Is it from my husband?" I demanded. I hardly knew what I hoped or expected, a possibility of release flashed up in me.

"It has been forwarded." She sat down on the bed beside me. "My poor Olivia . . . you must try to think of it as anything but a way out. Mr. O'Farrell will let you go for this. . . ." If it had to happen it couldn't have happened better.

"Give it to me—"

"Remember it is a way out."

I read it hastily:

> Mother had a stroke. Come at once.
> Signed: FORESTER.

Chapter 7

It was a common practice in Taylorville never to send for the doctor until you knew what was the matter with you. So long as the symptoms failed to align themselves with any known disorder, they were supposed to be amenable to neighbourly advice, to the common stock of medical misinformation, to the almanac or some such repository of science; and though this practice led on too many occasions to the disease getting past the curable stages before the physician was called, I never remember to have heard it questioned.

"You see," people remarked to one another at the funeral, "they didn't know what was the matter with her until it was too late," and it passed for all extenuation. It was natural then that my mother should have kept any premonitory symptoms of her indisposition even from Forester; close as they were in their affections she would have thought it indelicate to have spoken to him of her health. The first determinate stroke of it came upon her sitting quietly in her usual place at prayer meeting on a Wednesday evening.

It had been Forester's habit to close the shop a little early on that evening, going around to the church to walk home with her, getting in before the last hymn to save his face with the minister by a show of regular attendance. But on this evening customers detained him beyond his usual hour, so that by the time he reached the corner opposite the church, he saw the people dribbling out by twos and threes, across the lighted doorway, and noted that my mother was not with them. He thought she might have slipped out earlier and gone around to the shop for him as occasionally happened, but seeing the lights did not go out at once in the church, he looked in to make sure, and saw her still sitting in her accustomed place. The sexton and the organist, who were fussing together about a broken pedal, appeared not to have observed her there, and one of them was reaching up to put out the light when Forester touched her on the shoulder. She started and seemed to come awake with an effort, and on the way home she stumbled once or twice in a manner that led him, totally unaccustomed as he was to think of my mother as ill in any sort, to get a little entertainment out of it by gentle rallying, which was dropped when he discovered that it caused her genuine, pained embarrassment. The following Tuesday he came home to the midday meal to find her lying on the floor, inarticulate and hardly conscious. There must have been two strokes in close succession, for she had managed after falling, to get a cushion from the worn sitting-room lounge under her head and to pull a shawl partly over her. Effie, who was at Montecito, was summoned home, and that evening, by the doctor's advice, the telegram was sent which separated me so opportunely from the Shamrocks. By the time I reached her, speech had returned in a measure, and by the end of a fortnight she was able to be lifted into the chair which she never afterward left.

I remember as if it were yesterday, the noble outline of her face and of her head against the pillows, the smooth hair parted Madonna-wise and brought low across her ears, the blue of her eyes looking out of the dark, swollen circles, for all her fifty-two years, with the unawakened clarity of a girl's. Stricken as I was from my first realizing contact with sin, and my identification with it through the assumed passions of the stage, it grew upon me during the days of my mother's illness that there was a kind of intrinsic worth in her which I, with all my powers, must forever and inalienably miss. With it there came a kind of exasperation, never quite to leave me, of the certainty of not choosing my own values, but of being driven with them aside and apart.

It was responsible in part for a feeling I had of being somehow less related to my mother's house than many of her distant kin who were continually arriving out of all quarters, in wagons and top buggies, to express a continuity of interest and kind which had the effect of constituting me definitely outside the bond.

The situation was furthered no doubt, by the whisper of my connection with the stage which got about and set up in them an attitude of circumspection, out of which I caught them at times regarding me with a curiosity unmixed with any human sympathy. Yet I recall how keen an appetite I had for what this illness of my mother's had thrown into relief, the web of passionate human interactions, bone and body of the spirituality that went clothed as gracelessly in the routine of their daily lives as the figures of the men under the unyielding ugliness of store clothing. It came out in the talk of the women sitting about the base burner at night with their skirts folded back carefully across their knees, in the watches we found it necessary to keep for the first fortnight or so. I remember one of these occasions as the particular instance by which my mother emerged for me from her condition of parenthood, to the common plane of humanity, by way of an old romance of hers with Cousin Judd. Cousin Lydia sat up with her that night and Almira Jewett, a brisk, country clad woman of the Skaldic temperament who from long handling of the histories of her clan had acquired an absolute art of it. She was own sister to the woman who married my mother's half-brother, and the Saga of the Judds and the Wilsons and the Jewetts and the Lattimores ran off the points of her bright needles as she sat with her feet on the fender, with a click and a spark. Cousin Lydia never knitted; she sat with her hands folded in her large lap and time seemed to rest with her.

"It will be hard on Judd," Almira offered to the unspoken reference forever in the air, as to the possible fatal termination of my mother's illness.

117

"Yes, it'll be hard on him." A faint, so faint nuance of assent in Cousin Lydia's voice seemed to admit the succeeding comment, shorn of impertinence. I guessed that the several members of the tribe were relieved rather than constrained to drop their intimate concerns into Almira Jewett's impartial histories.

"I never," Almira invited, "did get the straight of that. Sally was engaged to him, warn't she?"

"Not to say engaged," Cousin Lydia paused for just the right shade of relation, "but so as to want to be. Judd set store by her; he'd have had it that way anyway, but Sally couldn't make up her mind to it on account of their being own cousins."

"I reckon she had the right of it; the Lord don't seem no way pleased with kin marrying."

"I don't know, I don't know;" Cousin Lydia dropped the speculation into the pit of her own experience. "It looks like He wouldn't have made 'em to care about it then. But being as she saw it that way, they couldn't have done different. Not that Judd didn't see it in the light of his duty, too." There was evidently nothing in the annals of the Judds and the Lattimores which allowed a violation of the inward monitor.

"Well, I must say, he has turned it into grace, if ever a man has. Not to say but what you've helped him to it." It was in the manner of Almira's concession of not in the matter, that Cousin Judd had chosen Lydia chiefly for her capacity not to offer any distraction to his profounder passion, and nothing in Cousin Lydia's comment to deny it. From the room beyond we could hear the inarticulate, half-conscious notice of my mother's pain. Cousin Lydia moved to attend her.

"All those years," I whispered to Almira, "she has loved him and he has loved my mother!" I was pierced through with the pure sword of the spirit which had divided them. But Almira was more practical.

"She was better off," Almira insisted. "Lydia hadn't no knack with men folk ever. She knew Judd wouldn't have loved her, but so long as he loved your mother she was safe. They got a good deal out of it, her knowing and sympathizing. She could sympathize, you see, for she knew how it was herself, loving Judd that way. It was no more than right they should get what they could out of it. It was the only thing they had between them."

"All those years!" I said again. I felt myself immeasurably lifted out of the mists and mires of the Shamrocks into clear and aching atmospheres.

"I will say this for Lydia," extenuated the Skald, "that though she hadn't no gift to draw a man to her, she know how to hold her hand off and let him go his own thought. It was religion kept your mother and Judd apart, and yet it was in religion they comforted one another. Lydia never put herself forward like she might, claiming it was her religion too. And she was one that appreciated church privileges."

But I wondered where my father came in. It had been, I knew, a passionate attachment.

"Like a new house," said Almira, "built up where the old one has been, but the cellars of it don't change. Real loving is never really got over." I felt the phrase sounding in some subterranean crypt of my own.

With this new light on it, it came out for me wonderfully in my mother's face, as I watched her through the anxious days, how much her life had been stayed in renunciations. I suppose my new appreciation must have shone out for her as well, for I could see rising out of her disorder, like a drowned person out of the sea, a bond of our common experience. We were two women, together at last, my mother and I, and could have speech with one another.

Something no doubt contributed to this new understanding by an affair of Forester's which, as I began to be acquainted with the incidents preceding it, I believed to be partly responsible for my mother's stroke. I have already sketched to you how Forester had grown up in the need of finding himself always at the centre of feminine interest without the opportunity of satisfying it normally by marriage, and how the too early stimulation of sentiment and affection had led to his being handed about from girl to girl in the attempt to gratify his need without transgressing any of the lines marked out by his profession as an eminently nice young man. It came naturally out of the mere circumstance of there being a limited number of girls at hand whom he might conceivably court without the intention of marrying, for him to fall into the society of others whom he might not court but who might nevertheless find it much to their advantage to marry him.

I do not know how and when it came to my mother's ears that he was calling frequently at the Jastrows; very likely they brought it to her notice themselves. They were a poor, pushing sort, forever exposing themselves to the slights arising from their own undesirability, which they forever tearfully attributed to an undeserved and paraded poverty. They paraded it now as the insuperable bar to all that they might have done for my mother, all that they actually had it in their hearts to do on their assumption of a right of being interested, an assumption which, even in her weakness, before she could trust herself to talk very much, I felt her dumbly imploring me to deny. The girl—Lily they called her —was not without a certain appeal to the senses; and knowing rather more of my brother's methods, I did not find Mrs. Jastrow's pretension to a community of interest in what might be expected to come of his attention, altogether unjustified. But in view of mother's condition and what Effie told me of the way business was going—rather was not going at all—any kind of marriage would have been out of the question. It was the way I put the finality of that into my dealings with Mrs. Jastrow, that drew mother over into the only relation of normal human interdependence I was ever to have with her. Whenever Mrs. Jastrow would come to call with that air she had, in her dress and manner, of being pulled together and made the best of, I could see my mother's fears signalling to me from the region of tremors and faintness in which she had sunk, and I would set my wits up as a defence against what, considering all there was against her, was a really gallant effort on Mrs. Jastrow's part to make out of Forester's philanderings a basis for a family intimacy. It was plain that neither my mother nor Mrs. Jastrow dared put the question to Forester, but rested their case on such mutual admission of it as they could wring from one another.

I could never make out on my mother's part, whether she was really afraid of the issue, or if in the preoccupation of their affection both she and Forester had overlooked his young man's right to a woman and a life of his own. Through all her dumb struggle against it, never but once did my mother openly face the ultimate possibility of his marriage with Lily Jastrow.

It was about the third week of her illness, and Mrs. Jastrow, making one of her interminable calls, had been brought so nearly to the point of tears by my imperiousness, that Effie had been obliged to draw her off into the kitchen to have her opinion about a recipe for a mince meat such as she knew the Jastrows couldn't afford to be instructed in, and so had gotten her out of the side door and started down the walk before the situation could come to a head. My mother watched her go.

"Do you think," she hazarded suddenly, "that Forester really is engaged to her?"

"To Lily? Oh, no; Forester doesn't get engaged to girls, he just —dangles." It was characteristic of my mother's partiality that even damaging insinuations such as this, slid off from it as too far from the possibility to be even entertained. Perhaps a trace of my old exasperation with the whole situation, and the glimpse I had of Mrs. Jastrow letting herself out of our gate with her assumption of being as good as anybody still to the fore but a little awry, prompted me to add:

"And it is only natural for her mother to make the most of it. She's looking out for her own, just as you are."

"A mother has a right to do that;" she protested, "to keep them from making themselves miserable. It is no more than her duty."

"Yes," I said; the remark had the effect of a challenge.

"Young people don't know how to choose for themselves; they make mistakes." She revolved something in her mind. "You, now . . . you're unhappy, aren't you, Olivia?"

"Yes; oh, yes." I had not thought of myself as being so particularly, but I did not see my way to deny it.

"I've been afraid . . . sometimes . . . since you wrote me about going on the stage, maybe you weren't exactly . . . satisfied. But it isn't that, is it?"

"No, mother, it isn't that."

"There! You see!" She shook off her weakness with the conviction. "And you mightn't have been if I hadn't looked out for you a little."

"Why, mother, what could you possibly—" She triumphed.

"You remember that Garrett boy that was visiting at his uncle's? He called that night; the night you were engaged to Tommy."

"Yes, I remember. You sent him away?"

"He wasn't suitable at all . . . smoking, and driving about on Sunday that way. . . ." Her tone was defensive. "He left a letter that night—"

"Mother! You didn't tell me!"

"I was thinking it over . . . I had a right . . . you were too young!"

"Mother . . . did you read it?"

"I . . . looked at it. You hadn't met him but once and I had a right to know; and that night you were engaged. I took it for a sign."

"And the letter?" It seemed all at once an immeasurable and irreparable loss.

"I sent it back . . . and, anyway, it turned out all right." I was possessed for the moment with the conviction that it was all dreadfully, despairingly wrong.

"I couldn't have borne for you to marry anybody but a Christian, Olivia!" I thought of Tommy's exceedingly slender claim to that distinction and I laughed.

"Tommy smokes," I said; "he says he has to do it with the customers."

"Oh, but not as a habit, Olivia." I overrode that.

"Tell me what became of him—of Mr. Garrett. Did you ever hear?"

"He went West," she recollected; "I asked his aunt. He quarrelled with them because his uncle wouldn't send him to school. At his age they thought it wasn't suitable. I wouldn't have wanted you to go West, Olivia."

I took her worn hands in mine. "It's all right, mother. I'm not going West. And I'm not going on the stage any more. I'm done with it." I felt so, passionately, at the time. We sat quietly for a time in that assurance and listened to Effie singing in the kitchen.

"Olivia," she began timidly at last, "aren't you ever going to have any more children?"

"Oh, I hope so, mother. I haven't been strong, you know, since the first one. We didn't think it advisable."

"Well, if you can manage it that way . . ." There was a trace in her tone of the woman who hadn't been able to manage. I wished to reassure her.

"When I was in the hospital the doctor told me . . ." I could see the deep flush rising over her face and neck; there were some things which her generation had never faced. I let them fall with her hands and sat gazing at the red core of the base burner, waiting until she should take up her thought again.

"I used to think those things weren't right, Olivia, but I don't know. Sometimes I think it isn't right, either, to bring them into the world when there is no welcome for them." She struggled with the admission. "You and I, Olivia, we never got on together."

122

"But that's all past now, mother." She clung to me for a while for reassurance.

"I hope so, I hope so; but still there are things I've always wanted to tell you. When you wrote me about going on the stage. . . . there are wild things in you, Olivia, things I never looked for in a daughter of mine, things I can't understand nor account for unless—unless it was I turned you against life . . . my kind of life . . . before you were born. Many's the time I've seen you hating it and I've been harsh with you; but I wanted you should know I was being harsh with myself . . ."

"Mother, dear, is it good for you to talk so?"

"Yes, yes, I've wanted to. You see it was after your father came home from the war and we were all broken up. Forester was sickly, and there was the one that died. So when I knew you were coming, I—hated you, Olivia. I wanted things different. I hated you. . . . until I heard you cry. You cried all the time when you were little, Olivia, and it was I that was crying in you. I've expected some punishment would come of it."

"Oh, hush, hush mother! I shouldn't have liked it either in your place. Besides, they say—the scientists—that it isn't so that things before you are born can affect you as much as that." She moved her head feebly on the pillows in deep-rooted denial.

"They can say that, but we've never got on. There's things in you that aren't natural for any daughter of mine. They can say that, Olivia, but we—we know."

"Yes, mother, we know."

I took her hands again and nursed them against my cheeks; after a time tears began to drip down her flaccid cheeks and I wiped them away for her.

"Don't, mother, don't! We get along now, anyway! And as for the things in me which are different, do you know, mother, I'm getting to know that they are the best things in me."

I honestly thought so; and after all these years I think so now.

I wheeled her into the bedroom presently, where she fell into the light slumber of the feeble, and seemed afterward hardly to remember, but I was glad then to have talked it all out with her, for though she lived nearly two years after, before I saw her again another stroke had deprived her of articulateness.

Chapter 8

I went home to my husband after it began to seem certain that my mother's condition would not change for some time, but I knew in the going that neither Tommy nor Higgleston could ever present themselves to me again in the aspect of an absolute destiny. By the incidents of the past few weeks I had been pulled free from the obsession of inevitableness with which my life had clothed itself until now; I stood outside of it and questioned it in the light of what it might have been, what it might yet become. Suppose I had received Helmeth Garrett's letter; suppose my interest in Mr. O'Farrell had wavered a hair's breadth out of the community of work into that more personal and particular passion—?

I quaked in the cold blasts which blew on me out of unsuspected doors opening on my life.

And still I went back to Higgleston. There seemed nothing else to do. I think I deceived myself with the notion that there was something in Tommy's resistance to a more acceptable destiny, that could be resolved and dissipated by the proper stimulus. But I knew, in fact, that he and Higgleston suited one another admirably. To my husband, that he should keep a clothing store in a town of five thousand inhabitants was part of the great natural causation. The single change to which our condition was liable was that the business might take a turn which would enable us to move out of the store into a house of our own. It had not occurred to Tommy to take a turn himself. The Men's Tailors and Outfitters lay like most business in Higgleston, in the back water, rocking at times in the wake of the world traffic, but never moving with it. There was a vague notion of progress abroad which resulted in our going through the motions of the main current. The Live Business Men organized a Board of Trade and rented a room to hold meetings in, but I do not remember that when they had met, anything came of it. The great tides of trade went about the world and our little fleet rocked up and down. If I had ever had any hope that Tommy and I might out of our common

124

stock, somehow hoist sail and make a way out of it, in that spring and summer I completely lost it.

I believe Tommy thought we were perfectly happy. Considering how things turned out, I am glad to have it so; but the fact is, there was not between us so much as a common taste in furniture. In the five years of married life, our home had filled up with articles which by colour and line and unfitness jarred on every sense. Tommy had what he was pleased to call an ear for music, and if the warring discords of our furnishings could have been translated into sound he would have gone distracted with it; being as it was he bought me a fire screen for my birthday. Miss Rathbone hand-painted it for the Baptist bazaar, and Tommy had bought it at three times what we could have afforded for a suitable ornament. It was his notion of our relations that we and the Rathbones should do things like that by one another. I suppose you can find the like of that fire screen at some county fair still in Ohianna, but you will find nothing more atrocious. Tommy liked to have it sitting well out in the room where he could admire it. He would remark upon it sometimes with complacency, evenings after the store was shut up, before he sat down in his old coat and slippers to read the paper. Occasionally I read to him out of a magazine or a play I had picked up, in the intervals of which I used to catch him furtively keeping up with his newspaper out of the tail of his eye.

Now and then we went out to a sociable or to the Rathbones for supper. Less frequently we had them to a meal with us. It was characteristic of business partnerships in Higgleston that they involved you in obligations of chicken salad and banana cake and the best tablecloth. Tommy enjoyed these occasions, and if he had allowed himself to criticise me at all, it would have been for my ineptitude at the happy social usage. Things went on so with us month after month.

And if you ask me why I didn't take the chance life offers to women to justify themselves to the race, I will say that though the hope of a child presents itself sentimentally as opportunity, it figures primarily in the calculation of the majority, as a question of expense. The hard times foreseen by Burton Brothers hung black-winged in the air. We had not, in fact, been able to do more than keep up the interest on what was still due on the stock and fixtures. Nor had I even quite recovered the bodily equilibrium disturbed by my first encounter with the rending powers of life.

125

There was a time when the spring came on in a fulness, when the procreant impulse stirred awake. I saw myself adequately employed shaping men for it . . . maybe . . . but the immediate deterring fact was the payment to be made in August.

I went on living in Higgleston where human intercourse was organized on the basis that whatever a woman has of intelligence and worth, over and above the sum of such capacity in man, is to be excised as a superfluous growth, a monstrosity. Does anybody remember what the woman's world was like in small towns before the days of woman's clubs? There was a world of cooking and making over; there was a world of church-going and missionary societies and ministerial coöperation, half grudged and half assumed as a virtue which, since it was the only thing that lay outside themselves, was not without extenuation. And there was another world which underlay all this, coloured and occasioned it, sicklied over with futility; it was a world all of the care and expectancy of children overshadowed by the recurrent monthly dread, crept about by whispers, heretical but persistent, of methods of circumventing it, of a secret practice of things openly condemned. It was a world that went half the time in faint-hearted or unwilling or rebellious anticipation, and half on the broken springs of what as the subject of the endless, objectionable discussions, went by the name of "female complaints."

In all this there was no room for Olivia. Somehow the ordering of our four rooms over the store didn't appeal to me as a justification of existence, and I didn't care to undertake again matching the adventures of my neighbours in the field of domestic economy with mine in the department of self-expression. Let any one who disbelieves it try if he can assure the acceptance of his art on its merit as work, free of the implication of egotism. You may talk about a new frosting for cake, or an aeroplane you have invented, but you must not speak of a new verse form or a plastic effect.

All this time, in spite of my recent revulsion from it, I was consumed with the desire of acting. My new-found faculty ached for use. It woke me in the night and wasted me; I had wild thoughts such as men have in the grip of an unjustifiable passion. All my imaginings at that time were of events, untoward, fantastic, which should somehow throw me back upon the stage without the necessity on my part, of a moral conclusion. Sarah Croyden, to whom I wrote voluminously, could not understand why I resisted it; there was after all no actual opposition except what lay inherent in my traditions. Sarah had such a way of accepting life; she used it and her gift. Mine used me. I saw that it might even abuse me. She went, by nature, undefended and unharmed from the two-edged sword that keeps the gates of Creative Art, but me it pierced even to the dividing of soul and spirit. My husband stood always curiously outside the consideration. I think he was scarcely aware of what went on in me; if any news of my tormented state reached him, he would have seen, except as it was mollified by affection, what all Higgleston saw in it, the restlessness of vanity, a craving for excitement, for praise, and a vague taint of irregularity. He was sympathetic to the point of admitting that Higgleston was dull; he thought we might join the Chatauqua Society.

"Or you might get up a class," he suggested hopefully; "it would give you something to think about."

"Teach," I cried; "TEACH! when I'm just aching to learn!"

"Well, then," he achieved a triumph of a reasonableness, "if you don't know enough to teach in Higgleston, how are you going to succeed on the stage?"

It was not Tommy, however, but a much worse man who made up my mind for me. He had been brought out from Chicago during my absence, to set up in Higgleston's one department store, that factitious air of things being done, which passed for the evidence of modernity. He had, in the set of his clothes, the way he made the most of his hair and the least of the puffiness about his eyes, the effect of having done something successfully for himself, which I believe was the utmost recommendation he had for the place. He preferred himself to my favour on the strength of having seen more than a little of the theatre. Very soon after my return, he took to dropping into my husband's store which, in view of its being patronized by men who were chiefly otherwise occupied during the day, was kept open rather late in the evenings. From sheer loneliness I had fallen into the habit of going down after supper to wait on a stray customer while Tommy made up the books. Mr. Montague, who went familiarly about town by the name of Monty, would come in then and loll across the counter chatting to me, while Tommy sat at his desk with a green shade over his eyes, and Mr. Rathbone, who never came more than a step or two out of his character as working tailor, clattered about with his irons in the back, half screened by the racks of custom made "Nobby suits, $9.98," which made up most of our stock in trade.

I had already, without paying much attention to it, become accustomed to the shifting of men's interest in me the moment my connection with the stage became known: a certain speculation in the eye, a freshening of the wind in the neighbourhood of adventure; but by degrees it began to work through my preoccupations that Mr. Montague's attention had the quality of settled expectation, the suggestion of a relation apart from the casual social contact, which it wanted but an opportunity to fulfill. It took the form very early, when Tommy would look up from his entries and adding up to make his cheerful contribution to the conversation, of an attempt to include me in a covert irritation at the interruption. If by any chance he found me alone, his response to the potential impropriety of the occasion, awoke in me the plain vulgar desire to box his ears. But no experience so far served to reveal the whole offensiveness of the man's assurance.

The week that Tommy went up to Chicago to do his summer buying, we made a practice of closing rather early in the long, enervating evenings, since hardly any customer could have been inveigled into the store on any account. I found it particularly irritating then, to have Mr. Montague leaning across the counter to me with a manner that would have caused the dogs in the street to suspect him of intrigue. The second or third time this happened I made a point of slipping around to Mr. Rathbone with the suggestion that if he would shut up and go home I would take the books upstairs with me and attend them.

I was indifferent whether or not Mr. Montague should hear me, but I judged he had not, for far from accepting it as a hint that I wished to get rid of him, that air he had of covert understanding appeared to have increased in him like a fever. He made no attempt to resume the conversation, but stood tapping his boot with a small cane he affected, a flush high up under the puffy eyes, the corners of his mouth loosened, every aspect of the man fairly bristling with an objectionable maleness. I made believe to be busy putting stock in order, and in a minute more I could hear old Rathbone come puttering out of his corner to draw the dust cloths over the racks of ready-made suits and, after what seemed an interminable interval, fumbling at the knobs of the safe.

"Oh," I snatched at the opportunity, "I changed the combination; let me show you." I was around beside him in a twinkling.

"Good-night," I called to Montague over my shoulder.

"Good-night," he said; the tone was charged. The fumbling of the locks covered the sound of his departure. I got Mr. Rathbone out at the door at last, and locked it behind him. I turned back to lower the flame of the acetylene lamp and in the receding flare of it between the shrouded racks I came face to face with Mr. Montague. He stood at the outer ring of the light and in the shock of amazement I gave the last turn of the button which left us in a sudden blinding dark. I felt him come toward me by the sharp irradiation of offensiveness.

"Oh, you clever little joker, you!" The tone was fatuous.

I dodged by instinct and felt for the button again to throw on the flood of light; it caught him standing square in the middle of the aisle in plain sight from the street; almost unconsciously he altered his attitude to one less betraying, but the response of his mind to mine was not so rapid.

"I'm going to shut up the store," I was very quiet about it. "You'll oblige me by going—"

"Oh, come now; what's the use? I thought you were a woman of the world."

I got behind the counter, past him toward the door.

"You an actress . . . you don't mean to say! By Jove, I'm not going to be made a fool of after such an encouragement! I'm not going without—"

"Mr. Montague," I said, "Tillie Hemingway is coming to stay with me nights; she will be here in a few minutes; you'd better not let her find you here." I unbarred the door and threw it wide open.

"Oh, come now—" He struggled for some footing other than defeat. "Of course, if you can't meet me like a woman of the world—you're a nice actress, you are!" I looked at him; the steps and voices of passersby sounded on the pavement; he went out with his tail between his legs. I locked the door after him and double locked it.

I climbed up to my room and locked myself in that. The boiling of my blood made such a noise in my ears that I could not hear Tillie Hemingway when she came knocking, and the poor girl went away in tears. After a long time I got to bed and sat there with my arms about my knees. I did not feel safe there; I knew I should never be safe again except in that little square of the world upon which the footlights shone, from which the tightening of the reins of the audience in my hands, should justify my life to me. I was sick with longing for it, aching like a woman abandoned for the arms of her beloved. I fled toward it with all my thought from illicit solicitation, but it was not the husband of my body I thought of in that connection, but the choice of my soul.

People wonder why sensitive, self-respecting women are not driven away from the stage by the offences that hedge it; they are driven deeper and farther into its enfoldment. There is nothing to whiten the burning of its shames but the high whiteness of its ultimate perfection. It is so with all art, not back in the press of life, but forward on some overtopping headland, one loses behind the yelping pack and eases the sting of resentment. I did not agree in the beginning to make you understand this. I only tell you that it is so. All that night I sat with my head upon my knees and considered how I might win back to it.

I tried, when my husband came home, to put the incident to him in a way that would stand for my new-found determination. I did not get so far with it. I saw him shrink from the mere recital with a man's timorousness.

"Oh, come—he couldn't have meant so bad as that." His male dread of a "situation" pled with me not to insist upon it. "And he went just as soon as you told him to. Of course if he had tried to force you . . . but you say yourself he went quietly."

He was seeing and shrinking from what Higgleston would get out of the incident in the way of vulgar entertainment if I insisted on his taking it up; by the code there, I shouldn't have been subject to such if I hadn't invited it.

"Of course," he enforced himself, "you did right to turn him down, but I don't believe he'll try it again."

"He won't have a chance. I'm going back on the stage so soon;" the implication of my tone must have got through even Tommy's unimaginativeness; he said the only bitter thing that I ever heard from him.

"Well, if you hadn't gone on the stage in the first place it probably wouldn't have happened."

He came round to the situation in another frame when he learned that I had written to Sarah putting matters in train for an engagement.

"You will probably be away all winter," he said. "It seems to

130

me, Olivia, that you don't take any account of the fact that I am fond of you." We were sitting on a little shelf of a back balcony we had, for the sake of coolness, and I went and sat on his knee.

"I'm fond of you, Tommy, ever so. But I can't stand the life here; it smothers me. And we don't do anything; we don't get anywhere."

"I don't know what you mean, Olivia; we're building up quite a business; we'll be able to make a payment this year, and as the town improves—"

"Oh, Tommy, come away; come away into the world with me. Let us go out and do things; let us be part of things."

"Higgleston's good enough for me. We're building up trade, and everybody says the town is sure to go ahead—"

"Oh, Tommy, Tommy, what do I care about a business here if we lose the whole world—and we'll be old and gray before we get the business paid for. Oh, it isn't because I don't care about you, Tommy, because I am not satisfied with you; it is the glory of the world I want, and the wonder of Art, and great deeds going up and down in it! I want us to have that, Tommy; to have it together . . . you and I, and not another. It's all there in the world, Tommy, all the colour and the splendour . . . great love and great work . . . let us go out and take it; let us go. . . ." I had slipped down from his knees to my own as I talked, pleading with him, and I saw, by the light of the lamp from within, his face, charged with pained bewilderment, settle into lines of habitual resistance to the unknown, the unknowable. My voice trailed out into sobbing.

"Of course, Olivia, I don't want to keep you if you are not happy here, but I have to stay myself." His voice was broken but determined, with the determination of a little man not seeing far ahead of him. "I have to keep the business together."

I went, as it was foredoomed I should, about the middle of September. Sarah and I had been so fortunate as to get engagements together. My going, upheaving as it had been in respect to my own adjustments, made hardly a ripple in the life around me. Even Miss Rathbone failed to rise to her former heights, but was obliged to piece out her interest with her customary dressmaker's manner of having temporarily overlaid her absorption in your affair with an unwilling distraction.

The rest of Higgleston received the announcement with the air

131

of not supposing it to be any of their business, but that in any case they couldn't approve of it. Mrs. Harvey put a common feminine view of it very aptly.

"I shouldn't think," she said, "your husband would let you." It was not a view that was likely to have a deterrent effect upon me.

Chapter 9

We had the good fortune that year, Sarah and I, to be with a manager who redeemed many O'Farrells. The Hardings—for his wife, under her stage name of Estelle Manning, played with him and was the better half of all his counsels—were of the sort of actor-managers to whom, if the American stage ever arrives at anything commensurate with its opportunity, it will owe much. They were not either of them of the stripe of genius, but up to the limit of their endowment, sound, sincere and able to interpret life to the people through the virtue of being so humanly of the people themselves. It was very good for me to be with them, not only for the stage craft they taught me, but for the healing of my mind against the contagion of irresponsibility. The Hardings taught me my way about the professional world, the management of my gift, its market value, but I am not sure I do not owe much more to the fact that they loved one another quite simply and devotedly, and to the certainty which they seemed to make for us all that loyalty, truth, and forbearance were part of the natural order of things.

I was aware, when I was with the Shamrocks, of a subconscious current against which any mention of my husband appeared a kind of gaucherie; it was wholesome for me then, to find it expected of me by the Hardings that I should act better after I had received a long, affectionate letter from Tommy, and to be able to refer to it quite unaffectedly. Everybody in the company took the greatest interest in his coming on at Christmas to spend four days with me.

We had a carefully chosen company, and clean, straightforward plays which met with gratifying success. At the end of February, when traffic was tied up during the great ice storm, I was near enough to get home to Taylorville and spend a week there.

Tommy came to meet me and we were all happy together, mother sitting nearly inarticulate in her chair, pleased as a child to see me doing all the parts in our repertory, and Effie reading my press notices to whoever could be got to listen to them. I seemed to have found the groove in which the wheels of my life went round smoothly; I was justified of much that in my girlhood I had been made to feel so sorely, set me reprehensibly apart. I remember Forester telling how he had heard Charlie Gowers retailing the incident of my having slapped him when he tried to kiss me, getting a kind of reflected glory out of the incident being so much to my credit.

I went back to Higgleston in May and was happier than I had been in the six years of my married life. I had my work and my husband; all that I wanted now was to bring the two into closer relation; it seemed not unlikely of accomplishment. With what I had saved of my salary, Tommy was able to make quite a payment on the business, and with the release of that pressure the whole grip of Higgleston seemed to be loosed from him. When I suggested that I might get permanent engagements in Chicago or St. Louis, where he could establish himself, he was disposed to view it as not unthinkable in connection with what might be expected from a live business man.

I had to leave home early in the autumn for rehearsals, and to leave Tommy, by some chance of the weather a trifle under it. I felt I shouldn't have been able to do so if my husband and Miss Rathbone hadn't been eminently on those terms that fulfilled Tommy's ideal in respect to the womenfolk of his partner. Very likely, as she maintained, it was a feeling of caste that rendered her professional affectionateness offensive to me. One had to admit that when she applied it to her shuffling, peering old father, with red-lidded eyes and a nose that occasionally wanted wiping, it was every way commendable. At any rate I was glad on this occasion to take what she did for old Rathbone as an assurance that if Tommy fell ill, or anything untoward, he wouldn't lack for anything a woman might do for him.

That winter Mr. Harding starred me, and what a wonderful winter it was! Sarah says, taking account of the cold and the condition of the roads, it was rather a hard one, but I was floated clear of all such considerations on the crest of success. Nothing whatever seemed to have gone wrong with it except that Tommy failed me at Christmas. He was to have spent a week, but wired me at the last moment that he could not leave before Wednesday, and then when he came stayed only until Saturday. He had something to say about the pressure of the holiday trade in neckties and cuff links such as the ladies of Higgleston habitually invested in, on behalf of their masculine members, and all the time he was with me, wore that efflorescence of appreciation which I have long since learned to recognize as the overt sign of male delinquency.

If I thought of it at all in that connection, it was clean swept out of my mind by meeting early in January with Mr. Eversley and hearing him first apply to myself that phrase which I have chosen for the title to this writing. Mark Eversley, the greatest modern actor! So we all believed. He had been an old friend of Mr. Harding's; they had had their young struggles together; we crowded around our manager to hear him tell of them; struggles which, in so far as they identified themselves with our own, seemed to bring us by implication within reach of his present fame. Eversley played in St. Louis while we were there, and having an evening to spare, in spite of all the eager social appeal, chose to spend it with the Hardings. They had had dinner together, and as Mr. Harding did not come on until the second act, the great tragedian sat with him in his dressing room, visiting together between the cues like two boys in a dormitory. That was how Eversley happened to be standing in the wings in my great third act, and as I came out between gusts of applause after it, he was very kind to me.

"You will go far, little lady," said he, his lean face alive with kindliness, "you will go farther and have to come back and pick up some dropped stitches, but in the end you will get where you are bound." It was not for me to tell him how the mere consciousness of his presence had carried me that night to the utmost pitch of my capacity; I stood and blushed with confusion while he fumbled for his card.

"I will hear of you again," he said; "I am bound to hear of you; in the meantime here is my permanent address. It may be that I can be of use to you when you come to the bad places."

"Oh," said Mrs. Harding, whose failure to win any conspicuous distinction for herself had not embittered her, "she seems to have cleared most of the hard places at a bound."

"My dear young lady," Eversley appealed to me with a charming whimsicality, "whatever you do, don't let them put that into your head; you will indeed need me if you get to thinking that. You are, I suspect, a woman of genius, and in that case there will always be bad places ahead of you—you are doomed, you are driven; they will never let up on you."

Well, he should know; he was a man of genius. I hope it might be true about me, but I was afraid. For to be a genius is no such vanity as you imagine. It is to know great desires and to have no will of your own toward fulfilment; it is to feed others, yourself unfed; it is to be broken and plied as the Powers determine; it is to serve, and to serve, and to get nothing out of it beyond the joy of serving. And to know if you have done that acceptably you have to depend on the plaudits of the crowd; the Powers give no sign; many have died not knowing.

There is no more vanity in calling yourself a woman of genius if you know what genius means, than might be premised of one of the guinea pigs set aside for experimentation in a laboratory; but the guinea pigs who run free in the garden impute it to us. I wrote my mother and Tommy what Eversley had said, but I knew they would see nothing more in it than that he had paid me a compliment which it would not be modest to make much of in public.

The successes of that year prolonged the season by a month, and by the time I got home to Higgleston the leaves were all out on the maples and the wide old yards smelled of syringa. I came back to it full of the love of the world, alive in every fibre of my being, and the first thing I noticed was that it caused my husband some embarrassment. There was a shyness in his resumption of our relations more than could be accounted for by the native Taylorvilian gaucheries of emotion.

"My dear," I protested, "you don't seem a bit glad to see me."

"You are away so much" he excused. "You're getting to seem almost a stranger."

"Getting? I should say I am. This morning it seemed to me almost as if I waked up in another woman's house." I meant no more than to suggest how little the walls of it, the furniture, the draperies, expressed my new mood of creative power, but suddenly I saw my husband colour a deep, embarrassed red.

"You never did take any interest in our life here . . . in the business . . . in me." He seemed to be making out a case against me.

"Don't say in you, Tommy; but the life here, yes; there is so

135

little to it. Another year and Mr. Harding says I could hope to stay in Chicago." My husband pushed away his plate; we were at breakfast the second morning.

"Higgleston's good enough for me," he protested. He got up and stood at the window with his back to me, looking out at the side street and the tardy traffic of the town beginning to stir in it. "When you hate it so," he said, "I wonder you come back to it." But my mood was proof against even this.

"Oh, Thomas, Thomas!" I got my hands about his arm and snuggled my head against it. "And you can't even guess why I come back?" He looked at me, vaguely troubled by the caress, but not responding to it.

"Do you care so much?"

"Ever and ever so." I thought he was in need of reassurance.

I hardly know when I began to get an inkling of what was wrong with him; it trickled coldly to me from dropped words, inflections, sidelong glances. Whenever I went out I was aware of all Higgleston watching, watching like a cat at a mouse-hole for something to come out. What? Reports of my success had reached them through the papers. Were they looking for some endemic impropriety to break out on me as a witness to what a popular actress must inevitably become? By degrees it worked through to me that all Higgleston knew things about my situation that were held from me. What they expected to see come out in my behaviour was the stripe of chastisement.

When I had been at home four or five days it occurred to me Miss Rathbone had not yet run in to see me with that quasi-familiarity which had grown out of the business association of our men. Old Rathbone had said that she had the trousseau of one of the Harvey girls in hand, but I knew that if the courtesy had been due from me, I couldn't have neglected it without the risk of being thought what Miss Rathbone herself would have called uppish. So the very next afternoon, having fallen in with some Higgleston ladies strolling the long street that led through the town from countryside to countryside, passing her gate, it struck me that here was an excellent opportunity to run in and exchange a greeting with her. I said as much to Mrs. Ross and Mrs. Harvey, as I swung the picket gate out across the board walk; there was something in their way of standing back from it that gave them the air of sheering off from any implication in the incident. They looked at the sidewalk and their lips were a little drawn; I should have known that look very well by that time. I threw out against it just that degree of impalpable resistance that was demanded by my official relation to the women of my husband's business partner, and clinched it with the click of the gate swinging to behind me, but as I went up the peony-bordered walk I wondered what Miss Rathbone would possibly have done to get herself talked about.

I was let into the workroom by Tillie Hemingway, in the character of a baster, with her mouth full of threads; Miss Rathbone came hurrying from a fitting, and in the brief moment of crossing my half of the room to meet her I was aware that she had turned a sickly hue of fear. She must have seen me coming up the street with the other women, I surmised, and guessed that I knew. I felt a kind of compulsion on me to assure her by an extra graciousness that I did not know, and that it wouldn't make any difference if I did. She was not changed at all except perhaps as to a trifle more abundance of bosom and a greater insensibility to the pins with which she bristled. There was the same effect of modishness in the blond coiffure with the rats showing, and the well cut, half-hooked gown, but she seemed to know so little what to do with my visit that I was glad to cut it short and get away into the wide, overflowing day. I went on under the maples in leafage full and tender, following the faint scent of the first cutting of the meadows, quite to the end of the village and a mile or two into the country road, feeling the working of the Creative Powers in me, much as it seemed the sentient earth must feel the summer, a warm, benignant process. I was at one with the soul of things and knew myself fruitful. At last when the dust of the roadway disturbed by the homing teams, collected in layers of the cooler air, and the bats were beginning, I tore myself away from the fair day as from a lover and went back to Tommy waiting patiently for his supper. While I was getting it on the table I recalled Miss Rathbone.

"What," I said, "has she been doing to get herself talked about?" Suddenly there whipped out on his face the counterpart of the flinching which I had noted in the dressmaker.

"Who said she had been talked about? What have they been telling you? A pack of lying old cats!"

"So she *has* been talked about?" I put down a pile of plates the better to account to myself for his excitement.

"I might have known somebody would get at you. Why can't they come to me."

137

"Tommy! Has Miss Rathbone been talked about with *you?* Oh, my dear!" I meant it for commiseration. Tommy went sullen all at once.

"I don't want to talk about it. I won't talk about it!"

"You needn't. And as for what the others say, you don't suppose I am going to believe it?" He turned visibly sick at the assurance.

"I'll tell you about it after supper," he protested. "I meant to tell you." I kept my mind turned deliberately away from the subject until it was night and I heard the last tardy customer depart, then the shutters go up, and after a considerable interval my husband's foot upon the stairs.

I hope I have made you understand how good he was, with what simple sort of goodness, not meant to stand the strain of the complexity in which he found himself. He wanted desperately to get out of it, to get in touch again with straight and simple lines of living. As he stood before me then his face was streaked red and white with the stress of the situation, like a man after a great bodily exertion. I was moved suddenly to spare him—after all what was the village dressmaker to us? Tommy flared out at me.

"She is as good as you are . . . she's as pure . . . as kind-hearted. It's as much your fault as anybody's. You were away; you were always away." His voice trailed out into extenuation. There fell a long pause in which several things became clear to me.

"Tell me," I said at last.

Tommy sat down on the red plush couch. He had taken off his coat downstairs, for the evening was warm. There was pink in his necktie and the freckles stood out across his nose. I was taken with a wild sense of the ridiculous. Miss Rathbone, I knew, was six years my husband's senior.

"I went there a good deal last winter," he began. "I never meant any harm . . . my business partner . . . it was lonesome here. Of course I ought to have known people would talk. Nobody told me. She was brave, she bore it a long time, and then I saw that something was the matter. I didn't know until she told me, how fond of her I was—"

"Tommy, Tommy!" Strangely, it was I crying out. "Fond of her? Fond of *her?*"

"I was fond of her," he insisted dully. "She suffered a lot on account of me." The words dropped to me through immeasurable cold space. I believe there were more explanations, excusings. I was aware of being wounded in some far, unreachable place. I sat stunned and watched the widening rings of pain and amazement spread toward me. By and by tears came; I cried long and quietly. I got down on the floor at my husband's knees and put my arms about his body, crying. After a time I remember his helping me to undress and we got into bed. We had but the one. I know it now for the sign that I never loved my husband as wives should love, that I felt no offence in this; sex jealousy was not awake in me. We lay in bed with our arms around one another and cried for the pain and bewilderment of what had happened to us.

Chapter 10

As if the attraction Miss Rathbone had for my husband had been a spell, the mere naming of which dissipated it, we spent the ensuing three or four days in the glow of renewal. It was Miss Rathbone herself who drew us out of that excluding intimacy; set us apart where we could feel the cold stiffness of our hurts and the injury we had inflicted each on the other.

Whatever there had been between them, and I never knew very clearly what, they had failed to reckon on the recrudescence of the interest I had always had for my husband, and the tie of association. At any rate Miss Rathbone failed. I must suppose that she loved Tommy, that she was hungering for the sight of him, needing desperately to feel again the pressure of whatever bond had been between them. She came into the store on the fourth evening after my husband's admission of it, on one of the excuses she could so easily make out of her father's being there. I was sitting upstairs with some sewing when she came and neither saw nor heard her, but the unslumbering instinct, before I was half aware of it, had drawn me to the head of the stair.

As I came down it, still in the shadow of the upper landing, I saw her leaning across the counter with that factious air of modishness which was so large a part of her stock in trade with Higgleston. She had on all her newest things, and I think she was rouged a little. Even with the width of the counter between them she had the effect of enveloping my husband with that manner of hers as with a net; to set up in him the illusion of all that I was in fact; mystery, passion, the air of the great world. I was pierced through with the realization that with men it is not so much being that counts, as seeming. There was a touch of the fatuous in the way Tommy submitted to the implication of her attitude as she took a flower from her breast and pinned it in his coat. The foot of the stair came almost to the end of the counter where they stood, and a trick of the light falling from the hanging lamp threw the upper half of it in shadow. I stood just within it with my hand upon the rail. Something in the avidity of yielding in my husband's manner was like a call in me; I moved involuntarily a step downward.

They heard and then they saw me; they stopped frozen in their places and the thing that froze them was the consciousness of guilt. They stood confessed of a disloyalty. I turned full in their sight and walked back up the stair. It was very late that night when Tommy came up to me.

"If that is going on in the house," I notified him, "you can't expect me to stay."

"I dare say you'd be glad of a chance to leave."

"Is that why you are offering it to me?"

It was by such degrees we covered the distance between our situation and the open question of divorce. But there were lapses of tenderness and turning back upon the trail.

"I don't want anybody but you, Olivia," Tommy would protest. "If you would only stay with me!"

"Oh, Tommy, if you would only come away with me!"

If either of these things had been possible for us, I think Tommy would have recovered from his infatuation and been the happier for it. Or even if Miss Rathbone had kept away from him. But that is what she couldn't or wouldn't do. She might have thought that by being seen coming in and out of the store, she could stave off criticism by the appearance of being on good terms with us. At any rate she came. I think her coming caused my husband some embarrassment, and, manlike, he made her pay for it. As I think of it now, I realize that I really did not know what went on in her; whether she had set a trap for my husband or yielded to an unconquerable passion. In any case she had imagination enough to see that unless she could maintain the tragic status, she cut rather a ridiculous figure. Sometimes I think people are drawn into these affairs not so much by the hope of happiness as the need, the deep-seated, desperate need of emotion, any kind of emotion. I think if we had taken her note, had had it out on the world-without-end basis, she would have been almost as well satisfied by a recognized romantic loss as by success. But I never knew exactly. She was equally in the dark about me. Now and then I had a glimpse of the figure I was in her eyes, in some stricture of my husband's on my behaviour—some criticism which bore the stamp of her suggestion; it was as if he was being dragged from me by an invisible creature of which I knew nothing but an occasional scraping of its claws. I try to do her the justice in my mind, of thinking that the situation which she had built up out of Tommy's loneliness was as real for her as it was for him. Nobody in Higgleston had ever taken my natural alienation from the people there as anything but deliberate and despising. To her, my husband was the victim of a cold, neglectful wife, and to him she contrived to be a figure of romance.

"I owe her a lot," Tommy insisted; "she has suffered on account of me." He went back to that phrase again, "I owe her a lot."

"What do you owe her that you can't pay?"

"Well, I couldn't marry as long as you—"

"You want to marry her?" I cried. "You want to marry *her*?"

"I couldn't expect you to appreciate her," Tommy was sullen again; "you're so full of yourself." I held on to a graver matter.

"You want us to be divorced?" I can hear that sounding hollowly in a great space out of which all other interests in life seemed suddenly to shrink and shrivel. I had learned to talk of divorce in the great world, but to me my marriage was one of the incontrovertible things.

"We might as well be," I heard my husband say; "you are never at home any more." Then the reaction set in. "Stay with me, Olivia. I don't want anybody but you; just stay with me!"

"You want me to give up the stage and live here in Higgleston *forever*?" The unfairness of this overcame me.

"Well, why not, if you're married to me?"

I believe he would have done it. He would have wasted me like that and thought little of it. I was married, and not altogether to Tommy, but to Higgleston and the clothing business. The condition he demanded of me was not of loving and being faithful, but of living over the store. Until now, though I knew I did not love

141

my husband as life had taught me men could be loved, I had never given up expecting to. Somewhere, somehow, but I was certain it was not in Higgleston, the transmuting touch should find him which would turn my husband into the Lord of Life. Now I discovered myself pulled over into another point of view. He had become a man capable of being interested in the village dressmaker. The farther she drew him from me the more the stripe of Higgleston came out in him.

I had planned to go up to Chicago for a week in August; to consult with Mr. Harding about the plays he was to produce the next season. I had not signed with him yet, but I knew that I should, that I could no more dissever myself from that connection than I could voluntarily surrender my own breath; I might try, but after the few respirations withheld, nature would have her way with me. It was not that I came to a decision about it; the whole matter appeared to lie in that region of finality that made the assumption of a decision ridiculous. I do not know if I expected to divorce my husband or if he or Miss Rathbone expected it. I think we were all a little scared by the situation we had evoked, as children might be at a dog they let loose. We felt the shames of publicity yelping at our heels.

The day before I left, I went to see Miss Rathbone; I had to have a skirt shortened. It was absurd, of course, but there was really no one else to go to. If there had been I shouldn't have dared; all Higgleston would have known of it and drawn its own conclusion. As it was, Higgleston was extremely dissatisfied with the affair. It did not know whom properly to blame, me for neglecting my husband or Miss Rathbone for snapping him up; they felt balked of the moral conclusion.

I hardly know what Miss Rathbone thought of my coming to her. I think she had braved herself for some sort of emotional struggle sharp enough to drown the whisper of reprobation. My quiet acceptance of the situation left her somehow toppling over her own defences. Sometimes I think the emotionalism which the attitude of that time demanded to be worked up over a divorce, drew people to it with that impulse which leads them to rush toward a fire or hurl themselves from precipices. Miss Rathbone must have been aching to fling out at me, to justify her own position by abuse of mine, and here she was down on the floor with her mouth full of pins squinting at the line of my skirt. It was then that I told her what I was going to Chicago for. "You'll be away from home all winter, then?" The question was a challenge.

"I don't know, I haven't signed yet." For the life of me I couldn't have foreborne that; it was exactly the kind of an advantage she would have taken of me. If I chose not to sign for the next winter, where was she? She stood up blindly at last. "I guess I can do the rest without you," she said. Some latent instinct of fairness flashed up in me.

"But I think I shall sign," I admitted. "I couldn't stand a winter in Higgleston." I was glad afterward that I had said that; it gave her leave for the brief time that was left to them, to think of him as being given into her hands.

I was greatly relieved to get away, even for a week, from the cold curiosity of Higgleston which, without saying so, had made me perfectly aware that I showed I had been crying a great deal lately. But no sooner was I freed from the pull of affection than I began to feel a deep resentment against Tommy. His attempt to charge his lapse of loyalty, on my art, on that thing in me which, as I read it, constituted my sole claim upon consideration, appeared a deeper indignity than his interest in the dressmaker. It was all a part of that revelation which sears the path of the gifted woman as with a flame, that no matter what her value to society, no man will spare her anything except as she pleases him. At the first summer heat of it I felt my soul curl at the edges. His repudiation of me as an actress began to appear a slight upon all that world of fineness which Art upholds, a thing not to be tolerated by any citizen of it. In its last analysis it seemed that my husband had deserted me in favour of Higgleston quite as much as I had deserted him, and it was for me to say whether I should consent to it. In that mood I met Mr. Harding and signed with him for the ensuing season, and then quite unaccountably, ten days before I was expected, I found myself pulled back to Higgleston. I had wired Tommy, and was surprised to have Mr. Ross meet me at the station.

"Mr. Bettersworth is not very well," he explained, as he put me into Higgleston's one omnibus. "It came on him rather suddenly. Some kind of a seizure," he admitted, though I did not gather from his manner that it was particularly serious until the 'bus, instead of stopping at our store, drove straight on up the one wide street.

"I thought you'd want to see him immediately," the attorney interposed to my arresting gesture. "You see he was taken at his partner's house." He seemed to avoid some unpleasant implication by not mentioning Rathbone's name.

I scarcely remember what other particulars he gave me at the time; my next sharp impression was of my husband lying white and breathing heavily in the bed in the Rathbone's front room, the drapery of which had been torn hastily down to make room for him, regardless of the finished pieces of Miss Harvey's trousseau still crowding the chairs upon which they had been hastily thrust. Empty sleeves hung down and vaguely seemed to reach for what they could not clasp; strangely I was aware in them of an aching lack and loss which must have sprung in my bosom. I took my husband's hand and it dropped back from my clasp, waxlike and nerveless. I think I had been kneeling by the bed for some time, talk had been going on whisperingly around me; finally the light faded and I discovered that the doctor had gone. The beribboned bridal garments hung limply still on the chairs and mocked me with their empty arms. Presently I was aware that Miss Rathbone had come in with a lamp. She stood there on the other side of the bed and we looked at him and at one another.

"How long?" I asked her.

"Two or three days maybe, the doctor says."

"Will he know me again."

"The doctor says not."

"Oh, Tommy, Tommy!" I began to shake with suppressed sobbing. Miss Rathbone looked at me with cold resentment.

"You can cry as much as you like, it won't disturb him," she said.

She seemed to have taken the fact that she wasn't to cry herself, as final. In a few minutes old Rathbone shuffled in from the shop and stood peering at Tommy with his little red-lidded eyes, wiping them furtively. I believe the old man was fond of his partner and it was not strange to him that Tommy should be lying ill at his home. Miss Rathbone came and took him by the shoulders as one does to a grieving child and turned his face to her bosom. She was a head taller than he, and as she looked across him to me there was compulsion in her look and pleading.

"He is never to know," the look said, and I looked back, "Never."

It was then that I realized how genuine her affection was for the feeble, snuffling old man; she would suffer at being lessened in his eyes.

Some one came and took me away for a while, and by degrees I got to know the story. It had been the night before, just about the time I was taken with that strange impulse to return, that Tommy had shut up the store and gone over to the half-furnished room belonging to the Board of Trade, which had become a sort of club for the soberer men of the community. A great deal of talk went on there which gave them the agreeable impression of something being done, though there must have been much of it of the character of that which was going on in a group around Montague when Tommy came in at the door. He came in very quietly, blinded by the light, and they had their backs to him, shaking with the loose laughter which punctuates a ribald description. Then Montague's voice took it up again.

"Rathbone'll get him," he said. "She's got the goods. The other one has probably got somebody on the side; these actresses are all alike."

There was a word or two more to that before Tommy's fist in his jaw stopped him. Montague struck back, he was a heavier man than my husband, but in a minute the others had rushed in between them. They were drawn back and held; Tommy's nose bled profusely, he appeared dazed, and accepted Montague's forced apology without a word. The men were all scared and yet excited; some of them were ashamed of themselves. They suspected it was not the sort of thing that should go on at a Board of Trade, and agreed it ought to be kept out of the papers. Some one walked home with my husband, and on the way he was seized with a violent fit of vomiting.

"Who was it hit me?" he asked at the door, and seemed but vaguely to remember what it was about. The next morning he opened the store as usual and appeared quite himself to old Rathbone, who came shuffling and sidestepping in to his nest at the accustomed hour. About half-past ten the tailor was made aware by the rapping of a customer on the deserted counter, that Tommy had gone out without a word. He must have gone straight to Miss Rathbone; those who met him on the street recalled that his gait was unsteady. She must have been greatly concerned to have him there at that hour, for people were moving about the streets and customers beginning to come in, and in the presence of Tillie Hemingway he could offer her no adequate explanation.

She was desperately revolving the risk of taking him into the front room to have out of him what his distrait presence half declared, when he was taken with a momentary retching; she went into the next room to fetch him a glass of water and a moment after her back was turned she heard him pitch forward on the floor.

When Rathbone had sent for me by the wire that passed me on the way home, he sent also to Tommy's father, who got in before noon the next day. I remember him as a quizzical sort of man always with his hands in his pockets, and a bristling brown moustache cut off square with his upper lip, and a better understanding of the situation than he had any intention of admitting. I had by some unconscious means derived from him that though he was fond of Tommy, he never had much opinion of his capacity. I think now it must have been his presence there and his manner of being likely to do the most unexpected thing, that pulled those same live business men who had stood listening in loose-mouthed relish of Monty's ribaldry, out of the possibility of entertainment in the case that might be made out of his implication in my husband's death, to the consideration of the town's repute as a place where such things could not possibly happen. By the time Forester came on, a covert discretion had supplied the event with its sole consoling circumstance of secrecy. Not even my family got to know what led up to that blow which had precipitated an unsuspected weakness. It was quite in accordance with what they believed of the life I had chosen, that my husband's death in a brawl should be among its contingencies. Poor Tommy's end took on a tinge of theatricality.

It was toward the end of the second day that he began to respond to the stimulants the doctor had been pouring into him. He opened his eyes and looked at us, conscious, but out of all present time. Feebly his glance roved over the figures by the bed, and fell at last on me.

"Ollie," he whispered, "Ollie!" It was a name he had not called for a long time.

"Oh, my dear, my dear!" I took his hand again and felt a faint pressure. Miss Rathbone hardly dared to look at him with the others standing about. I whispered her name to him, and his partner's, but he did not so much as turn his eyes in their direction. I could see him studying me out of half-shut glances; there would be an appreciable interval before the sense of what he saw penetrated the dulled brain; I thought I knew the very moment when the significance of our standing all about his bed crying, took hold of him. All at once he spoke out clearly:

"Is my father here?" I fancied he must have hit on that question as a confirmation; but before there could be any talk between them he slid off again into the deeps of insensibility. At the end of half an hour or so he started up almost strongly.

"Ollie!" he demanded, "where is the baby?"

"Asleep," I told him.

"Then I will sleep too," and in a little while it was so.

The Odd Fellows took charge of my husband's funeral, his body was moved from the Rathbones', to their hall and did not go back again to the rooms over the store. Miss Rathbone made up my crape for me. I believe it gave her a little comfort to do so. Forester came and settled up my husband's affairs; he was rather inclined to resent what he felt was an effort of the Rathbones to claim a larger share in the business than the books showed, but he thought my indifference natural to my grief. He was shocked a little at my determination to go on with my engagement; we were not so poor he thought, that I could not afford a little retirement to my widowhood. But in that strange renewal of communion after death, I felt my husband nearer than before. He would go with me at last out of Higgleston. Strangely, I wanted to see Miss Rathbone, but she kept away from me. That was as it should have been in Higgleston. She had tried to get my husband, she had been, in a way, the death of him. It was hardly expected that I could bear the sight of her, though it would have been Christian to forgive her.

I did see her, however, the night before I went away. It was the dusk of the first of September. There was a moon coming up, large and dulled at the edges by the haze, and that strange earthy smell with the hint of decay in it, kept in by the banded mists that lay below the moon. The darkness crept close along the earth and spread upward like an exhalation into the sky where almost the full day halted. I had slipped out down a side street and across an open lot to the cemetery. I would have that hour with my dead free from observation.

I went between the white head stones and the flower borders. As I neared my husband's grave, something moved upon it. It arose out of the low mound as I approached; for one heart-riving second I stopped, speechless; it moved again and showed a woman.

147

"Miss Rathbone!" I called. "Henrietta!" I had not used her name before; I have just now remembered it.

"You might have left me this," she said. I saw that she had covered the mound with flowers, and I was glad I had not brought any.

"I am leaving," I answered. "I am going tomorrow . . . where my work is."

"Yes, *you* can go. But I have to stay . . . where my work is. I stay with him. You can go . . . you always wanted to go. And I, I have been talked about and I daren't even cry for him, not even at night, for my father hears me." She was crying now, deeply, bitterly. "You never cared for him," she insisted, "and now he knows it; he knows and has come back to me . . . to *me*."

"He comes back," I admitted. I was stricken suddenly with the futility of all human conviction. Moving about the house that day I had been conscious of him beside me then, and now, lying there beside my boy, touching him . . . mine . . . sealed to me in the certainty of death. And he had come back to *her*. I did not know even now what she and my husband had been to one another.

It swept over me somehow, drowningly, that this was the secret that the dead know, how to belong to all of us. They had no bond, how could they be unfaithful? For a moment I was caught up by the thought to nobility.

"Look here, Henrietta, if you feel that way, I'll leave it to you. I'll not come here any more." I did not know what else I could do about it.

"It's the least you *can* do." She was accepting it as her right. Any woman will understand how I wanted to lay my hand there, above his breast. She must really have believed I did not love him. I turned back across the borders.

"Good-bye, Henrietta." She made a nearly inarticulate sound. The last I saw of her in the dusk she was tucking her flowers into the fresh sod as one tucks a coverlet about a child. He had been, I suppose, both man and child to her.

148

BOOK III

Chapter 1

I have to take up my story again about eighteen months later at the point of my going out to Suburbia to ask Gerald McDermott for a part in his new play, which was being rehearsed with Sarah in the *rôle* of *Bettina*. But before that there had been some rather mortifying experiences to teach me that though I was done with Higgleston, it was, to a certainty, not done with me. In any case I suppose the shock of my husband's death must have affected my work unfavourably, but the knowledge of his secret defection, and the excuse he found for it in what was best in me, made still corroding poison at the bottom of my wound.

What it all amounted to in my career was that the season which should have swept me back to Chicago in triumphant establishment of my gift, trickled out in faint praise and cold esteem. It was not that you could place your finger and say just there was the difficulty, but what came of it was another year on the road with Cline and Erskine, in stock. The Hardings, notwithstanding their disappointment in what they expected to make of me, managed to be kind.

"You'll pull up," they assured me; "it's because you are really an artist that you show what you've been through!" And they didn't know the half of what that was.

To Henry Mills my engagement with Cline and Erskine, was a step forward into that blazoned and banal professionalism which passes in America for dramatic success; but Sarah knew, and I think I knew myself, that the dance they led us in the spotlight of copious advertisement, was a dance of death to much that the plastic art should be. In this instance it was demonstrated even to the hopeful eye of Henry Mills, for the play chosen proved so little suited to the semi-rural, Middle West cities where we played it, that before the season was half over we were recalled, and, after an empty interval, finished out the engagement in one of those sensation mongering shows with which such combinations as Cline and Erskine clutch at the fleeing skirts of a public they never understand.

It was about a month after the closing of this engagement that I took Sarah's suggestion about applying to Gerald McDermott, but not before I had tried several other things. The truth was, as I knew very well when I faced it, that I had at the time nothing in me. To those who haven't it, a gift is a sort of extra possession, like an eye or a hand that can be commanded to its accustomed trick on any occasion; but to the owners of it it is a libation poured to the Unknown God. I had emptied my cup of its froth of youth, and as yet nothing had touched the profounder experience from which it should be fed and filled again, and I had no technique to supply the insufficiencies of my inspiration. Somewhere within me I felt the stuff of power, stiff and unworkable, needing the flux of passion and the shaping hand of skill.

Looking back now from the vantage of a tolerable success, if you were to ask me what, more than any other thing, prevents the fulness of our native art, I should say the blank public misapprehension of its processes. Turning every way to catch the favourable wind, what met me then, was the general conviction on the part of my friends that if you had talent you succeeded anyway, and if you weren't succeeding it was because you hadn't any talent. I suffered many humiliations before I learned how absolutely, by that same society that so liberally resents the implication of any separateness in art, the artist is thrust back upon himself. To do what seemed necessary for the development of my gift, to have a year or two to travel and study, to connote its powers with its limitations, required money; and though there in Chicago there was money for every sort of adventure that stirred the imagination of man, there was none for the particular sort of investment I represented. At least not at the price I was prepared to pay.

The half of what had been put into setting my brother on his feet would have served me, but I learned from Effie, that as much of my mother's capital as had been put into Forester's business, was not only impossible to be withdrawn from keeping him upright, but threatened not to hold him so for as long as it was necessary for mother to see in him the figure of a provider. This had been made plain at Christmas, when Effie had written me that a particular wheeled chair which my mother had set her heart upon because of a hope it held out of church-going, would be impossible unless I came forward handsomely. I did come forward on a scale commensurate with the Taylorville estimate of my salary, which was by no means comparable to its purchasing power in Chicago; and now I was beginning to realize that unless some one came forward for me, I stood to lose the Shining Destiny to which I felt myself appointed. I was slow in understanding that it was not to be looked for by any of the paths by which interest and succour are traditionally due. Not, for instance, from Pauline and Henry Mills.

I was seeing a great deal of them since I had come to Chicago, not only because of our earlier friendship, but because I found myself constantly thrown back on all that they stood for, by my distaste for much that I saw myself implicated in as a theatrical star who had not quite made good. I hated, quite unjustly, I believe, the players with whom for the time I was professionally classed; I loathed the shallow shop talk, the makeshift rooms we lived in, the outward smartness and the pinch of anxiety it covered. I was irritated by my external and circumstantial resemblance to much that I felt instinctively, kept them where they were, and vexed at some cheapness in myself which seemed to be revealed by the irritation. I had been thrown up out of the freemasonry of the preliminary struggle into a kind of backwater of established second-rateness, where there were also second-rate manners and morals and social perceptions. It was a great relief to get away from it to Pauline's home in Evanston, and the air it had of being somehow established at the pivot of existence. Pauline had two children by now, and a manner of being abundantly equal to the world in which she moved, a manner which I was only just realizing was largely owing to the figure of her husband's income. What Pauline furnished me at her home, over and above the real affection there was still between us, was a sort of continuous performance of the domestic virtues.

That faculty for knowing exactly what she wanted, which had led her to make the most of her housekeeping allowance in the days when making the most of it was her chief occupation, now that the centres of her activity had been shifted from the practical to the social and cultural, stood her in remarkable stead. I was so constantly amazed by the celerity and sureness with which she seized on just the attitude or opinion which suited best with the part she had cast herself for as the perfect wife and mother, that it was only when I discovered its complete want of relativity to the purpose of the play or to the rest of the company, that I was not taken in by it. I doubt now if Pauline ever had an idea or permitted herself a behaviour which was not conditioned by the pattern she had set for herself, which she intrigued both Henry and myself into believing was the only real and appreciable life.

At the time of which I write it was a great comfort to me to get away from my own dreary professionalism, to the nursery at Evanston, or to add my small flourish to the *scene à faire* of Henry's homecoming, made every day to seem the one event for which the household waited, from which, indeed, it took its excuse for being. For all of this was so well in line with what Henry, who with the amplification of his income had taken on a due rotundity of outline and a slight tendency to baldness, conceived as proper for a man's home to be, that he played up to it as much as was in him. He had still his air of knowingness about the theatre, and if there was at times in his manner a suggestion that he might have found it pleasanter to adjust his relation to me on the basis of what I was as an actress, if I had not been quite so much the friend, it was so far modified by his genuine admiration for his wife and his cession to her of every right of judgment in the home, that I was inclined to accept him at his own and Pauline's estimate as the model husband.

It was only a few days before my visit to Gerald McDermott, that I had undertaken to state to Pauline the nature of the help I required and my title to it. I had gone out to dinner and found her putting on a new gown, one of those garments admirably contrived between the smartness of evening dress and the intimacy of negligée, in which Evanston ladies of that period were wont to receive their lords.

"I'm needing something new myself," I said for a beginning, "and I'm divided between the certainty that if I don't get an engagement I can't afford it, and if I don't afford it I probably won't get an engagement." Pauline stopped in the process of hooking up, to take stock of me.

"You absurd child!" The note of amused admonition with which she ordinarily accepted my professional exigencies turned on the note of correction. "Don't you think you put too much stress on those things?"

154

"What things?" She had touched upon the spring of irritation.

"Clothes, you know, and appearances. Isn't it better just to do your work well and rest upon that?"

"Pauline, if you had ever looked for an engagement you would know that getting it is largely a matter of appearing equal to it, and clothes are the better part of appearing."

"But if you know that your work is good, what do you care what people think of you?" I dodged the moral situation about to be precipitated on me.

"It's about the only way you know it is good, knowing what people think of it."

"Now see here," Pauline protested, reinforced by the evident superiority of her viewpoint to mine, "you're getting all wrong; these things you are thinking of, they are not the real things; they don't count, not in the long run; it's only the spiritual things that really matter." She had put on all the plastic effect of nobility that was part of her stock in trade with Henry Mills. I thrust out against it sharply.

"Do you realize, Pauline, that if I don't get an engagement soon I shan't be able to pay my board?"

"Oh, you poor dear!" She came over and took my hand. I don't know why women like Pauline do that, but when they do it it is a sign they are not equal to the situation and are trying to fake it with you.

"I know it is hard"—she found the cooing note with facility—"but it will come right; it always does. I've always found that there is a way provided."

Something flashed into my mind that I had read in the newspapers recently about the corporations Henry worked for, and I wondered if Pauline had the least notion how the way, for her, was humanly provided, but the sound of Henry's latchkey put an end to the conversation, which I hadn't felt sufficiently encouraging to warrant my taking up again.

I went from Pauline's, at the very first opportunity, to Sarah Croyden, who was playing in Chicago, and doing her kindliest to blow the wind of hope into my sagging sails. I met Cecelia Brune there. It had been to me the witness of how far I had fallen from my mark, that I had been thrown with her again in my last engagement. Hers was the sort of talent that Cline and Erskine could play up to the limit of the inadmissible. There were not

155

wanting intimations that Cecelia had moved her own limit a notch or two in that direction. She had taken a characteristic view of my reappearance in her neighbourhood.

"Got into the band-wagon, didn't you?" she remarked. "I saw Dean on the road last year and she said you was going in for high-brow stunts. Nothin' to it. You stay with Cline and Erskine; they get you on like anything." Her own notion of getting on was to figure as the sole female attraction in a song and dance skit in what she pronounced "Vawdville."

"It's the only place havin' a figgur does you any good!" That she did not recommend it for me must be taken for her estimate of mine. Nevertheless I was amused by her, and Sarah, I knew, was even a little fond. Sarah's affections were a sort of natural emanation from her, like the rays of a candle, and warmed all they lighted on. On this afternoon I found Cecelia drinking tea there and I wasn't able to conceal my professional depression from her sharp, shallow inquisitiveness. There were never two or three players got together, I believe, but the talk turned on the comparative ineffectiveness of Merit as against Pull in the struggle for success.

"There's no two ways about it," insisted Cecelia Brune; "you gotta get a hold of some rich guy and freeze to him." The extent to which Cecelia had blossomed out in ostrich tips and orchids that bright spring afternoon, might have suggested to an experienced eye, that the freezing process had already begun. I say might have, because Sarah and I found it difficult to disassociate her from the hard, grubby innocence in which our acquaintance had begun. Sarah, I know, believed in her and had her in often to informal occasions as a bulwark against what, with all her faith and pains, she didn't finally save her from.

"You can talk all you want to," Cecelia asseverated, "about man being the natural provider. I've noticed he don't work at the job much without he's gettin' something out of it. If you're sufferin' with that little old song and dance about men doin' for you because you're a woman and need it, you gotta get over it. There's nothin' laid down over that counter unless you deliver the goods." She was nibbling lumps of sugar moistened in her tea, and the wild rose of her cheeks and the distracting rings of her hair made her offensiveness a mere childish impertinence.

"Look at Helen Matlock," she ran on, "gettin' five hundred a week. And when old Sedgwick put it up to her she said she'd die rather; and then she went home and found her mother sick, and what did she do? Never batted an eye, but told her she'd got an engagement, and went back and made it good. An' now she's gettin' five hundred. That's what I call doin' well by yourself."

"She can't mean it," Sarah extenuated when Cecelia had gone; "she's too frank about it. When she stops talking I shall begin to suspect her."

"But is it true, about Miss Matlock, I mean?" Just at that juncture Helen Matlock was doing the work I felt most drawn to, most fit to undertake.

"I suppose so," Sarah allowed; "it's a common saying that the way to the footlights in the Majestic is through the manager's private room." She came over and sat beside me on the bed, which, under a Bagdad curtain, did duty as a couch. "There are other theatres besides the Majestic," she said.

"None that want me," I averred.

"Oh," she cried, "you don't mean—?"

"No," I had to own, "I don't mean that I have a chance to get on even by misbehaving myself. I'm not the kind to whom that sort of chance comes." Sarah stroked my hand a while.

"I've been thinking, if you could get a small part or a season, you could take it under another name until you are quite yourself again. It's often done." I could see she had gone much farther than that with it in her thought. It was just such cover as that I was seeking for the renaissance of my acting power.

And that was what led to my going out to Suburbia to see Gerald McDermott about the part of *Mrs. Brandis* in "The Futurist."

It was out quite in the frayed edge of outer fringe of real estate ventures which hedged Chicago round, in a district which was spoiled for country and not quite made into town, and from the number of weedy plots not built upon between the scroll-saw cottages, had almost a rural air. Leaning trolleys went zizzing along the banked highways, and at the ends of the unpaved avenues there were flat gleams of the lake. Depressed as I was by the consciousness of having fallen from the estate of actresses who command engagements to those who seek them, I was still able to be touched a little by curiosity by what Sarah had told me of McDermott and his wife, whom he had married for her pretty, feminine inconsequence, who, having no point of attachment to her husband's life but femininity, was able to imagine none for any other woman, and suffered incredibly in consequence.

"If one could only discover why clever men marry that sort of women!" I wondered.

"Oh, Jerry thought he was going to bend her to his will," Sarah explained. "But that kind don't bend, they just slump." I had hardly knocked at the door before I had an inkling of how painful to the author of "The Futurist" the process of slumping might be.

I could hear the fretting of a child, hushed suddenly by my knock, then the patter of little feet across the floor and voices startled and pitched low. I was just debating whether I shouldn't pretend I hadn't heard anything and go away again, when Mr. McDermott opened the door. I had met him once at Sarah's and should have known him again by the pallor of his countenance against the dead blackness of his hair, straight and shining like an Indian's. The effect of boyishness that one derived from his tall, thin figure was increased now by the marks of weeping about his eyes. In the glimpse of the room behind him I was aware of a disorder only excusable in the face of a family catastrophe; one of the children that ran to his knee was still in its little petticoat, without a slip, and had not been washed or combed that day. I wavered an instant between the obligation of politeness to ignore the situation and the certainty that I couldn't.

"Oh!" I cried. I snatched at my repertory for the proper mixture of commiseration and consternation. "Is any one ill?"

His desperate need of help opened the door to me.

"My wife" . . . he began, but the state of the room accounted for that, as he perceived, taking it in afresh through my eyes. Mrs. McDermott was lying on the sofa in the coma of exhaustion. She lifted her face to me for a moment, swollen with crying, and then let herself go again into that pit in which a woman sinks an impossible situation. She was really faint, poor thing, and, if I judged by the state of the house, had had no luncheon. I took all that in at a glance, but it was none of my business.

"Is it her heart?" I wanted to know of her husband as I bent over her. He caught up the suggestion eagerly.

"Yes, her heart . . . she is very weak." He did whatever I suggested on that explanation. I would have proposed putting her to bed if I had not feared that that would involve more revelations of the family disorder than I was willing to tax him with.

We got her out of her faintness presently and found her a safety valve in pitying her poor children with that sloppy sort of maternal affection which is not inconsistent with a good deal of neglect. I wasn't working for anything but to save Jerry—I came to call him that before many weeks—from the embarrassment of what I was sure had been a family fracas which threatened at every moment to break out again. I suggested tea, for I was satisfied that both of them wanted food, and while I was making toast before the sitting-room fire, Mrs. McDermott managed to get herself and the children into some sort of order. I could see then how pretty she had been in a large-eyed, short-lipped way, and how charming in her youth had been the inconsequence which as the mistress of a family made her a sloven. Not to seem to notice too much the superficial air of being prepared for company which she managed to give the children by washing their faces surreptitiously, I explained to Mr. McDermott that I had come about the part of *Mrs. Brandis*.

"Oh, you'll do," he assented heartily. "You'll do just as you are. *Mrs. Brandis* is a widow you know . . . that is, the *Mrs. Brandis* that I created—"

"Just as you conceived it of course," I insisted, "I should want to play it that way."

"The trouble is that Moresco isn't satisfied so easily; he wants me to make changes in the part."

"Well . . . " I was prepared to make concessions.

"I'm afraid he has somebody in mind . . ."

"Fancy Filette," his wife broke in, "a painting, flirting, immoral . . .!" Jerry scraped his chair back along the floor to cover the word, but I knew where I was in a twinkling.

"Fancy Filette! She'll play it in short skirts!"

"I'll be lucky if she doesn't insist on a song and dance."

"He doesn't need to have her unless he wants to." Mrs. McDermott was positive on that point. She was sitting with both children on her lap, chiefly in order to keep up the fiction that I didn't know she had just been having hysterics, I had cautioned her against letting them climb over her, and she promptly let them, because the idea that she was tending them at a risk to her health, rather helped out with her own notion of herself as a misused but devoted wife and mother.

Jerry looked at me over her head in a mute appeal to me to understand.

"Unless Moresco puts on my play there is no chance for it," he protested. "I've been to the others. I'll tell you, though, if you go to him just as you are, he may think better of it. He can't possibly get anybody so good."

We neither of us believed that Mr. Moresco would turn down Fancy Filette for anybody, but we kept up the game of thinking so from sheer desperation. I played too at the pretence that Jerry's wife was a delicate, idealized sort of creature who did not understand the great hard world. That was no doubt what had appealed to him in the beginning, but she wasn't made up for the part. She had begun to put on weight after she had children, and her hair wanted washing. I got away as soon as I could and went straight to Sarah.

"They'd been having some kind of a row," I told her.

"Oh, it must have been Fancy Filette who set her off," Sarah was certain. "She took to you as a relief, but you'll be in for it too if you get the part."

I had to admit to myself after I had been to Mr. Moresco, that there was not much likelihood that I would get it. He laid the tips of his pudgy fingers together and addressed me with the slight blur in his speech which convinced one of the racial affinity which he commonly denied.

"Mr. McDermott thinks it will suit me admirably," I told him.

"Ah, yes, the author," the manager mentioned him as though it were a fact indulgently admitted to the discussion, "but then, my dear Miss Lattimore, we have to think of the audience."

There was this peculiarity of Moresco's handling of an audience, that he treated it as an entity, a sort of human stratification of which the three front rows were lubricious, the body of the orchestra high-brow, the first balcony sentimental and virtuous, the gallery facetious. As far as possible he arranged his plays to meet the requirements.

"Now we have Miss Croyden for *Bettina,* she is your type."— He meant as a woman, not as an artist; Sarah and I were both serious and respectable.—"For *Mrs. Brandis* I think we should have something a little more snappy."

"It isn't written snappy in the play," I reminded him.

"Ah, no, that is the trouble; I have spoken to Mr. McDermott; he will perhaps change it."

"And if he doesn't you will keep me in mind for it." I kept my voice with difficulty from being urgent. "You see, I don't feel like

playing a heavy part this year." I glanced down at my mourning;
I hoped he would accept it as an explanation. Two or three days
later I saw Sarah and she remarked that Jerry was rewriting some
parts of his play at the request of the manager.

"The part of *Mrs. Brandis?*" Sarah nodded.

"Mr. Moresco want's it more—more—"

"Snappy," I supplied. "And who is to have it, have you heard?"

"Fancy Filette!"

"Oh, well, she's snappy enough, I suppose."

"I know; I don't even like to be billed with her; but, anyway,
the part wasn't worthy of you." But I felt as I went home to my
lodging that that was only Sarah's kind way of putting it.

Chapter 2

I saw more than a little of Jerry McDermott during the spring and
summer that I stayed in Chicago, haunting managers' offices in
my winter's suit and a fixed determination not to let any of them
suspect that I knew I couldn't, for the moment, act at all. Where
the gift had gone I did not know, nor when, in some desperate
encounter with the chance of an engagement, I attempted to
draw about me the tattered remnants of my old facility, had I any
notion what would bring it back again.

Effie wrote me to come home for the hot weather, but though
I regretted afterward not having done so I could not make up my
mind to leave Chicago. It seemed to me then that the deadly
quality of Taylorville lay waiting like a trap, which in my present
benumbed condition might close on me if I put myself in the way
of it. I thought that if I got out of reach of the flare of light from
the theatre doors, of the smell of back scenes and the florid grip
of the posters, that I should never in this world win back to them.
A summer in Taylorville would have saved me money, would
have rested and perhaps restored the balance of my powers, but
the inward monitor of which I was the mere shell and surface,
clutched upon the city with the grip of desperation. I hung upon
whatever slight attachments to the theatre my circumstances
afforded, like the drowned upon a rope, and waited for the resus-

161

citating touch. Somewhere beyond me I was aware of succor; not knowing from whence it should come, I grasped at everything within reach and was buffeted and torn about in the eddy of reverses.

What more even than his need of me, drove me back on Gerald McDermott, was the certainty that he was deriving from Fancy Filette the quality I missed. She was playing in one of the cheaper theatres in one of those entertainments that men are supposed to resort to when their families are out of town, and I had a moment's feeling that he exposed his sex to ridicule by the avidity with which he surrendered himself to her perfectly obvious methods. Until he sent his family north to one of the lake resorts for the hot weather, I found myself involved in certain obligations of visiting at his house, where I saw that his wife created for him by her incompetence much the same sort of background that my bereaved and purse-pinched condition made for me, and watched with alternate sympathy and resentment his flight from it to the effective self-complacency which Miss Filette induced in him.

I don't mean that Jerry wasn't fond of his wife in a way, and faithful to her, in so far as she didn't interfere with his male prerogative of being played upon by other women, but I do not think he had ever an inkling that the vortex of anger and despair which she forced him to share with her, in lieu of the passion which she couldn't any more excite, was of the same stripe as his need of the high, inflated mood that Miss Filette provided for him with her little bag of tricks. For from the first Jerry seized on me, poured himself out, despoiled himself of all the hopes, conjectures, half-guesses of his career, and that without in the least discovering that I was in need of much the same sort of relief myself. After his wife had taken the children to the country— though she used even then to come down on him suddenly with both of them and break up his work for days, or just when it was running smoothly, wire to him to rush up to Lake View and allay the horrors of her too active imagination—often evenings after the day's work, he would take me to dine at queer little French or Italian restaurants which were supposed to be preferred on account of the "atmosphere" rather than their cheapness, and uncoil for me there all the intricate turnings of his work upon itself, and the rich shapes and colours it took, played upon by the slanting eyes and carmine smile of Miss Filette. He would sit

162

opposite me with a cigarette and a glass of "Dago red," his black, shining hair, which he wore too long, slanting above his forehead like a boding wing, uncramping his soul; and though I liked him as a friend, and as a playwright thought him immensely worth while, I was divided between exasperation at his tacit exclusion of me from the world of excited powers in which any stimulation of his maleness threw him, and fear that in missing his capacity for quick, shallow passions, I had missed the one indispensable thing for my art.

"It is the chance of a lifetime," Jerry would be reassuring me, "to delineate a character that will be so intimate an expression of the one who is to play it . . . it's really extraordinary that she should have been named Fancy . . . it's symbolic."

"Oh, if you imagine she is really in the last like the *Mrs. Brandis* you are creating . . . besides, I happen to know her name is Powers, Amanda Powers." He caught at this delightedly.

"Ah, she's a poet, a poet! Such self-knowledge! To think of her knowing what would suit her so exactly!"

But I was not in the least interested in Miss Filette's psychology. What I was trying to get at was the source of the creative mood which I was sensible did not arise from anything Miss Filette was, but from what Jerry was able to think of her. I admitted it was a mood you had to be helped to, but I wasn't going to accept it from any male compliment to his inamorata. I set up Jerry's case alongside of Miss Dean and Manager O'Farrell, and a kind of fine intolerance drove me from it as ships are driven apart upon the tide.

It drove me back in the first instance upon what Pauline and Henry Mills stood for in my life. I was full of a formless importunate capacity, like the motor impulses of a paralytic, and I imagined a relief from it in the shadow of some succoring male who, by assuming the traditional responsibility of getting a living, should leave me free to produce the perfect flower of Art. At the time I was as far from realizing as Pauline, that she was eminently the sort of woman the sheltered life produced; had Henry Mills been upon the market I should have seized upon him promptly as the solution of all my difficulties.

Pauline did her best for me—that is to say, she brought out for me an infinite variety and arrangement of the sentimentalized sex attractions with which she charmed dull care from Henry's brow. It was only by degrees that I perceived that the utter want of

163

relativity of the quality that was known in Evanston as True Womanliness, was due to its being conditioned very much as I thought of myself as happiest to be. It was not until Pauline went to the country for the hot weather without making any sensible change in my affairs, that I began to understand how little she contributed. What I chiefly missed was a place to walk to when I went out for exercise.

I spent a great deal of time just walking, for there was not much doing in the theatrical line to interest me, and I was sustained and tormented by intimations that somewhere, not far from me, my Help walked too. I don't know where this conviction came from that there was help somewhere in the world; but by the middle of the summer the terrible, keen need of it walked with me through all my days and lay down with me at night. There were times when the certainty that it was there seemed almost enough to lift me again to a plane of power, other times when the sheer hunger of it bit into the bone. It was most like the sense I had had as a child of the large friendliness that brooded over Hadley's pasture; it was like the promise of the shining destiny that had moved between my youth and the common occurrence; but now at times, just along the edge of sleep, or out of the thick, waking drowse of heat, it shaped familiarly human. I think about that time I must have dreamed again the dream I had of Helmeth Garrett just after I had seen Modjeska, writing that letter in his uncle's house; and with the help of what my mother had told me I was able to read it plain. I do not distinctly remember dreaming this, but there were times when, just after waking, my mind would be full of him, and there would be a stir in me of the wings of power. But in the broad day, though I thought of him often, I could not so much as recall his face clearly.

The one thing that I remembered about him was that I had pleased him. It was a mortifying certainty that Jerry's ready acceptance of me as a woman of whom his wife could not possibly be jealous, had defined for me, that I didn't in general know how to please and interest men. They often were interested in me, but I was never in the least conscious of what drew them or caused them to sheer away. I had a suspicion, doubtless of Taylorvillian extraction, that there was a sort of culpability in knowing; but it came back to me now almost with a thrill that I had known with Helmeth Garrett. I had been able, out of all the possible things which might be said, to choose the thing that swayed him. I hadn't known ever for what things my husband loved me; but in a brief hour with Helmeth Garrett I was conscious of much in my manner to him arising from his conscious need. And I had no more than shaped this in my mind than I felt a faint stirring within me as of power.

About this time I began to be more aware of the Something Without, toward which my work tended, just after I had been asleep, as if the self of me had gone on seeking more successfully in the silences. I would arise very early with such a faint consciousness as a vine might have toward the nearest wall, and get up in the blue of the morning to go for long walks through the pleasant, empty streets, sometimes out to the lake shore where the glint of the moving water under the mist, struck faint sparkles from my stagnant surfaces. I would come back from these excursions beginning to faint with the day's heat, to wear through the afternoon with books and long drowses, and then in the cool of the evening it would call me again, and I would seek It until late at night, sometimes in the lit streets, fetid with the day's smells, sometimes on a roof garden or at a park concert, where the lights, the gayety, and the music served merely as a drug to my outer sense, which went on busily at its absorbing quest. Sometimes men spoke to me in these lonely wanderings; I would remember it afterward as one recalls little, unnoticed incidents in the midst of great excitement; but for the most part I was, except for the invisible presence, as unaccompanied as if the city had been quite empty. If I could have laid the anxiety of my diminishing bank account and the dread of not getting an engagement, I should have been almost happy.

It was along early in August that Chicago was greatly stirred by the visit of one of the Presidential candidates—for that was a Presidential year—who was also a popular hero. It had come rather unexpectedly and the preparations for it were of the hastiest. There was to be speaking at Armory Hall, and a reception afterward, and I thought I would go and clasp hands with the great man, as if, perhaps, I might find in it, as many of his admirers did, a sort of king's touch for the lethargy of my spirit. The meeting began early in the sweating afternoon and dragged out three heavy hours. Nothing of any importance transpired there until we were moving up the right side of the hall toward the receiving committee. The hall was split lengthwise by a bank of chairs, and down the left aisle the company of those who had

already gripped the broad palm of the candidate, had been elbowed to oblivion by the committee. It was in the very beginning
of the handshaking and there were not so many of them as of us.
They lingered in groups and talked with one another. I was about
midway of the aisles and several persons deep in the crush, when
I saw him. How well I knew the lock falling over his forehead, and
the quick unconscious motion of the head that tossed it back!
There was the indefinable air of the outdoor man about him,
though he was quite correctly dressed and had a lady's light wrap
over his arm.

"Helmeth! Helmeth!" I cried out to him from the centre of my
will. I fought my way to the outer edge of the moving crowd, I
caught at chairs and struggled to maintain my position opposite
him. He was talking to two or three men, and just at the edge of
the group a woman stood with an air of waiting. I resented her
immobility, so near him and so little moved by him.

"Helmeth, Helmeth, Look! Look at me!" I demanded voice-
lessly across the bank of chairs.

He heard me; slowly he turned; his attention wandered from
the group.

"Helmeth! Helmeth!" All my will was in my cry. Now he looked
in my direction. There was that in his face that told me my cry
had touched the outer ring of his consciousness. Then the lady
who stood by, took advantage of his detachment to touch him on
the arm. Only a man's wife touches him like that. I knew her at
once; she was the type of woman who subscribes to the _Delineator,_
and belongs to the church because she thinks it is an excellent
thing for other people. She had blond hair, discreetly frizzled
about the temples, and her dress had been made at home.

As soon as she touched him, Helmeth Garrett turned to her
with divided attention. I saw her take his arm; he looked back; the
cry held him; his eyes roved up and down; the moving mass
closed between us and carried me completely out of sight.

It was fully a quarter of an hour before the crowd released me,
and by that time he had quite vanished. I hung about the entrance
to the hall, I pushed here and there in the press, elbowed out of
it by resentful citizens. At last when the hall was closed and even
the policemen had gone from before it, I went home, to lie awake
half the night planning how to get at him. And the moment I
woke from the doze of exhaustion into which I finally fell, I knew
that the thread which bound me to Chicago had snapped. I stayed

on two or three days, vaguely hoping to come across him. I even looked in the hotel registers before I accepted Sarah's urgent invitation to spend the rest of the month with her at Lake View.

One night when the wind out of the lake was fresh enough to suggest, in the closed window and the drawn blind, a reciprocated intimacy, I told Sarah all about Helmeth Garrett.

"And to think," I said, "how different it all might have been if only I had got that letter."

"Yes," Sarah admitted, "but that doesn't prove you'd have been happy."

"Not if we loved one another?"

"Oh, I am not sure loving has anything to do with happiness, or is meant to. Sometimes I think God—or whoever it is manages things—has a very poor opinion of happiness, because you don't find it invariably along with the best of experiences. It happens, or it doesn't. If love does anything for you it is just to give you the use of yourself."

"But it hasn't," I protested; "I'm just stumping along."

"You haven't really had it—just being kissed once, what does that amount to?"

"Oh, Sarah, Sarah, that is what hurts me! I haven't really had it. I'm never going to. I'll just go halting like this all my life."

"No, you won't," Sarah shook her head, piecing her own knowledge slowly into comfort for me. "You remember what I told you that time when you found out about Dean and Mr. O'Farrell? There's a kind of feeling that goes with acting that is like loving, only it isn't. I don't know where it comes from. Maybe it is what they call genius, but I know you can slide off from loving into it. That is what makes Jerry think he has to be in love all the time; it is a little stair he climbs up, and then he goes sailing off. You don't think Fancy Filette really does anything for him?"

"Goodness, no; she hasn't a teaspoonful of brains!"

"Well, then," she triumphed. "After a while his genius will be so strong in him that he won't need that sort of thing and he will think it ridiculous."

"And you think that will come to me?"

"It did come. You didn't have to be in love to begin," Sarah objected.

"Sarah, I will tell you the truth! I was in love all the time, I didn't know with whom, but always wanting somebody . . . trying to get through to something; trying to mate. That was it. Nights

167

when I would do my best, and the house would be storming and cheering, I would look around for . . . for somebody. And I would go to my room, and he wouldn't be there! I used to think Tommy would be He, I wanted him to be. I thought some day I would turn around suddenly and find him changed into . . . whatever it was I wanted. But I know now he never could have been that. And all this summer . . . I've heard it calling. I've walked and walked. Sometimes it was just around the corner, but I never caught up with it. And when I saw Helmeth Garrett, *I knew!*"

I had leaned back out of the circle of our small shaded lamp to make my confession, but Sarah came forward into it the better to show me the condoning tenderness of her smile.

"It's no use, Sarah, I'm no genius; I have to be in love like the rest of them." She shook her head gently.

"You'll get across. Love would help; I wish you had it. But I'll confess to you; I had love and it only opened the door. There's something beyond, bigger than all men. You must reach out and lay hold of it. Oh, if it were love one needed, I should die—I should die!" I had never seen her so moved before.

"Tell me, Sarah; I've always wanted to know."

"I want you to know, but it isn't easy! I didn't know anything about love . . . how could I the way I was brought up! My father was a Baptist preacher. I had been taught that it was wrong to let anybody . . . touch you; and when he kissed me I felt as if he had the right. . . ."

"I know, I know!" I had been kissed that way myself.

"How can anybody know? I loved him, and I was the only one of many. He left me without a word. . . . like a woman of the street . . . not looking backward." She got up and moved about the room, the thick coil of her rich brown hair slipping to her shoulders, and her bodily perfection under the thin dressing gown distracting me even from the passion of her speech. I had a momentary pang of sympathy with the delinquent Lawrence, I could see how a man might be afraid almost, of the quality of her beauty.

"Sometimes," she said, "I think marriage is a much more real relation than people think—that something real but invisible happens between them so that even if they are parted they are never quite the same again. It is like having a limb torn from you; you ache always, in the part you have lost." I knew something of

168

what that ache could be, but I could only turn my face up to hers that she might see my tears.

"You have enough of your own to bear," she said. "I must not lay my troubles on you; but I wanted to tell you how I know it is not love that makes art. I was dying for love when Mr. O'Farrell put me to acting. I was bleeding so . . . and suddenly I reached out and laid hold of Whatever is, and I found I could act. It was as if the half of me that had been torn away had been between me and It, and I laid hold of It. That's how I know." She came behind me, leaning on my chair, and I put up my hands to her.

"Oh, Sarah, Sarah, help me to lay hold of it, too!" But for all her shy confidences, deep within I didn't believe her.

Toward the first of September we went back to the city, Sarah to begin rehearsals for *The Futurist,* and I to take up the dreary round of managers' offices and dramatic agencies. The best that was offered me was poor enough, but it had a faint savour of a superior motive clinging to it. It was from a Mr. Coleman, an actor manager of the old, heavy-jowled Shakespearian type, who was projecting a classic revival with himself in all the tragic parts, and I signed with him to play *Portia, Cleopatra,* and the wife of *Brutus.* We had been busy with rehearsals about ten days when I had a telegram from Forester saying that mother had died that day and I was to come immediately.

It was late Sunday evening when I received it and I hunted up the manager at the hotel.

"I'm going," I told him.

"Well, of course, your contract—"

"I'm going anyway . . . and I know the lines." He was as considerate, I suppose, as could be expected.

"I can give you three days," he calculated.

"Four," I stipulated.

"Well, four," he grudged. That would allow two days for the funeral.

Chapter 3

As it turned out I was more than a month in Taylorville and so saved myself from the Coleman players for a more kindly destiny, though at the time it did not appear so. It grew out of my realizing, in Effie's first clasp of me, something more than our common loss, more than family, something that I felt myself answer to before we could have any talk together that did not relate to the funeral and the manner of my mother's death.

They thought from little things that came to mind afterward, that she must have been prepared for it, but forebore to trouble them with a presentiment of what could not in any case have been much longer delayed: she had clung to them more and been still more loath to trouble them with her wants. The Saturday before, she had made Effie understand that she wished all the photographs of my father brought together, queer, little old daguerrotypes of him as a young man, a tintype of him in his volunteer soldier dress, and a large, faded photo of him as an officer leaning on his sword. She kept them by her and would be seen poring upon them, as though she tried to fix the identity of one about to be met under unfamiliar or confusing circumstances, though they did not think of this until afterward. The Sunday of her death Cousin Judd had come in to sit with her, as his custom was, an hour earlier than the morning service. He had read the day's lesson from the Bible and sung the hymn, and then after an interval Effie, who was busy about the back of the house, heard him sing again my mother's favourite hymn,

> "Come, Thou fount of every blessing.
> Tune my heart to sing Thy praise."

and as he sung she saw the tears rolling down his face. So she turned her back on them and let them say their good-byes without her, though she had no notion how near the final parting was.

Forester was dressing—he and Effie had taken turns at church-going ever since mother's stroke—and he was surprised to find that Cousin Judd had gone off without him. Mother clung to him when he went to kiss her good-bye; she struggled with her impotence, but they made out that it was not because she wanted him to stay at home with her; and for the first time since her illness she wished not to be propped up at the window where she could sign to the neighbors going by, but seemed to want greatly to sleep. Effie wheeled her into the corner of the sitting room: and a little later she noticed that mother's head had slipped down on the pillow as it did sometimes, past her power to lift it up again. So my sister straightened the poor head with a kiss and went back to getting the dinner. She moved softly because mother seemed asleep, but at last when she went as usual to tell her that Forester was visible at the end of the street, on the way home, she saw that the head had slipped down again, and this time as she lifted it up there was no life in it at all.

One of the strange incidents of that morning, and yet not strange when you think how much they had been to one another, was that Cousin Judd, though he had started home directly after church, could not get there, but when he had driven a little way out of town, drawn by he knew not what unseen force, turned back and pulled up in front of our door just as the doctor who had been summoned hastily was saying that mother had been dead an hour.

It was Monday morning when I arrived, and the funeral could not be until Tuesday, to allow time for the news to penetrate to all the distant country places from which my mother's relatives would be drawn to it, moved and anxious to come, though many of them had not seen her for a matter of years. I think I realized at once how it would be about my getting back to Chicago, especially when I spoke to Effie about it. She cried out and clung to me in a way that made me see that I stood for something more to her than just sisterliness. Without saying anything I wrote to Mr. Coleman that I should be detained a week or longer, and that though I hoped he would be able to save my place for me, I didn't really expect that he would.

It was not in the Taylorville cemetery that we buried my mother, but in a little plot set aside from the old Judd place, along with the rest of the Wilsons, Judds, and Jewetts, those that had dropped back peacefully to their native sod, and those sent home from Gettysburg and Appomattox. It was a longish ride; from turn to turn of the country road, teams dropped into the procession that led out from town. On either side the woods blazed like the ranked Cherubim, host on host; great shoals of fiery leaves lay in the shallows of the burying ground. At the last, shaken by the light breeze that sprung up, little flamy darts from the oak whirled into the grave with her. They were to say in their own fashion that there was nothing more natural. I think my mother must have found it so.

We had scarcely got home again, still sitting about, veiled and voluminous, when I was drawn out of grief to meet Effie's emergency. It was Almira Jewett who brought me face to face with it. Almira had taken off her things and was getting tea for us in her brisk, capable way.

"Anyhow," she said, "I 'spose you'll stay with your sister until she gets sort of used to things." It flashed on me that what she was expected to get used to, was going on just as she had been without the excuse of my mother's needing her.

"Oh, I'll stay till the breaking up," I met her promptly.

"My land!" said Almira Jewett, "you talking of the breakin' up and your mother ain't hardly out of the house yet. They do say there's nothing like play-acting to make you nimble in your feelings." I knew of course that they would lay it to the defibricating influence of my profession that I should take the breaking up of my mother's home so lightly, but I had caught a brief hiatus in Effie's sobs and I realized that what the poor child was afraid of, was being hypnotized into a situation against which her natural good sense revolted. I was bracing myself against the tradition of filial obligation that I felt was going to be put in force against me, when suddenly help arrived from an unsuspected quarter.

"I 'spose you're going with a troupe yet?" Cousin Lydia interposed, for the first time in her life, I believe, delivering herself of a conclusion. "It's a pity, because if you was anyways settled you could take Effie with you. Forester was a good son;" she ruminated on that for a while. "He was what you call a real model son, but I don't know as I want to see Effie married to him the same as your mother was." It gave me a shock to think that all these years she must have been seeing how things were.

"She shan't," I assured her, "not if I have to stay with Forrie myself." I had thought a good many times what was to become of Effie. I couldn't take her with me, of course, but I wasn't in the least prepared to see her intrigued by the popular séntiment into becoming a mere figurehead for Forester's rôle of provider.

"Keeping up a home" they called it in Taylorville, as though the house and furniture and the daily habit of coming back to it, were the pivotal facts of existence.

It almost seemed as if it might come to that. After the others were all gone and the night closed in on us three, the spirit of the dead came and stood among us. Effie wept in Forrie's arms and said that he should not be quite bereft, he should have her anyway.

"You poor child . . . you've got a brother left; you too, Olivia. You shan't want for a home while I live." That of course was the sort of thing Taylorville expected of him. It began to seem as if I might have to make good my word about staying with my brother to let Effie free. I believe he would have accepted that without even a suspicion of what I surrendered by it. If anything, he would have seen in it only another dramatization of his *rôle* of dutifulness. That a woman had any preferred employment beside cushioning life for the males of her family, had not impinged on the consciousness of Taylorville.

But the very next morning I awoke anew to the purpose of rescuing Effie, and to the recollection of an incident of the funeral, noted but not taken into the reckoning in the stress of more absorbing emotions.

"Effie, wasn't that Mrs. Jastrow I saw at the cemetery yesterday with her head done up in a black veil—crape, too? I have just recalled it." Effie nodded.

"One would have thought," I resented, "that she was one of the family."

"Ah, that's it; she thinks she is."

"One of the family? Oh! you don't mean that Forrie—Where was Lily then?" I demanded.

"She wouldn't come, of course, not being recognized as one of the family and yet counting herself one."

"But, explain . . . how could she? I thought that was broken off long ago."

"When mother was first taken," Effie agreed, "but you see she made such a dead set at him, she had to keep it up somehow; she couldn't admit that Forrie hadn't wanted her. So they made it up between them, Lily and her mother, I mean, that she and Forrie had really been engaged, but it had been broken off because Forrie couldn't marry so long as mother—" She broke off with tears again, remembering how mother was now.

173

"That was two years ago; you don't mean to say they've kept it up all the time?"

"They've had to. You see Lily hadn't been careful about not getting herself talked about with Forester. Oh, not scandal, of course, but you know how it is when a girl is crazy after a man; everybody gets to hear of it. And then they had to make so much of the engagement never coming to anything on mother's account, it quite spoiled Lily's chances, and you know, Forester. . . ."

"Oh, he was taken in by it, no doubt; it was something to sentimentalize over and be self-sacrificing about."

"Well, of course, he couldn't quite abandon the poor girl; and she really *is* fond of him."

"And perfectly safe to philander with. Well, now that he has no one depending on him I suppose he will marry her!"

"That's what is worrying me," protested Effie; "you see it all depends on whether I go on depending on him." She broke down over that. Mother hadn't wanted Forester to marry Lily Jastrow, and everybody by the mouth of Almira Jewett, had thought it was Effie's duty to keep him from it if she could.

"And I could, by just staying on. It's mother's money in the business, you're and mine as much as his, and this house . . . it's partly ours . . . if we stay in it."

"Well if you *want* to. . . ."

Effie came over and sobbed on my shoulder, "Oh, I don't," she said. "I suppose it is horrid and selfish. I'm fond of Forrie, but I want to do things in the world . . . like you have . . . and I want to marry and have babies. Oh, oh!" She was quite overwhelmed with the turpitude of it.

"You shall, you shall," I determined for her.

"Oh, Olivia, I have *wanted* you so. I knew you'd understand. It was all right so long as mother lived; I could do anything for her, but now I want—I want to be *me!*" I understood very well what that want was. But first off I had to explain to Effie why I couldn't take her with me. It was wonderful how she entered into my feeling about my work, and my lack of success in Chicago.

"*Of course,* you ought to go to New York. You'll be a great tragic actress, Olive, I know *that.* You could go, too, if you could get your share out of the business. You could have mine and yours!" She glowed over it. But the fact was we couldn't get the money out of the business. As it stood we couldn't have sold the shop

174

for what mother had put into it, and, besides, we should have had to deal first with Forester's conviction that he was taking care of our shares for us. I needn't have worried about Effie; she was too pretty and competent not to have arranged for herself. The principal and his wife drove over from Montecito to say that they would be glad to have her come back and finish the course interrupted within a few months of graduation by my mother's illness. And for her board and tuition she was to act as the principal's secretary. Within a year she wrote that she was engaged to their son.

In the meantime I undertook to stop the capacious maw of Forrie's need of being important; and the only way I saw to do it, involved my surrender of any hope I had of finding my own release in what my mother had left us of my father's hard won savings. I shouldn't have had any compunction, so fierce was my own need of success, about forcing my brother's hand, but I meant definitely not to leave any gap in his life for Effie to be drawn back into. Before we had come to this point, the second afternoon after the funeral in fact, circumstances had begun to work for me. Effie and I, looking out of the window, saw Mrs. Jastrow coming along by the front fence with all her gentility spread, as it were, by the feeling she had of her call on us being a diplomatic function.

"She's coming to see how we take it," Effie averred.

"Her coming to the funeral as one of the family? Well, how do we take it, Effie?"

"Mother couldn't bear the idea of it." Tears came into my sister's eyes; I could see the wings of self-immolation hovering over her.

"Look here, Effie, you go and take home Mrs. Endsleigh's spoons." There had been so many out of town connections dropping in for a meal that we had been obliged to fall back on our nearest neighbour.

"Lily's respectable, isn't she? and Forester has encouraged her. Well, you don't want to spoil the poor girl's life, do you?"

"Oh," said Effie, "oh, Olivia!" I could see she was torn between compunction and admiration for my way of putting it on high moral grounds. I heard her counting out the spoons in the kitchen as I went to let Mrs. Jastrow in.

I think she didn't know any more than Effie did, what to make of my manner of receiving her. She sat on the edge of a chair and snivelled a little into a handkerchief which was evidently her husband's, but it was chiefly, I could see, because she had come prepared to snivel and couldn't quickly adjust herself to my change of base.

"Poor Lily," she moaned, "she thought such a lot of Mr. Lattimore's mother; but I tell her she must bear up."

"She must indeed," I assured her. "Forester needs all the sympathy he can get just now." I could see her peeping over the top of her handkerchief, trying to guess what to make of that; but the sentimental was easy for her.

"That's what I tell her; they'll have to comfort each other. Them poor young things, they'd ought to be together. But Lily's so sensitive she couldn't bear to put herself forward."

"I'll tell Forrie you called," I assured her.

Mrs. Jastrow fanned herself with her damp handkerchief; her poor little pretence broke quite down under my friendliness.

"He's got to marry her," she whispered. "Lily's been talked about, and he's *got to.*" I could guess suddenly what it meant to her to have reached up so desperately for something better for her daughter than she had been able to manage for herself, and to come so near not getting it. I was able to put something like sympathy into my voice when I spoke to Forester at supper.

"Mrs. Jastrow called to-day. She says Lily isn't bearing up as she might. I suppose you ought to go and see her!"

Effie's eyes grew round at me over the teacups, but after all Forrie didn't know what had passed between mother and me in regard to Lily. If I chose to take his relation to her as a matter of course, he couldn't object to it. We heard Forrie in his room changing his collar before he went back to the shop again.

"He'll go to her to-night after he closes up," Effie told me. "It will end with her getting him."

"So long as he doesn't get you—" But it was unfair to put ideas like that in Effie's head. "After all it is a very good match for him in some ways; she'll always look up to him, and that is what Forrie needs."

It was natural to Effie to judge every situation by what it had for those concerned; she wasn't troubled as I was by the pressure of an outside ideal. By the end of a month, when I thought of going back to the city, it was tacitly understood that as soon as convenient Forester was to marry Lily Jastrow. He meant, however, to be fair with us both about the property; he had given us notes for our share, and expected to pay interest. The note wasn't negotiable, as I learned immediately, and the interest wasn't any more than Effie would need for her clothing. I felt that the jaws of destiny which had opened to let Effie out, had closed on me instead. I returned to Chicago early in November; my place with the Coleman players had long been filled, and there was nothing whatever to do.

Chapter 4

Jerry's play, which had had its premier while I was away, was going on successfully. One of the first items of news Sarah told me about him was that his wife was expecting another child, undertaken in the hope that, if she couldn't hold her husband's roving fancy, she could at least fix his attention on her situation. All that she had got out of it so far, was a reason for staying at home, which left Jerry the freer to bestow his society where it was most acceptable.

"Does she know—Miss Filette, I mean—about the child."

"Not unless Jerry has told her—which he'd hardly do." Sarah laughed a little, and that was not usual with her; she had very little humour. "Fancy is so up in the air about the success of the play, she thinks she inspired it. I imagine they'd feel it an indelicacy of Mrs. McDermott to have intruded her condition on their relation. Of course it is understood that there's nothing really wrong about it . . ."

"It is wrong if his wife is made unhappy by it." I hadn't Sarah's reason for being lenient. "Somebody ought to speak to Jerry."

"You might—he would listen to you. It is just because there is so little in it that it is so hard to deal with."

I suppose I took to interfering in the McDermott's affairs because I had so little of my own to interest me. Besides, I was fond of Jerry and didn't see how he was to be helped by getting his family into a muddle.

"But after all," Sarah reminded me, "it is his own wife and his own inspiration." It wasn't in me to tell her, even if I had understood it myself at the time, that the secret of my resentment was that it should be so accepted on all sides that one must choose between them. I wanted, oh, I immensely wanted, what Jerry was getting out of his relation to Miss Filette, but I wanted it free of the implication that my abandonment of my husband to the village dressmaker put me in anything like the same case.

"The real trouble with you," Jerry told me, "is that you are trying to live in Chicago and Taylorville at the same time."

Not being able to make any headway with him, I went to call on Miss Filette. I wasn't on terms with her that would admit of an assault on her confidence, I didn't know her well enough to call on her in any case, but I wasn't to be thwarted of good intention by anything so small as a breach of manners in doing it. It wasn't so much the offense of my undertaking it that counted, I found, as Miss Filette's determination not to hear anything that would ruffle the surface of her complacency. I had to drop plumb into my revelation out of the opportunity she made for me in the question, as to whether the play would or would not go on the road before Christmas.

"I should hope so," I dropped squarely on her; "Jerry's wife needs him. There's a child coming in April."

"Yes," said Miss Filette; she was giving me tea and she poised the second lump over my cup with an inquiring eyebrow. "Have you seen what we have done with the second act lately?"

"Anyway," I said to myself as I went, "she knows. She can't skid over the facts as she has my telling her."

But it was the certainty that, knowing, she kept right on with Jerry, that drove me back on Pauline and Henry Mills. I fled to them to be saved from what, in the only other society I had access to, fretted all my finer instincts; to be ricocheted by them again on to that reef of moral squalour upon which the artist and woman in me were riven asunder.

What I should have done was to take my courage in my hands and have gone on from Taylorville to New York. But the most I was equal to was a fixed determination to accept anything which would take me nearer Broadway, which, even then, was to the player world all that the lamp is to the moth. In the meantime I had settled in two housekeeping rooms in a street that I wouldn't have dared to give to a manager as an address; one of those neighbourhoods where there are always a great many perambulators, and waste paper blowing about. There was never anything for me, in the frame of life called Bohemian, more than a picturesque way of begging the question of poverty. What I looked for in a lodging, was escape from the bedraggled professionalism which went on in what were called studios, by means of a cot bed, an oil stove, and a few yards of art muslin. That I hadn't managed it so successfully as I hoped, was made plain to me a few days after I had moved in, by the discovery of a card tacked on the opposite door, that read, "Leon Griffin, the Varieté." It was the same theatre at which Cecelia Brune was playing the chief attraction in song and dance. In the glimpses I had of Mr. Griffin in the dark hall going in and out, I was aware that he gave much the same impression of unprofitable use that was associated in my mind with the Shamrocks.

All this time I kept going through the motions of looking for an engagement. Now and then some shining bubble of opportunity seemed to float toward me, to dissolve in thin air as soon as I put my hand out to it. One of these brought me to Cline and Erskine's waiting room on the day that Cecelia Brune elected to register her complaint against what she considered a slight of her turn at the Varieté. She flounced about more than a little, not to let the rest of us escape the inference that she was not used to being kept waiting. When she had hooked and unhooked her handsome furs for the fourth time, she introduced me to Leon Griffin, who except for the name, I shouldn't have recognized for my hall neighbour. It was like being slapped in the face with my own hard condition to have him crowded on me in that character before the whole roomful. Life seemed so to have beggared him. In broad day he looked the sort of a man who has failed to sustain himself in the man's world, and must reinforce his value with the favour of women. Little touches of effeminacy about his dress failed to take the attention away from its shabbiness. His hair had the traditional thespian curl in spite of being cropped short, to allow of various make-ups, one surmised, and his very blue eyes were in a perpetual state of extenuating the meagreness of his other features. Being ashamed of my shame at meeting him there, I began to be very nice to him. Cecelia, in spite of her magnificent raiment, perhaps on account of it, had been disposed to graciousness. She drew us together with a wave of her hand.

"She ought to be doin' *Ophelia* on Broadway," she introduced me handsomely; "wouldn't that get you!"

"I saw you with the Hardings last year," Griffin assented, almost as though I might think it a liberty. "Where are you playing now?" He had the stamp of too many reverses on his face not to estimate mine at its proper worth. He had fine instincts too, for as soon as I told him that I was out of an engagement that season, he put himself on record quite simply. "My turn goes off next week—I'm trying to get Cline to put it on the circuit." When we came out of the office together he fell into step with me. One of the young women ahead of us made the shape of a bubble with her hands and blew it from her. "Pouff" she said. "There goes another of my chances." She laughed with a fine courage.

"They all go through with it," Griffin affirmed. "There's Eversley—" I have forgotten which of the well-known incidents he related.

"Eversley told me I might come to it. What made you think of him?" I demanded.

"I saw his name in the paper; he's to play here this winter. He's a wonder."

"He said wonderful things to me once." I had just recalled them.

"They'll come true then. Eversley never makes a mistake. Why, I remember once—" He broke off as though he had changed his mind about telling me. I was wondering if I couldn't get rid of him by stopping in at Sarah's, when he broke out again suddenly.

"To think of you being out of an engagement and a girl like Cecelia Brown—yes, I know her name is Brown, Cissy Brown of Milwaukee—"

"I've always suspected it," I admitted, "but it is her looks of course, and the clothes; Cecelia has lovely clothes."

"Well, so could you if . . ." He checked himself. "I don't mean to say anything against a lady . . ."

"I've always suspected that, too," I admitted, "but one doesn't like to say it."

"Well, you know what she gets—thirty-five a week. A girl doesn't wear diamond sunbursts on that."

"Mr. Griffin, I wish you'd tell me what sort of man it is that gives diamond sunbursts to Variety girls: I've never seen any of them."

"You have probably, but you don't know it. You meet their wives in society."

"Henry Mills." I don't know what made me say it; the image of him came tripping along the surface of my mind and slid off my tongue without having more than momentarily perched there.

"Is he in business downtown, and has he got a perfectly proper family and too many dinners under his vest?"

"Mr. Mills's home life is ideal; but I didn't mean—"

"Neither did I, but that's the type. They mostly have ideal families, but they couldn't live up to them if they didn't have Cecelia Brunes on the side . . . I beg your pardon."

He had looked up and caught me blushing a deep, painful red, but it wasn't on account of what he had intimated. I was blushing because of the discovery in myself of needs which, compared to the ideal of life I had set for myself, were as much of a defection as anything our conversation had suggested for Henry Mills. I was conscious in those days of a slow, steady seepage of all my forces toward desperation.

"You'll have to take a company out for yourself," was Jerry's solution. "I'll write you a play. I've got a ripping idea—a man, with a gift, and two women, good women both of them—that's where I score against the eternal triangle—each of them trying to save him from the other and breaking him between them." Jerry's plays were never anything more than dramatizations of his immediate experience. "You and Sarah Croyden, you set each other off; I'll write it for both of you." He walked up and down in my little room with his hands in his pockets and his shining black hair rising like quills.

"Jerry, how long will it take you to write that play? And how much will it cost to produce it?"

"Ten thousand dollars," he answered to the last question. "About eighteen months if I go right at it."

"And I've money enough to last me to the end of February. No," to his swift generous gesture. "You have to live eighteen months on yours—and another child coming." I made up my mind that I should have to speak to Pauline and Henry Mills.

Greater than any mystery of creative art to me, is the mystery by which the recipients of its benefits manage to keep ignorant of its essential processes. I have never been able to figure to myself how Pauline and Henry escaped knowing that the creative mood, the keen hunger of which is more importunate than any need of food or raiment, was to be had for very little more than they spent fattening their souls on its choice products. For it is always to be bought; it is the distinction of genius as against

181

talent, always to know in what far, unlikely market the precious commodity is to be bought. How was it that Henry escaped knowing that the appealing femininity which plays so large a part in the success of an actress with an audience of Millses, is largely the result of having been the object of that solicitious protection which it is supposed to provoke? With what, since it was agreed between Pauline and me that I was not to pay down on that counter what Cecelia and Jerry parted with cheerfully, was I ultimately to pay for it? Now that I had on all sides of me the witness of desperation, I began to be irritated at the way in which, in view of our long friendship, they accepted it for me.

As the holiday season approached, without any change in my circumstances other than a steady diminution of my bank account, I came to the conclusion that the only possible move was toward New York and that I should have to ask Henry to advance me the money for it. In view of what came to me afterward it was a reasonable proposition, but I reckoned without that extraordinary blankness to the processes of art which is common to those most entertained by it.

It was a day or two after Christmas, from which I had been excused by my recent bereavement, that I went out to dinner there with the determination to bring something to pass commensurate with their usual attitude of high admiration for and confidence in my gift. We had gone into the library after dinner, at least it was a room that went by that name, though I don't know for what reason except that Henry smoked there and the furniture was upholstered in leather, as in Evanston it was indispensable that all libraries should be.

Here and there were touches that suggested that if Henry moved his income up a notch or two, Pauline's taste might not be able to keep pace with it. Henry warmed his back at the gas log and wished to know how things went with me.

"As well as I could expect them *here*. I've made up my mind to try for New York as soon as I can manage it."

"What's the matter with Chicago?" Henry's manner implied that whatever you believed about it, you'd have to show him.

"Well, I'd have to be capitalized to do anything here the same as in New York, and the field there is larger." I went on to explain something of what the metropolis had to offer.

"I guess the worst thing about Chicago is that you're out of a job. People don't get sore on a place where they are doing well."

"No. They generally light out for a place where there are more jobs." I thought I should get on better if I took Henry in his own key, but he forged ahead of me.

"If there's anything the matter with your acting, why don't you ask somebody?"

"There's nobody to ask. Besides, there isn't anything the matter with it; the matter is with me."

"Well, I must say I don't see the difference."

"Oh!" I cried. I hadn't realized that they wouldn't just take my word for it. "It is because I am empty—empty!" I trailed off, seeing how wide I was of his understanding. I shouldn't have questioned Henry Mills's word about the capitalization of a joint stock company; and I resented their discounting my own statement of my difficulties. Pauline got hold of my hand and patted it. I wondered if it was because all her own crises were complicated with Henry Mills that she always thought that affectionateness was part of the answer.

"It is only that, with all your Gift, Henry can't understand how you need anything else," she extenuated.

"I need food and clothes," I blurted out; "pretty soon I shall need a lodging."

"Oh, my dear!" Pauline was shocked at the indelicacy. I don't know if she didn't understand how poor I was, or if it was only the general notion of the sheltered woman, to find in complaint a kind of heresy against the institution by which they are maintained. "After all," she caught up with her accustomed moral attitude, "there's a kind of nobility in suffering for your art. It's what gives you your spiritual quality." I thought I recognized the phrase as one that was current in the women's clubs of that period. I took hold of my courage desperately.

"Well, I'm offering you a chance to suffer two thousand dollars' worth." Pauline's tact was proof even against that.

"You Comedy Child!" she laughed indulgently.

"You're getting ideas," Henry burbled on cheerfully; "all these long-hairs and high-brows you've been associating with, they've filled you up. That friend of yours, McDermott, somebody had him to the club the other day, talking about the conservation of Genius. Nothing in it. Let them work for their money the same as other people, I say."

"You know you didn't have any money to begin with," Pauline reminded me. I was made to feel it a consideration that she hadn't pressed the point that if I couldn't do again what I had done then, there was something lacking in the application. They must have taken my gesture of despair for surrender.

"I guess you were just getting it out of your system," Henry surmised comfortably.

It was not the first nor the last time that I was to come squarely up against the lay conviction that whatever might be known about the processes of art, it wasn't the artist that knew it. Later, when Henry took me out to the car, he came round to what had been back of the whole conversation.

"I suppose you could use more money in your business; most of us could," he advised me, "but you don't want to let people find it out. There's nothing turns men against a woman so much as to have her always thinking about money."

It was a very cold night as I came down the side street to my door, deserted as a country road. The narrow footpath trodden in the pavement looked like the track of desolation, the cold flare of the lamps was smothered in sodden splashes of snow. There had been the feeling of uneasiness in the air that goes before a storm all that forenoon, and in the interval that I had been revaluing a lifelong friendship in terms of what it wouldn't do for me, it had settled down to a heavy clogging snow. I was startled as I turned in at the entry to find a man behind me. He had come up unsuspected in the soft shuffle and turned in with me.

By the light that filtered through the weather-fogged transom I saw that he was Griffin of the Varieté. Now as I fumbled blindly at the latch he came close to me.

"Beg pardon!" He had put out his hand over mine and turned the key for me.

"My fingers are so cold," I apologized. I turned my face toward him with the stiffness of cold and tears upon it and there was an answering commiseration in his eyes. I reached out for the key and he took my hand in his, holding it to his breast with a movement exuding human kindness. If the gesture was at all theatrical I did not feel it. I let him hold it there for a moment before I went in and shut the door.

Chapter 5

Depression, as well as the storm which held on heavily all night and the next day, kept me close, and the state of my coal bin kept me in bed most of the next day. Along late in the afternoon I was aroused from a lethargy of cold and crying, by Leon Griffin tapping at the door to know how I did. The snow by this time had settled down to a blinding drift, and the thermometer had fallen into an incalculable void of cold. Griffin was in his overcoat as though he had just come in or was just going out, though I learned later he had been sitting in it all day in his room. The impression it created of his being in the act of passing, led me to open my door to him, as I otherwise might not have done. A terrible, cold blast came in with him and a clattering of the shutters on the windward wall of the house. Outside, the day was falling dusk; there was no light in the room but the square blank of the window curtained by the sliding screen of snow, and my little stove which glowed like a carbuncle in its corner.

"You're cozy here"—he put it as an excuse for lingering, for I hadn't asked him to have a chair—"you hardly feel the wind. On my side there's a trail of snow half across the room where the wind whips it in between the casings."

Though he had come ostensibly to offer me a neighbourly attention, he was plainly in need of it himself; it was his last night at the Varieté and, between the storm and the depression of having nothing to turn to, he was coming down with a cold. I had him into my one easy chair and suggested tea.

"I hardly slept any last night," he apologized over his second cup, "the shutter clacks so." I could hear it now like the stroke of desolation.

That night when I heard him stamping off the snow in the hall, I had a hot drink for him, but when I saw him, by the rakish light of the hall lamp, wringing his hands with the cold before taking it, I insisted he should come on into my still warm room. I had to turn back first to light my own lamp and, in respect to my being in my dressing gown with my hair in two braids, to slip into my bedroom and experience, as I looked back at him through the crack in the door, the kind of softening a woman has toward a man she has made comfortable. The light of my lamp, which was shaded for reading, like a miniature calcium, brought out for me the frayed edge of his overcoat and all the waste and misuse of him, the kind of faded appeal that sort of man has for a woman; forlorn as he was, as he put the bowl back on the table, I was so much more forlorn myself that I was glad to have been femininely of use to him.

Pauline wrote me to come out and stay with her during the protracted cold spell, but owing to the difficulty in delivery, the invitation failed to reach me until the severity of the weather was abated. In any case I was still too sore at what seemed to me the betrayal of my long confidence, to have been willing to have subjected myself to any reminders of it. And whatever kindness Pauline meant, it could hardly have done so much for me as Leon Griffin did by just needing me. It transpired that he had no stove in his room, and the heat from the register for which we were definitely charged in the rent, scarcely modified the edge of the cold. For the next two or three days we spent much of the time huddled over my stove. Snow ceased to fall on the second day, and nothing moved in our view except now and then the surface of it was flung up by the wind, falling again fountainwise into the waste of the untrampled housetops that stretched from my window to the icy flat of the lake darkening under a dour horizon. Somehow, though I had never been willing to confess to my friends how poor I was, I made no bones of it with Griff, as I had heard Cecelia call him, a name that seemed somehow to suit the inconsequential nature of our relation better than his proper title. We frankly pooled our funds in the matter of food, which one or another of us slipped out to buy, and cooked on my stove. I took an interest in preparing it, such as I hadn't since the times when I imagined I was helping Tommy on the way to growing rich, and when the room was full of a warm savoury smell and the table pulled out from the wall to make it serve for two, we felt, for the time, restored to the graciousness of living. We fell back on the uses of domesticity, by association providing us with a sense of life going on in orderliness and stability. It came out for me in these moments that it is after all life, that Art needs rather than feeling, and that, to a woman of my capacity, was to be supplied not by innocuous intrigues like Jerry's but by the normal procedure of living. I believe I felt myself rather of a better stripe, to find it so in the domestic proceeding, though I do not really know that my necessity was any whit superior to Miss Filette's, except in offering the minimum possibility of making anybody unhappy by it. But because I knew my friends would think it ridiculous that I could lay hold of power again by so inconsiderable a handle as Leon Griffin, I suffered a corroding resentment. Griffin was getting up a new act for himself, and evenings as I helped him with it, I felt a faint stirring of creative power. When he had finished, I would take the shade off the lamp and render scenes for him from my favourite Elizabethan drama; and in the face of his unqualified admiration for me, I could almost act.

Toward the end of the week as the cold abated, Mr. Griffin asked me to see a play in which some of his friends were playing; and Jerry being prodigal of favours, I responded with an invitation to "The Futurist." I hadn't mentioned Griff to Sarah, I never more than mentioned him to any of my friends, but I saw no reason why I should not speak of them to him, especially when they were so much upon the public tongue as Sarah was just then.

"Croyden?" he said; "isn't that an unusual name?" He appeared to be puzzling over it. "I seem to remember a town somewhere by that name."

"In New York," I told him. I was on the point of telling him how Sarah came by it, but an impulse of discretion saved me. I had seen "The Futurist" so many times now, that, once at the theatre, I occupied myself with looking at the audience and took no sort of notice of my escort until after Sarah's entrance near the close of the first act.

"Well?" I laid myself open to compliments for my friend. I was startled by what I saw when I looked at him. He had shrunk away into the corner of his seat farthest from me, like a man whose garment had fallen from him unawares. The stark naked soul of him fed visibly upon her bodily perfection; Sarah's beauty took men like that sometimes when they were able to see it—there were those who thought her merely nice-looking. I could see his tongue moving about stealthily to wet his dry lips. I couldn't bear to look at him like that; it seemed a pitiful thing for a man to ache so with the beauty of a woman he had long ceased to deserve; it was as though he had laid bare some secret ache in me.

Coming out of the theatre he surprised me with a knowledge of Sarah's affairs. He knew that she had begun with O'Farrell.

"I played with him myself," he admitted; "that was before Miss
—Miss—"

"Croyden," I supplied; "that was the town she came from; I
shouldn't have told you except that you seem to know."

"I was expecting another name. Wasn't she—wasn't she married once? A fellow by the name of Lawrence."

"Oh, well, you may call it married. He was a cur."

"You can't tell me anything about him worse than I know
myself." From the earnestness of his tone I judged that he had
suffered something at the hands of Lawrence. "But I'll say this
for him, he didn't stay with the other woman; she followed him
and found him, but he wouldn't stay with her."

"I don't see that that proves anything except that he was the
greater scoundrel. The other woman was his wife."

"It proves that he loved Miss Croyden best—that he couldn't
bear the other woman after her." I thought it was no use matching ethical ideals with him and I let the matter drop. It came back
to me next day that if he had been with O'Farrell in Lawrence's
time, he might have known something of the other Shamrocks.
I meant to ask him about it in the morning, but put it off as I
observed that the recollection of it seemed to have stirred him
past the point of being able to sleep. He was pale in the morning,
and the rings under his eyes stood out plainly; he had the
whipped look of a man who has been so long accused of misdemeanour that he comes at last to believe he has done it. I could
see the impulse to confess hovering over him, and the hope that
I might find in his misbehaviours the excusing clue which he was
vaguely aware must be there, but couldn't himself lay hands on.
I suppose souls in the Pit must have movements like that—seeking in one another the extenuations they can't admit to themselves.

We didn't, however, strike the note of confidence until it was
evening. Griffin kept up the form of looking for an engagement,
which occupied his morning hours, and in the afternoon Jerry
came in to see how I had come through the cold spell, and to win
my interest with his wife to consent to his going as far as St. Louis
with "The Futurist." I forget what reasons he had for thinking it
advisable, except that they were all more or less complicated with
Miss Filette.

"But, heavens, Jerry, haven't you ever heard of the freemasonry of women? How can you think my sympathies wouldn't be

with your wife? Especially in her condition."

"It's only for a week; and, you know, except for her fussing, she is perfectly well. And look here, Olivia, you know exactly why I have to have—other things; why I can't just settle down to being —the plain head of the family." His tone was accusing.

"I know why you *think* you have to. Honest, Jerry, is it so imperative as all that?"

"Honest to God, Olivia, unless I'm . . . interested . . . I can't write a word." His glance travelling over my dull little room and makeshift furniture, the cheap kerosene lamp, the broken hinge of the stove. "You ought to know," he drove it home to me. I felt myself involved by my toleration of Griffin in a queer kind of complicity.

"What do you want me to do?"

"Tell her you think it is to the advantage of the play for me to be there in St. Louis for the opening. It's always good for an interview, and that's advertising." After all I suppose I wouldn't have done it if I hadn't found his wife in a wrapper at four o'clock in the afternoon, when I went out there. If she wouldn't make any better fight for herself, who was I to fight for her? And as Jerry said, for him to be with the play, meant advertising.

I talked it over with Griffin that evening, as we sat humped over my tiny stove before the lamps were lighted. Outside we could see the roofs huddling together with the cold, and far beyond, the thin line of the lake beaten white with the wind in a fury of self-tormenting. It made me think of poor little Mrs. Gerald under the lash of her husband's vagaries.

"I can't help think that she'd feel it less if she made less fuss about it," I protested. Griffin shook his head.

"It's a mercy she can do that; it's when you can't do anything it eats into you."

I reflected. "There was a woman I knew who looked like that. O'Farrell's leading lady; she was jealous and there was nothing she could do. She looked gnawed upon!"

"Miss Dean, you mean?"

"I forgot you said that you knew her." I wanted immensely to know how he came to be mixed up with her. "She was jealous of me, but there was no cause. How well did you know her?"

"I . . . she . . . I was married to her." His face was mottled with embarrassment; it occurred to me that his confusion must have been for his complicity in the fact of their not being married now, but he set me right. "I oughtn't to have told it on her, I suppose. She married me to go on the stage. I was boarding at her mother's and I couldn't have afforded to marry unless she had. You don't know how handsome she was. I knew she couldn't act. . . . I can't myself, but I know it when I see it. Her father had been an actor of a sort; he had taught her things, and I thought I could pull her along."

"She *has* got on." I let the fact stand for all it was worth.

"Yes, she had something almost as good as acting . . . she could get hold of people."

"She had O'Farrell. Was it on his account you separated?"

"Long before that. You see she could handle the managers in her own interest, but she didn't know what to do with me. So I —I got out of her way." Griffin's clothes were too loose for him, and his hair, which wanted trimming, disposed itself in what came perilously near to being ringlets, accentuating the effect of his having been shrivelled, and shrunk within the mark of his capacity. There was a certain shame about him as he made this admission, that made me feel that though to leave his wife free to seek her own sort of success had been a generous thing to do, it was all he could do; his moral nature had suffered an incurable strain.

"Griff, did they tell you when you were young, that love was all bound up with what you should do in the world and what you could get for it?"

"They never told me anything; I had to find it out."

"Jerry too; he thought he was going to have a graceful, docile creature to keep him in a perpetual state of maleness. I should have thought you'd have left the stage after that," I said, reverting to the personal instance.

"I ought to have, but somehow I kept feeling her; even when I wasn't thinking of her I could feel her somewhere pulling me. It was like living in the house where some one has died, and you keep thinking they're just in the next room and you don't want to go away for fear you'll lose them altogether."

"I understand."

The afternoon light had withdrawn into the bleak sky without illuminating it. I threw open the stove for the sake of the ruddy light, and the intimacy of our sitting there drew me on to counter confession.

"It's like that with me all the time," I said, "only there hasn't really been anybody. Sarah says there doesn't have to be anybody; that we only think so because we have felt it that way once. She thinks it is just . . . Personality . . . whatever there is that we act to."

"Well, I know you have to have it, anyway you can get it."

"O'Farrell used to call it feeling your job. I wonder where he is now." So the talk drifted off to the perpetual professionalism of the unsuccessful, to incidents of rehearsals and engagements. I believe it would have been good for me to have run my mind in new pastures, but there was nobody to open the gates for me.

I said as much to Sarah the very next time I saw her; it seemed a way of getting at what I hadn't yet told her, that I was within a week or two of the end of my means. I had the best of reasons for not calling my case to her attention, in the readiness with which she offered herself to my necessity.

"You must go to New York of course; I've three hundred dollars, and I could send you something every month——" I cut her off absolutely.

"I'd rather try Cecelia Brune's plan first," I assured her.

"Not while you have me;" she was firm with me. "Besides, you don't really know that Cecelia——"

"Didn't buy her diamond sunburst on thirty-five a week!" I told her all that Griffin had said. Sarah looked worried.

"I'll tell you about the diamonds. About a year ago, while you were with the Hardings, she got into trouble. Oh, she loved him as much as she was able! He gave her the diamonds; but Cecelia cared. And then when the trouble came, he deserted her. That's what Cecelia couldn't understand. She had never given anything before, and she didn't realize that that had been her chief advantage. It gave her a scare."

But in spite of Sarah's confidence in Cecelia's bitter experience keeping her straight, I could see that she had taken what Griffin had told me to heart. A day or two later she referred to the matter again.

"If she goes over the line once, and doesn't have to pay for it, she is lost." She was standing at my window looking out over the roofs and chimneys cased in ice, and she might, for all the mark her profession has left on her, been looking across the pasture bars. I was irritated at her detachment, and her interest, in the face of my own problem, in an affair so unrelated as Cecelia Brune's.

"Why do you care so much?"

191

"You'd care too, if you had seen as much of her; it's like watching a drowning man; you don't stop to ask if he's worth it before you plunge in!"

"I can't swim myself," I protested.

I didn't want to be dragged in, rescuing Cecelia; I had myself to save and wasn't sure I could do it. It was after this talk, however, that Griff, who still hung about the Varieté from habit, told me that Sarah had fallen into the way of stopping to pick up Cecelia on her way home from her own theatre. He thought it a futile performance.

"Nothing can stop that kind; they don't always know it, but that's what draws them to the stage in the first place. It's a kind of what-do-you-call-it, going back to the thing they were a long time ago."

"Atavism," I supplied; I thought it very likely. All the centuries of bringing women up to be toys must have had its fruit somehow. Cecelia was made to be played with; she wasn't serviceable for anything else. And what was more, I didn't care to be identified with her even in the Christian attitude of a rescuer. I said as much to Sarah one evening about a week later, when I had gone with Jerry to give my opinion of some changes in the cast, preparatory to going on the road with his play, and in the overflow of his satisfaction at the way the audience rose to them, he had asked me to go to supper with him. Then as Sarah joined us and the spirit of the crowd caught him, pouring along the street, bright almost as by day and with the added brightness of evening garments, Jerry, always open to the infection of the holiday mood, proposed that for once we stretch a point by going to supper at Reeves's. Sarah and I demurred as women will at such a proposal from a man whose family exigencies are known to them, but Sarah found a prohibitory objection in a promise she professed to have made, to go around for Cecelia on her way home, which Jerry promptly quashed by including her in the invitation. I protested.

"Supper at Reeves's is quite enough of an adventure for one time. Cecelia paints."

"Not really," Sarah protested. "It's only that she uses so little make-up that she doesn't think it necessary to take it off."

"All the better," insisted Jerry. "I never did take supper at Reeves's with a painted lady, and I'm told it is quite one of the things to do."

I let it pass rather than spoil his high mood. It was not more than three blocks to the Variété, and at the stage door Sarah insisted on getting out herself.

"Why did you let her?" I protested to Jerry.

"Because it will please her, and Miss Brune will be gone; Sarah doesn't realize how late we are." I could see her returning through the fogged glass of the stage door.

"Cecelia's gone! The man said she was going to Reeves's too; we can pick her up there."

"Oh," I objected, "I can stand Cecelia, but I draw the line at her gentleman friends. She didn't go there alone, I fancy."

"We'll have a look at him, anyway, before we give him the glad hand," Jerry temporized.

The cab discharged us into the press of black-coated men and bright-gowned women that at that hour poured steadily into the anteroom of Reeves's, which was level with the pavement, divided from it by a screen of plate glass and palms. Beyond that and raised by a few steps, was the palm room, flanked on either side by dressing rooms; and opening out back, the great revolving doors, muffled with crimson curtains, that received the guests and sorted them like a hopper, according to the degree of their resistance to the particular allurements of Reeves's. There was a sleek, satin-suited attendant who swung the leaves of the door at just the right angle that inducted you to the public café, or to the corridor that led to private rooms, and was famed never to have made a mistake. Jerry dared us hilariously as we went up the steps, to put his discrimination to the test.

"You and I alone then; Olivia's black dress would give us away," Sarah insisted.

"I want you to stay here and watch for Cecelia," she whispered to me; "I must see her; I *must.*"

Her going on with Jerry would give her an opportunity to look through the café; if Cecelia hadn't already arrived, I would be sure to see her come in with the crowd that broke against the bank of palms into two streams of bright and dark, proceeding to the dressing rooms, and returning by twos and threes to be swallowed up by the hopper turning half unseen behind its velvet curtains. I slipped behind a group of bright-gowned women waiting for their escorts under the palms. I was hypnotized by the movement and the glitter; I believe I forgot what I was looking for; and all at once she was before me.

The theatrical quality of Cecelia's prettiness and the length of her plumes would have picked her out anywhere even without the blackened rim of the eyelids and the air she had always of having just stepped into the spot light.

She had stationed herself, with her professional instinct for effect, just under the Australian fern tree, waiting for her escort, and in the moment it took me to gather myself together he joined her. I had come up behind Cecelia and was brought face to face with him; it wasn't until he had wheeled into step with her that he saw me and his face went mottled all at once and settled to a slow purple. Cecelia was magnificent.

"Oh, you here! How de do!" She slipped her hand under her escort's arm and sailed out with him. I caught the glint of the brass-bound door under the curtains. I don't know how long I stood staring before I started after her, to be met by the leaves of the revolving door which, reversing its motion, projected Sarah and Jerry into the palm room beside me.

"I have been all over the café—" Sarah began.

"Didn't you meet her?"

"In the café? I was just telling you . . ."

"No, no. In the corridor, just now; they went through."

"But they couldn't," urged Sarah. "I was standing at the door of the café with Jerry . . ." The truth of the situation began to dawn on her.

"There's such a crowd, of course you missed her." Jerry began to build up a probability by which we could sustain Sarah through the supper which followed. We all of us talked a great deal as people will when they are anxious not to talk of a particular thing. When we were in the dressing room again, putting on our wraps, Sarah turned on me.

"She wasn't in the café at all," she declared.

"I never said she was. I said she went through into the corridor." In the silence I could feel Cecelia dropping into the pit.

"Did you know the man?"

I nodded. "It was Henry Mills!"

Chapter 6

Before I had an opportunity to talk the incident over with Sarah, she had seen Cecelia.

"She is perfectly furious with you," she reported. "She hasn't heard from Mr. Mills since, and she thinks it is on your account; that you have taken steps for breaking it off."

"Well, if she admits there was something to break off . . . I tell you, Sarah, you are fretting yourself to no purpose, the girl had been there before."

"I'm afraid so." Sarah's taking it so much to heart was a credit to her, but I was more curious than commiserating.

"Tell me, what is in the mind of a girl when she does things like that? What does she get out of it?"

"Excitement, of course; the sense of being in the stir, and the feeling of being protected. She says Mr. Mills has been kind to her. It is odd, but she seems to think it is all right so long as it is going on; it is only when it is broken off she can't bear it. That is why she is so angry at you."

"There might be something in that," I conceded. "When it is broken off she is able to realize how cheap and temporary it has been; while it is going on she can justify it on the ground that it is going on forever. That *would* justify it, I suppose." I did not know how I knew this, but lately I had discovered in myself capacities for understanding a great many things of which I had had no experience. What concerned me was not Cecelia's relation to the incident.

"Whatever am I going to do about going there again, to Pauline's, I mean?"

"You can't tell!"

"And I can't go there and not tell. I've got to choose between deceiving Pauline and condoning Henry, and I've no disposition to do either." Sarah thought it over.

"There is only one thing you can do. You'll simply have to go to New York."

"For a great many reasons besides. You needn't tell me that. But how? How?"

"You know what I offered—"

"What I refused. It is out of the question. Don't speak of it."

"I suppose after this you couldn't ask the Millses?"

"Sarah . . . I did ask."

"Well?" All her interest hung upon the interrogation.

"They told me it was good for my spiritual development to suffer these things." We faced one another in deep, unsmiling irony. "Sarah, what do you suppose it costs a man for supper and a private room at Reeves's?"

"Don't!" she begged. "It's only a step from that to Cecelia."

"Yes; I remember she said that men never afforded protection to women except for value received."

"You must go to New York," Sarah reiterated. "You must!"

The truth was I had never told Sarah exactly how poor I was. In the end I let her go away without telling; at the worst I thought I might borrow from Jerry, who had given up the notion of going to St. Louis, largely no doubt because I had failed to back him up in it completely, and then just at the end changed his mind and went anyway. I knew nothing about it until Jerry wrote me from Springfield, for I had grown shy of going there where all Mrs. McDermott's conversation was set like a trap to catch me in something that would convict Jerry of misdemeanour. Jerry asked me to visit her in his absence, but I put it off as long as possible. I had to settle first about going to Pauline's. I arranged to spend the afternoon there, meaning to come away before dinner and so by leaving Henry to discover my attitude in the circumstance of my having been there without destroying his home, open the way to my meeting him again without embarrassment. To do that I should have left the house before the persuasive smell of the dinner began to creep up the stairs into the warm, softly lighted rooms, but from the beginning of my visit, Pauline, in order that I might not feel her failure to put her affection more cogently, had wound me about as with a cocoon of feminine devices, from which I hadn't been able to extricate myself earlier. I am not blaming her. I am not sure, indeed, seeing how completely she justified herself to Henry Mills by what she had to offer, that I had any right to expect her to understand how completely her playful and charming affectionateness failed of any possible use to me. But I felt myself so far helpless in the presence of it, that I stayed on until the smell of the roast unloosened all the joints of my resolution. I hadn't

196

realized how hungry I was until I found myself at a point where what Henry might think of me became inconsiderable before the possibility of my being put out of the house before dinner was served.

At the same time I could have wept at the indignity of wanting food so much. I remember to this day the wasteful heaping of the children's plates, and my struggle with the oblique desire to smuggle portions of my helping home to Griff, who looked even more of a stranger than I to soup and fish and roast, to say nothing of dessert.

It wasn't until we had got as far as the salad that I had leisure to observe Henry grow rather red about the gills as he fed, and speculate as to how far it was due to his consciousness that I could bring down the pillars of his home with a word, and didn't intend to.

There was nothing said during dinner about my prospects or the stage in general, but when Henry took me out to the car about nine o'clock, he cleared his throat several times as though to drag the subject up from the pit of his stomach, where it must have lain very uneasily.

"You know," he began, "I've been thinking about that scheme of yours of going to New York. I am inclined to think there is something in it."

"I haven't thought about it for a long time," I told him, which was only true in so far as I thought of it as a possibility.

"It would freshen you up a whole lot," Henry insisted. "Everybody needs freshening. I have been taking a little stir about myself." So that was the way he wished me to think of his relation to Cecelia!

"I've given it up," I insisted.

We were standing under the swinging arc light in a bare patch the wind had cleared of the fine, white February grit. Little trails of it blew up under foot and were lost among the wind-shaken shadows. I could see Henry's purpose bearing down on me like the far spark of the approaching trolley.

"I wouldn't do that," he advised. "It looks like pretty good business to me. You'd have to stay there some time to learn the ropes and if a few hundred dollars——"

"I've given it up," I said again. The car came alongside and Henry helped me on to it.

"If you were at any time to reconsider it, I hope you will let me know——" The roar of the trolley cut him off.

I knew I was a fool not to have accepted the sop to my discretion; I don't know for what the Powers had delivered Henry Mills into my hands, if it wasn't to get out of his folly what his sober sense refused me. Without doubt there are some forms of integrity that, persisted in, cease to be a virtue and become merely a habit; I could no more have taken Henry Mills's money than I could have gone to New York without it. I went home shivering to my fireless little room. I put on my nightgown over my underwear and my dressing gown over that, and cried myself to sleep.

It was a day or two later that I recalled that Jerry had asked me to go out and see his wife, and I thought if I must ask Jerry for help, it would be no more than prudent for me to do so, but I wasn't in the least prepared as I went up the path, from which the snow of the week before had never been cleared, to find the house shut and barred, and no smoke issuing from it. I made my way around to the kitchen door to try to discover some sign which would give me a clue to the length of time it had been deserted, if not the reason for it.

While I was puzzling about among the empty milk bottles and garbage cans, a neighbour woman put her head out of a nearby window and announced the obvious fact that Mrs. McDermott wasn't in.

"But in her condition——" I protested as though my informant had been in some way responsible for it.

"Well, if her own mother's isn't the best place for a woman in her condition! . . . Three days ago," she answered to my second question. Mrs. McDermott's mother lived in Peoria, and I knew that when Jerry left there had been no such understanding, but as lingering there ankle deep in the dry snow didn't seem to clear the affair, I undertook to rid myself of a sense of blame by writing all that I knew of it to Jerry within the hour. It was the third day after that he came storming in on me like a man demented. He had been to Peoria immediately on receipt of my letter and his wife had refused to see him. It hardly seemed a time for indirection.

"Jerry, what have you done?" I demanded.

"Nothing—not a thing." I waited. "There was a fool skit in one of the St. Louis papers," he admitted. "The fool reporter didn't know I was married."

"It was about you and Miss Filette?" He nodded.

198

"She had bought all the St. Louis papers," he said, meaning his wife.

"Well, that was natural: she wanted to read the notices; she was always proud of you."

"She believed them, too," he groaned. "And she's talked her mother over. They wouldn't even let me see the children." He put his head down on my table and sobbed aloud. I thought it might be good for him, but by and by my sensibilities got the better of me.

"Would it do any good if I were to write?"

"You? Oh, they think you're in it . . . a kind of general conspiracy. You know you said that—that one of the things nobody had a right to deny an artist was the source of his inspiration."

"Jerry! I said what you asked me." I was properly indignant too, when I had been so right on the whole matter. Besides, as Jerry had written little that winter except some inconsiderable additions to his play, I was rather of the opinion that he measured the validity of his passion by its importunity, rather than its effect on the sum of his production. "Besides, I told you you would never get your wife to understand."

"If she would only be sensible," he groaned.

"She isn't," I reminded him; "you didn't marry her to be sensible, but for her imagined capacity to go on repeating the tricks by which Miss Filette keeps you complacent with yourself. The trouble is, marriage and having children take that out of a woman."

"An artist ought never to marry. I will always say that."

I began to wonder if that were true, if Cecelia Brune were not after all the wiser. We beat back and forth on the subject for the time that I kept Jerry with me. The evening of the second day came a telegram. Jealousy tearing at the heart of poor little Mrs. McDermott had torn away the young life that nestled there.

Jerry wrote me later that the baby had breathed and died and that his wife was likely to be ill a long time. In view of the extra expense incurred, I didn't feel that I ought to ask him for the loan I was now so desperately in need of.

It was about this time that Griffin and I began to avoid one another about meal time. I have read how wild animals in sickness turn their backs on one another; one must in unrelievable misery. . . . we dodged in and out of our hall rooms like rabbits in a warren. And then suddenly we would meet and walk along the

199

streets together, mostly at night when the alternate flare of the lamps and the darkness and the hurrying half-seen forms, numb the sense like the flicker of light on a hypnotist's screen, and we moved in a strange, incommunicable world out of which no help reached us. We saw women go by with the price of our redemption flashing at their breasts or in their hair. We saw men hurried, overburdened with work, and there was no work for us. In our own land we were exiled from the community of labour and we sighed for it more than the meanest Siberian prisoner for home. And then suddenly communication seemed to be reëstablished. Effie for no reason sent me half of the rent money. "I don't need it here, and I think maybe I shall get more out of it by investing it in you," she wrote. She had always such a way of making the thing she did seem the choice of her soul. I bought meat and vegetables and invited Griff to dinner. He took me that night to that sort of dreary entertainment known as musical comedy. He could often get tickets and it was a way of spending the evening that saved fuel. As we tramped back through the chill, trying for an effect of jocularity in his voice, so that he might seem to have made a joke in case I shouldn't like, Griff said to me.

"I suppose you wouldn't go with a musical comedy?"

"My dear Griff," I answered him in the same tone, "I'd go with a flying trapeze if only it paid enough."

"I'm acquainted with Lowe, the tenor. I've been thinking I'd ask him——" We were as shy of speaking of an engagement as though it were wild game to be scared away by the mere mention of it.

There was no reason why Griffin shouldn't have succeeded in musical comedy, he had a fairish voice and had turned his gift as many times as the minister's wife in Higgleston used to turn her black silk. It was not more than two days or three after that, as I was coming back to my cold room in the twilight—I had spent the day in the public library on account of the heat—and as I was fumbling at the lock as I had been that first evening he had spoken to me, I heard Leon Griffin come up the stair three steps at a time, and I knew before I heard it in his voice, that the times had turned for him. I struck out fiercely against a sudden blankness that seemed to swim up to the eyes and throat of me.

He was trembling too as he came into the room.

"Olive," he cried, "Olive, I've turned the trick. I'm going with the 'Flim-Flams.'" That was the wretched piece we had seen together. He had never called me by my name before, and I had no mind to correct him. In the dusk he ran on about his engagement; they would go on the road presently and settle for the summer in some city. I heard him speak far from me. I was down, down in the pit of the cold room with the shabby furniture and the bleak light that disdained it from the one high window.

"Don't take off your things," I heard him say. "I came to get you. We'll have a blow-out somewhere. Olive, Olive!" His quick sympathy came out, and the excusing charm. "Oh, my dear, you're crying!"

"Griff, you're leaving me." It was as if I had accused him. I sank down in a chair; I was dabbling at my eyes and trying to get my veil off with cold fingers.

"Not if you feel that way about it." He came and put his arms about me and constrained me until I leaned against his body. I knew what he was, what a man of that stamp must be feeling and thinking, and, knowing, I permitted it. I was crying still, I think . . . his hands came fumbling under my veil . . . presently he kissed me.

"Olivia?"

"Well, Griff!"

"You know—it is for you to say if I shall leave you."

"You mean that you will give up . . . but how can you, Griff; it is the only thing that's been offered." We were sitting still on the low cot in my room and there was no light but the dull glow of the stove and the last trace of the day that came in at the window. We had not been out to dinner yet, and Griffin's arm was around me. I could feel it slack a little now as if he definitely forebore to constrain me.

"I mean, Lowe could get you a place in the chorus."

"But, Griff, I can't sing."

"You can sing enough for that, and Lowe would get you the place if—if you belonged to me." I knew exactly what this implied, but no start responded to it. The nerve of propriety was ached out.

"Of course I know I'm not in your class," Griff was going on. "I wouldn't do such a thing as ask you to marry me. But I'm awfully fond of you . . . and you're up against it."

"Yes, Griff, I'm up against it."

"Your fine friends . . . what would they do for you?"

"Nothing whatever."

"Well, then . . . you needn't go under your own name, and this is a chance; you could live and maybe get somewhere. Lowe told me he meant to strike for Broadway. You aren't insulted, are you?"

"No, I'm not insulted." Curiously that was true. I was drunk and shaking inside of me; I seemed to be poised upon the dizzying edge, but I was neither angry nor insulted.

"And I'd never come back on you if you got your chance for yourself . . . honest to God, Olive. I've had my lesson at that. You believe me, don't you?"

I believed him. I hadn't any sense whatever of the moral values of the situation. It was too desperate for that.

"I guess I ought to tell you . . . I'm a bad sort . . . bad with women. After I knew that my—that Miss Dean didn't want me, I didn't care what became of me. There was a woman in the company . . . she liked me, and I thought it would give Laura a chance. That was what the divorce was about. I thought I could make it up to the other woman by marrying her. But that didn't work either." He was silent a while, forgetting perhaps that he had begun to explain himself to me. "There's a way you've got to like a person to live with them . . . and, anyway, I'm not asking you to marry me." He got as much satisfaction out of that as if it were a superior abnegation.

"You've got to decide, right away," Griffin urged me.

"I must have a day to think," I insisted, not because I hoped that anything would interfere between me and disaster, but I wanted to be able to throw it up to the Powers that I had given them an opportunity.

I knew what he was. I had always known. When he put his cheek against mine to kiss me I had felt the marks there of waste and looseness, just as I felt now that native trick he had for extenuation, for putting himself on the pathetic, the excusing side of things. But I did not shrink from him. I suppose it was because just then he was a symbol of the protection which I had so signally gone without. The need of trusting is stronger in women than experience. Nothing saved me but the persistent monitor of my art. Here, when all else was numbed by loneliness and hunger and unsuccess, it waked and warned me. I had not drawn back from Griffin nor the relation he proposed to me; but I couldn't stand for *Flim-Flam*. I think just at first, though, I made myself believe I was considering it.

I went out to see Pauline the next afternoon. Not that I expected anything from her. It was merely that she represented all that stood opposed to what I was being coerced into, and I meant to give it a chance.

"I am thinking of going with "Flim-Flam," I told her.

"Oh, but my dear—surely not with that!"

"I'll get eighteen dollars a week and my expenses."

"Well, of course, if you want to sell yourself just for a salary!" Pauline's attitude could not have been improved on if she had known all that the engagement implied, but it wasn't in her to be ungracious for long. "I suppose you'll get experience?"

"I'll get my board and clothes out of it," I told her bluntly. "And whether I like it or not, it is the only thing offered."

"And you are just taking it on trust? I suppose that is the right way; you can never tell how things will be brought about." I don't know how much of this was honest, and how much derived from the capacity for self-deception which grows on women whose sole business in life is getting on with a man. At any rate, having shaken my situation around to the shape of a moral attitude, as a robin does a worm, nothing would have prevented her from swallowing it whole.

Faint as I was I refused her invitation to dinner. With what I had in mind to do I didn't care to meet Henry Mills again. I was fiercer in my detestation of him and Cecelia than I had been before I had thought of being in the same case myself. I resented them as a ribald commentary on my necessity.

As I rode home on the car, all my outer self was in a tumult, dazed and buzzing like a hive. I was dimly aware of moving, sitting upright, of paying my fare, and of great staring red posters that flashed upon me from the billboards. I remember that it occurred to me several times that if I could only understand what I read on them, it might be greatly to my profit. Somewhere deep under my confusion I was aware of being plucked by the fringes of my consciousness. Something was trying to get through to me.

I refused to see Griffin at all that evening, and got into bed early, staring into the dark and seeing nothing but fragments of red letters that seemed about to shape themselves into the saving word, and then dissolved and left me blank. I tried to pray and realized that I had no connecting wires over which help might come.

Belief in the God I had been brought up to, had been beaten

out of me at Higgleston, very largely by the conviction of those who professed to know Him best, that He couldn't in any case be the God of my Gift. And I hadn't been thinking since then of the Something Without Us to which I acted, as Deity. Now it occurred to me, lying there in the dark, that if the God of the Church had cast me off, there must still be something which artists everywhere prayed to, a Distributor of Gifts who might be concerned about the conduct of His worshippers.

I reached out for Him—and I did not know His name. I must pray though, I must pray to something which stood for Help. Slowly, as I cast back in my mind to find the name for it, I remembered Eversley. Eversley was everything which any player might wish to be, and Eversley had been kind. I would pray to Eversley. All at once there flashed across the blank of my mind, his name in letters of red. That was it! That was the name on the billboards! Eversley was in town. I recalled that Griff had spoken of it. I hadn't been able to spare a penny for a paper for a long time, or I should have known it. I would see Eversley. I got up and groped around in the cupboard for a piece of dry bread and ate it. Then I went back to bed and dropped asleep suddenly with the release of tension. To-morrow I would see Eversley.

Griffin failed to understand my change of mood in the morning.

"You aren't afraid that I shall try to hold you?"

"No I'm not afraid."

"Or that anybody will find it out?"

"I shouldn't care if they did," I told him. "I'm going to see Eversley. I suppose it's fair to tell you, you'll be the last resort, Griff."

"I'll be the foundation of your fortune, if Eversley will let me, but he won't." I think there was regret in his voice, but it was never in anything he said to me.

"I know you're not mean, Griff; that's why I told you."

"Oh, I'll tell you, too. I was mean once; I didn't mean to be, but it turned out that way." He was on the point of admitting something to me that I felt if I was to depend upon him I shouldn't hear.

I got out as early as possible and walked until I found a billboard. Eversley was at the Playhouse; he had been playing here for three days. I walked past it several times considering the possibility of getting his address from the stage doorman, though I knew I couldn't.

It was clear and bright, few people moved in the street. I walked between the alleyways and a row of ash-cans waiting for the belated carts of the cleaners. "Eversley, Eversley!" I called over and over as if it had been a charm. Suddenly in the still cold brightness, a torn fragment of newspaper flapped in the ash-can, it lifted and made a clumsy flight like a half-fledged bird and dropped beside me. Its one torn wing flapped gently as I passed it, and showed me part of a pictured face. I said to myself that I was in a pretty state when even a torn face in a paper looked like Eversley. I had gone on three steps, and suddenly I stopped. It was Eversley, of course; his picture would be in the papers. I went back and lifted the printed scrap. It was part of an interview with the great tragedian, three days old, and it told me the address of his hotel.

It was nearly eleven when I arrived there. The foyer was crowded with people among whom I fancied I recognized several of my profession. They had the same desperate air that I knew must stand out on me. I thought the clerk recognized it.

"Mr. Eversley is not in this morning," I was told. They pretended, too, not to know when he would be in. I understood that this meant that he was in, but probably asleep or breakfasting. I found a chair close to one of the elevators and waited. The room was warm and I was faint. I do not know how long I sat there; I must have been almost unconscious. Suddenly I snapped alert. There was Eversley and two or three others stepping into the elevator on the opposite side of the room. I was too late of course to catch them.

"Mr. Eversley's apartments," I said to the elevator boy.

"First turn to the left," he told me when he had let me out on the fourth floor. I was afraid to ask the number of the room lest he should suspect me of intruding. There were five or six doors down the left corridor. I knocked at one at a hazard, and was rejected by a large woman in deshabille. I was discouraged; somehow the prospect of knocking at every one of those doors and inquiring for Mr. Eversley daunted me. I was dividing between my dread of that and a still greater dread, if I should be found loitering too long in the corridor, of being taken for a suspicious person. In a few moments, however, a woman came out of one of the doors farthest down and moved toward me. I thought it was she I had seen getting into the elevator with Mr. Eversley; she had the gracious air of women who know themselves relied upon. She stopped, hypnotized by my evident wish to speak to her.

"Mrs. Eversley?" She acknowledged it. "I am trying to find your husband; I have his permission," I interpolated as I saw her pleasant, open countenance close upon me. I learned afterward how much of her life went to saving him the strain of publicity, and I did not blame her.

"My husband never sees visitors in the morning."

"If you would show him this card," I begged. "Perhaps he would make an appointment." She recognized the writing on the card, and I saw her relenting. Mr. Eversley, it proved, would see me.

He pretended kindly to have recognized me at once, but he didn't ask after the Hardings. He saw that it was the last lap with me.

"My dear Miss Lattimore, sit here. Now, tell me."

"So," I concluded at the end of half an hour, "I thought you could tell me if it is all gone. If I am never to have it back again, I can go with a musical comedy." I hadn't told him, of course, what the conditions were of my having even that, "but if you think it could be brought back again . . ." I could hardly formulate a hope beyond that.

"Never in the old way," he answered promptly. "*You* wouldn't wish that. What you did at twenty you must not wish to do at thirty, for then there is no growth. What do you really feel about it?"

"I feel," I said, "as if I could do something—something pressing to be done, but somehow different, so different that I do not know how to describe it to anybody nor to get them to believe in it."

"And so you have begun to doubt it yourself?"

"I shall believe you," I said.

He sat still after that for a while, staring into the open fire and rubbing his fine expressive hands together in a meditative way. It was good to me to see him, just touched mellowly with age, the delicate carving in his face of nobility and gentleness. There were men like that then, men who made by their mere being, something more than a shibboleth of the traditional dependability. He seemed to be far away from me, groping around the root of truth in respect to that gift with which he was so richly endowed. He rose presently and took a play-book which lay face downward on the table.

"Could you do a bit of this with me?" he suggested. ' "It will help me get my lines." The play was "Magda," new then on the American stage. Eversley was getting up the part of Colonel Schwartz. He explained the story to me a little and I began reading and prompting him. Presently I felt the familiar click of myself sliding into the part. All my winter in Chicago rose up in the part of *Magda* to protest against the judgment of Taylorville.

I knew better too than to attempt any sort of staginess with Eversley; I said the words, trying to understand them, and let the part have its way with me. It was not until we had laid down the book that I remembered I was still waiting judgment, and did not feel to want it.

"I won't take up any more of your time," I suggested. "You have been very good to me." I got up to go. After all what was there that Eversley could do for me.

"Well," he said, "and is it to be musical comedy?"

"No," I told him, "no, it may be starvation or the lake, but I'll not let myself down like that . . . . Was that why you asked me to do the part?" I said after a while, in which he had sat gazing into the fire without taking any note of my standing.

"Sit down," he said. "Have you ever heard of Polatkin?"

I shook my head and sat provisionally on the edge of my chair.

"Polatkin is a speculator; he speculates in ability. I think on the whole the best thing I can do for you is to introduce you to Polatkin."

Mr. Eversley thought of Morris Polatkin because he had met him the day before in Chicago. Before I left the hotel it was arranged that I was to see him the next day, and if he liked me —by the tone in which Mark Eversley spoke of him I knew that was foregone—he would take me on to New York with him and put my gift on a paying basis.

So suddenly had the release from strain come that I found myself toppling over my own resistance. I went out in the street and walked about until reminded by the gnawing in my stomach, that I had had nothing but the brewing of my twice-boiled coffee grounds for breakfast, I turned into the first attractive café and paid out almost my last cent for a comforting luncheon. It would have gone farther if I had bought food and cooked it at home, but I was past that. I had pinched and endured to the last pitch; I could no more. And besides the assurance of Mark Eversley, which as yet I could scarcely believe in, there had come a strange new courage upon me. For as I had suffered and struggled with *Magda*, suddenly from some high unknowable source, power descended. I had felt it fluttering low like a dove, hovering over me; it had perched on my spirit. I could feel it there now brooding about me with singing noises. It had come back! I rushed to meet it as to a lover.

As I walked back to my lodging, a flood of hopes, half shapes of conquests and surmises, bore me like a widening flood apart from all that the last few months stood for. Suddenly at the door I realized how far it had carried me from Griffin; the figure of him was faint in my mind as one seen from the farther shore. I considered a little and then I wrote him a note and slipped it under the door. I went out again, and walked aimlessly all the rest of the afternoon, and when it was dark I stole softly up to my room again, but he heard me. He came knocking almost immediately, full of the appearance of rejoicing, but even the dusk didn't conceal from me that embarrassment was on him. He looked checked and confounded as when he had told me about his relation to Miss Dean, like a man caught in an unwarrantable assumption. Whatever Dean had done to him, it had broken the back of his egotism completely. He knew well enough he had no business with a woman like me, a friend of Mark Eversley's, and he was ashamed to have been caught thinking he had. He sidled and fluttered for an interval, making up his mind to a resumption of affectionateness, and finally making it up that he couldn't and remembering an engagement somewhere for the evening.

It was about eleven of the next day that I had a note from Eversley to come to his rooms to meet Mr. Polatkin. I went in a kind of haze of excitement, numb as to my feet and finger-tips, moving about by reflexes merely and with a vague doubt as each new point of the way presented itself, the car I took, the hotel stair, the length of the corridor, if I should be equal to any one of them, so far was my consciousness removed from the means of communication.

Eversley shook hands with me out of a cloud, moving in an orbit miles outside of my own, and when he left me, saying that Polatkin would come up the next moment, it was as if he had withdrawn into the vastness of outer space. In the interval before I heard Mr. Polatkin's knock I rehearsed a great many ways of meeting him, none of which were from the right cue.

I do not know why I hadn't been prepared by the name for his being a Jew, nor for the sudden shifting of the ground of our meeting which that fact made for me. So far as I had thought of him at all, it was in a kind of nebulosity of the high disinterestedness that was responsible for Mark Eversley's interest in me. It had been, his generous succour, all of a piece of that traditional protectiveness, the expectation of which is so drilled into women that it rose promptly in advance of any occasion for it. The mere supposition that he was to provide for me, had tinged my mind, unaware, with the natural response of a docility made ridiculous by the figure of Polatkin edging himself in through a door that an arrangement of furniture made impossible completely to open. His height did not bring him above the level of my eyes, and as much of him as was visible above his theatrical-looking, furred coat, was chiefly nose and pallid forehead disdained by tight, black, curly hair, and extraordinarily black eyes which seemed to have retreated under the brows for the purpose of taking council with the intelligence that informed them.

I had put on my best to meet him, and though my husband had been dead more than two years, my best was still tinged with widowhood, for the chief reason that once having got into black I had not been able to afford to put it off for anything more suitable. I had put a good deal of white about the neck trying for an effect which I knew, as Polatkin's eyes travelled over me, had been feminine rather than professional. Now as I realized how I had unconsciously responded to the suggestion of preciousness in the fact of his coming to take care of me, I felt myself grow from head to foot one deep suffusing red. It comes out for me in retrospect how near I was to the situation which had intrigued Cecelia Brune and her kind, put at disadvantage, not by a monetary obligation so much as by the inevitable feminine reaction toward the source of care and protection. At the time, however, I was concerned to keep the stodgy little Jew, who stood hat in hand taking stock of me, from discovering that I had come to this meeting with a degree of personal expectation which I should have resented in him. I hoped indeed that my blush might pass with him for a denial of the very thing it confessed, or at least for mere shyness and gaucherie. I was helped from my confusion by the realization that Mr. Polatkin was not so much looking at me or speaking to me, as projecting me into the future and gauging me against a background of his own creation.

I was standing still, after we had got through some perfunctory civilities, for I thought he would want me to act for him—but I found afterward that he had trusted Mr. Eversley for my capacity —and I had a feeling of being able to meet the situation better on my feet. I caught him looking at me with an irritating impersonality.

"Jalowaski shall make your corsets," he affirmed; "he makes 'em for Eames and Gadski—a little more off there, a little longer here . . . so . . . ." He did not touch me, he was not even within touching distance, but he followed the outline of my figure with his thumb, flourishing out the alterations which made it more to his mind. "Jalowaski would fix you so you wouldn't believe it was you," he concluded.

He appeared so well satisfied with his inspection that he expanded graciously. "And there is one thing you have which there is lots of actresses would give half they got for it. You have got imagination in the way you dress your hair. It is a wonder how some of them can act and yet ain't got no imagination at all about the way they look, only so it is stylish. For an actress it is all right for her to look stylish on the street, but there are times when she has to look otherways on the stage; y'understand me."

I slid somehow into a chair; I don't know exactly what I expected, but it certainly hadn't been this appraisement, which I had the sense to see was favourable and yet resented.

"The first thing we will see to yet, is some clothes; for you will excuse me, Miss Lattimore, but what you are wearing don't show you off at all. You don't need to wear black. Of course I know you are a widow, Mr. Eversley was telling me, but there are some actresses what make out like they was, because they think it becomes them, y'understand, but there is no need for you to wear it, for Mr. Eversley is telling me that your husband is dead more than two years already." He had loosened his coat to display an appropriate amount of gold fob dependent over a small balloon in the process of being inflated; now from somewhere in his inner recess he produced a folded paper.

"It is better we have a contract from the start. Though of course it is all right if Mr. Eversley recommends you, but it is better we don't have misunderstandings." He spread the paper out and weighted it with one of his pudgy hands.

"So you are going to take me . . . you haven't seen me act yet."

"Eversley has."

"Well . . . if you want to take his judgment . . . but he hasn't told me anything about *you* yet. What do you want of me; what are you going to do for me?"

If Eversley had told him how desperate my situation was, it wasn't a good move to try to hold out against him now, it might have given him the idea that I was ungrateful, but I couldn't stand for being handed about this way like a female chattel. That Eversley had told him, I saw by the expression of astonishment on his face which slowly changed to one of amusement.

"I'm going to save you from starving to death," he began, and then as the sense of my courage in the face of such an alternative grew upon him, "I'm going to make you one of the leading tragic actresses of America."

"And what am I to do?"

"Whatever I tell you. Eversley thinks you could study a while with Mrs. Delamater. She is wonderful, wonderful!" He described with his arms a circle scarcely larger than the arc of his cherubic contour, to show how wonderful she was.

"I should like some dancing lessons, too," I submitted.

"Do you dance? Ah, no, it is too much to expect; but if I could find me a dancer, Miss Lattimore, a born dancer!" He brought his arms into play again to describe a felicity which transcended expression. "But they are not so easy to find," he sighed audibly. "We must do what we can already."

Eversley told me afterward that Polatkin had the soul of an actor, but the only part which he had ever been able to play without being ridiculous, was Fagin, and now he was too fat even for that, so that he took it out vicariously in the success of those whose opportunity he made. It was the dream of his life to find a real genius, a dancer or a prima donna; I believe I was the nearest he ever came to it; and I owe it to him to say that I couldn't have arrived at more than the faintest approach to it without him.

It was that contract I signed with him there in Eversley's room which brought him in the end about three hundred per cent on the money he advanced me, but I never begrudged it. He gave me a check then and there, and an address of a hotel in New York where I was to meet him within five days. He looked me well over as he shook hands with me.

"You would be better if you would weigh about ten pounds more," he assured me, and I was mixed between resentment at his personality and thankfulness to have even that sort of interest taken in me. I had lunch with Mr. and Mrs. Eversley afterward; there was not time for half the things I wished to hear from him, but this sticks in my memory. I had put it to him that the meagreness of my personal experiences had, so far, tended to the skimping of my art.

"There's no question as to that," he told me, "but it is nothing compared to the effect that your art will have on your experience. It's a mistake to let it set up in you an appetite for particular kinds of it. There's the experience of having done without experience, you can put that into your acting as well as the other, and you'll find it is often the most valuable." I was later to find the worth of that, but like most advice, it only proved itself in the event of my not taking it.

There was not much to be done about my leaving Chicago; I had rooted there shallowly. I went out that afternoon to tell Pauline good-bye, for I wished to avoid Henry. It seemed a great step, my going away. There was a kind of finality about it. The casual character of my relation to the stage had disappeared; I was about to be married to it. Pauline cried a little; in spite of there being so much in my life that I couldn't tell her, I remembered how long we had been friends and that we were very fond of one another. She couldn't of course, quite abandon her favourite moral attitude.

"You have a great work, Olivia, a great responsibility. You must remember that you are the trustee of a rare gift."

"I'll take as good care of it," I assured her, "as those who sent it take of me." At the time I believe I felt that the Powers *had* taken notice of me at last.

I got away as soon as possible; it seemed kinder to Griffin. We had been divided as by a sword; he knew now there was nothing between us and he was abashed at the memory of having touched me. All that time we had lurked behind the pressure of packing and settling my affairs; we never came out squarely and faced one another. I think some latent manhood that had risen to my need

212

of him, slunk back with the certainty that I could do very well without him.

"You'll be sure and hunt me up if you come to New York?" I urged; I wasn't going to be accused of disloyalty because of the rise in my fortunes. He shook his head.

"You'll be up among the nobs then." He looked at me for a moment wistfully, "You'll remember that I said I wouldn't try to hold you?" I let him get what comfort he could out of the generosity he imagined in himself at that. Seen against the shining background which Polatkin's money had made for me, he looked almost wizened. "Good-bye," I said, with another handshake, and I set my face steadily toward New York.

BOOK IV

Chapter 1

The third season in New York found me in a very gratifying situation. I had made a public for myself, and friends, not only new friends but old ones drawn there by good fortune of their own. I had worked out my obligation to Polatkin, though I was still on such terms with him as allowed him to give me a good deal of advice, and for me to call him Poly in his more human moments. I used even to go out to his house at One Hundred and Twenty-Seventh Street to spend an hour with Mrs. Polatkin and the several little replicas of himself, of whom, in spite of their tendency to run mostly to nose and forehead, he was exceedingly proud. The help he had afforded me had uncovered new layers of capacity, to fill out satisfyingly the opportunities he created. I was a successful actress, there was no doubt whatever that I was a success; I would have been able to prove it by the figure of my salary. And often when the house rocked with applause, and I was called time after time before the curtain, I would question the high, half-lighted void. I would look and ache and cry out inwardly. For what? Well, I suppose I knew pretty well what I was looking for by the end of that year, though it wasn't a thing I could say much about, even to Sarah.

Sarah and I had a flat together on Thirty-first Street. The second winter we had played together, in a comedy Jerry had written for us, with so much success that it was impossible that we should remain together long. To have kept together two players of such distinguished and equal quality would have been to miss the lustre of achievement which they might each shed on a lesser group, wholly without any other excuse for coherence. Our managers, too, contrived to get us not a little advertisement out of the circumstance of our being friends and undivided by success. There was, however, one fact known to us both, though without any conscious communication, which we would not for worlds have made known to an unsuspecting public; and that was that while I was still on the hither side of my full power, Sarah had come to the level of hers.

Sarah was always wonderful in what I call static parts, parts all of one mood and consistency. She was notable as Portia; as Hermione, absolute. Perhaps the greatest favourite with her public was Galatea, which, besides being well within the average taste, allowed the greatest display of her bodily perfection. Yet with all this, Sarah knew that she was nearing the end of her contribution; knew it perhaps with that prescience of the Gift itself, folding up its wings for withdrawal. I have never been able to make up my mind whether she abandoned her talent because she had no more use for it, or if it left her because its time was served.

I think we arrived at this certainty about our powers, night by night, that year as we came together after the performance, Sarah as though she had come back from a full meal, with a sense of things accomplished, but I—I came hungry—*always!* Sometimes it was merely with the feeling of interrupted capacity, as when one has left off in the middle of the course; when I would continue acting in my room, going over my part, recalling others, trying experiments with them, pouring myself out until Sarah, poor dear, fell asleep in the midst of her effort to be interested. Other times I would rage up and down, all my soul baffled and aching with incompletion.

I do not mean to say I hadn't taken a healthy satisfaction in what had come to me, the knowledge of being worth while, of contributing something; not less in sheer bodily well-being, leisure, beautiful clothes, conscious harmony with my background. I had more feeling of home for that little flat of ours than I had ever known in my mother's house, or my husband's, for the plain reason that its lines and colours and adjustments were in tune with my temperament, as nothing I had had before had been. It wasn't until I had the means to give my personal preference full scope, that I discovered how much of gracelessness in myself had been but the unconscious reaction to inharmonies of colour and line. I had developed, in response to my environment, the quality called charm.

And I was a successful actress. I have to go back to that to get anything like the effect of solidity which my world took on with that certainty. I was developing too, as my critics allowed, and gave promise of steady growth. I was well paid and well friended. I don't mean to say, either, that I did not get something out of being a part of the dramatic movement of my time, knowing and known of the best it afforded. I was integrally a part of that half-careless, hard-working, well-living crowd so envied of the street: I knew a great many notables by their first names. And all the time I wanted something! At last I knew what I wanted.

"It will come," Sarah had faith for me. "Everything comes if it is called hard enough. But you mustn't allow yourself to be persuaded by your wanting it so much, to take any sort of substitute."

That was on an occasion when my Taylorville training had revolted against some of the things that, though they passed current in my world, wore to me the indelible stamp of cheapness. Every now and then some aspect of it struck across my hereditary prejudices, and gave me a feeling of isolation, of separateness which drove me back in time, to condone the offences which set me apart in an inviolable loneliness. It was something my manager had said in my hearing about liking his leading woman to have a liaison with the leading man because "it kept her limbered up."

"I might as well," I said to Sarah. "I could have my leading man any minute." This was true, though it was by no means the inevitable situation, and Sarah in acknowledging it had not spared to point out to me the probable outcome of such a relation.

"This is the way we all end, isn't it?" I demanded. "Why should I go looking for an exceptional experience. We both of us know that I shall never come to my full power without passion and I have a notion that with experiences as with everything else, we have to eat as we are helped. And my leading man is the only thing on the plate." And then Sarah had replied to me with the advice I set down a moment ago.

It wasn't, however, that I hadn't seen clearly and enough of the cheapness and betrayal that comes of such irregular relations, to be warned; if only it were possible for women to be warned against trusting. What I wanted, of course, was some such sane and open passion as I appreciated between the Hardings and Mark Eversley and his wife, noble, extenuating, without a shadow of wavering. How, when I was able to conceive such a relation and to discriminate it so readily from the ruck of affairs like Jerry's and my leading man's, I came finally to miss it, is one of the things that must have been written in my destiny. Perhaps the Distributers of the Gift were jealous.

The beginning of the new coil of my affairs was in Sarah's going on the road early in January and my finding myself rather lonely in consequence, and going out rather too often to the McDermotts'. Jerry had settled his family at Sixty-seventh Street, then in that intermediate region which was at that time neither city nor suburb. Mrs. Jerry insisted that it was for the sake of the park for the children, though most of Jerry's friends were of the opinion that it was rather for the very thing for which they made use of it, an excuse for calling infrequently.

No one could be on a footing of any intimacy with Mrs. Jerry without being set upon by the little foxes of suspicion and jealousy which gnawed upon the bosom that nursed them. Connubial misery was a kind of drug with her, the habit of which she could no more leave off than any drunkard, or than Jerry could his sentimentalized, innocuous infatuations. All this comes into my story, for slight as my connection was with Jerry's affairs, in my capacity as confidante, it served to set in motion the profound, confirming experience of my art. Or perhaps I merely seized on it objectively to excuse what was really the compulsion of the gods. I could have gone anywhere out of New York to separate myself from Jerry's affair; that I should have chosen to go to London is the best evidence perhaps, that I was not really choosing at all.

It began with my spending mornings in the park with Jerry's children, who were nice children except for the way in which they continually reflected in their attitude toward their father, a growing consciousness of slighting and bitterness at home. Mrs. Jerry made a point of her generosity in rather forcing him on me on these occasions, and on the long walks which I fell in the habit of taking very early, or in the pale twilight whenever affairs at the theatre would permit me.

I remember how the spring came on in the city that year. I saw it go with the children to school in a single treasured blossom, or trailing the Sunday trippers in dropped sprays of hepatica and potentilla back from the Jersey shore. Soft airs and scents of the field invaded the town and played in the streets in the hours when men were not using them. A spirit out of Hadley's pasture came

220

and walked beside me. But it was not due to any suggestion of what there was in the invading season for me, that Jerry occasionally walked along with me, for the chief use Jerry had of the earth was to build cities upon.

Jerry drew the sap of his being out of asphalt pavements, and the light that fanned out from the theatre entrances on Broadway was his natural aura. He had developed, he had branched and blossomed in the degree to which the inspiration of his work had been squeezed and strained through layers and layers of close-packed humanity; and the more he was played upon by the cross-bred, striped and ring-streaked passions and affections of society, the more delicate and fanciful and human his work became. His lean figure, now that it had filled out a little, was built to be the absolute excuse for evening clothes, and never showed to such an advantage as in their sleek, satiny blackness, with a good deal of white front, and the rather wide black ribbon to his glasses which brought out the natural pallor of his skin. His hair, which he wore parted very far at one side, and made to curve glossily to the contour of his head, was more like a raven's wing than ever, and had still its little trick of erecting slightly and spreading in excitement, especially when he was up for a curtain speech, and was, in the way he looked the part of the successful dramatist, a good half of the entertainment. His contribution to the occasion on which I was good enough to take his children for an outing to the Bronx or Van Cortlandt Park, was made by lying flat on his back with his hands clasped under his head waiting until I had exhausted myself with games before he was able to take any interest in me. I would come back to him after a while and sit on the grass beside him. Jerry's way of acknowledging the pains I had been at to amuse his offspring, was to pat one of my elbows with a hand which he immediately restored to its business of propping his head.

"Jerry," I said, "I am convinced that something very nice is about to happen to me. Run your hands over the tops of the grass here and you can feel news of it coming up through the stems."

"Well, at any rate you can take it when it comes," he reminded me. "There won't be anybody to be hurt by your good times but yourself."

"Jerry, is it as bad as ever?"

"So bad that if she doesn't let up on it soon I shall do something to bring on a crisis."

"And spend the rest of your life regretting it. Besides there is Miss Doran; you'd have to think of her." Miss Doran was a dancer with a spirit in her feet and a South Jersey accent, whose effect on him Jerry was translating into quite the best thing he had done. It wasn't, however, that I cared in the least what became of her that I had thrown out that saving suggestion, but because it had been little more than a year since Jerry had disturbed the peace and broken the—not heart—let us say the organ of her literary ineptitudes—of Mineola Maxon Freear who had interviewed him once, and taken him with the snare of a superior comprehension. Mineola had advanced ideas as to the relation of the sexes, and a conviction that she was fitted to be the mentor of a literary career, and had missed the point of Jerry's philanderings quite as much as his wife missed them. With Mineola in mind and the tragedy she came near making out of it for herself, I ventured on a word of caution.

"You don't want to forget, Jerry, that there's one good thing about your marriage; it keeps you from making another one just like it."

"You think I'd do that?"

"It is written in your forehead, Jerry, that you are to be attracted to the sort of woman whom you have the least use for. The kind that would make you a good wife, you couldn't possibly love well enough to live with her."

"I could live with you," he affirmed.

"Then it would be because you have never been in love with me. Look here, Jerry, what does the other all amount to? If you didn't have any one . . . like Miss Doran, I mean . . . do you mean that you wouldn't write plays at all?"

"I'd write them harder and I'd write them different. How can a man tell? This thing *is*. Once you know it is to be had, you just can't hold back from it."

"Not even if somebody else has to pay?"

"Why should they?" Jerry sat up and began to pull up the grass by the roots and throw it about. "Why can't they see that all a man wants is to do his work?" I could see at any rate that he was near the breaking point, and I knew that if the break came from Jerry himself, it would be irrevocable. That was what put me in the notion of going away immediately. I had barely saved my face with Mrs. Jerry in the Mineola affair, and I thought if there was to be another crisis I had better clear out before it.

I had put off deciding about my vacation until I could hear from Sarah, who was playing in the West and rather expected to go on to the coast, but now the idea of getting off quite by myself began to appeal to me. It was about a week after that at Rector's, where I had gone with a party of players on the spur of the moment, we saw Jerry come in with the dancer, and an air that said plainly that he knew very well what a married man laid himself open to when he came into a place like that with Clare Doran. I watched them by snatches all through the supper before I made up my mind to send the waiter to touch him on the sleeve and apprise him that I was there. What deterred me was the reflection that if it came into Mrs. Jerry's poor, befuddled head to make a case of his being seen there, the fact that I had stood her friend wouldn't in the least prevent her from having me up as a witness to her husband's private entertainments. I seemed to see in the set of Jerry's shoulders that he expected that his wife would do something, and that it would be unpleasant. The necessity of taking some stand myself, of living myself for or against Jerry's connubial independence, had cleared my soul of sundry vagrant impulses and left the call of destiny sounding plain above the din of supper and the gurgle of soft, sophisticated laughter. The authority of that call, coupled no doubt with some annoyance at Jerry for putting me in a place where I had to decide against him, led me to break it to him there that I was about to leave him with his situation on his hands, rather than at a less public occasion.

He came at once with his napkin trailing from his hand and his raven's wing falling forward over his pale forehead, as he stooped to me.

"I was wanting to see you," I said, as I put up my hand to him over the back of the chair. "I shall be leaving the next day after we close."

"For where?"

"London," I told him. "I shall be in time for the best of the theatrical season there." I hadn't thought of that as a reason until that moment. "Besides I am crazy to go; I smell primroses."

"Nonsense, that's Moet '85. Besides, you've never smelled them, so how should you know?" That was true enough; Sarah and I had had six weeks of Paris the summer before and a week in London in August, where it rained most of the hours of every day, but as I said the word I realized that what had been pulling at my heart was the feel of the London pavements with the smell of the dust in the hot intervals between the showers, and the deep red of the roses the boys cried in the street.

Jerry stood looking down on me, and his face was troubled.

"I don't blame you for going."

"Come too, Jerry; bring the wife and babies." Miss Doran was tired of sitting alone so long, she stood up as if for going. A flicker of consternation passed in his face between his divided interest and a suspicion of the reason for my desertion.

"Look here, Olivia—oh, impossible!" It was plain that the dancer was going to make it uncomfortable for him for taking so much time to his good-bye. "I'll see you at your steamer." He clasped my hand with a detaining gesture. I could see him looking back at me from the doorway as though for the moment he had seen my destiny hovering over me. I have often wondered if Jerry hadn't provided me with an excuse, what the Powers would have done about getting me to London on this occasion.

I had almost a mind the next day to go out to his house and persuade him to drop everything here and take his family abroad with me. That I did not was, I think, not so much due to what I thought such a plan might contribute toward the saving of Jerry's situation, as the conviction as soon as I had decided, that whatever it was that lay at the end of my journey, I was called to it. I was as certain that in London I would find what I went to seek as though it had been printed in my steamer ticket. I shut up the house and left the key of the flat at the bank. A letter I wrote to Sarah crossed hers to me saying that she thought she would stay on in the West for her vacation. Two days after the theatre closed for the season I sailed for London.

Chapter 2

For a week, perhaps, I was content merely with being there, simply happy and human. I had brought letters and addresses which I neglected. In spite of the excuse I had made to Jerry about it, I did not even go to the theatres. I turned aside from the traditional goals, to ride on the top of omnibuses and walk miles down the Strand and Piccadilly, touching shoulders with the crowd. The thing that I had striven for in my art, what men paint and write and act for, was upon me. Answers to all the questions about it that I had not the skill to put to myself, lurked for me behind the next one of the Greek marbles and the next. The pictures were luminous with it. In the soft spring nights it took the streets and turned the voices happy. It danced with the maids in the alleyways to the tune of the barrel organs. Then all at once I had a scare. That-Which-Walked-Beside-Me seemed about to take flight. I would be smiling at it secretly. I would catch myself in the motion of saluting it, and suddenly it would be gone. Mornings I would wake up in Chicago to the old struggle and depression; I would have to go out in the streets and court back my joy; it fled from me and concealed itself in the crowd. I followed it by the trail of the first name I lighted on in my address-book. It happened to be Mrs. Franklin Shane; I wrote her a note and then walked out in Hyde Park to see the last of the rhododendrons, and regretted it. Mrs. Franklin Shane was Pauline Mills raised to the nth power, which I did not fail to perceive was due to Franklin Shane being Henry multiplied by a million. The acute sense of values, which had established Pauline at the centre of Evanston, had landed Mrs. Shane at the outer rim of English exclusiveness. What she would do with her time and energy when she had penetrated to its royal core, interested me immensely.

I had been entertained at her house the previous winter when I had been studying a play that made me perfectly willing to be exploited by Mrs. Franklin Shane, for the sake of what I got out of it to fatten my part. There in London she called for me in her car the afternoon of the day that brought her my note. I don't remember that anything was expressly said about it, but it was in the air that Mrs. Franklin Shane had arrived, in her study of Exclusiveness, at knowing that the younger members of it were addicted to the society of ladies of my profession, and meant to make the most of me. I thought it might be amusing to see what, supposing with me as a tolerable bait, she could catch a younger son, she would do with him. She was clever enough not to put the use she was to make of me, too obviously. I was invited to an informal reception the next afternoon in which she found herself involved by her husband's business exigencies; I gathered from her way of speaking of it that the guests were chiefly Americans and that she had made the best of the situation, extracting from it for herself a kernel of credit by not turning down her compatriots, now that she was assured of having the English aristocracy to play with.

The house in front of which a hansom deposited me the next day, was notable; one could guess that the Franklin Shanes had been made to pay a pretty penny for the privilege of occupying it. It was stuffed full of the treasures of four hundred years of the selective instinct.

"You must really see the Velasquez," my hostess had confided to me as soon as I had shaken hands with her, and I judged from the fact of her not mentioning my name to any other of her guests, that she was saving me for a special introduction.

The Velasquez was very wonderful; there was also an early Holbein and a Titian so black with time that there was only one point in the room from which you could make out what it was about. I was slowly making my way to that point. I had been in the house half an hour and had met but one or two people whom I slightly knew, when I was aware of my hostess piloting toward me through the press, a black-coated male in whom I suspected one of the pegs upon which her social venture hung. It occurred to me that she had sent me to look at the pictures so that she might know where to find me. The room was packed with Americans, satisfying in the only way open to them, a natural curiosity as to the shell in which the only kind of society which wasn't open to them, lived, and the man blocking out a passage through it with his shoulders, was so tall that it brought my eyes on a level with his necktie. There was an odd freedom about it that set me at once to correct my impression of him by his face, and the moment I raised my eyes to him I knew him.

I could hear Mrs. Franklin Shane mumbling the phrases of introduction, rendered unimportant by the radiant recognition that for the moment enveloped us, that burst around us as a flame in which our hostess seemed to shrivel and go out in a thin haze of silk and chiffon. I remember looking around for her presently, and wondering how she had got away from us. We began again at the point where we had left off.

"So you did go on the stage then, in spite of Taylorville?"

"And you," I pressed my foot into the velvet pile of the carpet to make sure that I stood. "You are an engineer, I suppose?"

"In spite of my uncle!"

Somewhere in the next room some one began to sing. I did not

226

hear the song nor see the Titian. I was back in Willesden pasture and the soft rain of dying leaves was on my face. I was conscious of nothing but his hand which he had laid upon my arm to steady me against the pressure of the crowd which swayed and turned upon itself to let Mrs. Shane through, to drag me to be presented to the singer who was even more of a notability than I was.

There was an interval then in which I appeared to be going through the forms of society, and going through them under an intolerable sense of injustice in the fact that having found Helmeth Garrett at last, now I had lost him. It was one of those occasions when the inward monitor is so bent on its own affairs that the habit of living goes on automatically, or does not go on at all. It went on so with me for half an hour. By degrees, what seemed an immense unbearable throbbing of the universe, resolved itself at the renewal of that electrifying touch on my arm, to the thrum of an orchestra in the refreshment room. I felt myself carried along by the pressure of the crowd in that direction, but just at the turn of the stair that went down to it I was drawn peremptorily aside.

"Come," Mr. Garrett insisted, "come out of this. I want to talk to you." There was the old imperiousness in his manner, exclusive of all other considerations. He seemed to know the house. We took a turn through the hall came out presently at the *porte cochère* where a line of carriages waited, supported by a line of skirt-coated figures like little wooden Noahs before an ark. I let him put me into a closed carriage without a word of protest. I had not taken leave of my hostess; I had not so much as thought of her. I suppose he had been arranging this in the interval in which I had not seen him. The moment the door of the carriage was shut, we clasped hands and laughed shamelessly.

"You had three little freckles high up on your cheek, what became of them?" he demanded. All at once his mood changed again. "All the years I've been without you . . .! I saw a picture of you in a magazine three years ago in Alaska. I came near writing."

"You should have. What were you doing there?"

"Promoting Engineer, Alaska, Russia, Mexico." He began a gesture to include the whole round of the mining world, but left off to take my hand again. "The world *is* round," he declared, as though he had somewhat doubted it. "It brings us back again to the old starting points."

"They're always the same, I suppose, the places we set out from; but we . . . we are never the same."

"Is that a warning?" He looked at me, checked for a moment.

"Only a platitude." I had thrown it out instinctively against his engulfing manner, against everything that rose up in me to assure me that nothing whatever had changed, that it would never change. The life of the London streets streamed around us; crossing Piccadilly Circus we were held up with the traffic; the roar of the city islanded us like a sea.

"I suppose you know where we are going?" I suggested in one of the checked intervals.

"To your hotel; Mrs. Shane gave me the address. I told her we were old friends. You mustn't be surprised if you find she expects us to have gone to school together. I wanted to get away where we could talk." I gave him an assenting smile. Still neither of us showed any disposition to begin. He took off his hat in the carriage and ran his fingers through his hair. About the temples it had gone gray a little. Now and then he gave a short contented laugh as a man will, put suddenly at ease.

"I'm glad you kept the old name, Olivia Lattimore . . . Olivia. I shouldn't have found you without."

"You knew I had lost my husband."

"I read that in the magazine. There's where I have the advantage of you." He dropped his light banter for a soberer tone. "My wife died two years ago." We were silent after that until the fact had been put behind us by a space of time.

I don't know why London seems a more homey place than New York. It has been going on so long, perhaps, is so steeped in the essential essence of human living, and the buildings there are smaller, more personal, the mind is able to grasp them to the uttermost. I remember as we stopped at my hotel, being taken suddenly with a tremendous awareness of it all, the noble river flowing by, the human stream, miles on miles of homes, and the green countryside. I was aware of a city set in an island and an island in the sea, the wide immortal sea going around and around it, the coursing waves—I checked myself in an upward gesture of the arms, as though I had pulsed and surged with it. I caught in my companion's smile a delighted recognition.

"Sh—" he said, "what'll Flora Haines think of you!"

"Flora! Oh, Flora wouldn't even *think* about a play-actor. What would your uncle—"

"He's dead now." He stopped me.

"They are all dead," I told him, "all those that mattered to us."

We had another mood when we came to my rooms. I perceived suddenly what there was in him more than I had known. It was in his manner that he had commanded men. I was pierced through with a sense of his virility, the quality that goes to make a male. I was glad of an excuse to put away my hat and wrap, to escape for a moment from the effect he produced on me . . . from inordinate pride in him that he could so produce it. The room was full of the tumult we created for one another.

"Will you sit here?" I said at last. I believe I pushed a chair toward him.

"No, you." He must have turned it back toward me, otherwise I do not know how I came to be so near him.

"You know," I said, . . . "I never got your letter."

"I guessed as much when it came back to me. I should have come to you the next day, but I quarrelled with my uncle. I walked all the way to the railway station before I remembered. But what had I to offer you?"

"It was so long ago . . ."

"No, no, yesterday." His arms were around me. "Olivia . . . yesterday and to-day!"

I think I moved a little to be the more completely engulfed by him, to lay against his the ache of my empty breast; all these years I had not known how empty. We kissed at last and Joy came upon us. We loved; we kissed again between laughter. I remember little snatches of explanation in the intervals of kissing.

"All this time, Helmeth, I have wanted you *so.*"

"I was on my way to you. All last winter in Alaska . . . in the long night, Olivia. I should have come soon."

"Oh," I cried, "I have been drawn across the sea to you. All the way I felt you calling!"

"We had to meet again; had to!"

After a time I insisted that he should sit down. "You haven't had any tea." I tried to get control of myself. I was crossing the room to ring when he swept me up again.

"Look here, Olivia, I don't want any tea. I want you. God!" he said, "do you know how I want you?" All at once I was crying on his breast.

"Oh, Helmeth, Helmeth, do you know you have only seen me twice in your life."

"And both times," he insisted, "I've wanted to marry you."

It was two or three days before we spoke of marriage again. I believe I scarcely thought of it: we had all the past to account for, and the present. We had moments of strangeness, and then we would kiss, and all the years would seem to each of us as full of the other as the very hour.

"Where were you, Helmeth, the second summer after we met?" I had told him of my visit to Chicago and the dream of him I had had there.

"Out in Arizona, carrying a surveyor's chain, dreaming of *you!* Often when the moonlight was all over that country like a lake, I would walk and walk. I had long talks with you; they were the only improving conversation I had."

"For years," I said, "that dream of you was the only thing that kept my Gift awake. Times I would lose it, and then I would dream again and it would come back. I know now when I lost it completely, it was about a year before I saw you that time in Chicago." I had told him of that, too.

"That year I married." I could see that there was something in the recollection always that weighed upon him.

"I didn't," he said, "until after my aunt had told me about you. I went back there when she died; she was always good to me. You know, don't you, Olive, that in spite of everything . . . everything . . . there is only you."

"Let us not talk of it." I do not know how it is proper to feel on such occasions, but I supposed that he must have had as I had, stinging tears to think of the dead and how their love was over-matched by this present wonder. I would have had, somehow, Tommy and my boy to share in it.

I went rather tardily to make my apologies to Mrs. Franklin Shane. I hope they sounded natural.

"My *dear!* you needn't expect me to be surprised at *anything* Helmet Garrett does." She talked habitually in italics. "My husband says that it is only because he so generally does right, that it is at all possible to get along with him." I snapped up crumbs like this with avidity.

"His wife, too, you must have known her," I hinted. This was at the end of a rather complete account of Helmeth's business relations with Mr. Shane.

"Oh, well," I could see Christian charity struggling with Mrs. Shane's profound conviction of the rectitude of her own way of life. "She was a *good* woman, but no—imagination." She was so pleased to have hit upon a word which carried no intrinsic condemnation that she repeated it. "No imagination whatever. One feels," she modified the edge of her judgment still further, "that so much might have been made out of Mr. Garrett. These self-made men are so difficult."

"Are you difficult?" I demanded when I had retailed the conversation to him that evening.

"I suppose so; anyway I am self-made. She is right so far; I dare say it is badly done. You'll have to take a few tucks in me."

"Not a tuck. I like you the way you are. Oh, I like you . . . I like you *so!*" There was an interval after this before we could go on again.

"Tell me how you made yourself, Helmeth. Don't leave anything out, not a single thing."

"By mistakes mostly. Every time I had made one I knew it was a mistake and I didn't do it again. I don't know that I'm much of a success anyway, but I've got a large assortment of things not to do."

"That was the way I learned how to act; filling in behind!"

"I thought that came by instinct. What counts with a man, is not so much getting to know how to do it, but getting a chance to prove to other people that he knows how."

"I've been through that too," I told him, but he was bent on making himself clear.

"I suppose I ought to tell you, Olivia, I'm only a sort of scab engineer. I haven't any papers."

"But if you can do the work? Mrs. Shane said—"

"Oh, Shane will trust me; he's learned. What hurts is to have worked up a scheme to the point where it is necessary to have outside capital, and then have one of the outsiders stick out for a certificated engineer. That's what comes of my uncle's notion that a man should 'pick up' his professional training." There was the core of that old bitterness rankling in him still; he could not yield himself quite to consolation.

"But you have got on, Helmeth, you got *here.*" What "here" meant to me exactly, was more than my lover, more than the pleasant room behind us, the obsequious servitors, more even than the sleek, silvered river and the towered banks that took on shapes of romance under the London gray. There was something in the word to me of fulfillment, the knowledge of things done, the certainty of an unassailed capacity for doing. We were sitting with the broad window flung open, the top of a lime tree tapping the sill of it with soft shouldering touches, as of some wild creature against its mate, creaking a little in somnolent content. I put out my hand to touch his knee—oh, as I might have done it if the "here" had been the point toward which we had travelled together all these years. He laughed then as he often did when I touched him, a man's short full laugh of repletion. He thrust out his knee quite frankly till it touched mine, and closed his hand over my fingers; he returned to what had been in the air the previous moment with an effort. The suspicion that it was an effort, was all I had to prepare me for what was about to leap upon me.

"Oh, I've pulled through, I've pulled through. But I'm not where I might have been. And I'm not rich, Olivia. Not what is called rich."

"Is being called rich one of the things that goes with—what was it you called yourself—a promoting engineer?"

"It goes with it if you are any good at it. Not that I care about money except for what it stands for . . . and then there are the girls."

"You have—girls." It struck me as absurd that I hadn't thought of it until that moment.

"I thought Mrs. Shane would have told you. I have two. It isn't going to make any difference with you, Olivia?"

"Ah, what difference should it make!" I was apprised within me by the haste I made to cover my consternation, that there was more difference in it than my words allowed. "Children of yours?" I said. "So much more of you for me to love." The apprehension was whelmed in the possessing movement with which he drew me to his breast.

Chapter 3

We had to go back to the subject of course, it couldn't be left hanging in the air like that. It was a day or two later at Hampton Court, where we had gone for no reason really, except that it seemed a more commensurate background for what was going on in us, the identification in each by the other, of the springs of immortal passion. We had roved through all the rooms, recharged for us with the exceptional experience, and come out at last on the river bank where there was quite a holiday air among the houseboats.

Behind us we could hear the soft slither of the fountain in the sunk garden; the warm sun streaming on us through the filmy air, the flutter of curtains in the houseboats above the little pots of geraniums, the voices of young people laughing and calling across, began to steal across my mind with a sense of the extraordinary richness of life. Here was all the stuff of which I had built up my earliest dreams of the Shining Destiny . . . young people growing up about me . . . room to stretch my capacity to the uttermost . . . the orderly social procedure. For the moment I believed that I might turn back on that path my feet had failed in, and find in it all that I had missed. I recalled that there were always children in my dream. For the instant they were back . . . little heads and faces . . . all the eyes on me . . . soft curls, like wisps of gossamer. I suppose there must be such little unclaimed souls forever hovering and flitting, little winged things, to love's mighty candle. What should there be in the touch of a man's hand on a woman's that they should come crowding to it like homing doves?

There was a maid going by with her charge, one of those glowing fair-haired English children who supply us with the images by which we prefigure the angelic choirs. Helmeth held out his hand to the boy, and with that swift spark that passes between the young and those by whom they are beloved, he toddled forward and laid hold of the inviting finger.

If I had had more experience of the pang that shot through me then, I should have known it for jealousy. It drove me on toward what, until now, I had avoided.

"Tell me about your girls, Helmeth." He felt in the pocket of his coat.

"If you would care to see them—" He was so pleased and shy, I suppose he must have understood better than I how it was with me. "They are with an aunt in Los Angeles; it was handier for me to see them when I ran up from Mexico. They are rather decent kiddies. You'll see them when they come to New York this winter."

"Shall you be in New York?" It struck coldly on me that he should speak of plans that seemed to be going on regardless of the extraordinary interruption of our love.

"Until I get this Mexican scheme on its feet I shall be going back and forth."

"They look like their mother," I suggested. I was looking still at the small, rather pale photographs he had handed me.

"Because they look so little like me?"

"You forget I saw her once, in Chicago."

"I remember. You know, I think I went there that time because I heard you were playing there." He was silent a moment, pitching bits of sod into the river. "There is something that manages these things. If I had met you then we couldn't have been like this. And we might never have met again."

When he said "like this," he had touched my knee with his hand with that possessive intimacy with which a man may touch his own woman. I had to go back to the photographs of the children to save myself from the blinding lightning of his eyes.

"*Are* they like their mother?"

"I suppose so. I hope so—she was a good woman."

"I'm sure of that." He sat up with intention.

"Ah, it isn't just a sense of what is due her that makes me say that. She was thoroughly good. When I met her out in Idaho she was my chief's daughter and the only nice girl in the place. She wasn't what you are—no other woman is—but she was one of those plain, quiet women that have a kind of grip on rightness. There was nothing could make her let go."

"My mother was like that. I think I can understand."

"Well, it was mighty good for me. I'm a bad lot, I suppose. I always want things harder than most, and I think the wanting justifies me in getting them, but she taught me better. She did things to me that made me fit for you, and I don't want us to forget that."

"Oh, my dear, it is I who am not fit."

But I could see he did not believe that. He had come upon me that day in the woods when happily the mood of Perdita had shut round the odd, blundering Olivia like an enchanter's bubble, through which iridescent surfaces he was always to see me; and by the mere act of loving he had fixed me in my happiest moment. He was the only man I ever knew, whom I could handle like an audience, perhaps he was the only man who never knew me in any other character than the lady of romance.

We went that evening to see Beerbohm Tree in a Shakespearian piece, always so much more worth while in London than anything the same people can do on any other soil, as if the play had mellowed there by all the rich life it tapped with its four-hundred-year roots. Borne up by my mood and the beauty of the production, so much greater than anything we could manage in New York at that time. I was chanting bits of it all the way home, and when we came to my room again I moved before him in the part of Egypt's queen.

> "Who's born the day
> When I forget to send to Antony
> Shall die a beggar—"

"Oh, Helmeth, if you could just see me do it!" I was aching to lay up my gift before him as on an altar.

"You shall do them all for me when we are out in the shack in Mexico."

"Mexico!" I was blank for the moment.

"We'll have to live there for a few years, until I get this scheme on its legs. Look here, Olivia, you haven't said yet when you are going to marry me."

"I've only known you four days!" I tried for the note of feminine evasion.

"Four days and an afternoon, to be exact. What's that got to do with it, when you are made for me?"

"Don't you like this, Helmeth?"

He caught me to him with that frank delight in the pressure of his arm about my body, the feel of his cheek against mine that was as fresh to me as water in a wilderness. "It's not this I'm objecting to, but the trouble I shall have doing without you." He let me go at that, as though he would not add the persuasion of his touch to what he had to say.

"The truth is I've no business to ask a woman to marry me for the next two years. I'm pledged to this Mexican proposition. I've staked all I have on it, and I've asked other men to put their money in, and I can't go back on it. I shall have to be back and forth between London and New York and the mines, for at least a couple of years. If it wasn't for wanting you so . . . but now that I've found you again, I know there's no going on without you!"

He turned his face toward me that I might see the lines of anxious thought there, the buffetings and disappointings, and through it all, the plain hunger of the man for his natural mate.

I saw that and I didn't flinch from it. I took his face between my hands and drew it down to my breast.

"I'm under contract for the next year," I told him. "I signed just before I left . . . what does it all matter? Can't we be just . . . engaged."

"We'd be engaged to be married. And I couldn't take you to Mexico on an engagement."

"I'm under contract," I told him again.

"You mean to say that you'd go on acting after we were married?"

It isn't worth while retailing what we said after that. It has been said so many times. It was the same thing that Tommy said, better put, more fully. He was ready, you understand, to make concession to my liking for the stage, to feel himself sincerely a poor substitute for what I had got for myself out of living, but there it was at the end, that he couldn't make for his own work the concessions he demanded of mine.

"We would have to live in Mexico," he said at last. "That's incontrovertible. And besides there are the kiddies to think of. Their mother wouldn't want them brought up in the atmosphere of the stage." He had me there. I thought of Miss Dean and Griffin, of the Cecelia Brunes I had known, and Polatkin tracing the outline of my figure with his fat forefinger.

"I wouldn't either," and my frank admission of it brought us out of the atmosphere of controversy to the community of our love again.

"You understand, don't you, that I feel even more obligation to her *now.*" I nodded. I understood fully that obstinate trace of disloyalty that came of his having given himself to what she wouldn't approve of, to what he couldn't for decency's sake admit of giving her daughters.

"I know what people think of the life of the stage," I agreed; "and I know what's worse, that most of it is true. Not that it need to be; but it has got in the habit of being so."

"Well, then, if you feel that way—" The inference was plain that he didn't know in that case why I held on to it.

"It has got into my blood, Helmeth. I can't explain, and I didn't realize until we got to talking of it, but I don't believe I could live away from it. It is with me as it is with you about your engineering." If I had a momentary qualm lest that last should be not quite disingenuous, it passed in the realization that the compari-

236

son hadn't come home to him. I remembered how Forester would have accepted the abnegation of my gift to his necessity of being important, and I didn't hold it out against Helmeth that he failed to realize at all the place that my work occupied, just as work, in the scheme of my existence.

We came back to it the next day and the next. It would have been simpler, of course, if it hadn't been for the children, and for my being at one with him in the opinion that the stage wasn't the proper atmosphere for the rearing of young ladies. I was still of the opinion which was exemplified in so far as I knew it, by Pauline and Mrs. Franklin Shane, that the function of mothering could not go on except by complete separateness from the business of making a living. All my training and heredity had fostered an ideal of family life, which rendered obligatory a proper house and servants, in the neighbourhood of good schools, and the exclusion from it of everybody but those who found themselves in an identical situation. And if we had been able to imagine a compromise, Helmeth and I would have been hindered by the defrauded capacity for loving, from working it out logically. At the mere suggestion of anything to drive us apart, the mating instinct set us toward one another irresistibly. We would leave off any argument and fall to kissing. We were pierced through and through with loving.

"Let us not think of it any more; something will work out for us. Let us just be happy the way we are," I would protest.

"Oh, child, child, will you never understand that the way we are is what is so hard to bear!" Then he would snatch me up until the suffusing fire of his caress would steal through all my body and sing in me like bacchic sap of vineyards in the spring.

"You oughtn't to marry me unless you can't help yourself," he would laugh shamelessly. So we fell deeper in love and not out of our difficulties.

Toward the end of that week, the weather which had been thickening to a storm, brought us to one of those thunderous London days, full of a stifling murk that might have been breathed out by the nostrils of the greasy, hurrying snake that went by in the bed of the river. Inconsequential lightnings flashed in the smoky vault, from every quarter of which rolled unrelated thunder.

Helmeth came over from Mr. Shane's office in London Wall; the need we had of being together was oppressive like the day which, when we had sought it in the Park, we could hear like some great monster bellowing for its mate. We went out and walked about for a time under the trees, fancying the relief of freshness in the green obscurity that under the ranked trunks, thickened to blackness. No one was about but a few belated nursery maids, scurrying in silhouette against the pale glow of the light pinned down and imprisoned under the thick cloud of foliage. We were on the Broad Walk, when suddenly a wind tore loose in the firmament. It made a whirling chaos of the murk, it wrung the treetops, but the air along the ground was stagnant as a cistern. Now and then a few great drops spattered on the leaves of the limes. Over a quarter of a mile from us, near the Alexandria gate, the tension of the day snapped suddenly in flame, a bolt had shattered one of the great trees. Straight across the grass toward us the bolt sped like a ball of light. It skimmed the ground knee high, flame points on its edges, flickered viciously as it drove at us.

There was no time for anything. Helmeth cried out to me once and I stepped within the circle of his arms; we could hear the fire ball sizzling as it cleared the grass; within a yard of us it went out in a flare of gas and a crack like thunder. Suddenly buckets of rain were precipitated on us, we could hear the slap of them on the pavement as we ran.

I was crying hysterically by the time we came to my room in a cab. I remember Helmeth trying to rid me of my wet things and my clinging to him crying.

"Oh, my dear, my dear, it was so near, so near, I thought I was to lose you before I had had you—before I had had you at all!"

"No, no . . . not that, Olivia, not that!" His arms were around me and all my life up to that moment was no more to me than a path which led up to those arms. I remember that . . . and the world dissolving in the wash of the rain outside . . . and the lift of his breast; and deep under all, old, unimagined instincts reared their heads and bayed at the voice of their master . . .

Chapter 4

After the evening of the storm we talked no more of marriage for a while, and about a week later I went over to Paris ostensibly to shop, and was joined there by Mr. Garrett on the way to Italy. I suppose that Italy must always lie like some lovely sunken island at the bottom of all passionate dreams, from which at the flood it may arise; the air of it is charged with subtle essences of romance. One supposes Italy must be organized for the need of lovers. Nothing occurred there to break the film of our enchanted bubble. For a month we kept to the hill towns and to Venice, where we could go about in the conspicuous privacy of a gondola, and all that time we met nobody we had ever known.

It was all so easily managed—we had to think of the girls, of course—no one seeing our registered names side by side, Mrs. Thomas Bettersworth, New York, and Helmeth Garrett, Chilicojote, Mexico, would have thought of connecting them. Helmeth attended to all his business correspondence as though he were still in London, and nobody expected to hear from me in any case.

It is strange how little history there is to happiness. We had come together past incredible struggles, anxieties, triumphs, defeats; we had been buffeted and stricken, and now suddenly we were stilled. If at any time the ghosts of the uneasy past rose upon us, we kissed and they were laid. So long as we kept in touch, there ran a river of fire between our blessed isolation and the world. And for the first time we looked upon the world free of the obligations of our being in it. We looked, and exchanged our separate knowledges as precious treasure. My exploration of life had been from within—I knew what Raphael was thinking about when he painted that fine blue vein on his Madonna's wrist. But Helmeth had looked on the movement of history; what he saw in Italy was the path of armies, lines of aqueducts, old Roman roads to and from mines. Everything began or ended for him in a mine, in Gaul or Austria or Ophir; dynasties were marked for him by change in the ownership of mines. So he drew me the white roads out of Italy as one draws fibre from a palm, and strung on them the world's great adventures. There were hours also when we let all this great fabric of art and history float from us, sure that by the vitalizing thread of understanding which ran between us like a new, live sense, we could pull it back again . . . but we loved . . . we loved.

Nothing that happened to us there, came with a more revealing touch than the attitude in which I caught myself, looking out for and being surprised at not discovering in myself any qualms of conscience. All that I had known of such relations in other people, had made itself known by a subtle, penetrating, fetid savour, against which some instinct, as sure as a hound, threw up its head and bayed the tainted air.

But in my own affair, the first compulsion that irked me was the necessity I was under of not telling anybody. I wasn't conscious at any time of any feeling that wouldn't have gone suitably with the outward form of marriage; there were times even when I failed to see why one should take exception to the neglect of such form. I was remade every pulse and fibre of me, my beloved's . . . and so obviously, that the necessity of tagging my estate with a ceremony struck me as an impertinence. Marriage I think must be a fact, capable of going on independently of the prayer book and the county clerk. Whatever *you* may think, no god could have escaped the certainty of my being duly married.

There were days though, just at first, when I suffered the need of completing my condition by an outward bond. I knew very well where the custom of wedding rings came from; I should have worn anklets and armlets as well, if only they could have been taken as the advertisement of my belonging wholly to my man. Depend upon it, the subjugation of woman will be found finally to rest in the attempt visibly to establish, what the woman herself concurs in, the inward conviction of possession.

How much of what was in my own mind, was also in Helmeth's, I do not know, but because I had brought upon myself the condition of not being married, I failed to speak of what I found regrettable in it. What did come out for me satisfyingly, was the man's sheer content in his mate, the response, and our pride in it, of his blood and body to my presence, and the new relish it created in him for the processes of living, for his pipe and his meals, and his work. He had brought some estimates to figure out; evenings at work on these, he would call me to him and sit with his left arm thrown lightly about my chair, the pencil going as though my presence were an added fillip to activity. He took on weight in that holiday, and his mouth relaxed to a more youthful curve.

We spent the last three weeks of it at a quiet hotel on the point of land that divides Lake Como from Lecco, opposite Cadenabbia. Times yet I will wake out of dreaming, to find the pulse of the city transmuted into the steady lisping of that silver fretted lake. We had come to a phase like that in our relation, deep and full and shining. We spent hours sitting on the parapet in the sun, looking at it. I would sit on the stone ledge and Helmeth would stretch himself, with his pipe, along the ground.

"Helmeth," I said on such a morning, "do you know this is the first time I ever rested?" He gave a little gurgle of content; the sun turned on the sails of the fishing-boats and flashed us sympathy. "I'm afraid," I admitted, "I'm never going to want to do anything else."

"Oh, I'm going to want to. This is good enough, but it wouldn't be half so good if I couldn't take it along with me and do things with it—great things." He threw his arm across my knees with one of those quick, intimate caresses, flooding me full of the delighted sense of how completely I belonged to him. "I feel," he said, "as if I had been going about with one arm or one hand, and now I've got a full set of them. Wait until I show you!"

"When you talk of doing, Helmeth—that means leaving me."

"That's for you to say, Olive." That was as near as he had come yet to reminding me that it was I who had chosen this instead of a relation which would have implied my going with him wherever his work led him, and that the choice was still open to me. The night after the storm he had written me:

> "There is nothing that troubles me about to-night except the fear that you may regret it, that you might ever come to have a doubt of how I feel about it. I want you to feel that whatever you choose is right to me, and though I hope for nothing so much as to make you my wife, I shall not urge you beyond what you feel that you can do without urging."

It was a generous letter, and no doubt it had its weight in persuading me to trust the situation, in the face of that instinct which saves women, even from passions that seem their own

241

justification. If he had counted on the naturalness of love to set up its own public obligations, he had not been far wrong with me. If it had been practicable, I should have walked out with him any day those first weeks to be married. But marriage is a very complicated business in Italy. In a measure I had satisfied my fret for the visible tie, with a ring which he had bought me in Florence, which, as the stone flashed in the sun, turned me back on the thought I had when first he set it on my hand.

"Helmeth, do you suppose that we are pushed on to make laws and observances about marriage, because the bond that comes into being then has a consistency and validity beyond what we feel about it?"

"Oh, beyond what we feel about it, yes." He sat up then a little away from me, as he often did when he drew upon experiences lying beyond the points at which his life had been touched by mine, and began skipping little stones into the water. "Yes, I'm sure that what you feel about a thing that happens to you is not always the test of what it does to you. Sometimes I think feelings haven't much to do with our experiences except to get us into them." He left off skipping stones and began to pile them into a little heap. "I was thinking of Laura," he concluded. It was not often that he spoke to me of his wife.

"I can't remember that I had a great deal of feeling about her; I was too busy, I suppose, getting on with my engineering; but she had a grip on me. She had a grip. Look here, my dear, I ought to tell you this, you're the wonder of the earth for me, and I know very well that my wife's world was a very little one; it was bounded by the church on one side and by conventions on all the others. But somehow I don't want to get too far away from it, and I don't want the girls to get too far." He swung about to look squarely up at me. "This that you've given me, it's heaven; it's a thing for a man to die for and die happy; but there's the other too." He laughed a little awkwardly; he caught my feet in one of his strong hands. "Have I made you understand?"

"I understand that kind of life. It's like a clean, scrubbed room. I *know*. I was brought up in it. There have been times when I have been desperate because I couldn't go back and live there. But I ought to tell you, Helmeth, I can't find my way back."

"You! Why should you? You were made to live in Kings' houses. But I wanted to be sure you weren't going to be disappointed if I haven't the manners that always belong to palaces.

242

I've been in camps where a scrubbed room looked mighty good to me." He stretched himself and rolled over on the ground, lying with his back to the sun, soaking in it in simple, animal content. Little white flecks showed on the lake, the sails of the fisher-boats tilted slowly and composed themselves anew with the line of the shore and the flowing hills. Directly opposite, the walls of Cadenabbia showed white amid the green, like a little streak of Arcady.

"We've never been," I reminded him.

"I thought you wanted to leave it so you could always think of its being as romantic as it looks, without making sure that it isn't." That was the reason I had given him, but the truth was that Cadenabbia was on one of those tourist routes where, supposing anybody we knew to be wandering about Europe, we would be sure to run into them. This morning, however, I was seized with an irresistible desire to visit it.

"But supposing it isn't as interesting as it looks," I submitted, "if I go there with you I shall never know it. And think how disappointed I should be if I should ever come there without you and find that it is the one place we ought to have seen."

There was a little motor launch plying between the shores of the lake, and an hour before tea time we crossed in it. We spent the hour in the garden of the Duke of Saxe-Meiningen, and then along the parapet we strolled in search of tea. It was the height of the tourist season and the gay groups moving in the streets between the quaint low houses, gave it a holiday air. We heard them calling one to the other, exchanging appreciations and information. All at once we heard them calling us.

"Garrett, Garrett!" a party in the act of settling at a tea table in the garden of one of the hotels, dissolved and reorganized about us as the centre. There was laughter and garbled greetings and hand-shaking. Presently Helmeth began to introduce me. They were a party of Californians, all more or less acquainted and importunate; we were swept back by them to the table and tea. There were two married couples and one unmarried woman of about my age, and a boy of sixteen. I could see by the way she appropriated him, that his acquaintance with Miss Stanley had been of the degree that might have ripened into marriage, and that Miss Stanley had not wholly made up her mind that it wouldn't. She was one of those unmarried women who contrive by a multiplicity and vivacity of interests to deny what is explicitly advertised by their anxiety to have you understand that they consider themselves much better off just as they are. I could see her taking in all the details of my appearance, to find the key to what Mr. Garrett might presumably like in me, and striking out in her manner to him a quick sketch of me, bettered in the direction of what she believed it most to be. The other women, if they had been brought up in Taylorville, would have resembled Pauline Mills; that they didn't I could see was difference of geography. They were all full of gay talk and reminiscence of a mutual life in the West, on a footing that left me rather more than room to play the part, which I had cast for myself with celerity, of being a casual acquaintance of his, picked up at a hotel. He had introduced me to them as Mrs. Bettersworth, and whether they would have known me or not by my stage name, I took care they shouldn't have the opportunity.

Nothing would do but he must stay to dinner; I guessed that there was that degree of acquaintance between them which would have made it unfriendly of him to refuse. I could see Miss Stanley prick up at his manner of leaving the decision to me, and realized that whatever we might have agreed upon, there would be no keeping our relation from being at least a matter of curiosity to the women, the elder of whom had promptly included me in the invitation.

I invented a mythical travelling companion across the lake whom I must join, and managed to make my being in Mr. Garrett's company appear so casual that I came near to overdoing it by exciting his concern.

"What's the matter; don't you like them?" He wished to know as he saw me to the landing.

"Ever so," I insisted promptly, "but they wouldn't like me after a while. You behave as if we had been married five years."

"Oh, well, haven't we?" He looked back and his brow gathered a little. "For two cents I'd tell them." But after all there was nothing he could do but see me comfortably off and go back to them. He told me afterward that Mr. Harwood, the elder of the two gentlemen, had been useful to him in business.

It must have been close on to midnight when he waked me, sitting on the edge of my bed. He must have gone to his own room very softly, meaning not to disturb me; now I heard him calling my name in a whisper and his hand seeking for my face.

I reached up and drew his down to me.

"Oh, my dear—" I was startled at what I found there. "Beloved, why are you crying?" I could feel him shake with sudden uncontrollable emotion. I kept his head on my breast and comforted him.

"When did you come in?"

"An hour ago—you were asleep." The commonplace question seemed to quiet him.

"Was it something went wrong at the dinner?"

"Wrong, yes . . . but not there, not there. It's all wrong, it has been wrong from the beginning."

"Dear heart, tell me."

"Olive, marry me; say you'll marry me!" There was urgency in his whisper, there was pain in it. "Say it; say it!"

"I'll marry you. I've been waiting for you to ask."

"Oh, my dear, when I have begged you so. . . ."

"Tell me," I urged. . . .

"There isn't anything to tell, only . . . we walked along the parapet and were very happy together. They're a good sort. I've known them for years. And we found a peasant woman selling lace, good lace, the women said, and cheap . . . Harwood bought some for his wife . . . and Stanley bought his sister some. Harwood went back, pretending he'd forgotten something, and bought a piece his wife wanted and thought she couldn't afford. And I couldn't buy you any . . . not openly. I wanted Miss Stanley to select some handkerchiefs that I said were for the girls and she said girls shouldn't wear that kind. Oh, Olive, don't you understand?"

"I understand; you shall go back to-morrow and buy me some."

"But it won't be the same . . . and afterward . . . after dinner we sat in the garden and Harwood sat with his arm round his wife's chair. And you were over here . . . *hiding!* Oh, Olive, I want my wife, I want her . . . in the light, before everybody. I want her." I was crying now.

"It's all wrong," he insisted, "it's been wrong from the beginning. We belong together, before everybody." He kept repeating that phrase over and over. "All the years that we've been apart . . . and now just to have it in a hole in a corner!"

"No, no, my dear!" I protested. "Before God . . . it's been before God!" We sobbed together. By and by Love came and comforted us.

245

I suppose if it had been possible to go out and be married immediately we should have married the next morning; but in Italy there are observances—it would have taken three weeks at least and hardly less in Switzerland. In two weeks our vacation came to an end. Helmeth set out by the shortest route for Mexico and I interposed a week's shopping between me and Mrs. Franklin Shane to whom I had pledged myself for a week at her country house. In November I was to meet Helmeth Garrett in New York, "and settle things" he had stipulated. Somehow I could not bring myself to think of my relation to him as involving cataclysmal changes. I wouldn't say to myself that I intended to marry him, and I couldn't say that I wouldn't.

Chapter 5

Within a week after my return, Polatkin came to see me about a project of a theatre of my own, which had been on the horizon since the year before. Polatkin himself was to furnish the money, which, considering what he had made out of me under our earlier contract, he was not in the least loath to do. He couldn't understand why I hesitated.

"Is it that you think you are getting along without Polatkin? Well, you can try." I hastened to reassure him. "Well then—are you getting cold feet about that Ravenscroft woman? Understand me, she can't act at all. It's something scandalous the way she tries to act like you do, and she can't. If I was her manager I would introduce a tight rope into the third act and have her walk it, but what I would have something that wasn't copied from somebody else."

"I wasn't thinking of Miss Ravenscroft," I confessed. "I'm thinking of getting married."

"Married! Married! And leave the stage? My God—it is a sin—!" He clutched the air and shook handfuls of it in my face. "What do you want to get married for?" he demanded. "Ain't you getting on like anything? Ain't you popular? Ain't you making money?"

"All of those," I admitted.

"Well, then?" His wrath which had frothed white for a moment, cooled down into a fluid sort of bewilderment which seemed about to set and harden in a smile of disbelief.

"The man I am going to marry lives in Mexico."

"Mexico! Mexico!" he bubbled again. "I ask you is that any sort of a place for a man to live what married the greatest tragic actress ever was going to be?"

"Ach, my Gott," in moments of great excitement he reverted to the trick of the tongue to which he was born. "All these years I have waited for this, I have said Miss Lattimore is a great actress, she has talent, she has brains, and when she will have passion—Pouff!" He blew out his loose lips and made a balloon with his hands to express the rate at which I would rise in the scale of tragic actresses. "And now that it has happened, she wants to live in Mexico." He deflated himself suddenly, folded his hands over what he believed to be his bosom, and looked at me reproachfully. This being the first time he had studied my face directly since I came home, I suppose he must have seen there my doubt and indecision.

"Understand me," he said soberly, "I have known a lot of actresses, and I want to tell you that this marrying business don't pay. They got to come back to the stage; they got to. You ain't going to be any different down there in Mexico to what you are in New York, understand me. *Yah!* Mexico!" The word seemed to inflame him. But he had the sense to let me alone for a while.

A few days later I saw in the paper that he had taken the lease of the theatre he had mentioned to me, and I knew that he wasn't counting on my going to Mexico.

I suppose if I had had the courage to look into my own mind to find out what I wished to do, I might have surmised what was going on there from the fact that I didn't mention the idea of marriage to Sarah. I have tried—all this book has had no other purpose in fact, than to try to tell how I came to be in the relation I was to Helmeth Garrett, came into it as to a room long prepared for me, without any struggles or tormenting, and without thinking much about the effect that his presence in my life would have upon my work. I suppose that in as much as I had a man's attitude toward work, I had come unconsciously to the man's habit of keeping love and my career, in two watertight compartments. I found I was not able to think of them as having much to do with

247

one another. Still less had I the traditional shames of my situation.

I remember the first time I went to rehearsal, groping about in my consciousness for the source of what I felt suddenly divide me from the rest of my company, and finding it in the knowledge of myself as a woman acquainted with passion, with a secret, delicious life. And far from identifying me with the cheapness and betrayal which until now I had supposed inseparable from the uncertified union, it set me apart in the aloofness of the exclusive, the distinguishing experience. It remained for Sarah to pierce me, in spite of all I intrinsically felt my relation to Helmeth Garrett to be, with the knowledge of where I stood in the world which I still believed had the last word about human conduct.

It was not altogether the intent to deceive, that kept me from opening the matter to her in the beginning, but a feeling that the less advice I had about it the better. And if I did tell her, I wished first to arrange that I need not feel any constraint upon me of our habit of living together. I was anxious to have Helmeth find me when he came, free to be all to him that our love demanded, and in view of all the years in which Sarah and I had lived together, I did not know how to go about it. I began to think that I should have to tell her after all, when the Powers, who must have known very well what was going on, took that into account also.

Sarah's season began a week before mine, and I remember her saying that she would be glad when we could come home together, as she had had an uneasy sensation for the last night or two, of some one following her. Sarah had any number of admirers, but the sort of men who were attracted to her still splendour, were not the kind to follow her home at night.

"Turn them over to the police," I suggested. I had had to try that once or twice.

"Oh, I couldn't!" She turned scarlet. Even after all those years I had not realized how all her life was timed to catch the slightest approaching footfall of what, to her simple faith, must inevitably come. I found her waiting for me at the stage door on my first night—no matter how many of them you have, first nights are always in the balance—and we were so taken up with discussing how I had got on with it, that it wasn't until I was fitting the key in the lock that I was recalled to the occasion of her annoyance. Just below us there seemed to be a man dodging in and out of the blocks of shadow made by the high-railed stairways that led up to the first floor of the row of flats in which our rooms were located. Something in the figure, or in our standing there before the shadowed door with the dull light of the transom over us, brushed me with a light wing of memory; I seemed to recall some such conjunction before, but it was gone before I could connote the suggestion with time or place. All I said to Sarah was that if we saw anything more of that we would certainly speak to the police.

The next night we went to supper with friends, and it was after midnight when my cab—Sarah didn't afford cabs for herself—drew up at the door. The approach to it was by way of a handsome pair of stairs with an ornamental iron railing of so close a pattern that any one sitting on the steps in the dark, would be pretty well concealed by it. That there was some one so sitting, dropped there in a stupour of fatigue or drunkenness, we did not discover until we stumbled fairly on to him.

The exclamation we raised, awoke him; it arrested the attention of the cab driver just turning from the curb, he raised his lamp and sent the rays of it streaming over us. The man I could see, was shabby, ill and embarrassed, he ducked his head from the light, but his hat had fallen off on the step and as he threw up his arm to protect himself from recognition I knew him by the gesture.

"Griff," I cried. "Griffin! You!" I caught him by the arm. He let it fall at his side and stood looking at us pitifully, like a trapped animal.

"I wasn't doing any harm," he mumbled. The cab driver seeing that we knew him, let down his lights and clattered away. I thought quickly; he must have been in want, he had looked for me and at the last was ashamed to claim me.

"But, Griffin," I insisted, "you don't know how glad I am to see you—you must come in." He wasn't looking at me; he hadn't heard me.

"Look out," he said, "she's going to faint!" He brushed past me to Sarah. She leaned limp against the railing; he steadied her as a man might a sacred vessel in jeopardy. But Sarah didn't faint so easily as that, she gathered herself away from his hand.

"Come upstairs," she commanded. It was only one flight up. I don't know how we managed to get a light and to find ourselves in its pale flare, confronting one another. I could see then that my first surmise had been correct about Griffin, to the extent that he looked ill and in want. He was holding his hat, which he had picked up from the stairs, and fumbled it steadily in his hands. His hair, which wanted trimming more even than when I had last seen him, had still its romantic curl; he looked steadily out from under it at Sarah. I had an idea, though I think it must have been derived from my own dizziness at what rushed in upon me, that Sarah was floating in air, that she hung there swaying with the breeze from the open window, as a spirit. She was spirit white and her voice seemed to come from far.

"Leon! Leon!" How he knew what she demanded of him only the God who makes men and women to love one another, knows.

"She died," he said to the unspoken question. "She died two years ago. I've been all this time finding you." Suddenly a quick flame burst over Sarah.

"You came—you came to me!" I could see that she moved toward him, all her magnificent body alight, her arms, her bosom. I turned quickly through the door into the room beyond. I couldn't stay to see that. I went on into my bedroom and knelt down, hiding my face in the bedclothes. I think I meant to pray, but no words came. I rose presently and went into the kitchen. The maid did not sleep in the flat but came every morning at nine; on the table there was a tray as she left it always, with everything laid out in case we should be hungry coming late from the theatre. I moved about softly and made chocolate and sandwiches and arranged them on the tray; I knew Sarah would understand. About half an hour after I had gone to my room again, I heard her go out to find it.

From time to time I could catch a faint murmur from the front room. I put the pillow over my head and cried softly. I remembered how Griffin had looked at her that time in Chicago when I had taken him to "The Futurist," and how I had been ashamed ever to introduce him. I wondered whether his real name were Lawrence or Griffin. I had fallen asleep at last, and I was awakened by Sarah standing beside me in her white gown.

"May I sleep with you, Olivia? I've put . . . Mr. Lawrence . . . in my room." I drew her under the cover with me; she was cold and now and then a shudder passed through her from head to foot.

"You guessed, didn't you?" she whispered. "He said you knew him in Chicago. His . . . Mrs. Lawrence is dead . . . you heard him say that?" I understood she meant by that to extenuate his coming back to her. It was right for him to come if no other woman stood in the way; what there was in himself that stood in the way didn't seem to matter.

"He's been ill," she said. "I hope you didn't mind my keeping him in the house, Olive. . . . We can be married to-morrow."

I sat straight up in bed in my amazement.

"Sarah! You don't mean that you are going to marry him!"

"Why, what else is there to do?"

"But, Sarah . . ." I lay down again. After all what else was there to do?

"You know, Olivia, you have never really loved anybody." I had no answer to that; suddenly she broke out shaking the bed with her sobs. "Oh, my dear, my dear, it is true that he loved me. It is true. He came back to me as soon as he was free. Oh, Olive, if you had known what it is all these years not to know if it was *true!* If he hadn't only taken me just as a stop-gap . . . a fancy . . . how was I to know?"

I didn't think very much of the proof that he loved her now. Sarah, beautiful, prosperous, was a goal for any man to strive toward, even without the necessity which was written in every line of Leon Griffin Lawrence.

"Sarah," I questioned gently, "do you mean to say you've loved him all this time, that you love him now?" She left off sobbing to answer me with that steady, patient truth with which she met any issue of life.

"I loved him . . . all the love I had I gave him. It's not the same now, of course; its wings are broken, but it is his. Once you've given you can't take it back again."

"But he—he has no claim on you now. Sarah, do you need to marry him?"

"I am married to him."

"But, Sarah . . . look here, Sarah, it isn't true that I have never loved. I didn't love the man I was married to, but I have learned something about love; I've learned that marriage without it is a thing no self-respecting woman should go into."

"Love," said Sarah, "is a thing that once you've gone into, binds you by something that grows out of it that is stronger than love itself. Olivia, I am bound . . . if you want to know, I'd rather be bound to—Leon Lawrence by that tie than to the dearest love without it. Oh, Olivia, can't you see, can't you understand that I have to do *right* . . . that the way I see things there's a law . . . not

251

a civil law but a law of loving that goes on by itself; and being faithful to it is better to me than loving. You must see that, Olivia."

"I see that this is the happiest thing for you and I'll not put anything in your way, Sarah." I kissed her. What, after all, does one soul know of another.

It came to me as an extenuating circumstance when I looked him over the next morning, that Mr. Lawrence wouldn't live long enough to do her any particular harm. He had been so little of a man always to me, so much less so now, eaten through as he was by poverty and sickness, that I could never understand how he happened to be the vehicle of that appealing charm which even as I looked, drew me over to his side in something like a sympathetic frame.

I could see that he regarded me anxiously, and I thought it to his credit to be able to realize that there might be somebody not absolutely delighted at his marrying Sarah. But it wasn't, as I learned later, any sense of his shortcomings that waked in his eye toward me.

He was lying on the sofa in our little parlour, for the shock of the encounter had been too much for the abused and broken thing he was. Sarah had gone out, to consult Jerry, I believed about their marriage;—she wouldn't have asked me knowing how I felt about it. Griffin looked up at me with the old formless demand on my consideration.

"You've never told her, have you?"

"Told what?" On my part it was genuine amazement.

"About us, you know . . . there in Chicago." He dropped his eyes; something almost like a blush of shame overcame him. I stared.

"Good heavens, Griff, I'd forgotten it."

"Oh, well, I didn't know—some women—" He stopped, embarrassed by my sheer credulity of its having anything to do with his relation to Sarah. "I told you I was a bad lot," he protested, "but I swear that since my wife died and I could come back to her, I've been straight. You believe that, don't you?"

"Oh, I'll believe it if it's any comfort to you." When I talked it over with Jerry afterward I could see the queer, twisted kind of moral standard by which he made it appear that any irregularity of his during his wife's life, was unfaithfulness to her, and not Sarah.

She had come back with Jerry and I was walking with him to the City Hall for the license; he had begun by protesting just as I had, and had surrendered to his conviction that nothing less would satisfy Sarah.

"After all," I said, "it shows that there is some sort of harmony between them, that he should realize that the only reparation he could make would be to come back to her."

"Cur!" Jerry kicked at the pavement, "to pollute the life of a woman like Sarah with his wretched existence."

"That's how you feel," I reminded him, "but remember how all these years Sarah has felt polluted by the thought that she wasn't married to him."

"Oh, *damn!*"

"Sarah thinks, and I'm beginning to think so too, that there is something to marriage that binds besides the ceremony."

"I know." Jerry's wife had left him that summer and though he knew it was the best thing for both of them, he was trying to get her back again: "It binds of itself. If only they would tell us that in the beginning instead of putting up all this stuff about its being the law and religion. We think we can get out of it just by getting out of the law, and none of us know better until it is too late."

"People like Sarah know. They know just the way swallows know to go south in winter. You'll see; she will be happier married, not because it is pleasant but because it is right."

They were married that afternoon in our apartment, and it was not until I was settled in the hotel where I had elected to stay until I could find suitable quarters, that I realized that the chance of this marriage had accomplished for me the freedom that I had not known how to obtain for myself.

I lay awake a long time after I came from the theatre, and the mere circumstance of my being alone and in a hotel, as well as the events that led up to it, brought back to me the sense of my lover, of his being just in the next room and presently to come in to me. I felt near and warm toward him. And then I thought of Sarah and Griffin and how almost I had become the stop-gap to his affections that she dreaded most to find herself to have been. It didn't seem very real in retrospect. I shuddered away from it. Then I began to think how I had first been kindly disposed toward him, and that brought up an image of the dim corridor of the hotel where I had come to my first knowledge of such relations, and my abhorrence and terror of it. I thought of

O'Farrell and of Miss Dean, and that suspicion of sickliness which her personality had for me, and saw how it must have arisen from her consciousness of what she had done to Griffin rather than her relation to Manager O'Farrell. Then I thought of Helmeth Garrett and one night in Sienna when the moonlight poured white over the cathedral . . . and a linden tree in bloom outside the window . . . and a nightingale singing in it . . . Suddenly it was mixed up in my mind with the slanting chandelier and the tin-faced clock, and slowly a sense of unutterable stain and shame began to percolate through and through me.

Chapter 6

It is a great mistake to suppose that assertiveness is the only mannish trait taken on by successful women, nor is pliability the only feminine mark they lose. By what insensible degrees it came about I do not know, but I found myself on the peak of popularity, very much of the male propensity to be beguiled. I was willing to be played upon, and so it was skilfully done, to concede to it more than the situation had a right to claim for itself. I pulled myself up afterward, or was pulled up by the sharp rein of destiny, but for the time, while my success was new, I was aware not only of the possibility of my being handled, but of my luxuriating in it, of demanding it as the price of my favour, and in particular, of valuing Polatkin for the way in which, by my own moods, my drops and exaltations he brought me to his hand.

How much of the fact of my private life he was really acquainted with, I never knew, but he understood enough of its reaction to make even my resistances serve to push me on to the assured position of a theatre and a clientele of my own. It stood out for me as he described it, not so much as a means of dividing me from my beloved, but as a new and completer way of loving. I wanted more ways for that, space and opportunity. I wished to lay my gift down, a royal carpet for Helmeth Garrett to walk on; I would have done anything for him with it except surrender it. Not the least thing that came of my condition was the extraordinary florescence of my art.

Every night as I drew its rich and shining fabric about me I was aware of all forms and passions, the mere masquerade of our delight in one another. Every night I embroidered it anew, I adored and caressed him with my skill. Polatkin went about wringing his hands over it.

"You are a Wonder, a Wonder! And you are wasting it on them swine." That was his opinion of my support. "And to think you could have a theatre of your own, and what you like—"

"A theatre like me—*Me* spread over it, expressed, exemplified, carried out to the least detail?"

"You shall have it even in the box office!" he responded magnificently.

"How soon?"

"I will bring the plans this afternoon; I got 'em ready in case you came around." But he was much too intelligent to undertake to bind me to them at that juncture.

Things went on like this until the last week in November, then I had a telegram from Helmuth saying that he would be detained still longer. Every pulse of me had so been set to his coming on the twenty-seventh that I thought I should not be able to go on after that, I should go out like a light when the current is stopped. I had so little of him, not even a photograph, nothing but my ring and a few trinkets he had bought me in Italy. If I could have had a garment he had worn, a chair in which he had sat . . . I went round and looked at the Astor House, because he told me that he had stopped there once, years ago.

I stood that for three days and then I went down to New Rochelle where he had written me earlier, his girls were at school; not on my own account, you understand, but as a possible patron of the school on behalf of my niece, who was, if the truth must be told, less than two years old. While I was being shown about, I had Helmeth's children pointed out to me. They looked, as I had surmised, like their mother. If they had in the least resembled their father I should have snatched them to me. Everything might have turned out quite differently. They were, the principal said, nice girls and studious, but they did not look in the least like their father.

It was one of those dark, gusty days that come at the end of November, damp without rain, and of a penetrating cold. There had been a great storm at sea lately and you could hear the wash of its disturbances all along the Sound. There was no steady wind, but now and then the damp air gave a flap like an idle wing. It was like the stir in me of a formless, cold desire, not equal to the demand Life was about to make on it. As I turned into the station road after a formal inspection of the premises, I met the girls coming back from their afternoon walk with the teachers, two and two. The Garrett girls were next to the last, they were very near of an age; I waited half hidden by a tree to watch them as they passed.

They were well covered up from the weather in large blue coats with capes, and blue felt hats with butterfly bows to match at the ends of their flaxen braids. They looked like their mother . . . I couldn't see them growing up to anything that would fit with Sarah and Jerry and Polatkin. The wing of the wind shook out some gathered drops of moisture as they passed, the branches of the trees clashed softly together, and as they turned into the grounds I noticed that the older one had something in her walk that reminded me of her father.

I was pierced through with a formless jealously of the woman who had borne them in her body. I was moved, but not with the impulse to draw them to my bosom. I felt back in the place where my boy had been, for the connecting link of motherliness and failed to find it. I had had it once, that knowledge of what is good to be done for small children and the wish to do it, but it was gone from me. It was as though I might have had a hand or a claw, any prehensile organ by which such things are apprehended, and when I reached it out after Helmeth's children it was withered.

What I found in myself was the familiar attitude of the stage. I could have acted what swept through me then, I could have brought you to tears by it, but there was nothing I could do about it *but* act. I wrote Helmeth that night that I had seen the children and then I burned the letter.

He came at last. He was greatly concerned about his enterprise which was not yet established on that footing which he would like to have for it, and I think it was a relief to him to have me without the conventions and readjustments of marriage. It was tacitly understood between us that things were better as they were until that business was settled. I think he could not have had a great deal of money at the time; all that racing to and fro between London and Mexico must have cost something. His anxiety about the girls, which occasioned his sending them to the most expensive schools, and his affection for them, which led to their being carted about by their aunt to meet him occasionally at far-called places, was an additional drain.

We were very happy; there is nothing whatever to tell about it. We met in brief intervals snatched from our work and did as other lovers do. Sometimes he would come for me at the theatre —the freshness of my acting never palled on him. Other times I would find him waiting for me in the little flat I had expressly chosen and furnished to be loved in. The pricking warmth of his presence would meet me as I came up the stair. Not long ago I found myself unexpectedly in a part of the city where we used to walk because we were certain not to meet any of our friends there. There was a tiny café where we used often to dine, and the memory of it swept over me terrifyingly fresh and strong.

With all this, it was plain that we got on best when we were most alone. It was not that I did not every way like and was interested in the friends he introduced to me, outdoor men most of them, and their large-minded, capable wives. I got on with them tremendously, and found them as good for me as green food in the spring, sated as I was on the combined product of professionalism and temperament. It was chiefly that the simplicity and openness of their lives brought out for him the duplicity that lay at the bottom of ours. For it was plain that they wouldn't have understood, wouldn't have thought it necessary. They could have faced, those women, strange lands and untoward happenings, had many of them faced sterner things for the sake of their husbands, with the same courage and selflessness with which they would in my circumstances, have faced renunciation.

It was the realization of this, so much sharper in him who had seen and known, that checked and harassed Helmeth; he wished to be at one with them, to be felicitated on my success and my charm, to include me if only by implication, in that community of adventure with which these mining and engineering folk had ringed the earth. And the necessity of holding our relation down to the outward forms of friendship established on the supposition of our having grown up together, fretted him.

"It isn't honest," he broke out once after he had tried to persuade me to let him tell his friends that we were engaged. "It's all right between us; you are my wife in the sight of whatever gods there are, but that isn't what other people would call you."

"Somehow, Helmeth, so long as it is with you, I don't care much what they call me."

"Well, I care; I care a lot. You don't seem to remember you are going to be my girls' mother—sons' too, I hope. We ought to have some more children; Sanderson's got four." Sanderson had been our host at luncheon that day.

Helmeth was knocking out the ashes of his pipe on my hearthstone; he paused in the occupation of refilling it to look down at me in a moody kind of impatience that was the worst I knew of him. There was the suggestion of a cleft in his strong, square chin which came out whenever he bit hard on a difficult proposition. The play of it now was like the tiny shadow of disaster.

"I was down in old Brownlow's office the other day," he went on, "talking this Mexican scheme to him, and he had to break off in the middle of it to telephone to some chorus girl he had a date with. God! it made me hot to think of it!"

"Because I'm in the same—" He cut me off with a sound of vexation.

"Don't say it; don't even think of it! How long does this contract of yours last?"

"To the end of the season," I told him.

"Well, you chuck it just as soon as you can. I'll put this thing through somehow. We'll clear out of here." He had his pipe alight by now and began puffing more contentedly. "I don't think much of this burg anyway," he laughed as he settled himself in one of my chairs. "A man doesn't have a chance to get his feet on the ground."

There were times when he almost made me share in his distaste for it. That was when I had drawn him into the circle of my professional acquaintances which somehow shrivelled at his touch like spiders in the heat. Understand that I hold by my art, that I have poured myself a libation on that altar, that I value it above all other means of expressing the drama of man's relation to the Invisible, and that I do not think you do enough for it, prize it enough, or use it rightly. But I suppose there is a yellow streak in me, or I wouldn't sicken so as I do at what it brings to pass in the personalities by which it is most forwarded. For since it must be that art cannot be served to the world, except by a cup emptied of much that is most desirable in the recipients, it ill becomes them as long as they fatten their souls at it, to take exception to the vessel from which it is drunk. Nevertheless I used to find myself, when Helmeth was with me, sniffing at the spiritual garments of my friends for the smell of burning. I resented Mr.

258

Lawrence the most; it was not altogether for the incongruity of his possessing Sarah, her fine smudgeless personality and her lovely body, delicate and shapely as a pearl, but for the incontestable evidence he offered me of how low I had stopped. From the peak of my present prosperity, my troubles in Chicago, showed the merest accident, and the distance I had sprung away from them seemed somehow expressive of the strength with which I had sprung from all that Lawrence represented. Not all the care Sarah bestowed on him—and I think the best he could do for her was to provide her in his impaired health with an occasion for mothering—could quite distract the attention from the ineradicable mark of his cheapness.

He was as much out of key with the society in which Sarah's success and mine had placed him, as he was flattered to find himself there. It had brought out in him in the way privation had not, that touch of theatricality which intrigued Sarah's unsophisticated fancy in the first place. He let his hair grow into curls and made a mysterious and incurable pain of his broken health. And though he offered it as the best he had to offer, with humility, he suffered an accession of that devoted manner which had won his way among women of his own class, but which among the sort he met at my rooms was ridiculous. Jerry too, with his married life in dissolution, for what looked to Helmeth, and in the slight of his strong sense, was beginning to look to me like an aimless folly; out of all these blew a wind witheringly on the bloom of my happiness. We did best when we shut it out in a profound, exalted intimacy of passion.

What leads me to think that Polatkin must have watched me rather closely all this time, is the fact that he waited until Mr. Garrett was gone to London again in the latter part of February, to put it to me that if I really meant to leave the stage permanently, and it was a contingency which, in speaking to me of it, he had the wit to speak seriously, I could do no better for myself than to take flight from it from the roof of my own theatre. He put it to me in his own dialect, mixed of the green room and Jewry, that I had torn a large hole in the surrounding professional atmosphere by the vitality of my acting that winter, and that it would be a great shame to go out into the obscurity of marriage without this final pyrotechnic burst.

I could have, by his calculation, a short season to open with, and a whole year of brilliant success before—well before anything happened. I think by this time I must have known subconsciously that nothing would happen. It must be because no man naturally can imagine any more compelling business for a woman than being interested in him, that Helmeth failed to understand that he could as well have torn himself from the enterprise for which he had starved and sweated, as separate me from the final banquet of success. I had paid for it and I must eat.

We opened in May, not the best time of year for such an adventure; but I suppose Polatkin was afraid to trust me to the distractions of another vacation. It occurs to me now, though at the time I didn't suspect him, that we couldn't have opened even then if he had not been much more forward with the plan than at any time he had permitted me to guess. At the last I came near, in his estimation, to jeopardizing the whole business by opening with "The Winter's Tale" with Sarah in the part of *Hermione* and myself as *Perdita*. Jerry was writing me a new play, but in the process of breaking off a marriage that ought never to have been begun, he had found no time to complete it; but why, urged Polatkin, if we must fall back on Shakespeare, choose a part that did not introduce me to the audience until the play was half done? He stood out at least for *Juliet* or *Cleopatra*. "Why, indeed," I retorted, "have a theatre of my own if it is not to do as I please in it?" I knew however that what I could put into *Perdita* of Willesden Lake and the woods aflame, would have sustained even a more inconsiderable part.

Effie and her husband came on to my opening night. I want to say here, if I have not explicitly said it, that my sister is a wonderful, an indispensable woman. When I think of her, the mystery of how she came out of Taylorville, full-fledged to her time, is greater than the mystery of how I came to be at all. For Effie is absolutely contemporaneous. She lives squarely not only in her century, but in the particular quarter of it now going. No clutch of tradition topples her toward the generation of women past. Most women of my acquaintance are either sodden with left-over conventions, or blowsy with racing after the to-be, but Effie is compacted, tucked in, detached from but distinctly related to her background of Montecito. She was president of the Woman's Club, chairman of the book committee of the circulating library, and though she had a letter every morning and a telegram every night from the woman with whom she had left her two babies, it didn't prevent her in the week she spent with me, from getting into touch with more Forward Movements than I was aware were in operation in New York.

"But, good heavens, Effie, how can you find time for them? It's as much as I can do to attend to my own job."

"Oh, you! You're a forward movement yourself. All I am doing is herding the others up to keep step with you. You know, Olivia, I've wondered if you didn't feel lonely at times, so far ahead that you don't find anybody to line up *with*. Every time I see a woman step out of the ranks in some achievement of her own, I think, 'Now, Olivia will have company.' "

"But, heavens!" I said again. "I'm not thinking of the others at all. I don't even know that there are others, or at least who they are. I'm a squirrel in a cage. I go round because I must. I don't know what comes of it."

"I'll tell you what comes—women everywhere getting courage to live lives of their own. Do you remember what you went through in Higgleston? Well, the more women there are like you, the less there will be of that for any of them. It is the conscious movement of us all toward liberty that's going round with you." I was dashed by the breadth and brightness of her view.

"Effie," I said, "is this a new kind of toy to dangle before your intelligence to keep it from realizing it isn't getting anywhere?"

"Like the love affairs of your friends?" she came back at me promptly. "No, it isn't; it's—well, I guess it's a religion."

I believed as I dressed at the theatre that night, that it was the contagion of Effie's enthusiasm that keyed me up to a pitch that I thought I shouldn't have reached without Helmeth. I had counted so on his being there for the first night, but he was still in London, and for a week I hadn't heard from him.

I needed something then to account, as I proceeded with my part, for the extraordinary richness of power, the delicacy and precision with which I put it over line by line to my audience. I played, oh, I played! I felt the audience breathing in the pauses like the silent wood; the lights went gold and crimson and the young dreams were singing. So vivid was the mood that, when from time to time I was swept out on billows of applause before the curtain, I fancied I saw him there, leaning to me, now from a balcony, or standing unobserved in a box behind the Sandersons' and some friends of his who had pleased, on his introduction, to take a great interest in me. It was a wonderful night, flooded with the certainty of success as by a full moon; we danced under it in spirit—I believe that Polatkin kissed me; two of my young men I saw with their hands on one another's shoulders, capering in the wings as I was being drawn before the curtain again and again to bob and smile like a cuckoo out of a clock, striking the perfect hour. And through it all was the sense of my beloved, the leaf-light touch of his kiss on my cheek, the pressure of his arm, so poignant that as I came out of the theatre late with Effie and her husband, I thought I could not bear it to go back to my room and find it empty.

"Willis," I said to my brother-in-law, "you must lend me my sister to-night." I was sitting between them in the carriage, each of them holding a hand. I do not know what they were able to get of my acting, but nothing could have kept from them the knowledge of my tremendous success. I could see though, that in his excited state it wasn't going to be easy for him to spare his young wife, and that made it easier for me as we drew up in front of my door to change my mind suddenly and send her back with him. What really influenced me was the certainty that I could not bear even for Effie to disturb the sense of my lover's presence which I seemed to feel brooding over the room. I went up the steps warm with it.

I had a moment of thinking as I opened the door and found the lights turned on, that my maid had left them so in anticipation of my return, and then I saw him. He was sitting by the dying fire; he had not heard me come up the stair, for his head was in his hands. He turned then at my exclamation, and I had time, before we crossed the width of the room to one another, to think that the attitude in which I had found him and the new writing of anxiety in his face, as he turned it to me, had its source in his finding me in what looked like a permanent relation to a theatre of my own. For a moment I thought that, and then my apprehension was buried on his breast.

"Oh, my love, my love!" He held me off from him to let his eyes rove tenderly over my face, my breast, my hair. I do not know if he remembered the words he had spoken to me so long ago, or if they came spontaneously to the command of the old desire: "Oh, you beauty—you wonder. . . ."

Presently we moved to sit down, and stumbled over his bag upon the floor beside his chair. It brought me back to the miracle of his being there and to the certainly that he must have come to me direct from the steamer.

"On the *Cunarder*," he admitted, "six days and a half. O Lord!"

262

His gesture was expressive of the extreme weariness of impatience. "I came ashore with the quarantine officers. I couldn't cable. I left at two hours' notice."

It occurred to me that he must have at least come ashore before sunset, and in that case he couldn't have come straight to me. I began to feel something ominous in the presence there of his bag. His overcoat, though the evening was so warm, lay beyond him on another chair. It flashed over me in a wild way that he had come to some sudden determination—he had been at the theatre that night—he had taken my being there in that circumstance as final—perhaps he meant to abandon me to my art, to surrender me at least to its more importunate claim. He followed my thought dully from far off.

"I was at the theatre in time for your part," he said. "There wasn't a seat, but they knew me at the box office and let me in."

"Then it *was* you that I saw in the balcony, and in Sanderson's box? I thought it was a vision."

"I had business with Sanderson." He turned back to what was beginning to make itself felt through his profound preoccupation, the charm of my presence. "There was that in your acting to night that would have evoked visions," he smiled. "I had them myself." I knelt down on the floor beside his knees.

"Helmeth, tell me," I begged. He began to stroke my face with his hand.

"It doesn't seem so bad as it did a few moments ago, and yet it is bad enough. I must leave for Mexico in an hour."

"Leave me?" I was still, in my mind, occupied with what now began to seem a monstrous disloyalty to him, my obligation to Polatkin. There had been a great deal about our new venture on the programme, even if he hadn't seen the papers, he must have learned it as soon as he came into the theatre.

"Unless you can go with me in an hour . . . yes, my dear, I know it is impossible. . . ." He was silent a while, clasping and unclasping my hand on his knee, knitting his brows and staring into the fire with the expression of a man so long occupied with anxiety that his mind, in any moment of release, goes back to it automatically. I stirred presently when I saw that his perplexity had nothing to do with me. "I had a cable in London," he said. "Heaven only knows how long they were getting it down to the coast where they could send it; they have struck water in the mines." I failed to get the force of the announcement except that from the manner of his telling it, it was a great disaster. "I must leave on the

263

twelve twenty-three," he warned me. I did understand that.

"Oh, no, *no!* Helmeth!" I cried out. "Not now . . . not so soon!" I clung to him crying. "Stay with me to-night . . . just for to-night!" We rocked in one another's arms. I remember little broken snatches of explanation.

"I've worked *so,* Olivia . . . I've worked and sweated . . . and now. . . ." Presently he broke out again. "To have worked, and know that your work is sound, and to be played a trick, to lose by a ghastly trick! If there is a God, Olivia, why does He play tricks on a man like that?"

"Hush, my dear! Oh, my dear . . ."

"Do you know what I've been doing since I came ashore? I've been buying pumps, Olivia, pumps, and machinery to work them. Think of the delay; and I'll have to ask Shane for more money . . . more . . . and I meant to be paying dividends." He held me off from him fiercely with both hands. "Olivia, suppose to-night instead of applause you had heard hisses, and people going out, turning their backs on you in your best lines . . . oh . . ." He broke off and covered his face with his hands. I crept up to him.

"If they had, I should have come back to you, beloved. And I shouldn't have remembered it. Oh, beloved, what are all things worth except that they give us this?" I was on his knee now, and my hair was still in its maiden snood as it had been in the play. I drew it softly about his face.

"Oh, my dear, to be *this* to me, what does it matter about the mines? They will come straight again in a little time. But this . . . this is *now*. I could feel the yielding in his frame. He was my man and I did what I would with him.

Chapter 7

Among all the devices with which we confound the Powers forever fumbling at our lives, none must puzzle them more than the set of obligations and interactions that go by the name of business. Unless, indeed, there is a god of business, which I doubt.

Past all misguiding of our youth, past all time and distance and unlikelihood, the god who would be worshipped most by the welding of spirit into spirit, had brought us two together only to be rived apart by the necessity which tied us each, not only to our own, but to other people's means of making a living. The two or three hours following on Helmeth's announcement of the accident which had, who knows but at the instance of the Power which was bent upon uniting us, shattered the point of his attachment to the Mexican scheme, we spent in that drowning realization of the source of being and delight for each in the other, which is the process and the end of loving. And then the withdrawing of whole electric constellations from the city skyline and the clatter of the morning traffic in the street, and the dispersing blueness, let in with them the considerations which whipped us apart.

If there is a god of business he is of a superior subtlety, for even then we proposed to one another that the best way of being quit of the obligation was to serve our time to it; and it was in pursuance of some such idea that I found myself, toward the latter part of June, going out to Los Angeles to meet Mr. Garrett who would by that time, have come up the coast from Mazatplan to make purchases of supplies. I should have gone much farther than that merely to have touch with him, the warm pressure of his hand, his voice at my ear; all my dreams even, were tinged by the loss out of my life of his bodily presence. It was a singular flame-touched circumstance that the assured success of my new venture set up in me a fiercer need.

There had not been time for much in his letters but accounts of his struggle with conditions at the mine and his slow conquest of the water that flooded all the lower levels, of disheartening, incompetent labour and the multiplied difficulty of distance from any base of supplies. But that little was all timed to our meeting again. "I will explain all that when I see you," "We will talk of that later," were phrases that cropped out in his letters many times. I did not know, even in the act of going there, just what he expected to bring to pass in our affairs by my being in Los Angeles. I only know that I wanted desperately to see him.

One thing I gathered from his letters, that in the preoccupation and haste of his stay in New York he had wholly missed the significance of my new entanglement with Morris Polatkin. I have to suppose, to account for his never having any other conception of what my work was to me, that he had never known a professional woman or one who worked at anything except as a stopgap between the inconsequence of youth and marriage. He felt himself, humbly, rather a poor substitute for the colour, the excitement and gayety of my career—why should so many people suppose that an actress's life is gay—but he balanced that with what he meant to purchase for me by his own achievement. He had, without thinking it necessary to account for it, the idea that is so generally and unexcusedly entertained that I am sometimes hypnotized into thinking it must be the right one, that a woman in becoming a man's wife ceases to be her own and becomes somehow mysteriously and inevitably his. It was not that in all our talk about it, he had any conclusions about the stage as an unsuitable profession for women, but that he was inherently unable to think of it as possible for his wife. We were saved from dispute by the proof I had had in Italy that his inability to think of me as having a life apart, arose chiefly in his need of me, which had in it something of the absolute quality of a child's need of its mother. I am glad now, in view of all that came of it, that I was spared the bitterness of not seeing, in his inability to accept the finality of my relation to my work, anything nobler than an insufferable male egotism.

I have thought since, that we might have made more of our love, if we had but seen somewhere in the world the process of its being so made; if we could have moved for a time in a footing of intimacy among other pairs who had produced out of as unlikely material, a competent and satisfying frame of life. We did not know any but theatrical people among whom the wife had interests apart from her husband. That is where Taylorville betrayed us. And now you know what I meant when I said in the beginning that the social ideal, in which I was bred, is the villain of my plot; for we wished sincerely for the best, and the best that we knew was cast only in one mould. I have begun to think indeed, that this, more than anything else, accounts for the personal disaster which waits so often on the heels of genius, that we assume it to be the inalienable condition. For genius tends to spring from that stratum of society for which, when it has come to its full flower, it is most unfit, and it comes up slanting and aside like a blade of grass under a potsherd of the broken mould of unrelated ideals. Somewhere there must have been men and women working out our situation and working it out successfully, but the only example of life afforded us was not of the acceptable pattern. Still my agreement with Mr. Garrett, that it was after all *the* pattern, saved us from mutual accusation and recrimination.

Concerned as I was to make the most and the best of him, I kept looking out all the way after the train struck into the southwest, for every intimation of the life there which would have helped me to get at the springs of his behavior, and was by turns shocked away from its bleakness and drawn with a rush of sympathy toward what a man must endure to live in it. If I saw myself as he had sometimes sketched me, filling its bleak and unprofitable reaches with my gift as with flame and flower, I was as many times shudderingly brought face to face with the question as to where, in the wilderness, I was to find wherewithal to go on burning. At Los Angeles, a town of which I heard him speak as a place with a spirit with which he was in sympathy, I had nothing to look at for a week but a great deal of rather formless, wooden architecture expressing nothing so much as the attempt to reconcile Taylorvillian tastes and perceptions with a subtropical opportunity.

I do not know what that city may have become since I visited it, but at the time it was notable for a disposition to take the amplitude of its pretension for performance. Its theatrical season, if it had any, had dwindled to that execrable sort of entertainment which comes up in any community like a weed when the women are out of town; and if there had been anybody I knew there, I should have been debarred from making myself known to them until I had seen Mr. Garrett and learned his plans. I took to spending my time as far out of town as I could manage, and by degrees a strange, seductive beauty began to make itself felt with me, a large, unabashed kind of beauty that disdained prettiness and dared to dispense with charm. It was a land ribbed and sinewed with all I had set my hand to, making free with it as kings do with their dignity, and the moment Helmeth came, before the warmth of renewal had its way with us, I saw that the land had set its mark on him.

He was thinner, his manner hurried, obsessed. There are times, no doubt, when loving must be set aside for the sterner business of living, but it wasn't what I had come to Los Angeles for. I was flushed with success, I had spread the crest of my femininity, I was prepared to be adorable, enchanting; and I found that what was expected of me, was to sit by in my room in the hotel on the chance of his having time for me between the exigencies of buying cogwheels and iron piping. He was so tired at times that I was made to feel that my demand upon him for the

267

lover's attitude was an additional harassment. And there was so little else I could do for him! Not that I wouldn't have been glad to have done him a wifely service, laid out his clothes and seen to it that he had his meals regularly, but what I could do was subservient to the necessity of keeping our relation secret. It struck witheringly on all my sweet illusion of what I could be to him, to have it so brought home to me that the uses of affection are largely dependent on the habit of living together.

"At any rate," I said, consoling myself for his scant hours with me, "we shall have all day Sunday together. Helmeth, you don't mean to say—" something curiously like embarrassment suffused him.

"I shall have to spend most of Sunday at Pasadena . . . at the Howards' . . . the girls are there, you know." I didn't know, and the circumstance of its having been kept from me smacked of offence. Why, since I had been good enough to come all this distance to comfort him with loving, had he not explained to me that I must share him with the children; . . . why not have at least included me in a community of interest with them?

"I thought," he extenuated, "that the girls were the chief obstacle to your marrying me; that you might get to feel differently about them if you didn't have them thrust too much upon you."

"Oh, Helmeth!" I began to imagine a perversity in his avoidance of the main issue. "It isn't the girls—it isn't anything of yours, it is something of mine. It is my art you aren't willing for me to bring into the family with me."

"It is because, then, I'm not accustomed to think of the stage as being the sort of thing that belongs in a family. I thought you agreed with me about that?"

He had me there; if I had seen a way to separate all that I loved in my art, from all that was most objectionable in the practice of it, I should have married him and trusted to carrying my point afterward. I had a vision of Helmeth's girls overhearing Polatkin advising me about the fit of my corsets, and me calling him Poly. I came back on another path to my recently awakened resentment.

"Just the same you ought to have told me. Mrs. Howard is Miss Stanley's sister, isn't she?"

"They don't live together." He had answered my unspoken question, as though the ideas that were forming in my head had been in juxtaposition in his own before. "Miss Stanley and the young brother—you remember him at Cadenabbia?—live at the old place. She has been a mother to him."

"Ah," I couldn't forbear to suggest, "and she's mothering your children now."

"Good heavens, Olivia! you are not jealous, are you?"

"Yes, I am," I told him. "I'm jealous of every minute you spend away from me. I'm jealous of the men you do business with, men who can talk with you, hear your voice. Oh, my dear, my dear—" I put my hands up to his shoulders and cried a little upon his breast, his arms were about me; for me all time and place dissolved only to keep them there.

"Look here, Olivia, if you feel this way, let us go and be married to-day and then we can spend Sunday all together. I did not mean to urge you just now; things are pretty rough with me; it will be a year or two before I can straighten them out, but, after all, I guess our feelings count for something."

"I couldn't," I protested, "you don't understand; there's Polatkin and Jerry; he has written this play for me, we are all tied up together; you know how it would be if any of your partners should withdraw."

"A woman has no business to be tied up to any man but her husband—" he broke out, "think of any other man being able to tell my wife what she should or shouldn't do!" We went over that ground again until we ceased from sheer exhaustion.

It came to this at last, that he proposed that I should marry him at once; I could go back to Mexico with him. I hadn't to begin rehearsals until September; we could have the summer together and then I could go back to my work until he could claim me.

For a wild moment I yielded to the suggestion . . . if I could have him and my art . . . but I hope I am not altogether a cad. I saw what all his efforts could not keep me from seeing, that even to do that for me, to get me into his place in Mexico and back again would be a tax on him, and to ask him to do it with a reservation in my mind would be more than I would stand for.

"It isn't fair, Helmeth, my letting you think that anything could pull me away from the stage. It isn't that I don't agree with you about how a husband and wife ought to be with one another, nor that I am not entirely of the opinion that the atmosphere of the stage is not the place to bring up children the way you want yours brought up; it is because not even the kind of marriage you offer me would hold me."

"You mean that you'd leave me? That you'd go back to it?"

"Well, why not? I left my first husband. I know that wasn't the way it seemed to me then, but that's what it amounted to . . . and he fell in love with the village dressmaker." I had never told him that part of my life; I had never thought of it in the terms in which I had just stated it, I saw him grow slowly white under the sun-brown of his skin.

"I see . . . if your only idea in staying with me is that I might — Good God, Olivia, do you know what you've said to me?"

"Nothing except what is right for you to know. Do you remember, Helmeth, what I told you Mark Eversley called me?"

"A Woman of Genius; I remember." He was looking at me now as though the phrase were a sort of acid test which brought out in me traits unsuspected before.

"Well, then, I'm those two things, a woman and a genius, and the woman was meant for you; don't think I don't know that and am not proud of it with every fibre of my brain and body. I should have been glad once; if it were possible I'd be glad now to have kept your house and borne your children, and see to it that they brushed their teeth and had hair ribbons to match their clothes."

"Their mother thought that was important." He snatched at this as at an incontestable evidence of my being all that I was trying to show him that I was not.

"It *is* important . . . I remember to this day the effect on me of my hair ribbons—" He broke in eagerly.

"If you can see that . . . if you understand what their mother wanted . . . things I missed out of my life through having no mother, that I've heard you say you missed partly out of yours . . . birthdays and Christmas and good chances to marry when they grow up—"

"I do understand, Helmeth, but what I'm trying to tell you is that I can't go through with it. Those are the things that belong to the woman, that it takes all the woman's time to do the way their mother would have them done, and for me the woman has been swamped in the genius. Oh, I don't say that I'm not a better actress for having tried so long to be merely a woman, for being able even now, to know all that you mean when you say 'woman'; but there it is. I am an actress and I can't leave off being one just by saying so."

"And I can't leave off being a proper father to my girls. I owe them the things we've been talking about just as I owe them a

270

living. I suppose I should have married for their sakes, supposing I could get anybody to have me, even if I hadn't found you. And I don't want finding you to mean anything but the best to them." I had nothing to say to that, and he went back to a thought that had often been between us. "We ought to have married when we were young," he insisted as though somehow that made a better case of it, "if you hadn't begun you wouldn't have been called on to leave it off."

"The point is that it won't leave *me*. Genius—I don't know what it is except that it is nothing to be conceited about because you can't help it—isn't a thing you can pick up or lay down at your pleasure; it's a possession."

I could see that he didn't altogether follow me, that he was not very far removed, and that only by his admiration for me, from the Taylorvillian idea that to speak of yourself as a genius was to pay yourself an unwarrantable compliment, and that the most I could get him to understand of the meaning of my work, was what grew out of his being a most competent workman himself. He went back to the original proposition.

"Does that mean, then, that you are not going to marry me?"

"It means that I'm not going to leave the stage to do it."

"It seems to me to mean that you don't love me as you have professed to. Oh, I know how women love . . . good women."

"Helmeth!"

"I beg your pardon, Olivia." We stood aghast at what we had brought upon ourselves; across the breach of dissension we rushed together with effacing passion. After all, I believe I should have gone with him if he had had the wit to know that the point at which a woman is most prepared for yielding is the next instant after she has just stated the insuperable objection. Whether he knew or not, the whole of his outer attention was taken up with the purchase of pump fittings.

Understand that I didn't for a moment suppose that I had lost him, that I didn't believe anything but that I could go to him at any moment if the whim seized me, that I couldn't in reason pull him back if the need of him arose. I finished out my vacation at resorts up and down the California coast, warm with the certainty that I should see him in New York the next winter.

Chapter 8

The next season was a brilliant one, made so by the strength of
my wanting him, and by the sense of completeness and finality
which came to me out of the faith that we had been ordained to
be lovers from the beginning. It began to seem, in the fashion in
which we had been brought together as boy and girl and then
mated in ways which, creditable as they had been, yet offered no
obstacle to the freshness and vitality of our passion, that we had
been guided by that intelligence which in any emergency of my
gift, I felt rush to save it. That I had been prevented from any
absorbing interest until it had grown and flowered in me, appeared now to have come about by direct manipulation of the
Powers. I had curious and interesting adventures that winter in
the farthest unexplored territory of the artistic consciousness,
which tempt me at every turn to put by my story for the purpose
of making them plain to you, and I am only deterred from it by
the certainty that you couldn't get it plain in any case.

A few days ago I picked up a copy of Dante and found myself
convicted of shallowness in never having taken his passion for the
cold-blooded Beatrice seriously, by finding the evidence of its
absolute quality in the circle within circle of his hells and paradi-
sos, the rhythm of aches and exaltations. And if you couldn't get
that from Dante, how much less from anything I might have to
say to you. After all these years I do not know what is the relation
of Art to Passion, but I have experienced it. If I said anything it
would be by way of persuading you that loving is not an end in
itself, but the pull upward to our native heaven, which is no
hymn-book heaven, but a world of the Spirit wherein things are
made and remade and called good.

What I made out of it at that time was the material of a satisfying success, and though I got on without him much better than
I could have expected, the fact that after all, he did not get any
nearer to me than the Pacific coast, had its effect in the year's
adventures.

That I missed my lover infinitely, that I was thinned in the body by the sheer want of him, that I had moments of mad resolve, of passionate self-abandoning cry to him, goes without saying. One need not in a certain society, say more of love than that one has it, to be understood as well as if one displayed a yellow ribbon in the company of Orangemen, but since I couldn't say it, an opinion passed current among my friends that I was working too hard and in need of a holiday. It came around at last to Polatkin himself noticing it, though I believe with a better understanding of the reason why I should be restless and sleepless eyed. It was just after I had heard from Helmeth that he couldn't possibly hope to be in New York for another year, that my manager suggested that it might be good business policy for me to play a short tour in three or four of the leading cities, a strictly limited season which would be enough to whet the public appetite without satisfying it.

"What cities?"

I believe that I jumped at it in the hope somehow that it might be stretched to include Los Angeles, where Helmeth was at that moment, and where I felt sure he would come to me. When I learned, however, that nothing was contemplated farther west than Chicago, I lost interest. That very day I had a telegram:

"Will you marry me?
    "Signed: GARRETT."

It was dated at Los Angeles, and as I could think of no reason for this urgency, I concluded that it must be because the association there with the idea of me, had been too much for him, and in that new yielding of mine to the beguiling circumstance, I was disposed to interpret it as evidence that he was coming round. I wired back:

"If you marry my work.
    "OLIVIA."

and prepared myself for the renewal of that dear struggle which, if it got us no further, at least involved us in coil upon coil of emotion, making him by the very force he spent on it, more completely mine. I expected him in every knock on the door, every foot on the stair, and had he come to me then, would no doubt have provoked him to that traditional conquest which, as

273

it has its root in a situation made, affected for the express purpose of provocation, is the worst possible basis for a successful marriage.

On the day on which at the earliest, I could have expected him from Los Angeles, I sent my maid away in order that, if I should find him there in the old place waiting for me, there should be no constraint on the drama of assault and surrender for which I found myself primed.

Then by degrees it began to grow plain to me that he did not mean to come, that the question and my answer to it, had carried some sort of finality to his mind that was not apparent to mine. By the time I had a letter from him, written at the mine, with no reference in it to what had passed so recently between us, I understood that he would not ask me to marry him again. He had accepted the situation of being my lover merely, and I was not any more to be vexed by the alternative. I said to myself that it was better to have it resolved with so little pain, and that it should be my part to see that what we were to one another was to yield its proper fruit of happiness. I found myself at a loss, however, in the application; for though you may have satisfied yourself of the moral propriety of dispensing with the convention of publicity, you cannot very well, with a week's journey between you, get forward in the business of making a man happy. About this time Jerry began to be anxious about what I couldn't prevent showing in my face, the wasting evidence of love divided from its natural use of loving.

"You'll break down altogether," he expostulated, "and then where will I be?" He was tremendously interested in his new play, which was by far the best thing he had done, and in the process of getting it to the public he had so identified it with my interpretation that he was no longer able to think of the one without the other. There had come into his manner a new solicitude very pleasing to me, born of his sense of possession in me, in as much as I was the lovely lady of his play, and a sort of awe of all that I put into it that transcended his own notion and yet was so integral a part of it. It had brought him out of his old acceptance of me as a foil and relief for the shallow iridescence that other women produced in him. He had begun to have for me a little of that calculating tenderness with which a man might regard the mother of his nursing child. Night by night then as he came hovering about me he could not fail to observe, though he could hardly have understood it, the wearing hunger with which I came from my work, pushed on by it to more and more desperate need of loving, and drawn back by its unrelenting grip from the artistic ruin in which the satisfaction of that hunger would involve me. Now at his very natural expression of concern, I felt myself unaccountably irritated.

"Jerry," I demanded of him, "would it matter so much if we left off altogether writing plays and playing them? *What* would it matter?"

"You are in a bad way if you've begun to question that! What does living matter? We are here and we have to go on."

"Yes, but when we go on at such pains? Is there any more behind us than there is behind a ball when it is set rolling? Are we aimed at anything?"

"Oh, Lord, Olivia, what has that got to do with it?" He was sitting in my most commodious chair with his long knees crossed to prop up a manuscript from which he was reading me the notes of a tragedy he was about to undertake, and his quills were almost erect with the tweaking he had given them in the process of arriving at his climax. It was a curious fact that the breaking off of his marriage, which in the nature of the case could not be broken off sharp but had writhed and frayed him like the twisting of a green stick, by setting Jerry free for those light adventures of the affections which had been so largely responsible for the rupture of his domestic relations, instead of multiplying his propensity by his opportunity, had landed him on a plane of self-realization in which they were no longer needful. The poet in Jerry would never be able to resist the attraction of youth and freshness, but the man in him was forever and unassailably beyond their reach. I was never more convinced of this than when he turned on this occasion from the preoccupation of his creative mood, to offer whatever his point of attachment life had provided him, to bridge across the chasm of my spirit.

"I don't see why it is important that we should know what we are working for; we might, in our confounded egotism, not approve of it, we might even think we could improve on the pattern. I write plays and you act them and a bee makes honey. I suppose there's a beekeeper about, but that's none of our business."

"Ah, if we could only be sure of that—if He would only make himself manifest; that's what I'm looking for, just a hint of what He's trying to do with us."

"Well, I can tell you: He'll smoke you out of New York and into a sanitarium, if you don't know enough to take a change and a rest."

"Poly wants me to go on the road for a while; sort of triumphal progress. He thinks applause will cure me."

"You're getting that now. What would bring you around would be a good frost."

"You wouldn't want that in Chicago?" Jerry disentangled his limbs and sat up sniffing the wind of success.

"If I could have you to open with my play in Chicago," he averred solemnly, "I'd be ready to sing the Lord Dismiss Us." He really thought so. To go back to the scene of his early struggle with his laurels fresh on him, to satisfy the predictions of his earliest friends and confound his detractors, above all to be received in his own country with that honour which is denied to prophets, seemed to him then almost as desirable in prospect as it proved in fact not to be. I found another advantage in the confusion and excitement of touring, in being able to conceal from myself that I hadn't had a satisfactory letter from Helmeth since the pair of telegrams that passed between us, and no letter at all for a long time. It was always possible to pretend to myself that the letters had been written but were delayed in forwarding.

It was a raw spring day when we came to Chicago, the promise of the season in the sun, denied and flouted by the wind. It slanted the tails of the labouring teams and cast over the clean furrow, handfuls of the winter rubbish from the stubble yet unturned, and between field and field it wrung the tops of the leafless wood. Now and then it parted them on white painted spires without disturbing them or the rows of thin white gravestones. It laid bare the roots of my life to the cold blasts of memory, it rendered me again the pagan touch, the undivided part that the earth had in me. My dead were in its sod, in me the sap of its spiritual fervours and renunciations. What was I, what was my art but the flower, the bright, exotic blossom borne upon its topmost bough, its dying top; here in its abounding villages, in the deep-rutted county roads was the root and trunk. Outside, the wind flicked the landscape like the screen of the moving picture that the swift roll of the train made of it, and I felt again the pressure of my small son upon my arm, and the pleasant stir of domesticity and the return of my man. For the last hour Jerry had come to sit in my compartment, opposite me, and stare stonily out of the window; now and then his jaws relaxed and set again as he bit hard upon the bitter end of experience. No one, I suppose, can go through that country so teeming with the evidences of the common life, the common labour, the common hope of immortality, and not feel bereft in as much as the circumstances of his destiny divided him from it. We passed Higgleston; beyond the roofs of it the elms that marked the cemetery road, gathered green. The roofs of the town were steeped in windy light. I had no impulse to stop there. I withdrew from it as one does from a private affair upon which he has stumbled unaware. Rather it was not I who withdrew, but Life as it was lived there, turned its back upon me.

Getting in to Chicago through that smoky wooden wilderness, within which the city obscures itself as a cuttlefish in its own inky cloud, I felt again the wounding and affront, the cold shoulder lifted on my needs, the eager hand stretched out to catch my contribution. Chicago received me with its hat off, bowing to meet me, and when I remembered how nearly it had let me fall into the pit prepared for me by Griffin and the "Flim Flams," I burned with resentment.

It was seven years now since I had seen the city or Pauline, the only friend I had made there who could be supposed to take an interest in my coming again. I meant of course to see Pauline; we had kept up a correspondence which with the years had shown a disposition to confine itself to a Christmas reminder, and an occasional marked copy of a magazine, but I meant, of course, to see her. I had trusted to her finding out through the newspapers that I would be there and on such a date. It fell in quite naturally with my inclination, to have her card sent up to me the next morning a little after eleven. I was needing to be distracted. On my way up from breakfast I had met Jerry going down with his suit case.

"Back to New York," he admitted to my question, "as quick as I can get there."

"But with all this success . . . why, they fairly stood on their feet last night."

"I know, I know," he looked unendurably harassed. "I can't stand it, Olivia, I can't stand it. This place is full of ghosts." I remembered that both his children had been born there and that he had not seen them for more than a year, and I did not press him.

"I'll keep your end up for a week if I can," I assured him as he wrung my hand. He turned back when he was a step or two down the stair.

"Don't stay too long yourself," he admonished. "New York's the place."

I was feeling that when Pauline came to me. It wasn't until I saw her that I realized what a distance there was—in spite of our common youth, had always been—between us. It started out for us both in the first glimpse we had of one another, in the witness in all the inconsiderable elements of line and colour which go to make up a woman's appearance, of growth and amplitude in me and fulfilment in hers. Pauline had been in her girlhood, if not pretty, at least what is known as an attractive girl, and though there was only a matter of months between us, it came to me with a shock that she was now, not only not particularly attractive, but middle-aged. It was not so much in the fulness under her chin which apparently caused her no uneasiness, nor in the thickness of her waist, of which I was sure she made a virtue, but in the certainty that all that was ever to happen to her in the way of illuminating and self-forgetting passion, had already happened.

She had reached, she must have reached about the time I was taking my flight upward by the help of Morris Polatkin, the full level of her capacity to experience. She was living still, as I saw by the card which I still held in my hand, in Evanston, and she was living there because it was no longer within the scope of her possibility to live anywhere else. All this flashed through me in the moment in which Pauline, checked by what she was able to guess of unfamiliar elements in me, was crossing the room and taking me by the hands in the old womanly way, keyed down to the certainty of not requiring it in her business any more. It was so patent that Pauline was now in the position of having done her duty toward life and Henry Mills, and was accepting all that came to her from it as her due, that it almost seemed for a moment that she had said something of the kind. What did pass between us besides a kiss of greeting, were some commonplaces about my being there and how pleased Henry and the children would be to see me. We sat down on a sofa together and for a moment the old girlish confidence put forth a tender spring of renewal.

"So many years since we were at school together! You've gone a long way since then, Olivia."

278

"A long way," I admitted, but she didn't catch the double meaning the phrase had for me.

"Henry and I were talking about it this morning. And the times you had here in Chicago, you poor dear; you had to make a good many starts before you got on the right road at last."

"A great many."

"But you found out that it all came right in the end, didn't you? That it was best just for you to trust . . . you used to be bitter about it . . . but trusting is always best."

"Oh, if you think I've been trusting all these years . . . I've been working."

"Of course, *of* course." Much of her old manner came back with the occasion for moralizing. "But you were too amusing, you were quite fierce with Henry because he wouldn't do anything about it." She laughed reminiscently. "And now, you see. . . ." Her look travelled about the rose-coloured room, full of the evidence of prosperity.

"Pauline," I said, "if you are thinking that I could have gone to New York and become the success I am, *without* the help that you and Henry might have given me, you are making a great mistake. What did happen was that I had to accept it from a quarter where it wasn't so much to be expected, and was not nearly so agreeable."

"That man Mark Eversley found for you, you mean. Well, I suppose you did get on better for a little start."

"Start!" I cried. "Start! I had to have everything—food and clothes." A sudden recollection flashed upon me of those first days in New York, of myself become merely a dummy on which to hang a fat little Jew's notions of acceptable contours; the offence of it; the greater offence from which by the opportune appearance of the Jew I had so hardly escaped.

"Have you any idea, Pauline, what it means to have a man invest money in you? . . . a man like Polatkin. I was his property, a horse he had entered for the race. He had a stake on me . . ."

Pauline looked aghast; vague recollections of the actress heroines of fiction shaped her thought.

"You don't mean to say, Olivia, that you—that you were—"

"His mistress," I finished for her bluntly. "Is that the only thing your imagination takes offence at? Isn't it enough for me to tell you that he orders my corsets for me?" That did reach her.

279

I could see her struggle with the habitual effort to put the unwelcome fact down, anywhere out of sight and knowledge, under the cotton wool of a moral sentiment. Even now if she could escape being implicated in my predicament by avoiding the knowledge of it, she would not only do that but convict herself of superiority as well. My gorge rose against it.

"But if I didn't sell myself to the Jew," I drove it home to her, "it was chiefly because he was decenter to me than the circumstance gave me a right to expect. I came near doing it for a cheaper man and for a cheaper price, a man who had deserted one wife, and . . . a bigamist in fact. If you don't know that there were days when I would have sold myself for something to eat, it was because you didn't take the pains to."

"But you never said a word. Of course if you had told me the truth . . ." she floundered and saved herself on what she believed to be a just resentment, but I had no notion of letting her off so easily. I did not know exactly how we had got launched on the subject, it had not been in my mind to do so when she came in, but all the events of the past year seemed to lead up to it, to come somehow to the point of rupture against her smooth acceptance of my success as being derived from the same process as her own.

"I did tell you that I was in need of money to put me in the way of earning a living," I insisted. "I did not ask you for charity; what I offered you was the chance of a business investment, one that rendered the investor its due return. The fact that you did not know enough about the business to know how good it was"—I forestalled what I saw rising to her lips—"had nothing to do with it. You were my friend and professed to admire my talent; I had a right to have what I said about it heard respectfully." I had got up from the pink and white sofa where our talk had begun, and was trailing about the room in my breakfast gown, and the suggestion of staginess in the way the folds of it followed my movements, irritated me with the certainty that the effect of it on Pauline would be to mitigate the sincerity of what I said.

"You'd known me long enough," I accused her, "to know that I wouldn't have asked for money until I was in the last extremity, and then I wouldn't have asked it for myself. I don't know that it would have mattered if I had starved, but my Gift was worth saving."

"I didn't dream . . ." she began. "I hadn't any idea . . ."

"Well, why didn't you ask Henry, then? Henry knows what

becomes of women on the stage when they can't make a living."
This was nearer to the mark than I had meant to let myself go,
but I could see that it carried no illumination. She drew up her
wrap and braced herself for one more gallant effort.

"The things you've been through, my dear . . . I don't wonder
you feel bitter. But when it has all come out right, why not forget
it?"

"Oh, right! Right!"

The room was full of vases and floral tokens of the triumph of
the night before, and as I swung about with my arms out, disdain-
ing her judgment of rightness for me, I knocked over a great
basket of roses and orchids which had come from Cline and
Erskine. I don't suppose Pauline had ever knocked over anything
in her life, and the violence of my gesture must have stood for
some unloosening of the bonds of convention, with an implication which only now began to work through to her.

"You don't mean to say, Olivia, that you . . . that you are not
. . . not a good woman?"

"Oh," I said again, "good . . . good . . . what does it all mean?
I'm a successful actress."

"Olivia!"

"Well, no, if you insist on knowing, I'm not what you would call
a good woman." I threw it at her as though it had been a peculiar
kind of scorn heaped up on her for being what I had just denied
myself to be. I saw myself for once with all my thwarted and
misspent instincts toward the proper destiny of women, en-
meshed and crippled, not by any propensity for sinning, but by
the conditions of loving which women like Pauline set up for me.
"And if you want to know," I said, "why I'm not a good woman,
it is because women like you don't make it seem particularly
worth while."

"Oh," she gasped, "this is horrible . . . horrible!" The word
came out in a whisper. I saw at last that she was done with me,
that the only thought that was left to her was to get away, to put
as much space as possible between us. I got around with my hand
on the door to prevent her.

"Pauline, Pauline!" I cried almost wildly, as if even at the last
she could have helped me from myself. "Can't you remember
that we grew up together, that we had the same training, the same
ideals? Can't you remember that when we began I thought that
the life you had chosen for yourself was the best, that I thought

281

I had chosen it for myself too? Only—for heaven's sake, Pauline, try to understand me—there is something that chooses for us. Don't you know that I wouldn't have been any different from what you are if I hadn't been forced? Haven't you seen how I've been beaten back from all that I tried to be? All this"—I threw out my arms, as I stood against the door, to include all that had entered by implication in our conversation—"it had to come, and it came wrong because you won't understand that a Gift has its own way with us."

I could see, though, that she wasn't understanding in the least, that she was badly scared and even indignant at being forced to listen to a justification of what, by her code, could have no justification. She was standing not far from me, crushed against the wall, as though by the weight of opprobriousness that I heaped upon her, and her whole attention was centred on the door and the chance of getting out of it and away from what, in the mere despair of reaching her intelligence with it, I flung out from me now wildly.

"I suppose," I scoffed, "that it never occurs to you that a gifted woman could be as delicate and feminine as anybody, if only you didn't make her right to fostering care and protection conditional on her giving up her gift altogether. You," I demanded, "who tie up all the moral values of living to your own little set of behaviours, what right have you to deny us the opportunity to be loved honestly because you can't at the same time make us over into replicas of yourselves?"

I was sick with all the shames and struggles of the women I had known. I forgot the door and went over to her.

"You," I said, "who fatten your moral superiority on the best of all we produce, how do you suppose you are going to make us value the standards you set up, when the price you despise us for paying, nine times out of ten we pay to the men who belong to you? What right have you to judge what we have done when you've neither help nor understanding to offer us in the doing? What right . . . what right?" For the moment I had turned away in the vehemence of my indignation; I was pacing up and down. In the instant when my attention was distracted from the door, Pauline made a dart for it. I could hear her scurrying down the hall, but I went on walking up and down in my room and talking aloud to her. I was beside myself with the sum of all indignities. Was it not this set of prejudices which for the moment had presented itself in the person of Pauline Mills, which at every turn of my life had been erected against the bourgeoning of my gift? Was it not in the process of combating the tradition of the preciousness of women as inherent in particular occupations, that I had lost the inestimable preciousness of myself? Was it for what came out of Pauline's frame of life—I thought of Cecelia Brune here—that I had sacrificed my public possession of the man I loved. And what came out of it that was more to the world than what I had to offer? Had I cut myself off from the comfort and stability of a home, simply because in my situation as famous tragedienne I didn't see my way to bring up Helmeth's children so as to make little Pauline Millses of them? I was still raging formlessly in this fashion when Miss Summers, our ingénue, came to tell me that the cab waited to take us to the theatre for the matinée.

All through the performance, which I was told went remarkably well, I was conscious of nothing but the seismic shudders and upheavals of my world too long subjected to strain. It came back on me in intervals through the evening performance; I was physically sick with it. But by degrees through its subsidence, new worlds began to rise. By the time I left the theatre that night I knew what I would do.

It had been a mistake, a natural but cruel mistake, for Helmeth and me to suppose that a way of living could at any time be worth the very sap and source of life. Love was the central fact around which all modes and occupations should arrange themselves. Let us but love then, and live as we may. In all the world there was no need like the need I had for his breast, his arm.

Always the point of our conclusions had been that I agreed with him, that I *had* thought that failing to repeat the pattern of their mother in his children, I had failed in all, that I didn't any more than he see my way to keeping on with my work and meeting him at the door every night when he came home, in the sort of garment that, in the ladies' journals, went by the name of house gown. I laughed to think that we had not seen before that it was ridiculous. I had no more doubt now, no more trepidation. What burned in me was so clear a flame that he could not but be illuminated. Only let me find him, let me go to him again. At the hotel desk where I paused for my key I asked them to send up telegraph blanks to my room. With them came letters forwarded from New York. I started, as one does at an unexpected presence, to find an envelope among them with his familiar superscription. For the first time I would rather not have had a letter from him; it would be interposing a fresher picture between me and my new resolution, to put him for the moment farther from me.

I saw then that the letter in my hand had been posted at Los Angeles; it was as though he had leaped suddenly all that distance nearer than his Chilicojote, Mexico. I noticed that it was a very thin letter. A thousand conjectures rushed upon me, not one of them with any relativity to what I would find, for when I tore it open there floated out a printed slip. It was a clipping from a Pasadena newspaper and announced his engagement to Edith Stanley.

Chapter 9

There is very little more to write. I held myself together until I had written to Helmeth to say that I understood why he had done what he had done, and that I hoped he would be happy. The letter was not written to invite an answer; there was nothing he could say to please me that would not have been disloyal to Miss Stanley. Accordingly no answer came, though it was a long time before I gave over the unconscious start at the sight of letters, the hope that somehow against all reason . . . sometimes even yet. . . .

For I did not understand. I was married to him, much, much more married than I had ever been to Tommy Bettersworth, and it wasn't in me to understand how any man can take a woman as he had taken me, and not feel himself more bound than ever church and state could bind him. It was ten months since I had seen him, but that while my body still ached with the memory of him, he could have given himself to another woman, was an unbelievable offence. There are days yet when I do not believe it.

There was nothing any of my friends could do for me. I had the sense to see that and did not trouble them. Sarah, who was the only one who might have comforted me out of her own experience, was all taken up with her husband's declining health.

Mr. Lawrence died the next winter, and by that time my wound had got past the imperative need of speech. Effie was expecting another baby and wasn't to be thought of, so I turned at last, when the first sharp anguish was past, to Mark Eversley. He in all America stood for that high identification of his work with the source of power, that it is the private study of all my days to reach. I repaired to him as did Christians of old to favoured altars. That I did so return for comfort to that Distributor of Gifts by whose very mark on me I was set apart from the happier destiny, was evidence to me, the only evidence I could have at the time, that I had not been utterly mistaken in the choice I had made before I knew all that the choice involved. Eversley and his wife were Christian Scientists, and, though they did not make me of their opinion, I owe them much in the way of practice and example that keeps me still within the circle of communicating fire. I reestablished, never to be broken off again, practical intercourse with the Friends of the Soul of Man. I learned to apply directly for the things I had supposed came only by loving, and I found that they came abundantly. I grew in time even, to think of Helmeth without bitterness. What I was brought to see, over and above the wish to provide a home for his children, must have been at work in him, was much the same thing that had driven me to my work; the very need of me must have hurried him into the relief of being loved. It was the only way which his purblind male instinct pointed him, to find an outlet for what goes from me over the footlights night by night. For a man, to be loved is of the greatest importance, but with women it is loving that is the fructifying act.

That I was able to go on loving him was, I suppose, the reason why the shock I had sustained left no regrettable mark upon my career. The mark it left on me was none other than work is supposed to leave on every woman. What I am sure of now is that it is not work, but the loss of love that leaves her impoverished of feminine graces. I grew barren of manner and was reputed to be entirely absorbed in my profession. It was not, however, that I had excluded the more human interests, but they had taken flight. All the forces of my being had been by the shock of loss, dropped into some subterranean pit, where they ran on underground and watered the choicest product of my art. If I had married Helmeth Garrett, I might have grown insensible to him, as it was I seemed to have been fixed, though by pain, in the fruitful relation. The loss of him, the desperate ache, the start of memory, are just as good materials to build an artistic success upon as the joy of having. And I did build. I gathered up and wrought into the structure of my life the pain of loving as well as its delight. I am a successful actress. Whatever else has happened to me, I am at least a success.

I never saw him again. I never saw Henry and Pauline Mills but once, and some bitterness in the occasion, came near to driving me toward that pit into which Pauline was willing to believe I had already descended. It was the second season after I had parted from her in Chicago, that some sort of brokers' convention had brought Henry on to New York and Pauline with him, and to the same hotel where Mark Eversley was shut up with an attack of bronchitis. Jerry and I, going up to call on him, came face to face with them.

They were walking in the lobby. Pauline was in what for her, was evening dress, her manner a little daunted, not quite carrying it off with the air of being established at the pivot of existence which she could manage so well at Evanston. They were walking up and down, waiting, it seemed, for friends to join them, and they wheeled under the great chandelier just in time to come squarely across us. I could see Pauline clutch at her husband's arm, and the catch in her breath with which she jerked herself back from the impulse to nod, and looked deliberately away from me. For her, the evidence of my misdoing hung about me like an exhalation. She was afraid I should insist on speaking to her and some of her friends would come up and see me doing it. I didn't, however, offer to speak to her, I looked instead at Henry. I stood still in my tracks and looked at him steadily and curiously. I wished very much to know what he meant to do about it. He turned slowly as I looked, from deep red to mottled purple, and very much against his will his head bowed to me; his body, to which Pauline clung, dared not move lest she detect it, but quite above and independent of his smooth-vested, self-indulgent front, his head bowed to me. So went out of my life thirty years of intimacy which never succeeded in being intimate.

But though one may excise thirty years of one's past without a tremor, one may not do it without a scar. To allay the irritation of Pauline's slight, I came near to being as abandoned as she believed, as I had moments of believing myself. For the possibility that Helmeth Garrett had found in our relation of setting it aside, made it at times of a cheapness which seemed to extend

286

to me who had entertained it. I should have been happier, I thought, to have taken it lightly as he did. If so many women who had begun as I had begun, had gone on repeating the particular instance, wasn't it because they found that that was the easiest, the only possible way to bear it? How else could one ease the pain of loving except by being loved again? And if I was to lose the Pauline Millses of the world by what had been entered upon so sincerely, why, then, what more had I to risk on the light adventure? All this time I was sick with the need of being confirmed in my faith in myself as a person worthy to be loved, to feel sure that since my love had missed its mark, it wasn't I at least that had fallen short of it.

It was that summer Jerry had been driven by some such need I imagined, as I admitted in myself, to put his future in jeopardy by another marriage which on the face of it, offered even a more immediate occasion for shipwreck than the first, and I hadn't scrupled to put forth to save him, and the new capacity to charm which had come upon me with the experience of not caring any more myself to be charmed. I knew; it would have been a poor tribute to my skill as an actress if I hadn't by this time known, the moves by which a man who is susceptible of being played upon at all, can be drawn into a personal interest; and though I didn't then, and do not now believe that a love serviceable for the uses of living together, can be built up out of "made" love, I was willing for the time to pit myself against the game that was played by Miss Chichester for Jerry's peace of mind. I played it all the better for not being, as the young lady was, personally involved in the stake. That I thought afterward of doing anything for myself with what I had got, when at last I had by this means brought Jerry down from Newport to my place on the Hudson for a week end, was in part due to the extraordinary charm that Jerry displayed under the stimulus of a male interest in me, of whom for years he had thought of as being quite outside such consideration. There was a kind of wistfulness about Jerry when he was a little in love, that made him irresistible; no doubt I was also a little warmed by the fire which I had blown up.

He was to come from Saturday to Monday, and the moment I saw him getting down from the dogcart I had sent to the station for him, I knew that I had only to let that interest take its course, to find myself provided with a lover, whether or no I could command my heart to loving. I do not remember that I came to any conscious decision about it, but I know that I yielded myself to the growing sense of intimacy, that I consciously drew, as one draws perfume from a flower, all that came to me from him: his new loverliness, touched still with the old solicitous sense of the preciousness of my gift. I dramatized to the full the possibility of what hung in the air between us, I dressed myself, I set the stage accordingly.

It was Saturday evening after dinner that I sent him to the garden to smoke, keeping the house long enough to fix his attention on my joining him, by wondering what kept me, and so overdid my part by just so much as I made myself conscious of the taint of theatricality. For as I went down the veranda steps to meet him in the rose walk, the response of the actress in me to the perfectness of the setting and my fitness for the part of the great lady of romance, drew up out of my past a faint reminder of myself going up another pair of stairs so many years ago in the figure of an orphan child toiling through the world. Out of that memory there distilled presently a cold dew over all my purpose.

It was a perfect night, warm emanations from the earth shut in the smell of the garden, and light airs from the river stirred the full-leafed trees. At the bottom of the lawn the soft, full rush, of the Hudson made a stir like the hurrying pulse. Beyond the silver gleam of its waters, lay the farther bank strewn with primrose-coloured lights, and above that the moon, low and full-orbed and golden. Its diffusing light mixed and mingled with the shadow of the moving boughs. I was wearing about my shoulders a light scarf that from time to time blew out with the wind, and as we paced in the garden strayed across Jerry's breast and was caught back by me, but not before on its communicating thread, ran an electric spark. It must have been a good two hours after moonrise before we turned to go in, where the great hall lamp burned with a steady rose-red glow.

At the foot of the veranda a breeze sprang up fresher than before, that caught my scarf from me and wrapped us both in it as in a warm, suffusing mood. We were so close that I had instinctively to put up my hand as a barricade against what was about to come from him to me, and as I did so I was aware of something that rose up from some subterranean crypt in me . . . that old romance of my mother's . . . women like her, worlds of patient, overworking women who could do without happiness if only they found themselves doing right. Somehow they had laid on me, the necessity of being true to the best I had known, because it was the best and had been founded in integrity and stayed on renunciations. I knew what I had come into the garden to do. I had planned for it. I thought myself prepared to take up, as many women of my profession did, the next best in place of the best which life had denied me, but my past was too strong for me. The unslumbering instinct that saves wild creatures before they are well awake, had whipped me out of the soft entanglement, and before Jerry could grasp the change of mood in me, I was halfway up the stair.

"This wind," I said, "I think it will blow up a rain before morning." I went on up before him. "You can see the river darkling below its surface, it does that before a change." I went on drawing the chairs back from the edge of the veranda, I called Elsa to fasten all the windows. When at last we came into the glow of the hall lamp, I could see his face white yet with what he had missed; he thought he had blundered. He caught at my hand as I gave him his bedroom candle in an effort to recapture what had just trembled in the air between us.

"Olivia! I say . . . Olivia!"

"Your train leaves at nine-thirty," I reminded him. "I'll be up to pour your coffee."

I went into my room and blew out my candle. The warm summer air came in between the white curtains. I knelt down beside my bed; an old habit, long discontinued. I was too much moved to pray, but I continued to kneel there a long time listening to the soft shouldering of the maples against the wall outside the window. Far within me there was something which inarticulately knew that whatever the world might think of me, in spite of what I had confessed to Pauline, I was a good woman; I had loved Helmeth Garrett with the kind of love by which the world is saved. Past all loss and forsaking, past loneliness and longing, there was something which had stirred in me which would never waken to a lighter occasion; and whether great love like that is the best thing that can happen to us or the most unusual, it had placed me forever beyond the reach of futility and cheapness.

All this was several years ago. Jerry and I are the best of friends and I am far too busy a woman to miss out of my life anything Pauline Mills could have contributed to it. Besides, I am very much taken up with my nieces and nephews. Forester's oldest boy shows a credible talent for the stage, and I have him at school here where I can watch him. I shall try him out on the road next summer. Effie's husband is in the legislature now, and Effie looks to see him governor. I am very fond of my sister; we grow together. I owe it to her to have found ways of making things easier for women who must tread my path of work and loneliness. It is partly at her suggestion that I have written this book, for Effie is very much of the opinion that the world would like to go right if somebody would only show it how. Sarah also added her word.

"It is the fact of your telling, whether they believe you or not, of your not being ashamed to tell, that is going to help them," she insists. "At any rate it will help other women to speak out what they think, unashamed. Most women are not thinking at all what they are very willing to be thought of as thinking."

I am the more disposed to take their word for it, since as they are both happy, they cannot be supposed to have the fillip of discontent. Sarah left the stage a year after Mr. Lawrence's death, to marry a banker from Troy, and she has never regretted it. She calls her oldest girl Olivia. It is the sane and sympathetic contact with the common destiny, which I get at her house and my sister's that keeps me from the resort of successive and inconsequent passions, such as fill the void in the lives of too many women who are under the necessity of producing daily the materials of fire. But you must not understand me to blame women for taking that path when so many are closed to them. Haven't they been told immemorially that loving is their proper function, their only one?

Last year I walked in a suffrage parade because Effie wrote me that it was my duty, and the swing of it, the banners flying, the proud music, set gates wide for me on fields of new, inspiring experience . . . all the paths that lead to the Shining Destiny . . . why shouldn't women walk in them? I should think some of them might lead less frequently to bramble and morass.

"And after all," said Jerry, a day or two ago when I had read him some pages of my book, "you have only told your own story, you haven't found out why all the rest of us run so afoul of personal disaster. We, I mean, who as you say, nourish the world toward the larger expectation."

"And after all," said I, "what is an artist but a specialist in human experience, and how can we find out how the world is made except by falling afoul of it?"

"If when we fall we didn't pull the others down with us! I'm willing to learn, but why should others have to pay so heavily for my schooling? Where's the justice in making us so that we can't do without loving and then not let us be happy in it?"

"I don't believe it is the loving that is wrong; it is the other things that are tied up with it and taken for granted must go with loving, that we can get on with."

"Marriage, you mean?"

"Not exactly . . . living in one place and by a particular pattern . . . thinking that *because* you are married you have to leave off this and take up that which you wouldn't think of doing for any other reason."

"You mean . . . I know," he nodded; "my wife was always wanting me to do this and that, on the ground that it was what married people ought, and I couldn't see where it led or why it was important. But what if it should turn out that the others are wrong and we are right about it?"

"Oh, I think we are *all* wrong. People like us are after the truth of life, and marriage is the one thing that society won't take the trouble to learn the truth about. My baby, you know, I lost him because I didn't know how to take care of him, and there was nobody at hand who knew much more than I. But Effie's last baby came before its time and they saved it by science, by knowing what and how. Why can't there be a right way like that about marriage, and somebody to discover it?"

"Then where would we come in—after it was all found out— if we are the experimentors?"

"Oh, there'd be other fields. Why shouldn't it be that when we have found out our relation to the physical world—we are finding it, you know, radioactivity and laws of falling bodies—go on finding out the law of our relations to one another? And, when we've found that out, then there's all the Heavenly Host. We'd have to find out how to get on with Them."

"And in the meantime we are spoiling a lot of people's lives because we can't get on with one another—" He broke off suddenly. "My wife is married again. I don't know if I told you."

"Ah, then, you haven't quite spoiled her life; she has another

291

chance. And the children?" He had been very fond of them, I knew.

"I haven't done so much with my own life that I'd insist on controlling theirs."

"You've done wonders," I assured him. "Jerry, honest, do you mind it so much, not having a wife and family?"

"Oh, Lord, yes, Olivia; I need a wife the same as a man needs a watch, to keep the time of life for me." He faced me with a swift, sharp scrutiny. "Honest, do you mind?"

"Sometimes," I admitted, "when I think of what's coming . . . when I can't act any more."

"You'll be leading them all still when you are seventy. You do better every season." He threw away his cigar and came and stood before me, preening his raven's wing which now had a little streak of white in it. "Olivia, what's the matter with you and me being married? We get on like everything."

"There's more to it than that, Jerry."

"Being in love, you mean? Well, I don't know that I would stick at a little thing like that." He was looking down at me with an effect of humour which I was glad to see covered a real anxiety about my answer. "I've been in love lots of times; I've been mad about several women. I don't feel that way about you, and I don't know that I care to. But if wanting you is loving, if worrying about you when you aren't quite up to yourself, and being proud of you when you are, if liking to be with you and wanting to read my manuscripts to you the minute I've written them, if owing you more than I owe any other woman and being glad to owe it, is loving you, why, I guess I love you enough for all practical purposes."

"What would Tottie Lockwood say—or is it Dottie?" Miss Lockwood was Jerry's latest interest at the Winter Garden.

"Oh, *she*? She isn't in a position to say anything. It's only vanity on her part and the lack of anything to do on mine. There'd be no time for Totties if you married me."

"Jerry . . . since you've asked me . . . I suppose you know that I . . . that I . . ." He put up an arresting hand.

"I've guessed. There isn't anything you need to tell me. And I haven't an altogether clean record myself. But, I want you to know, Olivia, that there was never anything in my case that you could take exception to so long as my wife was with me. I

292

couldn't make her believe it but it's true. Except, of course, that I was a fool. I hope I'm done with that."

"I'd want you to be a bit foolish about me, Jerry,—that is, if I make up my mind to it." I had to defend myself against the encouragement he got out of my admission. "But, Jerry, when did you begin to think about—what you've just said?"

"About marrying you? Ever since that time I went down to your place . . . when that Chichester girl . . . ."

"When I wouldn't take her place, a *pis aller* merely. Well, suppose I had; suppose I had been . . . what the Chichester girl wouldn't . . . would you still have wanted to marry me?" I would not admit to myself why I had asked that question.

"I don't know, Olivia . . . men, don't you know, not often . . . but I want to marry you now. I want it greatly." I held him off still, trying to get my own experience in shape where I could leave it behind me.

"Such affairs never turn out well, do they?"

"Hardly ever, I believe."

"Unless you turn them into marriage," I hazarded.

"You know," he conjectured, "I've a notion that the kind of loving that goes to making such affairs, can't be turned into marriage very easily. It's a kind of subconscious knowledge of their unfitness that keeps us from turning them into marriage in the first place."

"I wonder."

He let me be for the moment revolving many things in my mind.

"It wouldn't be the vision and the dream, Jerry. You and I—"

"Well, what of it? It might be something better. Something neither of us ever had, really. It would be company."

"No, I've never had it." I remembered how blank the issue of my work had been to Helmeth Garrett.

"Well, then, . . . we have years of work in us yet. I'll buy Polatkin out of the theatre." He was going off at a tangent of what we might do together, but I had thought of something more pertinent.

"We might solve the problem of how to keep our art and still be happy."

"We might." He was looking down on me with great content,

293

but quite soberly. "Tell me, Olivia suppose we shouldn't, even with the unhappiness, with all you have been through, would you rather be what you are, or like the others?" We were silent as we thought back across the years together; there was very little by this time that we did not know of one another.

"No," I said at last, "if being different meant being like the others, I'd not choose to have it any different."

THE END

Afterword

Mary Austin (1868–1934) was a remarkable member of a revolutionary generation of American women. Born in Carlinville, Illinois in the aftermath of the Civil War and raised in a Methodist church-going household against which she rebelled, Austin joined her today better-known contemporaries Jane Addams, Charlotte Perkins Gilman, and Willa Cather in the first tide of career-minded new women to pull at the shores of middle-class convention.[1]

Typically from small towns and often the first women in their families to obtain the higher education their mothers could only dream of, in the last decades of the nineteenth century many of these new women migrated to the larger cities where a foothold in business and the professions might be attempted. Far from a silent tide, they left behind autobiographical accounts of their struggles and relations, both with the domestic culture they parted from and the professional world they entered. And although these economically independent, often single, publicly productive, and generally optimistic women constitute a significant demographic and political reality, their existence in the fiction of the Progressive Era is usually mirrored with one or another characteristic warp. In what might be called the "new woman" adventure story, high-spirited, untroubled, and thoroughly modern heroines accomplish almost by formula whatever they set out to do. In the darker tales, personal frustration and loneliness are the price of success, or death the punishment for failure: cheerful bachelor maids, rebels, and Patience Sparhawk *(Patience Sparhawk and Her Times)* on the one hand; Carrie Meeber *(Sister Carrie)*, Lily Bart *(The House of Mirth)*, and Edna Pontillier *(The Awakening)* on the other.[2]

Both kinds of fiction—whether considered popular or serious, whether written by women or by men—tend to present pictures of the new woman at odds with the portraits the women themselves painted in the autobiographical writings that look back to the turn of the century and earlier. Of course, the relationships of fiction to reality and reality to autobiography are always complex. In literature, Willa Cather noted, "success is never so interesting as struggle," a retrospective judgment she passed on her own study of the developing woman artist, the opera singer Thea Kronberg in *The Song of the Lark* (1915),[3] a novel directly influenced by the publication three years before of *A Woman of Genius,* and, like Austin's book, an exception to the rule that in major fiction disillusion and failure are somehow more aesthetic and culturally correct for women than self-fulfillment and triumph, unless, of course, the triumph is marriage.

Writing in the first person, the new woman often spoke to the obstacles that delayed fulfillment but had the understandable desire to smooth the lines of struggle, resolve the conflicts, and turn a firmly satisfied and accomplished face toward the world whose prejudices against aspiring women and their preferred radical social and economic reforms she knew only too well— whether the new woman autobiographer was Charlotte Perkins Gilman or Emma Goldman or Edith Wharton or Mary Austin herself. Some of the writers who buried their anger and bitterness in autobiographical retrospect had earlier bared their anguish at the cultural and emotional entrapments of women in their personal correspondence, as Goldman did, or in such chilling stories as Gilman's tale of marriage and madness, "The Yellow Wallpaper," and in the early fiction of Edith Wharton and Mary Austin. Such literary documents complement the public records these women left and enrich the complex institutional and personal history of a turbulent era.

A Woman of Genius (1912) partakes of the cultural complexity of social ideas and people in transition and deploys elements of both autobiography and fiction. As literature it is the rare reflection of a phenomenon we know occurred more frequently in the life of the period and subsequently: the woman who says no to men and conventional marriage and yes to living and productive work. Far from simply promoting female self-determination, however, or celebrating the romantic right of genius to overrun all obstacles, including the human ones, the novel articulates the conflicts of a transitional generation of women who relinquished the perquisites of protected, genteel womanhood for the rewards and responsibilities of the pursuit of public achievement and service to the community. The novel bears close enough relation to the inner and outer contours of Austin's life to be termed autobiographical. Yet the story departs from the life in ways that illumine both the life and the writing and the context out of which each evolved.

Long out of print and the full text available since 1977 only in an expensive hardcover edition,[4] *A Woman of Genius* is, like Austin herself, an overlooked classic of feminism. Olivia Lattimore occupies a pivotal position in the long procession of gifted women in literature. Restoring her to the classical fictional heroines available to teachers and the general reader should advance Austin's reputation as a significant contributor to feminist analysis as well.

The Career and Reputation

Mary Austin recalled as a child wanting to write "all kinds of books."[5] Indeed she succeeded. She was responsible for some 250 periodical pieces and published over 30 volumes in a variety of literary and expository forms that ranged from history, anthropology, and the natural sciences, to metaphysics, culture, and the arts.[6] She commented on most of the important social and political questions of the day. Though she was heralded in her own time as an original American woman of letters, within a few years of her death she had been virtually forgotten, her work reduced to scattered footnotes in the histories written by subsequent generations, and her life became the subject of derisive antecdotes elaborating upon her foibles. Why, despite her impressive productivity and former acclaim, Austin is less familiar today than some of her contemporaries who also wrote realistically about the new woman—people like Theodore Dreiser, Sinclair Lewis, Ellen Glasgow, and Willa Cather—is suggested in the broad outlines of her career and style. In some respects her obscurity is representative and speaks to the devaluation of feminist writers when publishers no longer seek the "women's point of view."[7] In other respects her neglect is simply the result of shifting literary and ideological patterns of her own and subsequent times.

In a decade when many new women were graduating from college and heading for the cities, Austin went to the frontier. In the summer of 1888, just shy of her twentieth birthday and recently graduated from Blackburn College, the then Mary Hunter traveled by train with her widowed mother and younger brother from the fertile prairie of southern Illinois to join her older brother homesteading in the high desert country of southern California. Descendants of generations of pioneers, the family was leaving behind the established but opportunity-saturated townlife typical of the period for what would prove the arid promise of ranching on the frontier. Years later the mature woman recalled her younger self's relative indifference to setting forth on the family adventure. Her particular future lay in teaching school. For that, she reasoned, one state seemed as likely as another. In any case, she was biding her time until she could, in the new parlance of the era, establish her "career" as a writer.[8]

In an article sent back to her college journal the following winter, she describes with an élan calculated to impress her sedentary Midwest reader the final stage of the journey, the hundred-mile trek on horseback and in covered wagon from Pasadena to the eastern slopes of the Sierras, north of the Mojave Desert. The assured style and sweeping observations of the dramatic scene testify to the young woman's determination to make of herself a notable writer. The change of residence provided her with a terrain, a cast of characters, ways of life, and (eventually) a literary movement strikingly different from what she had encountered in her schooldays' reading—she once characterized a piece of juvenilia as "sired by Edgar Allen Poe upon [Augusta Evans], with Ralph Waldo Emerson at the baptismal font"[9]—or for that matter in her hometown of Carlinville. Teaching would become an unhappy, interim means of support, first for herself and then, after her marriage in 1891, for her frequently improvident husband and their severely retarded daughter. In the meantime, her determination unshadowed by intimations of future trials and incompatibilities, she was beginning to fill a ten-cent black notebook with the kinds of careful sketches of the nature, personalities, and folkways of the region that appear in her first and most popular book, *The Land of Little Rain,* published in 1903 under her married name, Mary Austin.

Income from that book and subsequent stories allowed her to buy land in Carmel, which in 1906 made Austin one of the first settlers in that seacoast bohemia of artists and writers with whom she is often identified to the exclusion of other associations and contexts. There she sought the intellectual companionship, shared interest in craft, physical and mental health, and unencumbered space and time for writing that the economically hard-pressed and lonely life in the small towns of Owens Valley, California, where she had mainly lived for fifteen years ill afforded. There too she sought to uncover and express the passionate sexuality that had been buried in her marriage—a revolutionary gesture in an era in which sexual desire was still not generally acknowledged in women much less talked about in fiction.

Earlier in the 1890s, Austin had made several forays to San Francisco and Los Angeles, seeking like-minded folk who could help her develop as a writer. At that time she believed that domestic life and a career were compatible. As she wryly notes in *Earth Horizon,* never having met a living writer, she had found no one to tell her differently. Traveling to Oakland soon after her marriage, she sought out Ina Coolbrith, poet, librarian, editor, and friend to young writers, who showed her how to prepare a manuscript for submission and was helpful in placing Austin's first two stories in *The Overland Monthly.* Later, in 1899, taking with her the six-year-old daughter whose care, always distressing to Austin, had become increasingly burdensome, Austin began a trial leaving of her marriage, the mismatched dimensions of which she captured in the portrait of Olivia and Tommy Bettersworth. In Los Angeles she found a position lecturing on western nature study at the Normal School and established close contact with Eve and Charles Lummis, the flamboyant editor of *Land of Sunshine,* and the circle of writers and radicals he mentored.

In her early stories and novels, Austin drew her subject matter from her own, at times mystical contact with the land and the miners, herders, desperados, entrepeneurs, Mexicans, and Indians who moved across it. In particular she studied and participated in the life of the Paiutes whose spiritual practices she emulated and whose women she identified with, and wrote about as artists and guardians of the community. She collected stories and legends, and created some of her own. She considered herself a maverick, one cut out from the herd. And, indeed, the townspeople considered her an oddity. But until she made contact with other writers and scholars, she had no way of knowing that her interests and even her personality were part of a larger movement of fiercely individualistic western populists. Ardent advocates of the scenic wonders of California, they saw themselves as pioneers in creating a new regional literature that celebrated the land and indigenous cultures, protested their depredation and exploitation, and promoted the egalitarian social values and unconventional life-styles they tried to live, sometimes with disastrous consequences. Explicitly and implicitly, such figures as Edwin Markam, Joaquin Miller, Hamlin Garland, Ina Coolbrith, and Charles Lummis thumbed their noses at the mores, subjects, and styles of the eastern literary establishment. Undoubtedly in their openness and heartiness they were more hospitable to the importunings of a fledgling writer like Austin than might have been the case in a more formal milieu, especially since from all accounts Austin presented herself with a difficult combination of bumptiousness and insecurity. Austin, however, also set her sights on cracking the eastern periodicals with her western material, which she did at the turn of the century with publications in the *Atlantic Monthly* and *St. Nicholas,* and she read Henry James, at least as a theorist of realism.

It was in this formative stage that Austin met and felt deeply drawn to Charlotte Perkins Gilman, whose pioneering work of theory, *Women and Economics,* had just been published (1898). It might well have been from Gilman, the first of her own generation of public feminists Austin had encountered, that Austin learned of Olive Schreiner, whose passionate *The Story of an African Farm* (1883) both found an essential text of feminism, and whose tragic Lyndall should be counted as one of Olivia Lattimore's foremothers. Austin was attracted to Gilman's ideas on reorganizing the domestic realm to liberate women, which paralleled and fed her own. She also sympathized with Gilman's divorce and her decision to leave her daughter to the care of others —a prospect Austin would face soon enough in institutionalizing her own daughter. Gilman recalls that Austin defended her against the charges of unnatural motherhood that dogged Gilman on the lecture circuit. The association between the two women remained fruitful for years.[10]

Even after Los Angeles, Austin's line to Carmel and freedom was not straight. She returned to Owens Valley to attempt a reconciliation with her husband Wallace that failed. In this period she pleased the miners but scandalized the Methodists by organizing and acting in a community theater group that performed Shakespeare, an experience she utilized in *A Woman of Genius.* Austin continued to write and to sell, and remained politically active on behalf of her old love, the Indians, and her new cause, the small ranchers and their losing battle to retain the area's water resources for their own and not Los Angeles's use. Long considered eccentric by family and neighbors, Austin found few in her community who understood her or her off-again on-again domestic arrangements.

When Austin joined Jack London, George Sterling, Jimmy Hopper, and their assorted visitors in Carmel, she was close to forty, heavyset in appearance, socially awkward, and apparently as unprepared as Olivia for the amorous politics of her new sylvan world. The official logic of the Carmelites claimed grand passions necessary to the poetic inspiration of the male. And although Austin's sense of the mysteriously "intertwined roots" of sensuality and creativity form a part of her study of Olivia, her politics on the subject are quite clear: love may enhance performance, but is no substitute for talent and hard work and may, for women, subvert both if it comes at the wrong time.

Austin's experience of the professional cum sexual relations of the group is partly summed up in "Frustrate,"[11] published in 1912 and a companion piece to *A Woman of Genius*. In the short story, an unprepossessing, middle-aged woman leaves an indifferent husband to find inspiration and self-definition among a colony of authors and painters whom she supposes will understand and respond to her needs. She soon discovers that the men require a comely appearance and feminine charm for their attention. They also mistake her eagerness for aggression. Just before returning home in defeat, she is noticed by a same-aged "writer woman" who seems respected by the men who read their manuscripts to her in corners but never ask out for a walk or take to watch the moon over the water. The female writer offers advice: "It is the whole art of putting yourself into your appearance. I have too much waist for that sort of thing. I have my own game." The seasoned warrior does not share the particulars of her "game" with the inexperienced player, but Austin's division of herself into the ordinary woman of blighted hopes and the extraordinary woman who rises above her vulnerabilities becomes thematic in the fiction of the middle period and emblematic of the life, even as the analysis of women's fear of rejection becomes a cornerstone in Austin's thinking about the causes of women's subjugation.

Whatever else was going on, including recurrent bouts with the pain of suspected breast cancer and a depression that appear in the fiction as metaphors of waste and burning, Austin wrote

301

steadily at Carmel and her work brought her enough income to permit, between 1908 and 1910, travel in Europe and residence in London. There she met H.G. Wells, who praised her work, and there too she renewed associations with her old California acquaintance Lou Henry Hoover (to whom she dedicated *A Woman of Genius*) and Herbert Hoover, at that time a prosperous and highly respected mining engineer and owner. The Hoovers introduced Austin to the assorted literary and publishing figures they thought could advance her career. (In the novel, Austin erased such indications of support in painting Olivia to heighten the rugged lines of her development as an artist.) In this period too Austin became active on behalf of suffrage, observing, however, with some perturbation the antagonism raised by the direct-action tactics of the Pankhursts and preferring on the whole the more intellectual approach to reform of the Fabians and the company of the literary lights of the Lyceum.

Something of the classic American-in-Europe quality of Austin's sojourn is expressed in the romantic summer of *A Woman of Genius*. And although Austin seems to have had at least one romantic escort of the road, she also pursued her own studies of Italian landscape and art, which she used in later writing, and the Catholic mystical practices she credited with her recovery from the cancer she was certain she had developed back in Carmel. Inez Haynes Irwin, herself on the way to becoming known as a writer and feminist, provides a vignette of Austin at this time that indicates her growing confidence and attraction for others. Irwin had admired "The Walking Woman" (1909), the tale of a soulmate partnership in love and work that also brought Austin to Wells's attention and provided the entrée for meeting Joseph Conrad. She was eager to meet Austin, and pleased to find her dressed in brilliant scarlet, her Norse-blonde hair coiled in thick braids atop her head, the "picturesque" and voluble center of the pension they were both staying at in Florence. One day, correcting book proofs, Irwin was approached by Austin for what Irwin later recalled as "one of the most pleasant, writing book talks I have ever experienced."[12]

Clearly Austin was beginning to receive the recognition she deserved after years of lonely struggle and to enjoy her life. That some of the praise came couched in language that implied condescensions to gender and subject did not faze her. She remembered with pride that H.G. Wells told her no woman in England

302

or Europe wrote like her (he mistakenly assumed that the Indian walking woman of the lost borders who bore her lover's child without demanding a permanent commitment was a personal endorsement) and Conrad said that "he never knew a woman to write so well," a remark Austin reported with satisfaction to her editor.[13] One of her admirers proved helpful in having Austin's first play *The Arrow Maker* (1911) produced in New York where Austin moved the same year to establish an East Coast base in the heart of the publishing center upon which the key contacts of her career would depend.

In New York Austin wrote *A Woman of Genius,* apparently while renewing her Carmel acquaintance with the utopian muckraker journalist Lincoln Steffens, who had earned a measure of fame for his *The Shame of the Cities.* According to an entry in a journal Austin kept at the time, Steffens challenged her to learn the ways of the city as thoroughly as she had the desert, a difficult assignment but one that ultimately provided her with a wealth of material for her social criticism. Although biographers term their affair "evanescent," Austin did not view it in that light. The memory of her first fully equal relationship remained with her for over a decade and became the subject of an intense, even obsessive analysis of the social parasite she called the love-grafter, the radical whose treatment of women contradicted his egalitarian rhetoric, a sexual-political theme women on the Left raised again in the 1930s and 1960s. Undoubtedly the sense of euphoria followed by the pain of betrayal that appears in *A Woman of Genius* owes something to the Austin/Steffens affair. But aside from the fact that the fictional Garrett and the real Steffens both smoked cigars and neither relationship ended in marriage, Austin drew her characters to reveal a far more generic point: the absence of models for combining two careers with a common domestic life, even as a new ideology and alignment of the sexes was emerging at the turn of the century.

Living in New York off and on from 1911 until 1925 (when Austin built a permanent home in Santa Fe) proved something of a compromise between necessity and desire. In New York Austin knew the "movers and shakers," in fact met many of them first through the gatherings of Mabel Dodge Luhan who later befriended her at a critical time in New Mexico. She also picketed, paraded, observed, criticized, and worked for such reforms as removing the restrictions against hiring married women as public school teachers (an issue she recalled from her own difficulty teaching as a married woman in California), birth control (which she considered the single most significant conquest of her time) and, during World War I, community gardens, kitchens, and canneries to conserve resources and free women to work at the jobs opened up by the war. (Austin's position on the American involvement was mixed. She called herself a "constructive pacifist" who distrusted war as a strategy of peace. Yet she belonged to a league of writers who favored preparedness and resigned from the Women's Peace Party over their position that peace was a women's special interest issue.) However, for all the sparks, even conflagrations of people, ideas, and events in the urban environment—for all the Emma Goldman, Big Bill Haywood, Max Eastman, and Elizabeth Gurley Flynn she knew and theories of capital and labor she heard debated—Austin increasingly felt cut off from the spiritual spareness and physical freedom she enjoyed in the West and cut off too from the agrarian-based life, people, and politics she understood the best. Particularly in the early days Austin found herself living on the margins of poverty, unable to afford even a bouquet of flowers to cheer her up while she wrote. At one point she took odd jobs —shop clerk, typist, manufacturer of artificial flowers in a factory —supposedly to learn the ways of the city but also to earn money. Sometimes she received healthy advances from her publishers, but her financial status was always precarious. In the later years of her decade in New York she suffered from the pressures of chronic overwork as she cranked out the articles she termed "glittery" intellectual exercises that drained creativity and diverted energy from what she considered her more personal and original work. Still, in 1922 she was honored by her publishers, editors, and fellow writers as an original American woman of letters with a testimonial dinner at the National Arts Club, where she delivered an address on the contribution such women writers as Harriet Beecher Stowe, Edith Wharton, and Zona Gale had made to the development of a pluralistic American literature based on their interpretation of the American experience in the home.

During this period she traveled to the West Coast when she could and, after the war, to England where she lectured in the Fabian Summer School and interviewed writers for publication. One of her interviews was with May Sinclair with whom she found

304

much in common, later recommending Sinclair's *Mary Olivier* along with the novels of Sarah Grand and Dorothy Richardson as works attesting to women's struggle to free themselves from family obligations and to use their talents on their own behalf and not for the advancement of brothers, husbands, or lovers. (This theme appears also in *A Woman of Genius* and Austin recalls in *Earth Horizon* how many professional women of her generation spoke to this issue.) While Austin continued to publish regularly, her fiction did not sell well, and she had to compete for assignments in the still more difficult magazine market. Increasingly, she relied on the lecture circuit to make ends meet.

In the post-war years, Austin began the process of relocating in the Southwest. She was drawn to the region by the promise of a new relationship that she celebrated in a poem entitled "Love Coming Late" and by the friendship of Mabel Dodge who had moved to Taos and begun her association with Tony Luhan. Austin seems to have often been disappointed in her intimate relationships. Long estranged from her husband she felt both freed and abandoned when Wallace sued her for divorce in 1914 on grounds of desertion. Similarly, though she had not seen her daughter for years, Austin grieved deeply at the news of her death in 1918. Relations with other family members were strained, some of the old California crowd had died, and most of the New York relationships she had formed were more professional than intimate. Still, for all the overwork and disappointments, when Austin headed to Arizona and New Mexico she went with wings spread and some disposition for flying. And at first things went well. At the Luhans, she was able to finish *No. 26 Jayne Street* (1920), her novel about the war as seen from a woman's point of view which is also an exposé of sexual politics on the Left. Here, she also met D.H. and Frieda Lawrence among the guests. But gradually depression caught up with her. Sporadically ill, unhappy with the way her new relationships were turning out, and disillusioned about her ability to bring to light the kind of intuitive apprehensions she felt were in her, Austin underwent a crisis that deepened as the new decade progressed. Even in this period, however, when she was in her fifties, her public persona faltering and her private self in despair, Austin brought out work, including *The American Rhythm* (1923) in which she argues that free verse is not a modern invention but founded on the aboriginal rhythms of Indians moving on the land and pioneers clearing it, and *Everyman's Genius* (1925), the fruit of her long preoccupation with the sources and fostering of creativity. She also found time to remain active in the Indian Arts Fund campaign for the preservation of Spanish colonial culture, and fight again for the water rights of the region.

In the mid-1920s as she began restructuring her life around the research and writing of her remarkable autobiography *Earth Horizon* (1932), two of her most important assessments of feminism were published. Biographers picture Austin in Santa Fe as the autocratic and grouchy dean of a group that included the young Ansel Adams, with whom she collaborated on a book, and the poet Witter Bynner. She turned Casa Querida, her beloved house and gardens, over to Willa Cather while she finished *Death Comes for the Archbishop,* and although Austin thought Cather sided with the wrong party in the French-Spanish colonial dispute that is in the background of the novel, they remained correspondents and friends. The final years were absorbed by reflections on her life and on the long process of dying, which she chronicled in *Experiences Facing Death* (1931). Productive until close to the end, Austin died of heart disease in 1934 still at work on the unfinished novel that she hoped would complete the trilogy on the new man capable of understanding the new woman that she had begun with *The Ford* (1917) and *Starry Adventure* (1931).

Of the various tributes and reviews of Austin's career published by her contemporaries, perhaps that from the folklorist and critic Constance Rourke in 1932 is the most perceptive of Austin's strengths and even interest for our time.[14] Earlier, such male critics of the day as Grant Overton and Carl Van Doren had grappled with what they saw as the puzzle of Austin's career: its simultaneous over- and under-achievement.[15] Both men thought Austin's finest writing came in the poetic prose inspired by the desert lands and people. Van Doren compared her vision of an austere and impersonal nature to Conrad's. Overton took Austin's concern for women seriously, as Van Doren did not, complaining that when Austin tried to speak for women she spoke only for herself. Both found her interests too widely roving and diffuse for success in a single genre, which was considered a standard of achievement.[16] To Rourke, however, reviewing the autobiography *Earth Horizon,* Austin's explorations of her own life lived in and sometimes against the culture and times had "the impactive power of character free in a natural medium. She is a born autobiographer, with an uncompromising interest in herself . . . [and in] the unfolding of a long creative absorption." The book would have been justified on the grounds of Austin's feminism alone, Rourke wrote, but it is also invaluable social history —an assessment that could stand for some of Austin's other work as well.

Austin's own estimation that her concerns for nature, the folk quality of experience, and behavior termed mystical were at best sporadically popular with the eastern literary establishment is also on target. On the other hand, what one reviewer termed the "uncannily Jamesian" style of some of the novels,[17] notably *A Woman of Genius* and *No. 26 Jayne Street*, earned her the reputation of being accessible only to the literati. In all probability, though, it was Austin's thorough-going insistence on and assertion of a feminist perspective on most subjects that as much as anything rattled even the liberal critics (for instance, her 1912 study of the madonnas in Renaissance art, *Christ in Italy*, was dismissed as "another feminist outbreak")[18] and accounts both for the satiric accounts we have of her life and the decline of her reputation even in her own time. In the 1920s, a back-to-the-family conservativism grew as the power of the women's movement waned. Unemployment, social unrest, and fascism became the key issues of the 1930s as depression ravaged the economy. Individualistic stances such as Austin's were literarily and ideologically unpopular; "the women's point of view" was not sought and when expressed not particularly heard. Among subsequent generations, feminism as a public issue all but died out.

With all that, however, Austin never totally disappeared from view. Some of the southwestern works have remained in print or been reissued. Several more and less helpful biographical and critical studies have appeared over the years. Both, however, are marred by the war between affection and exasperation, respect and dismissal, that appears to overtake many who try to write about Austin. The most recent and complete biography, Augusta Fink's *I-Mary* (1983), avoids some of the pitfalls in developing a sympathetic account of the life that is also sympathetic to the feminism, but does not attempt to put the life in the contexts developed by feminist analysis nor to analyze the themes and development of the work. The best published charting of the kind of questions that should be asked of Austin is the fine review by

307

Melody Graulick of Fink's biography in *The Women's Review of Books.* [19]

Feminism: The Early Years and *A Woman of Genius*

In "Woman Alone," the autobiographical sketch Austin published in 1927 in *The Nation* as one in a series of anonymous essays by leading feminists, Austin describes what she terms the "bias and method" of her feminism as rooted in her "own position in the family as an unwanted, a personally resented child" who at an early age learned to set aside her need for love and use reasoned argument to obtain "a kind of factual substitute for family feeling and fair play."[20] When Mary was born the fourth of seven children, only three of whom survived, her young mother had already lost two infants, her equally young husband was a semi-invalid with a Civil War-incurred disability, and their son was showing symptoms of permanent lameness.

As Elaine Showalter comments in introducing the essay in *These Modern Women,* "Austin's life is a testimonial to the tragedies of 'enforced maternity' and the double sexual standard." As an adult Austin came to understand and sympathize with her mother in a number of respects. Even as a youth she saw the loss of status her mother suffered after her husband died and she supported the family by going out to nurse. References to the absence of a knowledge of birth control in *A Woman of Genius* suggest Austin understood the pain of sexuality repressed by the fear of continuous childbearing, as well as the desire of young couples like Olivia and Tommy to establish their own relationship before tracing the silhouettes of parenthood in one another. Eventually Austin gained her mother's respect—and a gesture of friendship —by slapping a man who had abused his wife while she was in labor. Even though the mature Austin transformed elements of her personal story into theory and a dialogue that resonates in her fiction, the psychological consequences of the antagonism between mother and daughter were severe. Early it led Austin to create an alternate, transcendent "self" to cope with the rejection. Her mother's attitudes, reinforced by her own deep immersion in evangelical Methodism, generated pain and ambivalence even in later life. (Austin recalled that her mother greeted the news that Austin's daughter was brain damaged with "I don't know what you've done, daughter, to have such a judgement upon you."[21] She also remembered that her mother professed no enthusiasm or pride when Austin's first story was published. Yet when her mother died when Austin was twenty-six, she experienced the loss as the severance of the very "root of being.")[22] Austin's strategic withdrawal from her mother's sphere of influence illustrates a complex attitude toward the traditional ties and thinking of women's domestic culture, which she alternately avoided and celebrated as socially useful throughout her career.

In *Earth Horizon* Austin describes the early forging of a competent, independent, self-directive, assertive state of consciousness that she discovered in contemplating the letter "I" in her brother's primer and later came to associate with her own giftedness. She contrasts this self-possessed, transcendent "I-Mary," as she calls her, with the ordinary, vulnerable, conforming child in need of affection and acceptance, whom she termed "Mary-by-herself." When Olivia says at the beginning of *A Woman of Genius* that she is going to tell the story of "an accomplished woman, not so much of the accomplishment as of the woman,"[23] Austin signals both the division between the ordinary-by-herself woman and the consciousness of "Power and Gift" that comes ultimately to direct her life. In saying that she will tell the story to Pauline Mills, Olivia further suggests the antagonism between the gifted woman and the social and sexual mores of the time that Pauline embodies.

The bias and method Austin refers to in "Woman Alone" are formative in Olivia Lattimore's life as well. Olivia's response to dispossession of breast and lap when the next baby comes along is not to feel comforted when her mother does pick her up; rather, she is left with a lifelong desire for unqualified love that is never fulfilled. (Austin would seem to anticipate here, as in other areas of her thinking, or simply in the candid reflection of her own experience, understandings of women's relationships that have recently been recommitted to theory.) Similarly, Olivia's negotiations, first for an allowance like her brother's and then for her portion of her father's legacy, are softened reflections of events Austin recounted in *Earth Horizon*. For both the fictional representation and the actual Austin, the insistence on "rights" as opposed to reliance on personal indulgence is a strategy with a consequence in later life. As Olivia puts it: "What it might have made for graciousness for once in my life to have been the centre of that dramatic [family] affectionateness, I can only guess."[24] On the other hand, Austin cites the refusal to conform stereotypically to compliant female behavior or to manipulate men for private advantage and to insist publicly on the liberation of women for its own sake as contributions her generation made to the dialogue of feminism. The emotional independence and self-respecting attitudes that backed those contributions, however, had their own possible consequences, as the characterization "woman alone" suggests about how Austin saw her own life, if not her heroine Olivia's.

Austin's mother was one of what Carroll Smith-Rosenberg identifies as the "new bourgeois matron" who, in the post-Civil War era, responded to the call of both the Suffrage and the Women's Christian Temperance Union movements. Austin said that she grew up in a generally enlightened and humane household. Her grandfather and other family members had been Abolitionists. Her father was a lawyer and town magistrate who read widely. Books and ideas were discussed in the home. Her mother at once dreamed of her daughter's attending Mount Holyoke and feared that educating a woman was a waste of money. When Austin did graduate from Blackburn, Mrs. Hunter expressed the hope that her daughter would not now throw her education away on "some man." Austin remembered being taken to hear Susan B. Anthony speak in Carlinville, and although she credits Frances Willard and Anna Howard Shaw as early influences in self-realization, Austin clearly distinguishes her generation's thinking from theirs: the pioneer women's movement leaders accepted in their own lives the forced choice between marriage and public service (Austin was not thinking of Elizabeth Cady Stanton when she wrote that) while the "modern" woman of the time intended to combine work with a domestic life. (Austin recognized that, in so doing and in entering into direct competition with men in the workplace, her generation of career women drew the opprobrium that her mother's generation had escaped by confining its reform activities to the moral and temperance crusades that were perceived as legitimate extensions of concerns in the home, a strategy Frances Willard used to keep her followers within the pale of middle-class respectability.) Austin erased these lines in drawing Olivia's background to make her emergence all the more unusual for not being even ideologically supported in her environment. Thus, the circumstances from which she arose were all the more typical of the indifferent education offered to women in the nineteenth century, and other oppressions the majority of women endured. However, Austin kept in the portrait lines that are faithful to her own difficulty as a female child gifted with "wit, anger, and imagination"[25]—in gaining acceptance by and identity in the adult world.

Although Olivia's mother is referred to as "the best of women," Olivia does not see her as a model. Olivia would, perhaps, have turned to her father, but he, like Austin's own, died when she was quite young. In the early death, Austin lost one of her two perceived supporters in the family. (The other, her younger sister who died soon after the father, she resurrects as Effie in the novel.) For both Olivia and Austin the loss of the male parent meant a youth spent "at loose ends for . . . a man's point of view and the appreciable standards that grow out of his relations to the community."[26] Part of Austin's later critique of women's culture stemmed from its associations with her mother's reliance on affectional ties and personal standards of behavior in running the household, as well as with her dislike for her daughter's displays of individuality. Part of Austin's later identification with aspects of "male culture" came from the (at least putatively) objective standards she associated with functioning in the world of public performance and institutions, along with her father's encouragement of her originality and innovation.

When Olivia encounters the women's movement at the height of her career, she is introduced by her sister Effie, the highly efficient modern middle-class matron of the turn of the century who is president of her women's club, civically active, solicitous of her babies back home and the husband whom she accompanies on a business trip, and, while in New York, in touch with all sorts of progressive movements. When Olivia confesses that she has been too involved in building a career to notice such activism, it is Effie who says: "You're a forward movement yourself." As a woman of achievement who stands out from the crowd, Olivia gives, Effie says, "women everywhere the courage to lead lives of their own." It is the conscious movement of all toward liberty. And in the "breadth and brightness" of Effie's vision, Olivia gives one of the finest performances of her career.[27]

Undoubtedly as a theorist Austin believed more in the individual genius leading the group than in the group itself, about which she remained skeptical. Groups of women irritated her. She was not an affiliator. Perhaps she had suffered too much censure at the hands of middle-class matrons. She also thought that the clubwoman's executive talent emphasized efficiency over originality. Her relations even with radical women appear also to have been uneasy. Elizabeth Gurley Flynn recalled her as a member of the Greenwich Village feminist group Heterodoxy, but she apparently did not attend meetings regularly and does not mention the group in her autobiography.[28] Perhaps, like the older Charlotte Perkins Gilman, she wearied of the discussions of the new "sex psychology" that interested the younger members: hers was not the confessional mode.[29] She certainly wearied of Suffrage meetings, impatient with the "process" and, seemingly, with the women whose dress and manner irritated her. (Unfortunately, she reveals some class bias here. She was also of her time in ambivalence about eastern Europeans, which the personal quality of her characterization of Polatkin shows.) Austin, like Cather, was in some fundamental sense a loner, ideologically an individualist, even male-identified, not an uncommon stance among the members of her generation of professional women who, unmoored from the ties of common domestic concerns that supported their mothers, had to establish new criteria and a new ideology of relatedness for the new woman in the workplace. The kind of sisterly help that Sarah Croyden gives Olivia points the way to a noncompetitive mode. However, like Charlotte Perkins Gilman who ran *The Forerunner* as a one-woman enterprise, Austin often walked alone.

Yet Austin's consciousness of women in the mass was keen. Her early fiction explores the gender oppression doubled by racial oppression women suffered, particularly Indian women. She was in her expository and autobiographical writings an insightful historian of the phases and meanings of the women's movement of her time. She was particularly perceptive in analyzing the attitudes of her own late nineteenth-century intermediate generation whose upbringing produced sexual repression and even an adversion to physical sexuality, reinforced, as she notes, by the absence of even "a vocabulary by which measures of [escaping pregnancy] could be intelligently discussed," which led to "sex-antagonism" and the belief that "the chief obstacle to all they most wished for was to be found in the maleness of men." This attitude was foreign to the pioneers of women's right to be equal citizens and considered prudish and unjoyful by the modern woman of the first quarter of the twentieth century.[30] Upon reflection, she stated, feminists of the transitional generation came to recognize that it was not men per se but their own lack of training and experience in the discipline of the professions that proved the chief obstacle to advancement. (Austin more candidly added, in "Woman Alone," that discrimination against women was a reality.)

As a theorist, half a century before such contemporary writers as Carol Gilligan and Sarah Ruddick,[31] Austin identified the distinctive ways women think based on their historic experiences in the home and family. She described a characteristic mode of thinking she called "mother-mindedness."[32] Always the critic, she sought to transform aspects of women's traditional concerns, broaden the scope from the individual to the community. She argued that claiming peace, however, as a special women's issue played into the exaggeration of the differences between men and women that her generation tried to reduce and left women vulnerable to charges of an unhealthy essentialism. Her *The Young Woman Citizen* (1918) reads like a primer on how women can overcome their native suspicion of politics as a male game and function effectively in the political process for the benefit of their concerns. Finally, though, it is in her speculations about greatness in women that the separate strands coalesce in a way that perhaps also sheds light on *A Woman of Genius.* Ideas, she argues, invariably are generated in the minds of one or two greatly endowed individuals. The intellectual woman, like the good actress, uses her "mother-mindedness" to think for all women, as Mary Wollstonecraft and Olive Schreiner did, setting forth a socially prophetic and intellectually coherent vision such as Jane Addams's, in the charismatic style of a Frances Willard, who inspired individuals to coalesce in translating the idea into an action.[33]

The Dilemma of the Talented Woman

> Why on earth, or why in heaven
> for that matter, should anybody
> make a mind like mine and then
> not use it.[34]

In Elizabeth Stuart Phelps's *The Story of Avis* (1879), the young artist's dream vision of a long procession of heroically striving women of different classes and nations moving silently through time ends with the whispered command of the sphinx: "Speak for me." The vision challenges the artist to solve the riddle of being a woman, which means for Avis first living the life the majority of women have led—marriage, childbearing, making a home—before she can paint it. Living the life, however, consumes the artist in the woman. When she finally does complete the painting of the sphinx, she can at least state the problem. All the power of that great recumbent female form is checked, held in moral and mental thrall by the admonition to silence of the child who stands before her with finger raised to lip. When Avis returns to art after the deaths of her son and husband, it is with fingers and aspirations too stiffened to paint. She gives drawing lessons to support herself and her daughter "Wait." Her own career sacrificed, she invokes the eternal hope of mothers that somehow life be better for their daughters. "We have been told," Phelps says, "that it takes three generations to make a gentleman: we may believe that it will take as much, or more, to make a woman."[35]

Phelps was writing in part of her mother and of herself as the daughter. It took more than three generations in the nineteenth century to make full, free, strong women in fiction. Mary Austin wrote in a tradition of writers who explored the themes of women's lives and work. Among her immediate predecessors in American literature were Rebecca Harding Davis (*Life in the Iron Mills,* 1861), Elizabeth Stuart Phelps (*The Silent Partner,* 1871, and *The Story of Avis,* 1877, among other works), Kate Chopin (*The Awakening,* 1899), and Edith Wharton (*The House of Mirth,* 1905). In England, after a half century of such depictions of thwarted intelligence as Aurora Leigh (Elizabeth Barrett Browning's poet who chooses marriage over her career) and Dorothea Brooke (the George Eliot heroine who, unlike her author, finds no satisfying use for her power), Olive Schreiner pioneered the character who both in aspiration and in analysis was the prototype of the "new woman" (although in fate she was classically tragic) whom Sarah Grand named and described in achievement (*The Beth Book,* 1897).

Avis's immediate predecessor, the iron mill worker Hugh Wolfe in *Life in the Iron Mills,* carves from korl a huge, powerfully muscled sculpture of a woman, crouching, arms outflung, face raised hungrily, questioning. The korl woman mirrors the baffled aspirations of the sculptor and represents Rebecca Harding Davis's identification as a woman, one with the need to write, with

314

unnurtured genius, unawakened power. Awakening, both sexual and artistic, in Chopin's Edna Pontillier falters in mid-flight. Edna leaves her husband and children, but for various reasons, including perhaps the failure of both love and talent and conceiving of no way she might live with self-respect in the world without either, drowns herself in the sea—Chopin's strong statement about a society not ready for her heroine's discoveries.

Olivia Lattimore stands in this company as pivot of the column, as one who, along with Sarah Grand's Beth, overcomes the obstacles of childhood and marriage to find that she has work in the world she is good at and is actually allowed to do without self-censorship on the part of the author. Unlike Grand, however, who caps Beth's career as writer and orator with the return of her knight in shining armor, Austin reintroduces the knight in the third book of *A Woman of Genius* and when he refuses to marry both Olivia and her work, she does not fold Olivia's wings but keeps her airborne, albeit flying at a lower altitude.

Austin is an important link between the nineteenth- and twentieth-century writers in this tradition. The conflict between a woman and her talent, and that talent and the society the woman lives in, are themes Austin explored in her life and fiction both. A number of the sketches and portraits of women gifted with intelligence and imagination Austin wrote in the course of her career have in common the themes of this novel: the departure in the personal life from the social and sexual mores of the time and the prominence of work viewed both as self-realization and service to the community. At least in some of the fiction, Austin structures questions of value and conduct as either explicit or implicit dialogue between a transcendent and an earthbound woman (reminiscent of her own self-imagery I-Mary and Mary-by-herself) to expose the unhealed divisions in the life and in the culture. In point of view she is closer to such moderns as Wharton, Cather, and Glasgow. She is also working her way out of problems that appear in the fiction of Phelps, Mary Wilkins Freeman, Sarah Orne Jewett, and Kate Chopin.

Austin lets Olivia tell her own story in the form of memoirs, which allows her to be both the subject and the object as she explores the events of her life for their meaning (in fact, the autobiographical form), that are also an *apologia* to Pauline Mills, Olivia's girlhood friend turned adult tormentor. Pauline and Henry Mills embody the cultural complacencies, hypocrisies, prejudices, and double sexual standard that Olivia must battle both in her life and in the theater. Pauline also represents the protected status of the middle-class matron and the internalized values from which Olivia's life departs. Olivia's other battle is with herself, her own desire for a husband and children, which she believes is the "happier destiny of women."[36] It is in Olivia's ambivalence about her own gift that Austin shows her relation to the earlier writers. The genius for acting is seen as a gift of the gods, an impersonal force, a flood that overwhelms the woman and breaks through the dam erected in the early years to contain it. In an exact reversal of Avis's loss of the career in the woman, Olivia tells Garrett that the woman has been drowned in the career. However, Olivia finally is not made to pay with her life for the conflicts within her and with her culture. She emerges from the failure of her expectations as a woman "retarded, crippled in my affectional capacities, bodily the worse, but still with wings to spread and some disposition toward flying."[37] Her career is also intact. By the end of the novel Austin is much closer to saying that Olivia keeps on doing what she is doing not only because she likes the independent income and has responsibilities to Polatkin but because she is good at performing on the public stage and also enjoys the acclaim: her audience gives her a good life. Both positions—surviving disappointments and liking work for the life it gives—are close to the self-affirming attitudes of Cather's Thea Kronberg and Glasgow's Dorinda Oakley.

A Woman of Genius is a book about a woman's life and the possibilities she has in a small town Austin calls Taylorville in Ohianna in the last decades of the nineteenth century. Olivia marries both because she wants to and because that is all she can think of doing. Although she discovers in the childhood play of Hadley Pasture her gift for acting, it is exercised in a secret world, removed from the sphere of the mothers. The dominant scenario in town is "tayloring" young women for the roles of wives and mothers in a hazy sort of way that omits any discussion of what the experience might be like. The only education Olivia's talent receives are the elocution lessons that lead indirectly to her meeting Helmuth Garrett at a picnic where he is taken with the beauty of her reciting Shakespeare and kisses her in response. Tommy Bettersworth offers to marry Olivia to save her from the embarrassment of that public kiss. Olivia wonders if she asked her mother about the difference between that passionate embrace and Tommy's "mild osculations" whether her mother would put up a defense for her daughter. But she doesn't ask: on the major questions of life there is repression and the conspiracy of silence. When Olivia later asks her mother how to manage the interval between marriage and pregnancy, her mother is at first horrified and then, in one of the most poignant moments of the novel, says "I'm sorry, daughter . . . I can't help you. I don't know . . . I never knew myself."[38]

The cultural conspiracy against a woman's telling the truth about her own experiences is broken by this novel. In addressing a range of questions about women's sexuality, including its connection with the creation of art, *A Woman of Genius* makes a singular contribution to the genre. The modern reader may have some trouble discerning the outlines of the discussion. Many students read right past that exchange between mother and daughter and miss the import because it is not cast in the language they are accustomed to. One needs to recall Austin's words in "The Forward Turn": her generation had not even a vocabulary for discussing sex and for their mothers, sex was an experience to which God submitted women inscrutably. Similarly, the modern reader may have some trouble working through Olivia's use of mystical language when she talks about her creativity, what Elizabeth Hardwick termed the I-Mary/Shining Destiny/Power and Gift— "capitalized accomplishments to the mundane person."[39] Here, Austin is crafting sentences to follow Olivia's thought processes (which are her own). Passages of Austin may be placed side-by-side with those from Henry James who wrote also to uncover developing consciousness.

Olivia's truth-telling proceeds on several levels. The novel is noteworthy also for the attention it pays to the points of view of conventionally raised men. Had Olivia been what she seemed to Tommy, and to herself and family, all might have been well. When she thinks of the dreams her husband had of being in fact the "adored, dependable" protector and how he "blundered and lost himself in the mazes of unsuitability," she feels bitterness on his account, not her own.[40] Later, Garrett seems as baffled as Olivia about why their relationship is impossible. Both believe in the values of Taylorville, but they live at a time when there are no models for successfully combining two careers and a common domestic life. As Austin writes in the beginning: "This is the story of the struggle between a Genius for Tragic Acting and the

317

daughter of a County Clerk, with the social ideal of Taylorville, Ohianna, for the villain."[41]

Austin does not remit on Olivia's point of view, neither on the unfortunate aesthetics of her marriage (Tommy likes red plush on principle) nor on the pain of trying to scale her life to his lack of ambition and the values of small-town America. It is, in fact, in casting around for something to do after the death of her son and a subsequent miscarriage that she hits upon amateur theater and is set off on the road to discovery. *A Woman of Genius* is a fine novel to compare with Theodore Dreiser's *Sister Carrie* (whose first public edition appeared also in 1912), for whom getting into the theater works in the opposite way: Carrie Meeber's success in the theater saves her from a life of prostitution, though it plunges her into personal loneliness. Both novels detail realistically the human indignities of making it in the world of commercial theater, the sexual politics and the poverty as well. Olivia does not succumb to the temptation of using sex to gain her way, saved from that as much by her conventional morality as by the solicitude of her friend and colleague Sarah Croyden.

Finally, though, it is the force of Olivia's own talent that both drives and pulls her through to New York and a theater of her own. At the height of her achievement she and Helmuth Garrett meet again, and although the last book of the novel may strike the reader as a plunge back into the sentimental or romance genre of women's fiction, the denouement is hardly typical even of that feisty breed. Garrett telegraphs "Will you marry me?" "If you marry my work," Olivia responds.[42] In the ensuing silence, Garrett marries a woman who will conventionally mother his daughters, leaving Olivia to her work and eventually to a companionate marriage with a playwright who has himself been around the bend several times but with whom she can at least discuss her work.

In *Main Street* (1920), Lewis's revolt from the small-town novel that popularized the genre Austin did much to model, Carol Kennicott is not endowed with sufficient talent or an analysis to understand her conflicts. Olivia's analysis of her own is not "tutored" feminism. She is the rugged individualist who makes it. She does, however, eventually encounter organized feminism, but instead of being sent back home by it as Carol is, Olivia's encounter with the vision enhances her performance.

Elizabeth Gurley Flynn in writing Austin in 1930 recalled *A*

Woman of Genius as an inspiration to her when she was a young woman just regaining her bearings in the labor movement after the breakup of her marriage.[43] Austin's analysis that it is precisely the risk of not being liked and the fear of rejections such as Tommy and Helmuth's that keep women from leading lives of their own may threaten our complacency. While the diminished note of accepting friendship over passion might strike today's reader as middle-aged, there is overriding inspiration in a novel that says in the end one can have work in common and a friendship.

Nancy Porter
Portland State University
Portland, Oregon

Notes

1. I am indebted to Carroll Smith-Rosenberg for her discussion of the new woman in "The New Woman Androgyne" in *Disorderly Conduct: Visions of Gender in Victorian America* (New York: Alfred A. Knopf, 1985). I also wish to thank Elinor Langer, Dorothy Berkson and the Faculty Research Group of Lewis and Clark College, and Florence Howe for discussions that improved my understanding of women's culture and *A Woman of Genius*.
2. The work of Elizabeth Ammons first introduced me to the new woman in literature. See particularly *Edith Wharton's Argument with America*, Chapter 1, (Athens, Ga.: The University of Georgia Press, 1980).
3. Willa Cather, 1932 "Preface" to *The Song of the Lark* (Boston: Houghton Mifflin Company, Sentry Edition, n.d.).
4. Mary Austin, *A Woman of Genius* (Garden City, N.Y.: Doubleday, Page and Company, 1912; rpt. New York: Arno Press, 1977). As with other "lost" women writers, we are indebted to Tillie Olsen for bringing Austin to our attention. Until it went out of print, contemporary readers were able to find an excerpt of the novel in *American*

Voices, American Women, edited by Lee R. Edwards and Arlyn Diamond (New York: Avon Books, 1973).

5. Mary Austin, *Earth Horizon* (Boston and New York: Houghton Mifflin Company, 1932).

6. Estimates of the number of book and periodical publications vary. I choose the median figures.

7. See, for example, the several generations of professional women represented in *These Modern Women: Autobiographical Essays from the Twenties,* edited and introduced by Elaine Showalter (Old Westbury, N.Y.: The Feminist Press, 1978); Judith Schwarz, *Radical Feminists of Heterodoxy* (New Lebanon, N.H.: New Victoria Publishers Inc., 1982).

8. The biographical information comes from several sources: Helen MacKnight Doyle, *Mary Austin: Woman of Genius* (New York: Gotham House, 1939); Thomas Mathews Pearce, *The Beloved House* (Caldwell, Idaho: Caxton Printers, 1940); Thomas Mathews Pearce, *Mary Hunter Austin* (Boston: Twayne Publishers, 1965); Augusta Fink, *I-Mary: A Biography of Mary Austin* (Tucson, Ariz.: The University of Arizona Press, 1983); my own research of the Mary Hunter Austin Collection in the Henry E. Huntington Library, San Marino, Calif.

9. Austin, *Earth Horizon,* p. 159.

10. Mary A. Hill, *Charlotte Perkins Gilman: The Making of a Radical Feminist, 1866–1896* (Philadelphia: Temple University Press, 1980). The Hill biography was also helpful in setting the historical context in which Austin and Gilman met in California.

11. Mary Austin, "Frustrate," *Century Magazine* (January 1912): 467–71.

12. Inez Haynes Irwin, *Adventures of Yesterday* (General Microfilm, 1973), p. 297. Typescript in the Inez Haynes Irwin Papers, The Schlesinger Library, Radcliffe College, Cambridge, Mass. I want to thank Julie Allen of the University of Texas, Austin for sharing her work on Irwin.

13. Mary Austin to Ferris Greenslet, Houghton Mifflin, cited in Fink, *I-Mary,* pp. 147–49.

14. Constance Rourke, "The Unfolding Earth," *New Republic* (December 21, 1932): 166–67.

15. Grant M. Overton, *The Women Who Make Our Novels* (New York: Dodd, Mead Company, 1928); [Carl Van Doren], "Mary Austin" in John C. Farrar, *The Literary Spotlight* (New York: George H. Doran Company, 1924), pp. 164–74.

16. Like other women writers, including Alice Walker today, Austin wrote in multiple genres.

17. Review signed A.C.B., no date, no source in clippings in the Mary Hunter Austin Collection, Huntington Library.

18. Unsigned review in undated, uncredited clipping in Mary Hunter Austin Collection, Huntington Library.

19. Melody Graulich, "Mary, Mary, Quite Contrary," *The Women's Review of Books* (January 1984): 16–17. Graulich's review clarified my own thinking and emboldened me to consider Austin's feminism pervasive. When so few have read a writer such as Austin, "discussions" often take place cross-country and in print.

20. Mary Austin, "Woman Alone," *The Nation* (March 1927), reprinted in Showalter, *These Modern Women*, pp. 79–86.

21. Austin, *Earth Horizon*, p. 257.

22. Ibid., p. 273.

23. Austin, *A Woman of Genius*, p. 3.

24. Ibid., p. 48.

25. Austin, *Earth Horizon*, pp. 157–58.

26. Austin, *A Woman of Genius*, p. 27.

27. Ibid., p. 261.

28. Elizabeth Gurley Flynn, *The Rebel Girl* (New York: International Publishers, 1973).

29. Charlotte Perkins Gilman, *The Living of Charlotte Perkins Gilman* (New York: D. Appleton-Century, 1935).

30. Mary Austin, "The Forward Turn," *The Nation* (July 20, 1927): 58.

31. Carol Gilligan, *In a Different Voice* (Cambridge, Mass.: Harvard University Press, 1982); Sarah Ruddick, "Maternal Thinking," in *Mothering: Essays in Feminist Theory*, edited by Joyce Trebilcot (Totawa, N. J.: Rowman and Allanheld, 1983).

32. Mary Austin, "Woman Looks at Her World," *Pictorial Review* (November 1924).

33. Mary Austin, "Greatness in Women," *The North American Review* (February 1923): 197–203.

34. Mary Austin to D.T. MacDougal, October 27, 1923. Cited in Fink, *I-Mary*, p. 219.

35. Elizabeth Stuart Phelps, *The Story of Avis* (rpt. New York: Arno Press, 1977), p. 450.

36. Austin, *A Woman of Genius*, p. 78.

37. Ibid., p. 69.

38. Ibid., p. 75.

39. Elizabeth Hardwick, Introduction to Arno Press edition of *A Woman of Genius*.

40. Austin, *A Woman of Genius*, p. 69.

41. Ibid., p. 4.

42. Ibid., p. 273.

43. Helen Gurley Flynn to Mary Austin, January 24, 1930, in the Mary Hunter Austin Collection, Huntington Library.

FEMINIST CLASSICS FROM THE FEMINIST PRESS

Antoinette Brown Blackwell: A Biography, by Elizabeth Cazden. $16.95 cloth, $9.95 paper.

Between Mothers and Daughters: Stories Across a Generation. Edited by Susan Koppelman. $8.95 paper.

Brown Girl, Brownstones, a novel by Paule Marshall. Afterword by Mary Helen Washington. $8.95 paper.

Call Home the Heart, a novel of the thirties, by Fielding Burke. Introduction by Alice Kessler-Harris and Paul Lauter and afterwords by Sylvia J. Cook and Anna W. Shannon. $8.95 paper.

Cassandra, by Florence Nightingale. Introduction by Myra Stark. Epilogue by Cynthia Macdonald. $3.50 paper.

The Changelings, a novel by Jo Sinclair. Afterwords by Nellie McKay; and by Johnnetta B. Cole and Elizabeth H. Oakes; Biographical Note by Elisabeth Sandberg. $8.95 paper.

The Convert, a novel by Elizabeth Robins. Introduction by Jane Marcus. $6.95 paper.

Daughter of Earth, a novel by Agnes Smedley. Afterword by Paul Lauter. $7.95 paper.

The Female Spectator, edited by Mary R. Mahl and Helene Koon. $8.95 paper.

Guardian Angel and Other Stories, by Margery Latimer. Afterwords by Nancy Loughridge, Meridel Le Sueur, and Louis Kampf. $8.95 paper.

I Love Myself When I Am Laughing . . . And Then Again When I Am Looking Mean and Impressive, by Zora Neale Hurston. Edited by Alice Walker with an introduction by Mary Helen Washington. $9.95 paper.

Käthe Kollwitz: Woman and Artist, by Martha Kearns. $7.95 paper.

Life in the Iron Mills and Other Stories, by Rebecca Harding Davis. Biographical interpretation by Tillie Olsen. $7.95 paper.

The Living Is Easy, a novel by Dorothy West. Afterword by Adelaide M. Cromwell. $8.95 paper.

The Other Woman: Stories of Two Women and a Man. Edited by Susan Koppelman. $8.95 paper.

Mother to Daughter, Daughter to Mother: A Daybook and Reader, selected and shaped by Tillie Olsen. $9.95 paper.

Portraits of Chinese Women in Revolution, by Agnes Smedley. Edited with an introduction by Jan MacKinnon and Steve MacKinnon and an afterword by Florence Howe. $5.95 paper.

Reena and Other Stories, selected short stories by Paule Marshall. $8.95 paper.

Ripening: Selected Work, 1927–1980, by Meridel Le Sueur. Edited with an introduction by Elaine Hedges. $8.95 paper.

Rope of Gold, a novel of the thirties, by Josephine Herbst. Introduction by Alice Kessler-Harris and Paul Lauter and afterword by Elinor Langer. $8.95 paper.

The Silent Partner, a novel by Elizabeth Stuart Phelps. Afterword by Mari Jo Buhle and Florence Howe. $8.95 paper.

These Modern Women: Autobiographical Essays from the Twenties. Edited with an introduction by Elaine Showalter. $4.95 paper.

The Unpossessed, a novel of the thirties, by Tess Slesinger. Introduction by Alice Kessler-Harris and Paul Lauter and afterword by Janet Sharistanian. $8.95 paper.

Weeds, a novel by Edith Summers Kelley. Afterword by Charlotte Goodman. $7.95 paper.

A Woman of Genius, a novel by Mary Austin. Afterword by Nancy Porter. $8.95 paper.

The Woman and the Myth: Margaret Fuller's Life and Writings, by Bell Gale Chevigny. $8.95 paper.

The Yellow Wallpaper, by Charlotte Perkins Gilman. Afterword by Elaine Hedges. $3.95 paper.

OTHER TITLES FROM THE FEMINIST PRESS

Black Foremothers: Three Lives, by Dorothy Sterling. $6.95 paper.

But Some of Us Are Brave: Black Women's Studies. Edited by Gloria T. Hull, Patricia Bell Scott, and Barbara Smith. $9.95 paper.

Complaints and Disorders: The Sexual Politics of Sickness, by Barbara Ehrenreich and Deirdre English. $3.95 paper.

The Cross-Cultural Study of Women. Edited by Margot Duley-Morrow and Mary I. Edwards. $29.95 cloth, $12.95 paper.

Feminist Resources for Schools and Colleges: A Guide to Curricular Materials, 3rd edition. Compiled and edited by Anne Chapman. $12.95 paper.

Household and Kin: Families in Flux, by Amy Swerdlow et al. $8.95 paper.

How to Get Money for Research, by Mary Rubin and the Business and Professional Women's Foundation. Foreword by Mariam Chamberlain. $6.95 paper.

In Her Own Image: Women Working in the Arts. Edited with an introduction by Elaine Hedges and Ingrid Wendt. $9.95 paper.

Integrating Women's Studies into the Curriculum: A Guide and Bibliography, by Betty Schmitz. $9.95 paper.

Las Mujeres: Conversations from a Hispanic Community, by Nan Elsasser, Kyle MacKenzie, and Yvonne Tixier y Vigil. $8.95 paper.

Lesbian Studies: Present and Future. Edited by Margaret Cruikshank. $9.95 paper.

Moving the Mountain: Women Working for Social Change, by Ellen Cantarow with Susan Gushee O'Malley and Sharon Hartman Strom. $8.95 paper.

Out of the Bleachers: Writings on Women and Sport. Edited with an introduction by Stephanie L. Twin. $9.95 paper.

Reconstructing American Literature: Courses, Syllabi, Issues. Edited by Paul Lauter. $10.95 paper.

Salt of the Earth, screenplay by Michael Wilson with historical commentary by Deborah Silverton Rosenfelt. $5.95 paper.

The Sex-Role Cycle: Socialization from Infancy to Old Age, by Nancy Romer. $8.95 paper.

Witches, Midwives, and Nurses: A History of Women Healers, by Barbara Ehrenreich and Deirdre English. $3.95 paper.

With These Hands: Women Working on the Land. Edited with an introduction by Joan M. Jensen. $9.95 paper.

Woman's "True" Profession: Voices from the History of Teaching. Edited with an introduction by Nancy Hoffman. $9.95 paper.

Women Have Always Worked: A Historical Overview, by Alice Kessler-Harris. $8.95 paper.

Women Working: An Anthology of Stories and Poems. Edited and with an introduction by Nancy Hoffman and Florence Howe. $7.95 paper.

Women's Studies in Italy, by Laura Balbo and Yasmine Ergas. A Women's Studies International Monograph. $5.95 paper.

For free catalog, write to: The Feminist Press, Box 334, Old Westbury, NY 11568. Send individual book orders to The Feminist Press, P.O. Box 1654, Hagerstown, MD 21741. Include $1.75 postage and handling for one book and 75¢ for each additional book. To order using MasterCard or Visa, call: (800) 638-3030.